MURDER MILE

Lynda La Plante was born in Liverpool. She trained for the stage at RADA and worked with the National Theatre and RDC before becoming a television actress. She then turned to writing—and made her breakthrough with the phenomenally successful TV series Widows. Her novels have all been international bestsellers.

Her original script for the much-acclaimed *Prime Suspect* won awards from BAFTA, Emmy, British Broadcasting and Royal Television Society as well as the 1993 Edgar Allan Poe Award. Lynda has written and produced over 170 hours of international television. *Tennison* has been adapted by ITV and was broadcast in March 2017 in the UK; international broadcast will follow.

Lynda is one of only three screenwriters to have been made an honorary fellow of the British Film Institute and was awarded the BAFTA Dennis Potter Best Writer Award in 2000. In 2008, she was awarded a CBE in the Queen's Birthday Honours List for services to Literature, Drama and Charity.

If you would like to hear from Lynda, please sign up at www .bit.ly/LyndaLaPlanteClub or you can visit www.lyndalaplante .com for further information. You can also follow Lynda on Facebook and Twitter @LaPlanteLynda.

Lynda La Plante

MURDER MILE

ZAFFRE

First published in Great Britain in 2018 by

ZAFFRE PUBLISHING
80–81 Wimpole St., London W1G 9RE
www.zaffrebooks.com

First published in the United States of America in 2018 by Zaffre Publishing
Typeset by Scribe Inc., Philadelphia, PA.
Printed and bound in the USA

Trade paperback ISBN: 978-1-49986-146-4
Also available as an ebook.

10 9 8 7 6 5 4 3 2 1

For information, contact 251 Park Avenue South,
Floor 12, New York, New York 10010

Zaffre Publishing is an imprint of Bonnier Zaffre,
a Bonnier Publishing company
www.bonnierzaffre.co.uk
www.bonnierpublishing.co.uk

For Cass Sutherland and The Chartered Society of Forensic Sciences

GLOSSARY

A10	The Met's internal monitoring division, similar to internal affairs in the US
CID	Criminal Investigation Department
DC	Detective Constable
DCI	Detective Chief Inspector
DCS	Detective Chief Superintendent
DI	Detective Inspector
DS	Detective Sargent
FLYING SQUAD	Division of the Met that investigates robberies and any crime involving a gun.
OLD BILL	Slang for "the police"
PC	Police Constable
PLONK	Derogatory slang for female police used by male police.
SECTION HOUSE	Residential accommodation for unmarried police officers
SOCO	Scenes of crime officer, i.e. part of the forensic team
SPG	Special Patrol Group, a mobile squad of highly trained officers deployed to assist other divisions as needed.
THE MET	The Metropolitan Police
TO BE NICKED	Slang for "to be arrested"

TO NICK	Slang for "to steal"
WDC	Woman Detective Constable
WDS	Woman Detective Sargent
WPC	Woman Police Constable

CHAPTER ONE

Jane Tennison, recently promoted to sergeant, looked out of the passenger window of the CID car at the snow, which was falling too lightly to settle. It was 4:30 on a freezing Saturday morning in mid-February 1979 and recently the overnight temperatures had been sub-zero. The weather reports were calling it one of the coldest winters of the century.

Apart from a couple of minor incidents, Jane's CID night shift at Peckham had been remarkably uneventful, due to the bad weather. She looked at her watch: only another hour and a half to go before she finished her week of night duty and could get home to a warm bath, good sleep and some time off. She'd be back at Peckham on Monday for the day shift.

Detective Constable Brian Edwards, an old colleague from her Hackney days, had been her night duty partner through-out the week. He was so tall he had the driving seat pressed as far back as it could possibly go, but his knees were still almost touching the steering wheel.

"Can you turn the heating up?" she asked, as they drove along East Dulwich Road.

"It's already on full." Edwards moved the slider to be sure, then glanced at Jane. "I meant to say earlier: I like your new hairstyle. Sort of makes you look more mature."

"Is that a polite way of saying I look older, Brian?" Jane asked.

"I was being complimentary! It goes with your smart clothes, makes you look more business like . . . Especially now you've been promoted."

Jane was about to reply when Edwards suddenly slammed on the brake, bringing it to an abrupt halt. They both lunged forward, Edwards banging his chest against the steering wheel and Jane narrowly avoiding hitting her head on the windscreen.

"What? What's up?" Jane asked, startled, staring at Edwards.

"A rat . . . A bloody rat!" He pointed at the middle of the road in front of them.

Illuminated by the car headlights was a massive rat, a piece of rotting meat between its sharp teeth. The rat suddenly darted off across the road and out of sight.

Edwards shook his head. "I hate rats. They give me the creeps."

"Well, that's obvious! And yes, thank you, Brian, I'm OK—apart from nearly going through the windscreen."

"I'm sorry, Sarge. I didn't mean to hit the brakes so suddenly."

"I'm just touched that you didn't want to run the rat over, Brian," Jane said.

Edwards pointed over towards Peckham Rye Park to a pile of rubbish-filled black plastic bin and shopping bags. They were piled up five foot high and stretched over twenty feet along the side of the park. The stench of rotting rubbish slowly permeated its way into the stationary car.

"It's thanks to Prime Minister Callaghan and his waste-of-space Labour government that the bin men and other public-sector workers are on strike," grumbled Edwards. "Everyone's dumping their rotting rubbish in the parks and it's attracting the rats. No wonder they're calling it the 'Winter of Disconnect.'"

"It's 'Discontent,'" Jane corrected him.

"You're quite right—there's not much to be happy about! Mind you, if Maggie Thatcher wins the next election we might get a pay rise. She likes the Old Bill."

Jane was trying hard not to laugh. "It's the 'Winter of Discontent'! It comes from Shakespeare's *Richard III*: 'Now is the winter of our discontent, made glorious summer by this sun of York . . .'"

Edwards looked skeptical. "Really?"

"I studied *Richard III* for A level English."

"All that Shakespeare lingo is mumbo-jumbo to me. I left school at sixteen and joined the Metropolitan Police Cadets," Edwards said proudly.

"I didn't know you'd been a 'Gadget,'" said Jane, somewhat surprised. A "Gadget" was affectionate force jargon for a cadet.

"It was all blokes when I first joined the Gadgets," Edwards went on. "We lived in a big dormitory and got work experience on division alongside the regulars. It gave me a better understanding of police work than your average ex-civvy probationer who went to Hendon. No offence intended," he added hastily.

"None taken. If I'd known what I wanted to do at sixteen I'd probably have joined the cadets—though my mother would likely have had a heart attack." Jane liked Edwards, but he wasn't the brightest spark. He'd been transferred to various stations and hadn't lasted long on the Flying Squad. In her estimation, he'd probably remain a Detective Constable for the rest of his career.

"Tell you what: head back to the station so we can warm up with a hot drink and I'll type up the night duty CID report," she said.

Edwards snorted. "That shouldn't take long—we haven't attended a crime scene or nicked anyone all night."

Their banter was interrupted by a call over the radio. "Night duty CID receiving . . . over?"

Jane picked up the radio handset. "Yes, Detective Sergeant Tennison receiving. Go ahead . . . over."

"A fruit and veg man on his way to set up his market stall has found an unconscious woman in Bussey Alley. Couldn't rouse her so he called 999. There's an ambulance en route," the comms officer said.

"That's just off Rye Lane." Edwards made a sharp U-turn.

"Yes, we're free to attend and en route," Jane confirmed over the radio, switching on the car's two-tone siren.

"If she's been out drinking she's probably collapsed from hypothermia in this bloody weather. Or maybe she's been mugged?" suggested Edwards.

"Let's just hope she's OK," Jane said.

Rye Lane ran between the High Street and Peckham Rye Park. In its heyday it had rivaled Oxford Street as a major shopping destination and was known as the "Golden Mile." It was still a busy area, with a large department store, co-op and various small shops and market traders selling home-produced and ethnic goods from their stalls. During the 1970s, Peckham had gradually become one of the most deprived areas in Europe, with a notorious reputation for serious and violent crime, especially muggings, which were a daily occurrence.

Jane and Edwards arrived at the scene within two minutes. A man who looked to be in his mid-fifties was standing under the railway bridge at the entrance to Bussey Alley, frantically waving his hands. He was dressed in a dark-colored thigh-length sheepskin coat, blue and white Millwall Football Club scarf and a peaked cap. Edwards pulled up beside him and opened the driver's window.

"I thought you might be the ambulance when I heard the siren." The man crouched down to speak to them. "Poor thing's just up there. She's lyin' face down and ain't moved. I put one of me stall tarpaulins over her to keep off the sleet and cold. I was hopin' she might warm up and come round."

Jane put on her leather gloves, got the high-powered torch out of the glove box and picked up the portable Storno police radio.

"There's quite a lot of rubbish been dumped on one side of the alley, just up from where she is—be careful of the rats," the market trader said as they got out of the car.

Jane grinned at Edwards. He hadn't looked too happy at the word "rat." "You get the details," she said. "I'll check on the woman."

She turned on the torch, lighting up the dingy alley. The narrow path ran alongside the railway line. In the arches underneath were small lockups where the market traders stored their stalls and goods. Jane walked at a brisk pace, until about forty feet along she could see the green and white striped tarpaulin. Crouching down, she lifted it back and shone the torch. The woman beneath was wearing a thigh-length blue PVC coat, with the collar up, covering the back of her neck.

Removing her right glove, Jane put her index and middle fingers together, and placed them on the side of the woman's neck, in the soft hollow area just beside the windpipe. There was no pulse and the woman's neck felt cold and clammy. Jane felt uneasy. She stood up and slowly shone her torch along the body, revealing dried blood smears on the back of the blue coat. The woman's knee-length pleated skirt was hitched up to her thighs, revealing garters and black stockings. Near the body the torch beam caught three small shirt buttons. Peering closely at one of them, Jane could see some white sewing thread and a tiny piece of torn shirt still attached. It looked as if the button had been ripped off, possibly in a struggle.

A little further up the alleyway Jane noticed a cheap and worn small handbag. Wearing her leather gloves, she picked it up and opened it carefully, looking for any ID. All she found was a lipstick, handkerchief, a small hairbrush and a plastic purse. Inside the purse were a few coins and one folded five-pound note. There were no house or car keys to be found. Jane placed a ten pence coin down on the spot where she'd found it; it would go in a property bag later to preserve it for fingerprints.

Next, Jane shone the torch around the body. It was strange: she couldn't see any blood on the pavement around or near the victim, or on the back of her head. She crouched down and slowly lifted the collar on the PVC coat back, revealing a knotted white cord around the victim's neck and hair.

Shocked, Jane got to her feet and pulled out the portable radio.

"WDS Tennison to Peckham Control Room. Are you receiving? Over." She spoke with confidence and authority, despite the fact she'd only been promoted and posted to Peckham a few weeks ago.

"Yes, go ahead, Sarge," the comms officer replied.

"Cancel the ambulance. The woman in Bussey Alley appears to have been strangled. I've looked in a handbag for possible ID, but can't find any. I need uniform assistance to cordon off and man the scene at Rye Lane, and the far end of Bussey Alley, which leads onto Copeland Road."

"All received, Sarge. A mobile unit is en route to assist."

Jane continued, "Can you call DCI Moran at home and ask him to attend the scene? I'll also need the laboratory scene of crime DS here. Oh, and the divisional surgeon to officially pronounce life extinct . . . Over."

The duty sergeant came on the radio. "Looks like a quiet week just got busy, Jane. I'll call Moran and tell him you're on scene and dealing . . . Over."

Jane ended the transmission and replaced the tarpaulin over the body to preserve it from the sleet that was still falling, although not as heavily. Then she walked back to Rye Lane.

Edwards was still speaking to the market trader and making notes in his notebook. As she approached him, she gave a little shake of her head to indicate this was more than a collapse in the street or hypothermia, then went to the rear of the CID car. Taking out a plastic police property bag, she placed the handbag inside it.

"Is she all right?" the trader asked.

Jane shook her head. "I'm afraid she's dead, sir. Did you see anyone hanging about or acting suspiciously before you found her?"

The man looked shocked. "No, no one . . . Oh, my—the poor thing. What's happened to her?"

"I don't know, sir, I'm afraid. Further investigation is needed." Jane did not want to reveal more.

"Can I get me gear out the lockup and set up for business?"

"Sorry, not at the moment, but maybe in an hour or two," she said. "We'll need to take a more detailed statement off you later."

Jane took Edwards to one side. By now their hair was soaking and their coats sodden.

"I take it you're thinking murder?" he whispered.

Jane nodded. "Looks like she's been strangled with a cord. I've spoken with the duty sergeant who's informing DCI Moran. The market man's up a bit early—does his account of how he found her sound above board to you?"

"Yeah. His name's Charlie Dunn, he's sixty-two and he's been working the markets since he was twelve. He's always been an early bird. He said he's just been over to Spitalfields fruit and veg market to get fresh stock for the day. That's his white van under the railway bridge. He was unloading it to his archway lockup in the alley when he saw the woman on the pavement. I checked his van: it's full of fresh goods. He also showed me the purchase receipt for the fruit and veg and his market trader's licence. He sounded and acted legit to me."

"Well, she's stone cold, so it looks like she's been dead a while, anyway."

"Any ID on her?"

"Nothing in the handbag, not even keys. I haven't had a chance to check her coat pockets yet. I want to get both ends of the alleyway sealed off and manned by uniform first—all the market traders will be turning up soon and wanting access to their archway lockups."

Edwards nodded and blew into his freezing hands. He didn't question her authoritative tone; on the contrary, he liked the fact WDS Tennison was taking responsibility for the crime scene.

The market trader went to his van and returned with a Thermos flask.

"Hot coffee? You can have it, if you want. I'm going to go home and come back later."

"Thank you!" Edwards took the flask and poured some coffee into the removable cup and handed it to Jane. She took a mouthful, swallowed it, then let out a deep cough and held her chest.

"There's more brandy in that than coffee!"

Edwards promptly held the flask to his lips and took a large gulp. "So there is," he said with a grin.

"Put it in the car, Brian. We don't want Moran smelling booze on us—you know what he's like about drinking on duty."

Edwards took another gulp, then put the flask in the back of the car and got a packet of lozenges out of his pocket.

"'Be prepared,' as we used to say in the scouts. You see, I remember some famous quotes as well." Edwards took one for himself, then offered the packet to Jane.

"What are they?" Jane asked.

"Fisherman's Friend. They'll hide the smell of the brandy and warm you up at the same time. I take them fishing with me when it's cold like this."

Jane reached into the pack, took out one of the small, light brown, oval-shaped lozenges, popped it in her mouth and immediately began taking deep breaths. The menthol flavor was so strong her eyes began watering, her nose started running and her throat tingled.

"They taste awful!" she exclaimed, spitting out the lozenge and placing it in a tissue to throw away later.

Just then, two police constables arrived in an Austin Allegro panda car. They got out and approached Jane.

"What do you need us to do, Sarge?"

"I need the Rye Lane and Copeland Road entrances to the alley sealed off with tape and one of you to stand guard at each end."

"Will do, Sarge." They both set off and then one of them turned back. "Oh, the duty sergeant said to tell you DCI Moran's been informed and is on his way with DI Gibbs."

Edwards looked at Jane. "I thought DI Gibbs wasn't due to start at Peckham until Monday?"

Jane shrugged. "That's what I thought as well."

"Maybe Moran wants him to run the investigation."

"Why? Moran's the senior officer—he's in charge of the CID at Peckham," Jane pointed out.

"Don't tell anyone I told you this," said Edwards, "but I was in the toilet cubicle when I overheard Moran talking to the chief super. Moran said his wife was suffering from the 'baby blues.' Apparently the baby was crying a lot and he didn't know what to do. The chief suggested he take some time off when DI Gibbs arrived—so maybe Moran's called Gibbs in early to familiarize himself with everything before he steps back to spend time at home."

"I didn't know his wife had had a baby."

"Yeah, about a month before you started at Peckham." Edwards paused. "I've not seen Spencer Gibbs since our Hackney days, but I heard he went off the rails a bit after Bradfield was killed in the explosion during that bank robbery by the Bentley family."

Jane immediately became tight-lipped. "I worked with Gibbs in the West End at Bow Street when I was a WDC and he was fine," she lied.

At the time, Gibbs was drinking heavily to drown his sorrows, but managing to hide it from his other colleagues. She had always had a soft spot for Gibbs and didn't like to hear his name or reputation being tarnished. She suspected he must have overcome his demons, especially if he'd been posted to a busy station like Peckham. She also knew DCI Moran would have had to agree to Gibbs' transfer.

Jane and Edwards returned to the alley. Edwards went over to look at the body, whilst Jane picked up the coin she'd used as a marker and replaced it with the handbag, now inside the property bag. Lifting back the tarpaulin, they both checked to see if there was anything in the victim's pockets to help identify her, but there was nothing.

Edwards pulled up the left sleeve of the victim's PVC coat.

"She's wearing a watch," he said. "Looks like a cheap catalogue one; glass is scratched and the strap's worn. There's no engagement or wedding ring—they might have been stolen?"

"Possibly," said Jane, "but there's no white patch or indentation on the skin to suggest she was wearing either. Plus the handbag was left behind with money in it." She got the radio out of her coat pocket and handed it to Edwards.

"Call the station and ask them to check Missing Persons for anyone matching our victim's description. I'll do a search further up the alley towards Copeland Road to see if there's anything else that may be of significance to the investigation."

Edwards hesitated. "What should I tell Comms?"

Jane gave a small sigh. "Brian, just look at the victim and describe her when you speak to them, OK?"

"Oh, yeah, OK, I see."

Jane watched Edwards disappear down the alleyway, leaving her alone with the body. She replaced the tarpaulin on the body, then searched the rest of the alleyway, but found nothing of interest. It was still dark and now that the initial adrenalin rush was wearing off she was even more aware of the cold. She stamped her feet and flapped her arms across her chest to generate some warmth. A sudden noise made her jump, and swinging her torch around revealed a rat scurrying from a pile of rubbish that had been left rotting in front of one of the arches. She thought about the woman lying on the ground in front of her. What had she been doing here? Had she been on her own, like Jane was now, or was her killer someone she knew?

Footsteps approached from the Rye Lane end of the alley. Jane looked up, shone her torch and saw Detective Sergeant Paul Lawrence from the forensics lab approaching. He was accompanied by a younger man in civilian clothes. Even if she hadn't seen Paul's face, she'd have guessed it was him. As ever, he was dressed in his trademark thigh-length green Barbour wax jacket and trilby hat. Paul Lawrence was renowned as the best crime scene investigator in The Met. He had an uncanny ability to think laterally and piece things together bit by bit. Always patient and willing to explain what he was doing, Jane had worked with him several times and felt indebted to him for all that he had taught her. Now she felt relief at the sight of his familiar figure.

Paul greeted Jane with a friendly smile. "I hear it's Detective Sergeant Tennison now! Well done and well deserved, Jane. As we're the same rank, you can officially call me Paul." He laughed. She had always called him Paul when not in the company of senior officers.

"You were quick," Jane said, smiling back at him.

"I'd already been in the lab typing up a report from an earlier incident in Brixton," he said. "Victim stabbed during a fight over a drugs deal. Turned out the injury wasn't as serious as first thought and the victim didn't want to assist us anyway, so there wasn't much to do. No doubt there'll be a revenge attack within a few days."

Jane explained the scene to him, starting with the market trader's account and exactly what she and DC Edwards had done since their arrival at Bussey Alley. She also told him about the handbag and buttons.

"Good work, Jane. Minimal disturbance of the scene and preservation of evidence is what I like to see and hear. Peter here is the scene of crime officer assisting me. He'll photograph everything as is, then we can get the victim onto a body sheet for a closer look underneath."

The SOCO set to work taking the initial scene photographs of the alleyway and body. He stopped when the divisional surgeon appeared. Although it was obvious, the doctor still checked for a pulse on her neck before officially pronouncing that she was dead. As the doctor was getting to his feet, Detective Chief Inspector Moran arrived, carrying a large red hard-backed A4 notebook, and holding up an enormous black umbrella. Dressed smartly in a grey pin-stripe suit, crisp white shirt, red tie, black brogues and thigh-length beige camel coat, he nonetheless looked bad-tempered and tired.

"So, DS Tennison," he said. "What's happened so far?" He sounded tetchy.

Jane had worked with DCI Nick Moran when she was a WPC at Hackney in the early seventies, and he was a detective inspector. She knew to keep her summary brief and to the point, so as not to irritate her superior.

"The victim was found in here by a market trader. Edwards spoke with him and is satisfied he wasn't involved. I called DS Lawrence to the scene and the divisional surgeon, who's pronounced life extinct. From my cursory examination it appears she's been strangled. I haven't found anything to help us identify who she is, though a handbag was nearby, which I checked—"

Moran frowned. "I had expected you to just contain the scene until I arrived. It's my job to decide who should be called and what action should be taken. You should have left the hand-bag in situ as well. It's not good to disturb a scene."

Jane felt Moran was being a bit harsh. She, like everyone else, was working in the freezing cold and soaking wet. He should have realized she was trying to obtain the best evidence and identify the victim. She thought about saying as much, but wondering if his mood was connected to a sleepless night coping with the new baby, decided to say nothing.

Lawrence looked at Moran. "It's standard procedure for a lab sergeant to be called to all suspicious deaths and murder scenes at the earliest opportunity. Preserving the handbag for finger-prints showed good crime scene awareness by WDS Tennison."

Moran ignored Lawrence and spoke to the divisional sur-geon. "Can you give me an estimation of time of death?"

The doctor shrugged his shoulders. "There are many vari-ables due to the weather conditions, breeze in the alley and other factors, which can affect body temperature. It's hard to be accurate, but possibly just before or after midnight."

Just about managing to keep his umbrella up, Moran wrote in his notebook. Jane could see Lawrence was not pleased. She knew his view was that divisional surgeons were not experi-enced in forensic pathology or time of death, and should con-fine their role to nothing more than pronouncing life extinct.

Lawrence looked at Moran. "Excuse me, sir, but now the sleet's stopped, it would be a good idea to get a pathologist down to see the body in situ. He can check the rigor mortis and body temp—"

Moran interrupted him, shutting his umbrella. "The weath-er's constantly changing, and more snow is forecast, so I want the body bagged, tagged and off to the mortuary as a priority for a post-mortem later this morning."

Lawrence sighed, but he didn't want to get into an argument about it. Opening his forensic kit, he removed a white body sheet and latex gloves. Using some tweezers, he picked up the three buttons beside the body and placed them in a plastic property bag. Then he unfolded the body sheet and placed it on the ground next to the body.

Lawrence looked up at Jane and Edwards. "I want to turn her over onto the body bag. If one of you can grab her feet, I'll work the shoulders. Just go slow and gentle."

Jane took a step forward, but Edwards said he'd do it and grabbed a pair of protective gloves from Lawrence's forensic bag. As they turned the body over, Jane shone her torch on the victim, lighting up her contorted face and the rope around her neck. The strangulation had caused her tongue to protrude and her eyes were puffed and swollen. The victim wore little make-up, and looked to be in her late twenties to early thirties. She was medium height, with brown shoulder-length hair parted down the middle, and was wearing a pink blouse, which was torn, and her bra was pulled up over her breasts.

Lawrence pointed to the pavement area where the body had been lying. "It's dry underneath her," he observed.

"The sleet started about three a.m.," Jane said.

"Then it's reasonable to assume she was killed before then."

"How can you be sure it was three a.m., Tennison?" Moran snapped, tapping the ground with the steel tip of his umbrella.

Jane got her notebook out of her inside coat pocket. "We'd just stopped a vehicle and I recorded the details and time in my notebook. I remember the sleet starting as I was taking the driver's details. Let me find it . . ." She flicked through the pages. "Ah—here it is. Time of stop, 3:03 a.m."

"Well, I want it checked out with the London weather office in case it becomes critical to the case," said Moran. "The body is a stone's throw from Peckham Rye railway station. She might have been out late Friday night and attacked in the alleyway if using it as a cut-through to Copeland Road."

Lawrence shrugged. "She might have thrown it away, but there was no train ticket on her. She may have been walking from the Copeland Road end and heading towards Rye Lane. The fact there were no house keys on her could suggest she was returning home and expecting someone to let her in."

Moran nodded. "We can put out a press appeal with the victim's description and ask if anyone recalls seeing her on the train Friday night. Also we can run a check with Missing Persons for anyone matching her description."

"Already in hand, sir," Jane said, without receiving so much as a thank you back. She glanced at Edwards, reminding herself to check exactly what description he had given Missing Persons.

Lawrence crouched down next to the body, looked at Moran and pointed to the victim's torn blouse. "She may have been sexually assaulted as well. There's four buttons missing on her blouse. I only recovered three beside the body and there's no more underneath her."

Jane raised her finger. "I had a good look up and down the alley before DS Lawrence arrived and didn't find any more buttons."

Lawrence stood up. "Best we check the soles of our shoes in case one of us has accidentally trodden on it and it's got lodged in the tread. It won't be the first time something has unintentionally been removed from a crime scene in that way. When you see the market trader who found her, check his footwear as well."

Everyone checked the soles of their shoes.

"Someone tread in dog shit?"

Jane turned around. Spencer Gibbs was wearing a trendy full-length brown sheepskin coat. His hands were deep in the pockets, pulling the unbuttoned coat around his front to keep out the cold. He had a big smile and Jane could instantly see he was looking a lot better now than when she last saw him, almost younger, in fact. His hair had changed as well. It no longer stood up like a wire brush, but was combed back straight from his forehead.

Gibbs' smile widened when he saw Jane.

She held out her hand. "Hello, Spence. You look well."

"Jane Tennison—long time no see!" He pulled her forward to give her a hug.

Jane noticed that DCI Moran didn't seem too impressed and wondered if Gibbs' jovial mood was due to drink, although she couldn't smell any alcohol.

Gibbs walked over to Moran. "Good morning, sir," he said, and they shook hands. Gibbs' coat fell open to reveal a blue frilled shirt, tight leather trousers, blue suede shoes and a large peace sign medallion. Everyone went quiet.

Moran frowned. "So you really think that sort of outfit is suitable for a senior detective, DI Gibbs?"

"Sorry, guv. I did a gig in Camden town with my band last night, then stayed at my girlfriend Tamara's pad. Thankfully I'd added her phone number to my out of hours contact list at the old station. I didn't want to waste time by going home to change when I got the call-out, so after a quick dash of Adidas after-shave, I came straight to the scene by cab."

Gibbs' looks and patter had become even more "rock and roll" than they used to be.

"Your band do glam rock, guv?" Edwards asked, trying not to laugh at Gibbs' dress sense.

"No, we're more progressive. Serious rock and roll. Girl-friend's in the band as well. Looks like Debbie Harry—she's a real stunner."

"Well, you look like a real poofter in that gear," Edwards replied, earning a playful slap on the back of his head from Gibbs.

Moran coughed loudly to get Gibbs' and Edwards' attention. "Show a bit of respect, you two. We're supposed to be investigating a murder, not discussing bloody music!"

"Sorry, sir," they said in unison.

"What have you go so far?" Gibbs asked Moran.

Moran frowned. "A murder, obviously. I want you to organize house-to-house enquiries, DI Gibbs. Start with any flats in Rye Lane, and all the premises in Copeland Road. Tennison and Edwards can return to the station to write up their night duty report, then go off duty."

Jane knew that organizing house-to-house was normally a DS' responsibility and she was keen to be part of the investigation team.

"I should have the weekend off, sir, but I'm happy to remain on duty and assist the investigation. You've got a DS on sick leave, one at the Old Bailey on a big trial starting Monday, and one taking over nights from me tonight. House-to-house is normally a DS' role, so I could—"

Moran interrupted her. "I'm aware of all that, Tennison. If you're willing to work for normal pay and days off in lieu, as opposed to costly overtime, then you can head up the house-to-house. Edwards, same rule goes for you if you want to be on the investigation."

Jane and Edwards agreed. Earning extra money was a bonus, but never a big deal when it came to a murder inquiry; it was more about being part of a challenging case.

Moran closed his notebook and put his pen back in his jacket pocket. "Right, DI Gibbs will be my number two on this investigation. We'll head back to the station. I'll get more detectives in from the surrounding stations and contact the coroner's officer to arrange a post-mortem later this morning. Tennison—you head back to the station with Edwards. Do your night duty report first, then prepare the house-to-house documents and questionnaires. You can get uniform to assist in the house-to-house, as well as the Special Patrol Group. DS Lawrence and the SOCO can finish bagging the body and examining the scene. If possible, I'd like to know who the dead woman is before the post-mortem."

"I'll take a set of fingerprints while I'm here," Lawrence said. "Uniform can take them straight up the Yard for Fingerprint Bureau to check. If she's got a criminal record they'll identify her."

Moran nodded his approval. As he walked off with Gibbs, Edwards turned to Jane.

"He could have poked someone's eye out the way he was swinging that umbrella! I reckon he's in a mood because the baby kept him up, and his wife gave him a hard time about being called in."

Jane said nothing, but she suspected there was some truth in Edwards' comment. Just as she was about to follow him back to the CID car, Paul called out: "Can you grab the large roll of Scotch tape from my forensic bag?"

He and the SOCO had wrapped the body in the white body sheet and twisted each end tight. Jane knew the procedure and helped by rolling the tape several times around each twisted end to secure them. She always found it surreal that a bagged dead body ended up looking like an enormous Christmas cracker.

"Thanks, Jane." As the SOCO moved away, Lawrence asked, "Is Moran always so tetchy these days?"

"Wife had a baby recently; sleepless nights are probably getting to him."

"Well, he was wrong to have a go at you and ignore my advice. He should have called out a pathologist."

"He was probably just asserting his authority to let us know he's boss."

"He might be in charge, but he's spent most of his career on various squads like vice, so he's not had a lot of experience in major crime or murder investigations."

"He did solve the Hackney rapes and murder committed by Peter Allard, the cab driver," Jane pointed out.

"Yes—but I also recall he was accused of faking Allard's confession. If it hadn't been for your dogged work in that case, he wouldn't have solved it. He showered himself in glory because of you, Jane. He seems to have forgotten that you stuck your neck out for him that night in the park acting as a decoy. You were the one that got attacked by Allard, not him."

"I know, Paul, but I think he's mellowed since our Hackney days. Apart from this morning he's been OK towards me."

"Well, I'd be wary of him, Jane," warned Lawrence. "He likes to think he knows best, which puts not only the investigation at risk, but the officers on it as well."

CHAPTER TWO

After leaving the murder scene, Jane returned to the station to prepare for the house-to-house. It was 10 a.m. and she was in the canteen with DC Edwards and DI Gibbs, who was still dressed in his rock band gear and looked like someone working under-cover in Carnaby Street. She was ready to brief thirty detectives and uniforms—male and female officers—who had been called in to assist with the house-to-house from local stations. Placing thirty blue A4-size folders down on the table, she waited for Gibbs to address the officers first.

"H-to-H is your show, so tell 'em what you want done," Gibbs whispered to her, sitting on the edge of a canteen table.

It was the first time she'd briefed fellow officers as a DS, but despite feeling nervous, she spoke in a loud, firm voice.

"OK, listen up, please. I'm Detective Sergeant Jane Tenni-son, in charge of the house-to-house enquiries on this murder investigation. For those of you who are not aware, the body of a white female was found in Bussey Alley at four thirty this morning by a local market trader. It appears she's been stran-gled and possibly sexually assaulted. Misper enquiries have so far proved negative and it is imperative that we identify her as soon as possible. Thorough and detailed house-to-house enqui-ries are critical to the investigation." Jane paused. The room was silent, then an elderly PC spoke.

"You really a DS, love?" he asked in a condescending manner.

Jane was annoyed at being called "love," but before she could reply, Gibbs stood up and pointed at the officer.

"Yes, she is, and if you don't like it then I suggest you bugger off back to your station and tell them DI Gibbs kicked you off house-to-house because of your attitude."

There were raised eyebrows around the room. Due to his unusual attire, nobody had suspected that Gibbs was a DI.

"I'm sorry, sir," the offending officer replied.

Jane was irritated that Gibbs had spoken for her. "And you can call me Sergeant or Sarge," she said, looking at the PC, pausing briefly before continuing.

"Each folder contains a description of the victim. Every resident must be asked if they know or had seen anyone matching that description in the last twenty-four hours. I want full background details of all the occupants in every residence. There is also a questionnaire about their movements and whereabouts on Friday and the early hours of Saturday morning." Jane pointed to the blue folders on the table in front of her. "Help yourselves to a folder. Each one has the street and premises numbers to be visited on the front. If you feel that anyone is lying, hiding something, or being evasive, then inform myself, DI Gibbs or one of the Murder Squad. Please leave the completed forms and questionnaires in the CID office, which is being used as the murder incident room. I have marked up a desk tray as: 'In, completed H-to-H.'"

As the officers stepped forward and helped themselves to a folder, Gibbs leant towards Jane.

"Well done. Good briefing."

"Thanks. I could have handled that PC myself, you know, so next time, please don't . . ."

"Yeah, I know you could, Tennison. It's just that those mouthy uniforms really get up my nose, especially the old boys who try to impress the crowd."

"I'll keep an eye on him while I'm out monitoring the house-to-house."

"Edwards can do that. Post-mortem's set for eleven a.m. and you need to be there."

"Will Moran be OK about that?"

"You were first on scene, so officially you have to ID the body to the pathologist. I've not had much dealing with Moran before, other than briefly on that Allard case. Is he always so grumpy and serious?"

"He and his wife are struggling with a new baby, keeping them up a lot. Edwards thought Moran might take some time off and let you run the investigation."

Gibbs laughed. "He probably gets more peace and quiet here. Shitty nappies and sleepless nights don't appeal to me either. You must be knackered yourself, what with being up all night."

"No, I'm fine. I'll finish writing up my night duty report and give you a lift to the mortuary."

"I'm waiting for my girlfriend to bring me in a change of clothes from my flat, so I'll meet you there," Gibbs said, walking away.

Moran, Jane and Lawrence were in Ladywell mortuary, Lewisham, with Professor Dean Martin, the forensic pathologist. Lawrence knew Martin well, having worked with him on countless murder investigations. Jane had met him on previous murders she had been involved in.

Dean Martin made the usual crack about his name to the audience. "As good looking as I am, I'm not to be confused with the Rat Pack crooner."

As Jane watched him put on his green mortuary gown and black wellington boots, she thought that he had put on weight since she last saw him. He was now in his late fifties, the top of his head was bald with thinning grey hair at the sides, his half-moon glasses were perched unsteadily on the end of his bulbous red nose, his cheeks had become ruddier through alcohol consumption and he was walking with a limp.

"Have you hurt your leg, Professor?" Moran enquired.

"No, a build-up of uric acid crystals in my foot is giving me hell," Martin replied gruffly.

Moran looked confused, but Lawrence whispered an explanation. "The prof has gout due to too much booze. It's extremely painful so he may be crotchety throughout the PM."

The victim's body was already laid out on the steel mortuary slab, covered with a white sheet. Moran looked at his watch.

"Where is DI Gibbs? It's nearly ten past and I told him to be here for eleven."

"His girlfriend turned up with some more suitable clothes, so he went to the men's locker room to get changed before coming here." Jane thought it was strange that Moran wanted Gibbs to be at the PM. Normally only one senior officer attended, whilst the other looked after the incident room and made sure all the necessary actions were being undertaken.

The mortuary door suddenly flew open.

"Sorry I'm late." Gibbs sauntered in wearing a very fashionable tan-colored tweed suit, matching waistcoat, white button-down shirt, matching wool tie and brown slip-on boots.

There was a stunned silence as everyone took in what Gibbs was wearing.

"You forgot your deer stalker hat, Sherlock," Lawrence remarked.

Gibbs smiled. "I'll have you know that it's herringbone tweed and made to measure from a shop in Knightsbridge . . . Admittedly it's a second-hand shop where high society locals take their unwanted clothes, but nevertheless, great quality and a bargain."

Martin laughed. "It's probably a dead man's cast-off."

"That may be so, Prof, but it's better than the creased, shiny-arsed, grey pin-striped suits the rest of CID wear " Gibbs replied, pulling his tweed jacket forward by the lapels to accentuate how classy he thought he looked. Gibbs saw Lawrence nudge his head towards Moran, who was wearing a grey pin-stripe suit.

"Of course you're the exception to that statement, guv," Gibbs said sheepishly, in an effort to cover his faux pas.

Moran shook his head. "It's one extreme to the other where your dress sense is concerned, Spencer. Now, if you don't mind, I'm sure the professor would like to get on with the post-mortem."

Martin pulled the white sheet from the body, in the manner of a magician working an audience when they reveal something during a conjuring act.

"Do we have a name for this poor girl?" Martin asked.

"No. A dead set of fingerprints was taken to the Yard. No match so far, but they're still working on them," Lawrence replied.

"Unfortunately the pathologist is unwell, though I suspect it's an excuse as he was out on the booze last night. DS Lawrence, I'd be grateful if you would assist me as you have a great deal of experience in mortuary procedure."

Lawrence gowned up and asked Jane to list and package the exhibits, which she was happy to do. She identified the body as the one in Bussey Alley and confirmed that, as yet, Missing Persons and house-to-house enquiries had still not revealed who she was. Moran added that the divisional surgeon had stated time of death was just before or after midnight. Jane saw Lawrence discreetly raise his eyebrows at Moran's remark, as Martin lowered his head and glared over the brim of his half-moon glasses at Moran.

"A divisional surgeon should only pronounce life extinct; comments on injuries or time of death are *not* their domain. If I'd been called to the scene, I could have taken a rectal body temperature, checked hypostasis, state of rigor mortis, whether it was present, and or affected by weather conditions—all critical factors in determining a reasonably accurate time of death."

Moran looked embarrassed. By his silence he clearly knew he should have heeded DS Lawrence's advice at the scene. Tactfully not looking at Moran, Lawrence took some photographs of the victim before she was undressed and her clothing put in exhibit bags for forensic examination at the lab. Her blue coat, pink blouse and bra were removed first. Lawrence remarked that the clothes didn't look expensive and the blouse had a Littlewoods label inside the collar. Jane double-checked the blouse and confirmed that, although they had only recovered three buttons, four had come off, so one was still missing. She confirmed that the market trader's boots had been checked by a DC when he came in to make a statement, but no joy. As Lawrence removed the victim's pleated skirt, they could all see that she wasn't wearing any underwear.

"Her underwear may have been taken by the killer, as some sort of sick souvenir," Jane suggested.

"Or she may not have been wearing any," Gibbs added politely.

"Either of you could be right. However, there are no scratch marks around or below the hip area or upper thigh to suggest they were forcibly removed."

Lawrence took out the stockings and suspender belt, then handed them to Jane, who had a closer look.

"There's not a tear or ladder on either of these stockings, which seems strange if she was attacked in the alleyway and forced to the ground."

Martin looked closely at the victim's hands, knees and face. "Her hands are quite calloused—possibly from some form of manual labor. I can't see any abrasions consistent with being forced face down onto the pavement, or dragged along it. That's not to say she landed on her back in the first instance, but we'll get to that later. There are faint signs of old stretch marks on her tummy, so I'd say your victim has given birth, but not recently."

Martin took swabs from the victim's mouth, vagina and anus to be tested for semen.

"Has she been sexually assaulted?" Moran asked, pointing to some marks on her inner right thigh.

"The abrasions on the thigh are linear scratch marks, but there's no bruising to her vaginal or anal area. The abrasions are parchment-like, the surface is dry and there are no signs of bleeding or bruising, so in my opinion the scratches occurred after death."

"Sorry, but I'm not quite sure what you mean, Professor," Moran said.

"Her assailant may have committed necrophilia and that's why there's no vaginal bruising."

There was silence in the room as everyone felt sickened at the thought of such a depraved act. Jane was used to attending post-mortems, and although hardened to some of the horrific sights she saw, she always felt sad for the victims and the fear and pain they must have suffered at the hands of their killers.

At Martin's request, Lawrence helped him lift the victim's head and shoulders to sit her upright, so he could get a look at her back and the knotted end of the ligature on the nape of her neck. Martin pointed to a circular-shaped bruise in the middle of the victim's back.

"This is not uncommon when someone is on the floor being strangled from behind: the killer kneels on the victim to get a better grip on the rope and stop him or her getting up or struggling. However, if it happened like this, and she struggled, I'd expect friction abrasions on her forehead or nose from contact with the pavement—but as you can see, there are none, which is very unusual."

Lying the victim back down, Martin asked Lawrence for a small scalpel. Gibbs stepped back, thinking Martin was about to cut the body open for an internal examination. The last thing he wanted was anything splashing onto his tweed suit.

Martin placed the scalpel blade on the rope. "I don't want to disturb the ligature knot, so I will cut through the rope at the front." He took his time, slowly cutting through the cord before removing and handing it to Lawrence.

The deep black and blue bruising imprint of the rope around the victim's neck was now visible.

"Considerable force must have been used to strangle her," Martin muttered.

Lawrence placed the cord on top of a property bag for closer examination.

"It's not hemp, so probably cotton or synthetic. About one inch thick and slightly frayed at both ends, as if it has been cut with scissors or a sharp knife, but I'll get a scientist to look at it," Lawrence said.

"It's tied in a form of slip knot," Jane observed, wondering if the victim was attacked from behind in the alleyway.

"Like a hangman's noose," Gibbs remarked.

Moran leant over. "Looks like a sailor's slip knot to me."

Gibbs and Jane turned to Moran.

"You'd know, would you, guv?" Gibbs remarked.

"Yes. I've been in The Met sailing club for ten years, so I know a bit about knots and loops. I'd say that if you untied the knot and laid it out flat, the length would be about three foot."

Gibbs was impressed. "Good call, guv. Might help when we get a suspect, especially if he's into sailing."

Moran shrugged. "Possibly, Spence, but rock climbers, and even scouts, use the same or similar sorts of knots."

Lawrence was deep in thought and didn't hear Martin ask him for a large scalpel.

"Is something troubling you, DS Lawrence?"

"It's the lack of abrasive injuries on the front of the victim, plus there was some smeared blood on the back of her coat, which may have come from the suspect, yet there were no drops of blood on the pavement at the scene, which is making me wonder if she was murdered elsewhere and her body dumped in Bussey Alley?"

Jane always respected Lawrence's eye for detail.

"Very astute, DS Lawrence," Martin responded. "The settling of blood on the front of the body, known as lividity, is consistent with the position she was found in. However, lividity begins to work through a deceased within thirty minutes of their heart stopping and can last up to twelve hours. Only up to the first six hours after death can lividity be altered by moving the body, but—"

"So she could have been murdered elsewhere and moved," Moran impatiently interrupted.

Martin looked over the rim of his glasses, the habit that inevitably preceded a curt reply. "I wasn't called to the scene, DCI Moran, to examine the lividity on her body in situ, so in answer to your question, I don't know for certain, but she could have been. And before you ask, I will give an estimation of time of death after *my* post-mortem."

Moran looked annoyed by the professor's tone of voice. Martin was often blunt and to the point, but Jane felt he was being particularly condescending, especially as Moran was the senior officer in the room and in charge of the investigation.

Martin continuously made notes throughout the post-mortem and spent the next two hours dissecting the body, removing the internal organs and brain, weighing them and taking samples of blood and urine to test for drugs and alcohol. When he'd finished, he put down his clipboard of notes and removed his gown.

"What was the state of rigor on the body at the scene?" Martin asked Lawrence.

"Pretty stiff, but not fully when we lifted her onto the body bag."

"Right, the rigor was fully stiff when we started at eleven, the stomach contents contained some semi-digested food particles, which is common in people who died two to six hours after a meal. This is in no way conclusive, but assuming she last ate between twelve and two, that gives a possible time of death range anywhere between two p.m. and eight p.m., which suggests that your thoughts about the body being murdered elsewhere and dumped in Bussey Alley are correct, DS Lawrence."

"If that occurred, I am somewhat confused about the number of buttons we discovered at the site where we found the body. We found three buttons and, on checking both her overcoat and the torn blouse, it appears there was a fourth button that was not recovered." Lawrence said.

Jane nodded. "The missing button could possibly have been left at the actual scene of the murder, unless she lost it before."

Lawrence glanced towards her but no one else seemed interested.

"The alleyway would be regularly used by the public and train commuters on a Friday night, yet the body wasn't found until early Saturday morning. Makes sense he'd dump her after midnight when there's less likely to be anyone about," Gibbs added.

"He may have used a car and travelled some distance, or the murder scene may be in nearby premises and he carried her out to Bussey Alley," Jane stated, unintentionally yawning as she looked at the mortuary clock. It was just after 2 p.m.; she'd had no sleep for nearly twenty-four hours and was beginning to feel nauseous.

"Might be a good idea if Jane went home and got some sleep," Lawrence suggested to Moran.

Moran shook his head. "Not at the moment. Our priority is finding out who our victim is, as it may well lead us to her killer and the scene of her murder. House-to-house is critical to this investigation. I want the forms that have been completed so far checked for anything that might assist or need urgent attention. A DCS will be appointed to oversee the case by Monday. I'd like unanswered questions resolved by then—even better, her killer in custody." Moran closed his notebook and left the room.

Jane returned to Peckham with DI Gibbs. The three-story red-bricked Victorian station was like Hackney, but much bigger, with a warren of small overcrowded offices. The stone-flagged floors, metal staircases and high windows cast a dull greyness inside the building. Even the array of wanted and missing persons' posters looked well worn, like parts of the building itself that needed repair and a lick of paint.

The large green corkboard on the wall in the far corner of the CID office was now covered with photographs the SOCO had taken in Bussey Alley. The victim's facial description was written up with an approximate age of late twenties to early thirties. Next to her name, address and time of death were large question marks. Gibbs picked up a black felt-tip pen and started to write down Professor Martin's observations about the time of death span and the fact the body was dumped. He also wrote: *Murder scene unknown.*

DC Edwards sat at the indexer's desk, looking through some of the house-to-house forms. He looked up at Jane.

"Hope you don't mind, Sarge, but I've been checking the completed H-to-H forms the uniforms brought in. Being a Saturday morning, a lot of people were at home . . ."

"Which is where I wish I was right now, Brian."

Edwards lifted a pile of the forms. "Me too. Anyway, I've been through half of these questionnaires, but so far there's nothing to help us identify the victim. A few people had friends, or knew other residents, who were similar in description, but they were all checked out and none of them are missing or unaccounted for."

"Thanks, Brian. I'll have to go through them anyway and sign each one off as correctly completed."

"No, you don't," Gibbs said.

"Yes, I do. Not that I don't trust Brian's abilities, but you heard what Moran said at the mortuary. If something gets missed, I'm the one he'll will have a go at, not you or Edwards."

"You don't have to because I will check them. You're so tired you could easily miss something. Go on, the pair of you—scoot and get some sleep. Give me your home numbers, then if anything important comes in I'll ring you so you won't miss out."

Jane was about to leave when the uniform PC who had called her "love" at the earlier briefing walked in with more completed house-to-house forms. He asked her if she'd like them or should he put them in the appropriate tray. Jane held out her hand to take them but Gibbs stepped forward and took them from the officer.

"Anything of interest for me?" Gibbs asked the PC.

Jane frowned at Gibbs, feeling that he was undermining her. "Or that needs my urgent attention as the house-to-house supervisor?" she said.

The officer took out his notebook from his jacket breast pocket and glanced at them both. "There was a light blue 1976 Austin Allegro outside 86 to 96 Copeland Road—they're a two-story block of flats that I visited on my house-to-house enquiries—"

"And?" Jane interrupted, wanting him to get to the point.

"The vehicle looked a bit out of place as—"

Gibbs looked bemused as he interrupted, "Allegros are one of the most common cars on the road. It may have missed your attention but virtually every police force in the country uses them because they're so cheap to run."

"It was a top-end Allegro, 1976 Vanden Plas Princess 1500 automatic, deep-pile carpet, leather seats and walnut trims—all in pristine condition. I asked in the flats and no one owned it or had seen it there before. Admittedly it did have a flat front offside tire with a screw stuck in it."

Jane wondered if the PC was trying to impress them in an effort to make up for his earlier behavior towards her.

"Have you recorded the details about the Allegro in your house-to-house folder?" Gibbs asked, hoping he'd say "yes" and so wouldn't have to listen to the matter-of-fact, boring tone of the officer anymore.

"No, I couldn't find an owner for it in the flats, so I wrote my observations down in my notebook. The vehicle's reg is tango, lima, yankee, two, two, five, romeo. All the doors and boot were locked and it did not appear to have been hotwired. The radio was missing and the connecting wires were exposed, so it may have been nicked."

Jane took a deep breath. "Have you done a computer check on the car to see who the owner is, or if it's been reported lost or stolen?"

"Not yet. Wanted to report it to you first before any further action. I'll nip downstairs and do that right now," the PC said and started to walk off.

Jane tried not to smile as Gibbs clenched his fists towards her, indicating his frustration with the PC.

"No, no, we'll do the checks and make further enquiries about the car. Thanks for informing us—very diligent of you," Jane said, forcing a smile.

The PC handed Jane the copy of his notes and left.

"I'll pop over to Copeland Road and have a look at the vehicle on my way home, see if there's anything untoward and get it brought in if necessary."

Gibbs shook his head and took the notes. "You get off home. I'll make further enquiries, but looks like the PC, as irritating as he is, did a good job checking it out. If it's got a flat tire, that may be why it was left there. We should also check into the missing radio because it doesn't quite make any sense if it was stolen and then the thief locked up the car."

Jane struggled to concentrate whilst driving home along the Marylebone Road. She pulled up at the red traffic lights by the junction with Gloucester Place and nodded off whilst waiting for them to turn green. The sound of repeated beeping of the car horn behind made her muscles tense as she jerked awake. For a split second she wondered where she was, then raised her hand in an apologetic manner and pulled away, turning right into Gloucester Place, then into Melcombe Street, where she lived in a top-floor flat of a three-story Victorian building. Thankfully, being a weekend, the parking restrictions were lifted so she didn't have to drive up and down the back streets looking for a residents' space.

Jane had grown to like Melcombe Street, with its narrow three-story white stucco-fronted houses and its proximity to Regent's Park, where she regularly jogged. Baker Street tube was virtually on her doorstep and was handy for getting into central London, shopping in Oxford Street or a night out in the West End. It wasn't so great for getting to Peckham, however, which is why she used her car to travel to and from work. Spotting a space close to her flat, Jane parked the car, got out and locked it. Her first car had been a second-hand VW that was an unfortunate bright yellow, but she had now traded it in for a newer version, which the team had jokingly nicknamed "the Jaffa Cake" due to its orange body and black roof.

As Jane headed for her flat, she contemplated popping into the Spar shop to buy something to cook for supper, but she was so tired that she decided she would just heat up some leftovers.

She smiled to herself as she stopped to catch her breath on the stairs. She was fit and could normally manage the three flights at a brisk pace, but her body was physically drained from lack of sleep and food.

The flat had been in good condition when Jane first moved in almost three years ago. Other than a lick of paint here and there, and a few pieces of furniture, she'd done little to it by way of further maintenance. Although small, it had two bedrooms and a well-equipped kitchen incorporating a small dining area. There was no sitting room and her mother was always saying "the place is so small you can't even swing a cat in it." Despite the fact she'd nearly been murdered in her flat by an active member of the IRA, she felt safe there.

Natalie Wilde had deliberately befriended Jane to cajole police information out of her about IRA suspects, whilst at the same time planning to bomb Scotland Yard's annual CID Good Friday party. On realizing Jane had discovered her deceit, Natalie tried to murder her, and if it weren't for the intervention of one of her colleagues she would have died. At the time, she felt emotionally drained and depressed, but after the experience with Natalie she'd learnt to develop her own coping mechanisms, and face her demons head on.

Jane ate some reheated spaghetti bolognese, had a relaxing hot bath and went straight to bed. She was woken by the bedside phone ringing and, looking at her alarm clock, saw that it was only 6:30 p.m. Feeling groggy, she stretched out for the receiver, picked it up and heard her mother's voice.

"Hello, dear. I know it's a bit last minute, but your father and I were wondering if you'd like to come over for Sunday lunch? Pam and Tony are coming with baby Nathan."

"I'd love to, Mum." Jane's mouth was so dry she paused to lick her lips before continuing.

"Great. I'll do roast beef, Yorkshire puds and veg. We'll eat at one o'clock."

"Mum, I'm sorry, but I can't come as I've got to work tomorrow."

"I noted on the wall calendar that you were off this weekend, after a night shift?" her mother replied brusquely.

"We had a murder last night, Mum. I'm on the investigation team, so—"

"You've only been at Peckham two weeks and already someone's been murdered?"

"I don't think my arrival at Peckham has anything to do with it."

"Don't be flippant, dear. You know I worry about you, especially if you are having to arrest people who commit such violent crimes . . . Was it a woman or man that was killed?"

"A woman. I'm in charge of the house-to-house enquiries, not the arrest team, so don't worry yourself. I'm really tired and need to get some sleep, so I'll ring you later."

Jane didn't dare worry her mother more by telling her any details about the murder, especially as the victim was around the same age as her.

"You always seem to be busy with work, Jane. The family haven't seen you in ages. You should at least make the effort to see Pam and your new nephew."

"I saw Pam and the baby last weekend. I went round to her place and she did my hair before I started night shift."

"Oh, Pam didn't mention your visit to me," Mrs. Tennison replied, sounding annoyed that she wasn't told.

Jane was irritated. "Why should she, Mum? It was just a haircut. Look, I really need to get some sleep. I'm sorry about tomorrow but I'll let you know when I'm next free and can come over."

"It would be nice if you offered to babysit for Pam and Tony so they could have a night out together. Honestly, Jane, sometimes it feels like you put the needs of the police force before your family. I'm sure the CID could cope without you now and again . . ."

"So can you, Mum. I'm sorry if my work inconveniences you," Jane replied abruptly.

Mrs. Tennison said nothing and put the phone down. Jane instantly regretted her thoughtless remark. Despite her tiredness, she wondered if she should ring her back to apologize. However, not wanting to get into another argument, she decided not to until she'd had a decent sleep. Jane pulled the duvet over her shoulders and snuggled into the fetal position. No sooner had she closed her eyes than the phone rang again.

She picked up the receiver. "I'm sorry for upsetting you . . ."

"You haven't," a surprised Gibbs replied, curious about who Jane had just been speaking to.

"Sorry, I thought you were my mother. I was tired and I snapped at her . . . Has there been a development in the case? Do you need me to come in?"

"No. Just thought I'd let you know I've been up to Copeland Road to have a look at the Allegro car and it's not reported lost or stolen. It was locked, the ignition was not hotwired and the front tire was as flat as a pancake. I doubt the radio was nicked as the loose wires had tape on the end to stop them sparking if they touched. Definitely not the sort of thing a thief would do if they'd just nicked it."

"Do you think the car could belong to our murder victim?" Jane asked as she sat up in bed.

"No. Clean as a whistle inside, pair of driving gloves on the front passenger seat, with a tartan rug and cushions on the back seat. It's more an older person's type of car. The registered owner is ex-directory, lives in St. John's Wood, just by Regent's Park. It's probably not connected to the investigation, but you need to find out why it's been left in Peckham."

"I know where it is, but I'm in bed now. I've hardly slept . . ."

"You can do it in the morning on your way in. The address is—"

"Hang on, let me get a pen and paper." Jane opened the bedside cabinet drawer. She had quickly learnt that having a pen and notepad close to hand was crucial, even in bed. She told Gibbs to go ahead and he gave her the car registration as TLY 225R. The owner, shown on the police national computer, was a Mrs. Sybil Hastings, flat 42, Viceroy Court, Prince Albert Road.

"Have you checked her name against missing persons?" Jane asked.

"Of course. She isn't reported missing and there's no one on mispers matching our victim's description either."

"Anything else, or can I get some sleep now?" Jane asked irritably as she tore the bit of paper from the notepad.

"I'll meet you there at nine a.m.," Gibbs said.

"I'm quite capable of doing a simple vehicle enquiry on my own, you know."

"Yes, but I need a lift as my Triumph Stag's in the garage having a new head gasket fitted. Tamara's flat is in Mayfair so I'll get her to drop me off at Viceroy Court. We're doing a gig at a pub in Belsize Park tonight—why don't you come along, Jane?"

"No thanks, Spence, I just need to get some sleep. I'll see you in the morning." Jane put the phone down, realizing, with slight annoyance, that Gibbs had given her the vehicle enquiry so he could get a lift in to work. She didn't mind too much as he'd at least been to Copeland Road to check the vehicle out and someone would have to have spoken with the owner anyway.

Pulling the duvet over her head, Jane was in a deep sleep within seconds, all thoughts of the investigation pushed from her mind for the time being.

CHAPTER THREE

It was cold outside. Jane had the engine running and heating on as she sat in her car facing the entrance to Viceroy Court. The brick-built 1930s modernist building consisted of eighty luxury apartments, laid out in the form of an elongated "H," with an underground garage and a white four-column porte-cochère covering the main entrance. The apartments overlooked Regent's Park and, even though it was winter, the surrounding lawns and hedgerows were well maintained, and the flowerbeds were filled with an abundance of color from winter pansies, violas and cyclamen.

Looking at her watch, Jane realized that it was 9:15 a.m. and Gibbs still hadn't arrived. She wasn't sure if he was running late or had changed his mind about accompanying her, so she decided she'd make the enquiry at Mrs. Hastings' flat herself. Standing at the main entrance, she pressed the buzzer and a smartly dressed uniformed porter came to the door. Jane introduced herself and showed him her warrant card.

"Follow me, madam."

The reception area had a thick red carpet, a desk area for the porter and two large floral displays either side of a wide marble staircase to the upper floors. The porter, who looked to be in his late fifties, turned out to be a bit of a nosy "jobsworth," making Jane sign the visitors' book and asking what the purpose of her visit was. Jane told him it was a minor enquiry regarding the theft of property from a resident's car.

"May I ask which resident, madam?"

"I'm sure the resident will reveal his or herself to you if they feel inclined to do so," Jane said as she walked towards the lift.

"Would you like me to accompany you, madam?" he asked as he opened the old-fashioned sliding grille gate of the lift and ushered Jane inside.

"No, thanks," Jane replied, smiling as she closed the gate and pressed the button for the fourth floor.

Apartment 42 was to the left. Jane pressed the doorbell and after a few seconds the door was opened by a woman in her mid-sixties, wearing a floral pinafore apron over a white shirt, calf-length tartan skirt, dark tights and flat-sole black house shoes. Jane held up her warrant card.

"Mrs. Hastings, I'm Detective Sergeant Jane Tennison."

"I'm no' Mrs. Hastings, dear. She's no' in just noo. I'm Agnes Anderson, her housekeeper. I thought you might be Mrs. Hastings, or her son Andrew. I phoned him earlier. Did he call you?" The woman spoke quickly, but in a soft, almost melodic, Scottish highland accent.

Jane was confused by what Agnes was saying, and thought she seemed rather anxious about something.

"Is her husband in?" Jane asked.

"He's no' alive, dear. Passed away a few years ago now from a heart attack."

Jane reached into her coat pocket and got out the bit of paper she'd written the details on. "Does Mrs. Hastings own a light blue Vanden Plas Princess Allegro, registration TLY 2—"

"Yes. Oh my goodness. Has she been in an accident? Is she in hospital? Have you told Andrew?" Agnes looked very worried as she fired her random questions at Jane.

Jane didn't want to say she was investigating a murder, but needed to know more about the car. "There was a minor car accident that we believe Mrs. Hastings may have been involved in, but failed to stop and exchange details with the other driver. Can I come inside and speak with you, please?"

Jane followed Agnes down the interior hallway into a large, plush living room, which had two white sofas and two arm-chairs, with hand-embroidered cushions scattered over them. An expensive Persian rug lay at the foot of a large white marble fireplace, the centerpiece of which was a Regency-style brass and chrome electric fire, with colored glass coals that gave off a flickering flame effect. Carved teak cabinets and chests had porcelain and china ornaments displayed on them, as well as what appeared to be family photographs. Various oil and water paintings were hanging from the walls, and in front of the long balcony, which overlooked Regent's Park, was a carved eight-seater teak dining table and matching Regency-style chairs. It was clear that Mrs. Hastings was a woman of considerable wealth.

"Do you have any idea where Mrs. Hastings might be at present?" Jane asked.

"Noo. She went out late Friday afternoon in her car an' I havnae seen her since. To be honest, I'm a wee bit worried. It appears she's nay been home and usually she'd leave me a message. Mind, I was out Friday night and stayed over at a friend's, I got home late last night and went to bed, then this morning I went to check on Mrs. Hastings, to see if she wanted breakfast, but she was no' in her bed. I even checked the underground car park and her car was no' there. Where did this accident happen?"

Jane told Agnes it was in Peckham.

"Peckham? But her golf course is over in Coombe Hill. Ohh, now I'm confused. I cannae remember if she said on Friday that she was going to see a friend from the golf club or she was going to the golf club to see a friend Or was she going to see Andrew . . . ?"

Jane was finding it hard to keep up with what Agnes was saying. "You mentioned you phoned Mrs. Hastings' son, Andrew?"

"Aye, I called him about eight thirty this morning to say I was worried about his mother's whereabouts. Andrew said to stop worrying as his mum was probably visiting friends for the weekend, or decided to have a night or two away on her own in a hotel, which she has done before . . . Normally she'd always tell me or leave a wee note if she was going anywhere. Andrew said he'd make a few phone calls and get back to me."

Jane asked if Mrs. Hastings had any friends in the Peckham or Dulwich areas. When Agnes said that she didn't know of any, Jane, now becoming a bit concerned, asked Agnes what Mrs. Hastings looked like. She doubted, due to the apparent age of their victim, that it was Mrs. Hastings who had been murdered. Agnes went over to one of the teak cabinets, picked up a photograph and handed it to Jane, who could see it was two women and two men, standing by a putting green holding golf clubs.

"That was taken last summer at Coombe Hill in the mixed four-ball competition. Mrs. Hastings is on the left—she's a good golfer—and that's her son Andrew next to her—he's her only child. I don't know who the other two are."

"How old is Mrs. Hastings?"

"She's sixty-six now."

Jane estimated Agnes was a few years younger than Mrs. Hastings. It was clear from her age and the photograph that Sybil Hastings was not their murder victim. Jane realized there wasn't much more she could ask Agnes and it would be best to ring later to see if Mrs. Hastings had returned home. However, she could see Agnes was still worried so decided to stay and chat with her. Just then the doorbell rang, which made the nervous Agnes jump.

"I'll get it. It's probably my colleague, Detective Inspector Gibbs," Jane said in an effort to calm Agnes.

Gibbs looked disheveled and hungover. Jane introduced Agnes to him as Mrs. Hastings' housekeeper and Gibbs asked if he could have a glass of water. Agnes went off to the kitchen to get him one. Jane wondered if Gibbs was still drinking heavily, or had recently fallen off the wagon. He stood beside Jane, his hands deep in his coat pockets.

"Dickhead porter wanted to know the ins and outs of a duck's arse . . . 'May I ask why you are here, sir?'" Gibbs said, exaggerating the porter's ostentatious manner and tone. "The pretentious git shut up when I told him we'd had a complaint that someone in a porter's uniform was flashing at elderly women in Regent's Park."

Jane refrained from laughing. Only Gibbs could come out with quick put-downs like that. She told him she hadn't mentioned anything about the murder they were investigating to Agnes as she didn't want to unduly worry her. Jane showed Gibbs the photograph she was still holding and pointed to the woman on the left.

"That's Mrs. Hastings and her son Andrew next to her. As you can see, she's clearly not our victim. Sybil Hastings owns the blue Allegro, but she's been away since Friday afternoon. Her son thinks she could be with friends or having a weekend away somewhere on her own."

Gibbs shrugged his shoulders. "Then we're wasting valuable time here. The priority is identifying our victim."

Jane replaced the photo on the cabinet. "Seems strange she should just leave her car in Peckham without contacting her son or Agnes."

"She's a grown woman who can do as she pleases. She might even have a secret toy boy lover over Peckham way. Her whereabouts are not our problem," Gibbs said.

Agnes came back into the living room with a glass of water and handed it to Gibbs, who gulped it down. Jane thanked Agnes for her assistance, asked for the flat phone number and said she'd ring back later to see if Mrs. Hastings had been in touch. Suddenly they heard an aristocratic voice bellowing down the hallway.

"Have you heard from Mother yet, Agnes? I phoned a few of her friends but no luck."

"That's Andrew," Agnes whispered nervously to Jane and Gibbs.

"I was supposed to be playing golf this morning, you know, and I've had to ruddy well cancel it," Andrew said as he entered the living room. He looked every inch the sophisticated golfer in a white nylon turtleneck top, with a woolen magenta jumper over it, hound's-tooth pattern golf trousers and black brogues. He was good-looking, in his late thirties and six-foot tall, with swept-back blond hair, which he ran his hand through as he looked inquisitively at Jane and Gibbs.

"Who are you?" he asked, looking at them in a disparaging manner.

"They're police officers, Andrew," Agnes told him.

Andrew gave Agnes a stern look. "I told you not to call the police."

"I didn't," Agnes replied timidly, and gesticulated towards Jane. "Sergeant Tennison is investigating a car accident your mother was involved in. She's no' hurt, but she drove off without stopping. Come to think of it, maybe that's why she hasn't come home . . ."

"Utter nonsense, Agnes. You know as well as I do Mother is as honest as the day is long. She'd never drive off after an accident." He looked at Gibbs. "And who, may I ask, is Tennison's sidekick?"

Jane could see from the way Gibbs pursed his lips that Andrew's sidekick remark had irritated him.

"I'm Detective Inspector Gibbs and we're here—"

"On false pretenses, I suspect," Andrew interrupted. "I'm friends with a very senior police officer, so I know for a fact detectives wouldn't be investigating a minor car accident. So why are you really here?"

Jane looked at Gibbs, wondering if she should say something. She intended to be polite and tactful, but Gibbs, who had clearly taken a dislike to Andrew, spoke up before she could.

"We are investigating a murder of a female in Peckham."

Agnes gasped, then Gibbs continued with a hint of disdain towards Hastings. "Having seen a photograph of your mother, she's clearly not the victim, so you can go and play your golf match if you want."

Andrew looked offended. "I find your attitude most rude, officer!"

Gibbs smiled. "When your mother returns, could you ask her to contact Peckham CID so we can have a quick chat with her about why she was in Peckham and why her car is there?"

"Why do you need to speak with her? Why did you even think she might have been a murder victim?" Andrew asked in a raised voice.

Jane thought things were getting out of hand, but as objectionable as Mr. Hastings was, he deserved to know about his mother's car being the real reason for their visit.

"We didn't think she was a murder victim, Mr. Hastings. Her car was found near the scene of a murder in Peckham. It is standard procedure to check out nearby parked cars and speak with the owners in case they may have seen something suspicious," Jane said.

"Peckham? My mother doesn't have friends in rundown places like Peckham," Andrew said indignantly.

"She might know someone in Dulwich Village, which is nearby and more upmarket," Gibbs remarked.

"If she did, I think I'd know," Andrew replied.

"This is all rather distressing," Agnes said, looking close to tears.

"The car was parked neatly up against the curb and locked. Apart from a flat tire, it looked in good condition," Gibbs said.

"I can't see my mother leaving her car in Peckham for two days without contacting me."

"If you're worried about your mother then I suggest you report her missing," Gibbs said bluntly.

"Then you'd better take down her details, hadn't you, Inspector Gibbs?"

Gibbs looked at his watch as he spoke. "Reporting her missing is entirely up to you, but it needs to be done at your local police station, which is St. John's Wood. Thank you for your time, Mr. Hastings."

"I find your attitude insensitive and unhelpful. Where exactly is my mother's car, so I can arrange for it to be brought back here before it gets stolen or damaged?"

"If you have a spare key, we could drop you there on our way back to Peckham, then you could drive it back here yourself," Jane suggested, trying to be helpful.

"There's a spare key somewhere in the kitchen," Andrew said and went to look for it, closely followed by Agnes.

Gibbs glared at Jane and whispered, "You shouldn't have offered Little Lord Fauntleroy a lift. Egotistical people like him look down on the police, as if we're uneducated and only exist to do their bidding." He held his right thumb and index finger close together. "I'm that close to sticking my fist down his posh gob!"

Jane suggested he wait outside and calm down a little, but Gibbs decided he'd make his own way back to the station, rather than put up with any more of Hastings' arrogance, and left.

Andrew returned with the car key in his hand. "Where's Inspector Gibbs gone?" he asked Jane.

She decided to lie. "He's running late for a meeting at Scotland Yard and had to go."

"I find his attitude very unprofessional. He'd better hope that no harm has come to my mother."

"Would you like me to come with you to Peckham, Andrew?" Agnes asked.

"No, I would not. You stay here in case Mother calls. And the house looks like it could do with a clean . . ."

Jane looked around the room, which was spotless. She thought to herself it was the pot calling the kettle black after his remarks about Gibbs being rude.

Outside, when Jane pointed to her car, she could see Andrew Hastings looked somewhat shocked.

"Is this really a police car?" he asked, looking at the vehicle with disdain.

"No, it's a Jaffa Cake on wheels, according to my colleagues." Jane smiled.

As she drove out of Viceroy Court, Andrew cleared his throat and looked at her in what she felt was a haughty manner.

"Do you know Detective Chief Superintendent Michael Blake?"

Jane knew he was deliberately name-dropping and sensed he wanted her to ask how he knew DCS Blake.

"I've heard the name, but I don't know him," she said politely.

"He's a senior officer in the Serious Crime Office at Scotland Yard."

Although Jane had never worked with Blake, she was aware he was commonly known to many officers, especially females, by the nickname "WHAT," which was an abbreviation for Wandering Hand Trouble. He often tried to touch female officers inappropriately.

"Michael and I are good friends. We're members of the same golf club and often dine out together with our wives. He's very professional in everything he does—unlike your DI Gibbs.

Michael would have taken my mother's details for a missing person's report if I'd asked him," Andrew sneered.

Jane thought Gibbs was right about Andrew Hastings being an insufferable, arrogant arsehole. She wished she'd never offered him a lift, but realizing Andrew's remark was a veiled threat to tell Blake about Gibbs, she slipped her notebook and pen out of her jacket pocket and handed it to Andrew.

"If you'd like to write down your mother's details, date of birth, height etc. at the back of my notebook, I'll get a telex misper report sent to St. John's Wood from Peckham. I'll need your home address and phone number as well, so an officer can contact you as well as Agnes."

"There, that wasn't all that difficult after all, was it, DS Tennison?" Andrew said with a smug grin as he started to write in her notebook.

"When did you last see your mother?"

"Last Sunday, when I played golf with her."

"Bit cold for golf, isn't it?" Jane remarked.

"We're not just summer golfers; we play all year round, unless the course is closed due to severe weather conditions," Andrew replied condescendingly.

"Hopefully your mother will have had a relaxing weekend somewhere and return home later today."

"Well, she'll have ruined my day if that is the case."

Jane was appalled by his remark. She knew she should ask him to write down details of his mother's last known movements, but she couldn't bear to be in his company any longer.

Arriving at Copeland Road, Jane pulled up in front of the Allegro. Andrew confirmed that it looked like his mother's car, and on trying the key in the driver's door, the lock popped open. He looked at the flat front offside tire and kicked it.

"Flat as a pancake."

Jane wondered why men always felt the need to kick a flat tire when it was fairly obvious it had a puncture.

"Too flat to get it back to my mother's without damaging the wheel. I'll have to change the tire for the spare in the boot. Don't suppose you could help me, DS Tennison?"

"Sorry, I'm a woman—as you know, we don't have a clue about changing car tires. I need to get back to the station." Jane returned one of Andrew's irritating smiles as she walked back to the car, laughing to herself.

Suddenly Jane heard Andrew cry out and turned to see him stumbling backwards, away from the boot of the car, a look of sheer terror on his face. Jane ran to the boot. Inside was a body lying in a fetal position, wearing a full-length mink fur coat. There was an awful stench radiating from it. The face, the body and the coat were heavily blood stained, and Jane could see stab wounds and cuts to the face and back of one of the hands.

"My mother, my mother. . . . Oh dear God . . . Who's done this to her?" Andrew fell to his knees on the road, gasping for air and clutching his chest.

CHAPTER FOUR

"How the fuck could you two let this happen?" Moran shouted at Jane and Gibbs as he paced up and down his office.

"You're overseeing house-to-house, Tennison, so vehicles are your responsibility as well. You should have checked the bloody car out as soon as it was brought to your attention."

Jane looked at Gibbs.

"I told her to go home and get some rest. I checked the car out myself. There was nothing untoward so I rang—"

"Nothing untoward! Sybil Hastings' body was in the boot with multiple stab wounds. Some deranged maniac used her as a fucking pincushion. Anyone with a bit of common sense would consider that if the first body was probably dumped, then it might have been taken there by car, making the initial discovery of the abandoned vehicle highly relevant to the investigation."

"Sorry, sir. The car had a flat tire and we did follow it up by going to Mrs. Hastings' flat the next morning. I don't see what else we could have done at the time," Jane said.

Moran shook his head in disbelief. "You should have had the car checked out thoroughly before going off duty."

"I disagree," Gibbs said, much to Moran's obvious annoyance. "There were many cars parked in Copeland Road. We had no reasonable suspicion or power to force entry and search any cars without the owners' permission, or a warrant, which I doubt a magistrate would have granted under the circumstances."

"But you didn't bother asking a magistrate, did you, DI Gibbs?"

"Both victims were women but there was a big age gap. One was strangled and the other stabbed to death. Mrs. Hastings and the unknown alleyway victim could have been killed by different people and the proximity of their bodies was coincidental," Gibbs said in his defense.

Moran was not impressed. "Coincidence! Are you seriously saying the proximity of the bodies is mere coincidence?"

"The first victim's murder could have occurred in premises in Copeland Road, or nearby, and the body carried the short distance to the alleyway to be dumped, as opposed to driven there," Jane said.

Moran banged his hand on the table. "Stop trying to defend each other. You both screwed up. Once the press gets hold of it, they'll have a field day saying we're incompetent. Our first victim's fingerprints weren't on file, so she's got no criminal record. We don't know if she's connected to Sybil Hastings, so we need more from her son. What did the hospital say about his condition, Tennison?"

"He didn't have a heart attack, but is suffering from severe shock. He's under sedation and they're keeping him in for observation. I asked him if he wanted us to inform his wife, but he said she was out and he'd contact her himself later to tell her what had happened."

Gibbs shook his head. "There's something strange about Andrew Hastings' attitude. Although he's stuck up and arrogant, he didn't seem that concerned about his mother's whereabouts. He was more pissed off about missing his golf game. And he was aggressive towards the housekeeper when he thought she'd reported Mrs. Hastings missing to police without consulting him first."

"Do you agree?" Moran snapped at Jane.

Jane nodded. "He's certainly arrogant and was aggressive towards Agnes, the housekeeper, who seemed scared of him. Come to think of it, he hadn't thought about reporting his mother missing until DI Gibbs suggested it. Also, Agnes did say she thought Mrs. Hastings might have gone to see Andrew on Friday afternoon at his house in Kingston."

"Are you two suggesting he could be responsible for his mother's murder? Because if you are, that means he may also be responsible for our unknown victim's death."

Gibbs was quick to reply. "Mrs. Hastings is a widower and clearly very wealthy."

"Any other siblings?" Moran asked.

"The housekeeper said Andrew was an only child, so he will inherit it all now."

"What did you make of his reaction to finding his mother's body?" Moran asked Jane.

"Hard to say, really, as neither of us were expecting it."

"He could be a good actor, but the fact is we need to know more about him and his movements on Friday and Saturday," Gibbs said.

Moran nodded. "And we need to find out more about his relationship with his mother. Gibbs, I want you to go to Andrew Hastings' house, see if the wife is there and ask if she knows anything about her mother-in-law's movements—but be discreet."

"And if she's not there or there's anything untoward?" Gibbs asked.

"Speak with the neighbors first; if none of them have seen her since Friday, ring me and I'll consider a different plan of action. Tennison, you go back and speak with the housekeeper, inform her of Mrs. Hastings' murder and see what she has to say when Andrew isn't there. Take DS Lawrence with you, get him to check over the house in case, God forbid, she was murdered there. Also check for a will and any letters or paperwork that might help us."

Jane hesitated. "The unknown victim's age is believed to be late twenties to early thirties. I'd say Andrew Hastings was mid-thirties, so his wife would probably be about the same age."

"You're thinking the body in the alley might be his wife?" Moran remarked with surprise.

Jane nodded. "I know the woman in the alleyway wasn't wearing expensive clothes, but it's possible. Agnes never spoke with Andrew's wife about Mrs. Hastings' whereabouts."

Gibbs interjected. "Jesus, maybe he killed them both, so that everything would be his, and then dumped the bodies in Peckham."

"Until we make further enquiries, this is all conjecture and guesswork. Andrew Hastings may even have a firm alibi for his movements on Friday and Saturday." Moran replied.

"Yeah, but he could have hired someone to kill them," Gibbs added, looking serious.

Jane knew it was a valid point, but wondered if Gibbs' instant dislike of Andrew Hastings was beginning to cloud his judgment.

"Although Andrew Hastings' reactions may seem strange, it doesn't mean he's a murderer. The quicker he can be removed from the inquiry, the faster we can move on in the investigation. Get out there and find me something positive, but be—" Moran's phone rang and he picked it up.

Moran was addressing the caller as "sir," so they knew it must be a senior officer. His apologetic tone and the mention of "Mr. Hastings" indicated that he was talking about the discovery of Sybil Hastings' body.

Moran continued, "Yes, sir, I understand . . . I wasn't aware of that . . . DI Gibbs and DS Tennison are with me just now, sir . . . I'm short-staffed as it is . . . Thank you for bringing it to my attention . . . I can assure you it won't happen again." Moran put the phone down and glared at Gibbs.

"That was Chief Superintendent Michael Blake."

Jane exclaimed, "Oh, I forgot to tell you: Andrew Hastings mentioned to me that he's friends with Blake. They play golf together, and have dinner."

"That's all I needed to hear," Gibbs hissed to Jane. "What did WHAT want?" he asked Moran.

"Your bloody heads on a plate. And cut out the crap with calling him WHAT," Moran barked. "Blake has been told to oversee the investigation and we're to deal with both murders. It seems Andrew Hastings is a good friend and phoned Blake from the hospital. Hastings complained about your attitude, Gibbs. Blake was considering taking you both off the investigation until I mentioned I was short-staffed."

Gibbs was irritated. "Blake and Hastings are probably in the same Masonic lodge. Well, he's obviously not that unwell if he can call Blake. I'd like to go to the hospital and interview him."

"No way. I don't want you two anywhere near him. It could do more harm than good. I'll interview Hastings personally, with Blake's approval, once he's released from the hospital. If he complains to Blake that we spoke with his wife, I'll argue that we needed to know as much about his mother as possible to move the investigation forward. Now, the pair of you—get out there and start digging. Keep me updated."

Jane went to the Met forensic labs at Lambeth to speak to DS Lawrence, who was in the vehicle examination bay inspecting Sybil Hastings' Allegro. The car had been taken from the scene on a transporter, with the body still in the boot so they could remove it, and examine the car, away from the public and in weather-proof surroundings. A SOCO helped Lawrence lift the heavily bloodstained body from the boot and place it on a white plastic sheet.

"Hi, Paul. How's it going?" she asked.

"Haven't started on the inside yet. There's a handbag in the boot, which was under the body. Grab some gloves and have a look in it for me while I bag and tag the body."

"Is the PM this afternoon?" Jane asked as she took some latex gloves out of Lawrence's forensic kit bag.

"No. Prof. Martin's got his granddaughter's christening today so it'll be tomorrow morning at Ladywell mortuary, ten a.m. kick-off. The Prof. popped out to the scene for a quick look at the body this morning. He reckons that, from the skin discoloration, mild decomposition and the fact rigor had passed, she died on the Friday within the same time frame as the unknown victim."

Lawrence knelt beside the body to take a closer look. "From the multiple stab injuries to her face and body, this was a frenzied attack. The one to the heart probably killed her."

"Gibbs doesn't like Hastings and thinks he might be responsible for his mother's murder," Jane said, taking the handbag out of the boot and carrying it over to the examination table.

"As the textbook says—thinking something and proving it are very different, Jane. Without evidence, you have nothing," Lawrence said.

Jane looked at the handbag. It was an expensive Kelly bag, with a patchwork brown snakeskin exterior and leather-lined interior.

"Do you think the two murders could be connected?" She asked, removing the contents of the handbag and placing them on a brown paper exhibits bag.

"The methods are different, but who knows . . . Fibers might help us, especially if we find some from the unknown victim's clothing on Mrs. Hastings' clothing, or vice versa. But that's going to take time and they won't start work on the clothes until tomorrow."

The contents of the handbag included a make-up compact, lipstick, some leather gloves and a purse containing £50 in different bank notes. There were also a couple of credit cards and a cash card, all assigned to "Mrs. Sybil Hastings."

Jane held the money and cards up for Lawrence to see. "Doesn't look as though robbery was a motive." She double-checked the bag to make sure she'd got everything in it. "There are no keys of any kind in here."

"I checked her coat pockets and the inside of the car, but no keys there either. Suggests the killer drove her car to Copeland Road and has either still got her keys or disposed of them somewhere."

Spencer Gibbs arrived at Rookwood Close just after one o'clock. It was a quiet, opulent area, just off Kingston Hill, with four big houses, each built in a different architectural style. Andrew Hastings' residence was a large, six-bedroom, medieval Tudor house with big dormer windows and decorative half timbering. The roofs were steeply pitched, with side gables, and there was a massive stone chimney capped with an elaborate chimney pot. It seemed that Andrew Hastings was a man of wealth, but Gibbs knew that often things were not always as they appeared on the surface.

There was a 1978 grey Mercedes station wagon parked on the driveway, and Gibbs wondered if it was Hastings' wife's car, given that Andrew's car must still be at the mother's flat. Gibbs approached the oak front door and used the large brass lion knocker. It was opened by a very attractive woman in her early thirties. She was about five foot eight inches tall, with an hour-glass figure and long blond hair that flowed around her soft, glowing complexion and striking blue eyes. She wore black figure-hugging trousers and a white T-shirt. Gibbs was expecting a polished accent and was surprised when she spoke with an East London lilt.

"Whatever yer selling, I ain't interested, darlin'." She started to close the door.

Gibbs held up his warrant card, introduced himself and asked if she was Mrs. Hastings. She nodded and he asked if he could come in to speak with her about her husband.

"He's still at the golf club, love."

Gibbs thought it strange that Andrew hadn't phoned his wife from hospital to let her know what had happened.

"I'm afraid your husband's in hospital, Mrs. Hastings. It's nothing serious, he's just under observation after an incident earlier."

The young Mrs. Hastings didn't seem concerned as she opened the door and let Gibbs in. "The living room's this way. Has Andrew been hit by a golf ball?" she joked, closing the front door.

"No, Mrs. Hastings, he—" Gibbs started to explain as he followed her across the hallway, but was interrupted.

"He's crashed the Bentley, ain't he? I've told him time and time again not to drive home pissed from the golf club."

"No, he hasn't been involved in a car crash. It's to do with his mother, Mrs. Hastings."

She looked at Gibbs with a friendly smile. "Please, officer, you don't need ter be so formal. My name's Joanne, but everyone calls me Jo."

As they approached the living room, Gibbs heard the sound of children. Entering the vast room, he saw a young boy and girl chasing each other around a sofa. Joanne shouted at them to go upstairs and play in their rooms.

"We don't want to," they argued back, almost in unison.

"Inspector Gibbs is a policeman. He'll arrest yer if yer don't behave, so do as I say."

They ran out of the room without a backwards glance.

Gibbs always thought it was wrong of parents to make remarks like that to their children as it led to them regarding police officers in a negative light.

"So what did the old battle-axe do to put my husband in hospital?"

Gibbs asked Jo to sit down, then explained the full circumstances surrounding Andrew's discovery of Sybil Hastings' body and his subsequent collapse.

"My God! That's awful! Poor Andrew. What hospital's he in?"

"King's, in Camberwell," Gibbs replied, wondering why she was so calm. She didn't seem unduly concerned about her mother-in-law's death. "Mrs. Hastings was stabbed multiple times. It was a vicious attack and at present we have no idea who did it."

"You must think I'm a bitch for referring to me mother-in-law as a 'battle-axe.' Sybil and I didn't see eye ter eye and we didn't really speak."

Gibbs was keen to find out more about her husband's movements on the Friday and Saturday, so didn't continue asking about Jo's relationship with Sybil.

"Did your husband mention that Agnes was worried that something had happened to Mrs. Hastings and wanted to report her missing?"

Jo shook her head. "To be honest I wouldn't have been that interested if he had told me. He doesn't talk about his mother to me cos it usually ends up in a row. But I'm sorry she was murdered. She adored her grandchildren and they loved her."

"I thought Andrew might have phoned you from the hospital before I got here," Gibbs remarked, trying not to sound suspicious about him.

Jo shrugged. "He knew I was taking the kids to visit me parents in Bermondsey for the day, so he probably thought I was still there."

"But you didn't go?" Gibbs asked, wondering if he had misunderstood her.

"Shortly after Andrew left this morning, my mum rang to say there'd been a power cut in their block and they had no heating. With it being so cold, I decided to stay home."

"Is Bermondsey where you're from?" Gibbs asked, realizing it wasn't far from Peckham.

"Yeah, born and bred. Accent give me away, did it?" she asked with a cheeky smile.

Gibbs smiled back. "Just a little." He looked around the lavish living room. "Looks like life's a bit different for you now."

Jo frowned. "Yeah, but trust me, money don't always bring yer happiness."

"How did you meet Andrew?"

"Through work. I was a secretary at Hastings Haulage in Bermondsey in the early seventies, when Andrew's dad, Henry, owned it. Henry was a lovely man. From a poor background he became a self-made millionaire with three depots across London." Jo spoke affectionately about Henry Hastings and smiled as she recalled the memories.

"Sounds like Henry was a hard worker," Gibbs remarked.

"And down to earth. Andrew's not like his dad, though. He was brought up with a silver spoon in his mouth and Henry gave him everything. Now all he cares about is playing golf. He leaves the running of the haulage businesses to the managers. Don't think the company's anything like what it used to be when Henry was running it."

Gibbs was surprised at Jo's openness about the family. She clearly didn't want for anything materially, but he felt that she was unhappy.

Hesitantly, he spoke. "I need to ask where your husband was last Friday, Jo?"

"Playing in a golf competition all day, at Coombe Hill," Jo answered, with a hint of displeasure.

"What time did he get home?"

Jo paused before answering. "Ter be honest, I don't know exactly. I'd gone to bed. I remember I was annoyed as he said he wasn't going ter be late."

Gibbs took out his CID notebook and pen. "Can you recall what time you went to bed, and how long after that your husband might have come home?"

"You're not thinking Andrew killed his mother, are you?" Jo exclaimed. "She's wet-nursed him all his bloody life and could do no wrong in his eyes."

"I didn't mean to imply that, Jo, but under the circumstances I have to verify his movements—it's standard procedure. We just need to establish that he has an alibi so that we can eliminate him from our enquiries."

Jo sighed. "I'd been watchin' *Village of the Damned* on TV and went to bed when it ended, must have been around midnight. I fell asleep and didn't hear Andrew come to bed. I woke at about four a.m. as one of the kids was crying. Andrew was there then, snorin' in bed next to me."

"Did he say anything in the morning about where he'd been?"

"When I asked him why he was so late he said he'd forgot to tell me there was a meal and prize-giving after the competition. Said he got chatting with a friend at the bar afterwards and didn't realize the time."

"Did he say who the friend was?"

"Michael Blake—he's a copper as well."

Gibbs raised his eyebrows. "Funnily enough, your husband told my colleague he knew DCS Blake."

"They play golf together and are in the same Masonic lodge. Personally, I can't stand the bloke. He's a pervert and makes my stomach turn."

Gibbs snorted, causing Jo to look at him quizzically.

"Sorry, I wasn't laughing at you, Jo. Every WPC in the Met feels the same as you about Blake, and the male detectives don't have much time for him either. He's an arrogant, pompous man. Not that you heard me say that."

"Maybe that's why he and my husband are such good friends."

Gibbs jotted down some notes. He wanted to ask how Andrew seemed on the Saturday after the competition, but didn't want to push things with Jo. If Andrew Hastings was at the golf club until after midnight, and Blake could vouch for him, then he was off the hook for the murders of his mother and the unknown victim. However, it was possible that he could have arranged their murders and created an alibi for himself.

"Do you know if Mrs. Hastings had fallen out with anyone, or had any enemies?"

"What, besides me, Inspector Gibbs?" Jo asked provocatively.

"Was it always bad between you?" Gibbs asked, wondering if she was mocking him.

Jo sighed. "Sybil thought I was too common for her son. Bloody cheek given that she was no posh bird herself—she didn't have a pot to piss in until she met Henry. I tried to be nice towards her, but she was always so smug and up her own arse about anything I said or did—especially when she moved in here for a while after Henry died."

Gibbs was curious. "Why did Sybil move in if you and she didn't get on?"

"To spite me—and prove she had control over Andrew. It was ten months of hell. All she did was moan about my bad housekeeping, and how I dealt with the kids. She nit-picked about every little thing, and it affected our marriage."

"It must have been a relief for you and Andrew when she moved out," Gibbs commented.

"It was too late by then—the damage was done. Andrew and I live under the same roof but we have separate lives. He spends all his time on the golf course while I'm at home playing housewife and looking after the twins. We have a cleaner who comes in regularly, but she's not much use."

Gibbs hesitated. "I hope you don't mind me asking this, but do you think your husband may have been having an affair?"

Jo nodded. "I've had my suspicions, but never any proof. He always has an excuse for why he gets home late. If I had any evidence, it would be all I needed to kick him out."

Gibbs was surprised at Jo's frankness. "Can I ask you to do something for me, Jo?" he asked.

"Depends what it is," she replied coyly.

"Your husband has already made a complaint to DCS Blake about me, so it would be best if he doesn't know about my visit today."

"Fine by me. But what if the kids say anything about a policeman being here?"

"You could just say that a local officer came to inform you about Andrew being in hospital."

"S'pose I'll have to go and see him in hospital anyway. I'll say it was a local copper who told me what had happened and which hospital he was in."

Gibbs closed his notebook and placed it back inside his jacket pocket.

Jo looked at him with a smile. "Tell me, Inspector Gibbs: are you married?"

"No. Can't find a woman who'd want to settle down with me," he joked.

"Not even a girlfriend?"

Gibbs wondered if Jo was playing games with him, or whether she was genuinely coming on to him. He knew that any form of relationship or physical contact with her could get him in big trouble. He thought of Tamara, who was younger than Jo and just as attractive, but not as sexy.

Gibbs smiled. "No, no girlfriend. Used to have one, but she cheated on me with a younger bloke."

Jo touched his arm. "That must have been awful for you. Do you ever mix business with pleasure?" she asked, moving closer to him.

Gibbs was unsure how to handle the situation. He couldn't help being attracted to her, but just as he was about to reply, the children came running into the living room.

"What's for lunch, Mum? We're starving!"

Jo turned to them. "I'll get it in a minute."

Gibbs stepped back. "I think I had better be going, Mrs. Hastings," he said. "Thank you for your time. I'll see myself out."

Jo said nothing as Gibbs turned and left.

CHAPTER FIVE

Jane and DS Lawrence were together in her car, driving to Viceroy Court.

"You still going out with what's his name?" Lawrence asked.

Jane grinned. "Which 'what's his name' would that be, Paul?"

"The male nurse at St. Thomas."

"Michael. No, we split up some time ago."

"Sorry to hear that. He seemed like a nice chap."

"He is. In fact, he's one of the nicest men I've ever met—second to you, of course."

Lawrence laughed. "Flattery won't get you anywhere with me, Sergeant Tennison."

Jane smiled. "It all finished amicably. To be honest, our different shift patterns meant we weren't really able to spend much time together. Michael got offered a senior charge nurse's position in Liverpool. We discussed it and I told him to take it. Truth is, we were both more interested in advancing our careers than settling down. I miss him, but we keep in contact on the phone. So I'm footloose and fancy free . . . What about you?"

"Still haven't found the right one."

"Good things come to those who wait, Paul."

"Knowing my luck, that will probably be when I'm in my eighties!"

Jane had always had a soft spot for Lawrence. He was very amiable, willing to help others and had taught her so much about forensics and crime scenes since she'd joined the Met. She had rarely ever heard him complain, despite the stress of having to deal with dead bodies and horrific crime scenes. Few officers would have the stomach to handle what he did, day in and day out.

At Viceroy Court, the same jobsworth porter let Jane and Lawrence in through the main entrance. Jane informed him her colleague was a fellow detective, but the porter insisted on seeing Paul's warrant card and requested that they both sign the visitors' book.

"What's the purpose of your visit, madam?"

"The same purpose as last time," Jane replied, walking towards the lift.

Agnes answered the door and immediately said that she hadn't heard from Mrs. Hastings. Jane and Paul followed her into the lounge and Agnes turned to look at Jane.

"It's no' good news, is it, officer?"

Jane shook her head and asked Agnes to sit down. As Jane told her about Sybil's murder, Agnes broke down in floods of tears. When she explained that Andrew had discovered her body in the boot of the car, Agnes started wailing loudly, rocking back and forth on the sofa.

"Would you like me to call a doctor?" Jane asked, putting her arm around Agnes' shoulder.

"No, no, thank you. I'll be all right in a wee minute." Agnes wiped her tears away with a tissue then blew her nose on it. "It's all such a terrible shock. Who could do such a thing to Mrs. Hastings? And why? She's never harmed anyone . . . She was such a kind and generous woman."

Lawrence went to the kitchen to get some water for Agnes.

"DS Lawrence is here to look through Mrs. Hastings' personal belongings, to see if there's anything that might help the investigation."

Agnes nodded. Lawrence returned with the water and handed it to Agnes, who took a sip before addressing him.

"All Mrs. Hastings' paperwork is in a small filing cabinet in the spare room, out there on the left," she said, pointing to the hallway.

Jane took hold of Agnes' hand as Lawrence left the room. "I need to ask some questions that may seem a bit probing, but it's a necessary part of the investigation."

Agnes nodded. Jane took it slowly, to cause as little distress to Agnes as possible.

"How long have you worked for Mrs. Hastings?"

"I became Mr. and Mrs. Hastings' live-in housekeeper at their house in Coombe Hill about fifteen years ago. Andrew was there too, until he married Jo. After Henry died, they sold that house and Mrs. Hastings went to live with Andrew and Jo for about a year. I lived with my sister until Mrs. Hastings moved into Viceroy Court a year ago. She asked me to move back in as her housekeeper again." Agnes sipped some water.

"Have you spoken to Andrew's wife since Friday?"

"Noo. I rarely have reason to phone their house, and as far as I know Jo has never rung here. Between us, Mrs. Hastings and Jo didn't get on. They never have, really."

"Why was that?" Jane asked.

"I don't know all the reasons, and it wasn't my place to ask. Seems to me that Mrs. Hastings thought Jo wasn't good enough for her son."

"How did Andrew feel about his mother and Jo's relationship?"

Agnes shrugged. "I don't know, I never asked him. He never said anything to me, but I can tell you that he loved and cared for his mother very much. He took her in when she was grief-stricken after her husband's death and he dealt with the sale of the old house and the purchase of this place."

Jane asked Agnes if she knew of anyone Mrs. Hastings had fallen out with recently. Agnes shook her head and said that Mrs. Hastings was not the sort of person who upset people. She also told Jane that Mrs. Hastings didn't really socialize with other residents in Viceroy Court, although she still played golf regularly with friends at Coombe Hill, where she was a member. Jane made a note of the names Agnes gave her in her notebook.

"Did Mrs. Hastings have any young female friends in their late twenties or early thirties?"

Agnes shook her head. "Not that I know of . . . But maybe at the Samaritans."

"Samaritans? Was Mrs. Hastings upset about something?" Jane asked, wondering why Mrs. Hastings might need emotional support from the Samaritans.

Agnes smiled. "Noo, Mrs. Hastings didn't have any problems. She was a volunteer with the Samaritans."

Jane was surprised, but knew this could be important to the investigation. "Oh, right, I misunderstood you. What exactly did she do there?"

"She was a listening volunteer for a few hours a week, at the branch in Soho. She didn't talk about her work there, as it was obviously confidential. But I know she found the work very rewarding and she said it made her realize how fortunate she was compared to others who were suffering terrible misery."

Jane asked Agnes if she knew the address of the Soho branch, but Agnes shook her head.

"Do you know if she kept a timetable of the hours she worked?"

"Aye, she did, in a date book that she kept in her handbag. She used the same date book for appointments with her friends as well. As I recall, she was at the Samaritans last Thursday."

Having already examined the contents of Sybil's handbag, Jane knew the date book wasn't there. She left the distraught Agnes sipping her water and went to find Paul. He told her that he had checked the kitchen, bedrooms and bathrooms, but couldn't see anything that suggested Mrs. Hastings' murder had taken place in her own flat.

"Well, that's some form of relief, I guess. If it had happened here, it might have pushed poor Agnes over the edge."

"I'm not saying categorically that it didn't happen here, Jane. There's a marble floor in the kitchen and bathroom, which could easily have been cleaned up if there was blood on it. I did some KM testing, but got no positive hits for blood. While we were in the lounge, I couldn't see any signs that areas of the carpet had been cleaned or furniture moved."

"Do you need more time here?" Jane asked.

Lawrence nodded. "It would be helpful if you could take Agnes to the kitchen so I can have a closer look in the lounge. I removed some documents from Mrs. Hastings' filing cabinet relating to her bank and savings accounts." He handed Jane an opened envelope. "Her will is inside. She's left a couple of grand to Agnes and everything else to Andrew Hastings. Looking at some of her bank statements and taking into consideration the value of this place, she was more than well off."

"You didn't see a date book in the spare room, did you?" Jane asked.

"No, and I had a good look inside the car before it was taken to the lab and it wasn't there. Is it important?"

"Agnes says that Mrs. Hastings kept one, but it seems to be missing. Her killer may have taken it because there was something in it about him. Also, she was a volunteer for the Samaritans, at their Soho branch."

"I imagine there are a few unstable people who seek help there. Could be she met up with one of them on Friday?"

Jane nodded. "I'll phone Moran and update him."

Using Mrs. Hastings' bedroom phone, Jane dialed DCI Moran's direct office number. When he answered, Jane filled him in about Sybil Hastings' will, her connection with the Samaritans, and the date book.

"We need to find that date book," Moran said.

"It doesn't appear to be in the house and it definitely wasn't in her handbag or in the car. I wonder if her killer may have taken it."

"Or disposed of it, if his name's in it," Moran remarked.

"Lawrence doesn't think Mrs. Hastings was killed here," Jane told him.

"Gibbs rang to say that Andrew Hastings' wife is alive and well. Apparently Hastings has an alibi for his movements on the Friday. According to his wife, he was at a golf club do that went on late into the evening. Gibbs is going to the club to check it out."

"Looks like we might be wrong about Andrew Hastings then," Jane reflected.

"Yes, but on the positive side at least we can eliminate him from our enquiries. I'd like you to go to the Samaritans in Soho, find out exactly what Sybil Hastings did there, and the details of anyone she was dealing with."

Jane recalled that Moran used to work in the West End. "Do you know the address of the Soho branch?"

"Forty-six Marshall Street—it's just off Beak Street."

Jane jotted down the address in her notebook. "I know Beak Street—it's near the trendy shops in Carnaby Street." She was about to put the phone down when Moran continued.

"I've had an artist's drawing done of our unknown victim. Can you get a recent picture of Sybil Hastings so I can release the details to the press?" He put the phone down.

Jane asked Agnes if they could have a cup of tea in the kitchen, leaving Lawrence to check out the lounge, although he didn't find anything of interest. Before they left, Jane asked Agnes if she could have a close-up photograph of Sybil, which she duly provided. Then Jane dropped Lawrence off at the lab in Lambeth before continuing to the Samaritans branch in Soho.

Gibbs arrived at Coombe Hill golf club, turning off the A238. He couldn't help noticing the instant change in surroundings. It was like driving into the countryside, with an abundance of oak, pine and sycamore trees, and a few houses, even bigger and more expensive than Andrew Hastings', set back off the road amongst the trees. Gibbs was surprised at how many golfers were in the grounds, particularly as it was winter. Some were carrying their clubs to and from their cars, whilst others practiced on the putting greens and chipping areas. He searched for a parking space amongst the Jaguars, Bentleys, Rolls Royces, Mercedes and other sports cars, chuckling to himself about how out of place the unmarked CID Hillman Hunter was. Spotting a space next to the entrance, Gibbs parked and got out the car.

"Excuse me, what do you think you're doing?" an authoritative Surrey accent boomed, in a haughty manner. Gibbs looked up to see a tall, balding man in his mid-sixties standing by the entrance to the clubhouse. He was dressed in a blazer, blue shirt and striped tie, with beige trousers that were an inch too short and revealed his white socks. He marched forward with a stern expression and as he approached, Gibbs recognized the badge on his blazer as that of the Blues and Royals, part of the Household Cavalry.

"You'll have to move your car—that's the captain's space you've just parked in."

Gibbs held up his warrant card. "DI Gibbs. I'm here on official police business."

"It wouldn't matter if you were the Commissioner, young man—you'd still have to move the car. Park it over there in the area clearly signposted for visitors."

Gibbs took a deep breath. Not wanting to risk another complaint about his attitude, he bit his tongue, apologized, and went to move the car. Returning to the steps of the clubhouse, the secretary introduced himself as Major Whitehead and asked how he could help. Gibbs responded that it was a delicate matter and that he needed to speak to him in private.

"Very well. I'm just finishing dealing with an important matter, but perhaps you could wait in the players' lounge." Whitehead pointed to a sign in the hallway, turned and walked off.

The players' lounge overlooked the well-manicured eighteenth green and its attractive tree- and heather-lined fairway. The large room was filled with leather easy chairs, sofas and small circular tables, whilst cabinets of trophies and engraved honors plaques lined the walls. Gibbs noticed that the Club Captains Board for 1979 had A. W. Hastings written on it. The bar was busy with golfers chatting to each other about their handicaps, how well they had played and about the stock markets. Some wore club blazers and ties, whilst others were more casual in club motif woolen sweaters. A couple of men were dressed in plus fours with knee-length socks. There were no women in the room.

Gibbs had no interest in the game and had only ever played mini golf when he was a kid on a family holiday at Butlin's. He thought it ironic that Sybil Hastings, who lived and socialized in this upper-class world, should be found stabbed to death in the boot of a car in Peckham.

Gibbs went over to the bar and ordered a pint of lager.

The barman smiled. "Are you a member, sir?"

Gibbs smiled back. "No, just visiting."

The barman frowned. "Then I can't serve you, sir, but a member can buy you a drink."

Gibbs took out his warrant card and showed it to the barman. "Major Whitehead said I could have a pint on the house. We wouldn't want to upset him, would we?"

The barman was very apologetic and poured Gibbs a pint. He downed it quickly, licking his lips satisfactorily. Placing the empty glass on the bar, he asked for a refill. As the barman placed the replenished pint on the bar, Whitehead walked over.

The barman smiled. "Should I put the officer's two pints on your tab, major, or on the club hospitality account?"

Whitehead glared at the barman and was clearly not pleased. Gibbs didn't help matters by raising his glass and saying "bottoms up" before gulping half of the contents.

The disgruntled major led the way through to his large office, which also overlooked the eighteenth green. The walls were oak paneled and covered with an array of golfing photographs. Amongst them were pictures of George VI, Winston Churchill and celebrities such as Jimmy Tarbuck, Bob Hope and Sean Connery. The floor was covered in a thick red carpet and at the far end of the room were period leather armchairs and a sofa. The major's large Jacobean writing desk had a leather-inlaid top and matching oak high-back chairs either side of it. He pointed to the chair opposite him and invited Gibbs to sit down.

The major proudly puffed out his chest. "Before this golf course was built, the area was known as Gallows Hill. Many highway men and nefarious villains met their maker on the scaffold on Coombe Hill."

"Really? How interesting," Gibbs replied drily.

The major wafted his hand at the pictures on the wall. "As you can see, we have had Royal members as well as—"

Gibbs interrupted. "I'm investigating the murder of one of your members."

The stunned major listened as Gibbs continued.

"Mrs. Sybil Hastings was found stabbed to death in the boot of her car in Peckham."

Whitehead was visibly shocked and seemed close to tears. "My God . . . Poor Andrew, losing his father and now his mother, in such a horrific way. Sybil was a member here for many years. She was a private woman but incredibly generous, and helped with charity events and parties at the club. She was a very accomplished golfer, as was her late husband. How is Andrew? Is there anything I can do for him?"

"He's obviously distraught and in shock, but he's bearing up. I need to ask a few questions." Gibbs took out his notebook and pen. "Can you tell me who Mrs. Hastings regularly played golf with?"

"Well, Andrew, for one, but mostly at weekends with him. Then there were two or three local women that she regularly played with."

Gibbs asked for their names and addresses, but the major said he wasn't sure if he was able to provide personal details of members without their permission. Gibbs couldn't be bothered to argue with the pompous major and asked him to contact the women personally to request that they ring him at Peckham CID.

"Was Mrs. Hastings friendly with any of the male golfers?"

"If you are asking whether she was in a relationship with any of them, no, not that I know of. She was friendly with everyone, male or female. Even after her husband died, she continued supporting the club by attending functions with her son."

"I believe Andrew Hastings played golf last Friday, in a competition?"

"Yes, that's right, in the winter medal. He came second. Plays off a two handicap, you know."

Gibbs didn't have a clue what that meant, and wasn't about to ask.

"Yes, it was a pity he couldn't stay for the dinner and collect his medal."

Gibbs felt his heart race. "Oh, why was that then?" he asked casually.

"Apparently one of his children was taken ill, so he had to shoot off home."

"Oh dear. What time was that?" Gibbs continued.

"I'm not sure exactly. The meal started at five p.m., and I remember asking Michael Blake—he's one of your chaps, senior officer at Scotland Yard. Do you know him?"

"Yes. What was it you asked DCS Blake?"

"Where Andrew was. It was DCS Blake who told me he'd gone home, and why. I gave him Andrew's runner-up medal so he could pass it on to him. Gosh, you don't suspect him, do you?" The major's eyes widened.

"No, not at all. Seems he and his mother were very close. Right, that's all for now. Thanks for your help. We haven't released any details about Mrs. Hastings' murder to the press yet, so I'd appreciate it if this conversation remained confidential."

"As a fellow officer, you can rely on me, Inspector Gibbs." The major saluted.

Gibbs suspected that no sooner had he driven out of the car park that Whitehead would be in the bar boasting to everyone that he was assisting police in a murder investigation. He chuckled to himself at the way the major had inadvertently dropped Andrew Hastings in the proverbial shit, making him a possible suspect in his mother's murder.

If Sybil Hastings and the unknown victim's murders were linked, Gibbs was now even more determined to find the connection.

CHAPTER SIX

Many of the back streets in Soho, and in Marshall Street itself, were strewn with piles of rotting rubbish due to the bin men's strike. Jane was struggling to find a parking space, but eventually squeezed into a space between overflowing rubbish bags. The stench that filled the air as she made her way to the Samaritans branch reminded her of being at a post-mortem.

After ringing the doorbell, Jane was let into the building and approached a smiling young lady sitting behind a desk.

"I'm afraid all our volunteer listeners are busy at the moment, but if you'd like to take a seat in the waiting room, I'll get someone to come and see you as soon as I can."

Jane took out her warrant card and introduced herself to the young lady, who looked embarrassed.

"I'd like to speak to the manager, please. It's police business, not personal." Jane smiled.

"We have a leader on duty—I'll show you to her office."

After being shown Jane's ID, the leader shook her hand and invited her to sit down. She was a portly woman in her mid-fifties.

"How can I help you, Sergeant Tennison?"

"Does a Mrs. Sybil Hastings work here?"

"Yes, but she's not on duty today. Is she in trouble?"

"I'm sorry to have to inform you that she's been murdered. I'm part of the investigating team and we're trying to piece together her last known movements."

The leader was very distressed. "Sybil? Murdered? Are you sure?"

"Yes, I'm very sorry. Can you tell me when she was last on duty here, please?"

The leader's hand shook as she opened a calendar that was on her desk. Flicking through the pages, she stopped and looked up at Jane, her voice trembling with sadness as she spoke.

"It was last Thursday evening. Sybil did a two to eight p.m. shift." She closed the calendar.

"Do you keep a record of the calls Mrs. Hastings dealt with?" Jane asked.

"Yes, the details of all the calls we receive are recorded on a Samaritans call logging sheet."

"Could I have a look at them, please?" Jane asked politely.

The leader shook her head. "I'm sorry but it's Samaritans policy to treat all calls as highly confidential. I understand the seriousness of your investigation, but I'm not at liberty to divulge any information to you—unless you have a court order."

Jane was disappointed but understood the leader's position. "What was Mrs. Hasting's role with the Samaritans?"

"Sybil was a listening volunteer. She took phone calls and had one-to-one meetings with drop-in visitors who needed someone to talk to. Like all our volunteers, she was patient, open-minded and a good listener. As a leader I helped train Sybil. She knew never to discuss her conversations with anyone outside the branch." The leader's eyes welled up as she spoke of her colleague.

"How long had she been a volunteer?"

"About eighteen months now. She did a four- or six-hour shift per week, depending on what time of day it was. Every volunteer also commits to one unsociable shift a month—working late at night, or the early hours of the morning."

"You mentioned dealing with drop-in visitors. Did Mrs. Hastings see anyone on Thursday?"

"I'll need to check the callers log, but as I said, I can't give you any details if she did. To be honest, we don't get as many visitors as we do callers." The leader stood up and went over to a filing cabinet. She unlocked it and removed a file, which she put down on the desk. Sitting down, she opened the file and removed a few sheets of paper, which were clearly call logs.

"She had no drop-in meetings that day, but she dealt with several calls."

Jane asked when Mrs. Hastings had last dealt with a visitor and was told it was just over a week ago.

"Was it a male or female?"

The leader put the paperwork back into the folder. "I'm not supposed to say, but it was a male, aged in his twenties, who didn't give his name."

"Would a Samaritan ever meet up with someone away from the branch?"

"No, they shouldn't. But I suppose it's possible . . . I'm sorry I've not been able to help you much. I would love to give you the information you have asked for, especially if it will help your investigation, but I hope that you can appreciate our rules of confidentiality. What I will do is prepare a folder containing a copy of everything Sybil has dealt with in the last three months. Then, as soon as you have a court order, I'll hand it over to you. Often callers and visitors don't give us their names, or they use a false name."

Jane was frustrated. It was clear that the only way she could get the information she needed was if everything was done by the book.

On her return to Peckham, Jane went to see Moran about her visit to the Samaritans. As she updated him, she thought he looked tired.

"Shall I get a court order for disclosure of Sybil Hastings' Samaritans work?" Jane asked.

"It sounds as though we could be chasing a dead end if the callers give false names, or none at all."

"There are probably a lot of mentally ill people who call them, so her work with the Samaritans might be linked to her murder," Jane remarked.

"There's lots of 'ifs and buts,' Jane. Gibbs will be back from the golf club soon, so hold off on the court order until I've spoken with him. In the meantime, go through the completed house-to-house reports for anything that needs following up or might help progress the investigation."

Jane spoke up. "It won't take me long to get a court order. The Samaritans leader said she'd prepare all the documents relating to Sybil Hastings right away, and that there might be something useful . . ."

"I'm the one running this investigation, Tennison! Just do as you're bloody well told and don't argue with me," Moran barked.

The phone on his desk rang and he picked it up.

"DCI Moran . . . I've already told you, Fiona, I'm dealing with a double murder and don't know when I'll be home . . . I'm not neglecting you and the baby . . . I'll do whatever you need me to do when I get home, but please stop calling me at work." Moran put the phone down and sighed, looking crestfallen.

Jane was surprised at Moran's sudden change in temperament. It was as if he felt guilty about not being there for his wife.

"Are you OK, sir?" Jane asked hesitantly.

"Yes . . . My wife and I had been trying for children for years and now we have a little boy. He's our pride and joy, but it's all a bit of a nightmare. He cries a lot, Fiona is constantly trying to breastfeed him, and he doesn't sleep well. Poor Fiona is exhausted all the time. I want to be there for her, but I can't just drop everything and bugger off home every time she rings."

Jane smiled. "It must take its toll on you as well, sir. Maybe DI Gibbs could run the investigation for a few days while you take some time off and—"

Moran frowned. "*Time off*? I've got a double murder investigation to run. I'm not having people think I can't cope."

Jane realized she'd offended Moran's male pride and, under the circumstances, thought she should try and be a bit sympathetic.

"My sister's just had a baby boy and she and her husband are finding it really difficult as well. My mum says newborns are hard work, but it gets easier. What's your son's name?"

"Arthur. He's six weeks old now. He's lovely and we're so lucky to have him. It's the shitty nappies I can't stand. Fiona insists on using the toweling ones instead of disposables—they're not very absorbent and the poo leaks out the sides. Sorry, Tennison, I'm sure you don't want to hear all about dirty nappies."

"To be honest, having children is not high on my list of priorities . . ."

Moran smiled. "Probably best, if you want a long career and further promotion in the police service."

Jane didn't reply. She knew it was rare for a policewoman to return to work after having a child, and many male officers still thought a mother's place was in the home. As she turned to leave, Moran spoke again.

"One other thing: DCS Blake is coming over to see me. He's still pissed off with you and Gibbs about the way in which you handled Andrew Hastings, so you might want to keep out of his way."

"Does Blake know Andrew Hastings well?"

Moran nodded. "Hastings' wife told Gibbs they were in the same Masonic lodge and play golf together a lot."

Jane frowned. "So he must know Sybil Hastings as well?"

"Yes?"

"Surely there's a conflict of interest, if Blake is so close to Andrew Hastings and he also knew the victim?"

Moran looked displeased. "You should keep your opinions and thoughts to yourself, Tennison. It's not your place to question the rights and wrongs of Blake's involvement . . ."

"I'm just concerned that Blake's close relationship with Andrew Hastings might hinder the investigation."

Moran pointed his finger at Jane and raised his voice. "Blake's a seasoned senior detective and knows what he's doing. The fact he knows Andrew Hastings might actually help the investigation. If Hastings is involved in any way, Blake is better placed than us to know if he is lying or hiding something."

"I didn't mean anything derogatory, sir, I was just thinking about the investigation—"

Moran interrupted her. "Blake is a lot older and wiser than you, so don't go questioning his relationships with members of the public. As I recall, you screwed up a big Vice Squad operation due to personal feelings towards a young Colombian girl. Then there was that Natalie Wilde woman you befriended, who turned out to be a bloody IRA sleeper. Those incidents totally screwed any chance you ever had of getting on the Flying Squad, and that's why the Dip Squad didn't keep you on either. You don't know how close you were to getting kicked back into uniform—for the rest of your career!"

Jane was shocked at Moran's verbal attack. She was surprised he even knew about the Regina Hernandez and Natalie Wilde incidences, which had happened nearly three years ago. Even if the phone calls from his wife were making him irritable, Jane felt Moran was being a bit harsh.

"I know I've made mistakes, sir, but I have learnt from them. I've never taken people on face value since then, or got emotionally involved in a case. As for coming off the Dip Squad, DCI Church told me at the time he couldn't keep me on due to financial restrictions and he had to cut his numbers down on the team."

"Church lied. He had a soft spot for you and didn't want to hurt your feelings. If it was me, I'd have told you straight and got you back in uniform directing bloody traffic. Now go and check the house-to-house files." His manner made Jane feel even more offended and upset.

Biting back a further comment, she left Moran's office, closing the door firmly behind her.

As Gibbs drove back to the station, he couldn't stop thinking about the fact that Andrew Hastings had lied to his wife about where he was on Friday evening. There was a good chance he was seeing another woman, and Gibbs considered the possibility that Andrew Hastings had been involved in his mother's death, and that maybe the unknown victim was his mistress. It would be interesting to hear what Hastings would say when asked directly by Moran about his whereabouts on Friday evening. If Hastings claimed that he was at the golf dinner, then DCS Blake's own words, relayed to the major, would prove that he was a liar.

Gibbs smiled to himself at the thought of Andrew Hastings squirming in an interview. He sat back in the driving seat and thought of Jo Hastings. He couldn't get her out of his mind because he found her incredibly sexy and was certain that she had been coming on to him.

Gibbs stopped at the traffic lights by Camberwell Green. It suddenly struck him that it was strange that Blake hadn't told Moran he was playing golf with Andrew Hastings on the Friday, or that Hastings had gone home before the dinner because one of his children was unwell. Stranger still was the fact that, as an experienced detective, Blake would know that Hastings would be considered a suspect until he could be eliminated from the inquiry. Therefore his exact movements would be crucially important and would need to be corroborated. As the lights changed to green, Gibbs cut in front of the car beside him and turned right into Denmark Hill, towards King's College Hospital. It was time Andrew Hastings was confronted about his whereabouts on Friday night.

As Gibbs approached the main hospital reception area, he caught sight of Jo Hastings leaving, on her own. It was clear from the look on her face that she was upset. Although Gibbs called out to her, she didn't see him and climbed into her Mercedes station wagon. Gibbs ran up to the car door and could see she had been crying.

"Jo, have you just been to see your husband?" he asked.

"Yes. Don't worry, I didn't tell him you'd come to the house and I pretended I knew nothing about his mother's murder. He told me about finding her body, saying how rude and incompetent you and some woman detective were. He also said the body of a younger woman was found near to his mother's—is that right?"

"Yes. I didn't tell you earlier because we're not sure yet if the two murders are connected or just coincidence. And we haven't been able to identify the other woman yet."

"Please tell me honestly: do you think Andrew was involved?"

"I need to check out, in more detail, what he was doing on Friday. And obviously he has yet to make a statement," Gibbs replied.

Eager to continue their conversation, he suggested that he get into the passenger seat of her car. Jo nodded. Once he was inside she told Gibbs how desperate she was to find out if Andrew was having an affair. She had come to the hospital to try and trick Andrew by telling him she had smelt another woman's perfume on the shirt he had been wearing on Friday night.

"What was his reaction?"

"He was angry. Accused me of having a wild imagination, and saying that I was being very insensitive considering his mother had just been murdered, and that he was still in terrible shock."

Gibbs thought about telling Jo that Andrew hadn't been at the golf dinner. He knew she'd find out in the long run, but was worried if he told her now she'd storm back into the hospital and confront her husband, which could ruin the element of surprise in any later interview with him.

Jo shook her head in disgust. "I know he's lying. The idiot gave himself away by suggesting the perfume I smelt had rubbed off from a waitress when she leant over him to serve his meal at the dinner. I told him I wasn't stupid and didn't believe him. He told me to ask Blake, as he was with him the whole evening, then changed the subject back to himself. He went on and on about how distraught he was, how he thought he'd had a heart attack and that they were keeping him in for observation. He's very good at laying on the 'poor me' sob story. A few minutes later Blake walks into the room, much to Andrew's surprise by the look on his face."

"What did Blake have to say?" Gibbs asked.

"He offered his condolences about Sybil's death, told us he would be overseeing a thorough investigation and said if there was anything he could do to help, just ask. So I did."

Gibbs noticed the sly smile on Jo's face. "What did you ask?"

"I was still convinced Andrew was lying to me, so I asked Blake if he was with Andrew on Friday night. Andrew didn't look best pleased, but I didn't care."

"It must have come as a shock when Blake told you that Andrew wasn't at the golf club dinner," Gibbs said empathetically.

Jo looked confused. She tilted her head to one side and looked Gibbs in the eye. "No . . . ? Blake looked at Andrew, then at me, then said they were on the same table together at the golf club dinner on Friday night and that they both left the clubhouse shortly after twelve thirty p.m. Andrew had a smug look on his face, as if to say 'I told you so.' But I'm not stupid. There was something about the way they looked at each other."

Gibbs took a deep breath. "I'm really sorry, Jo, but Andrew is lying. And for some reason so is Blake." He filled Jo in about his enquiries at the golf club and recounted how the club secretary, Major Whitehead, had relayed what Blake had told him about Andrew leaving early because one of the kids was unwell.

Jo looked pale and shocked as she took in what Gibbs had said. "Why didn't you tell me this before? If I'd known, I could have gone in there and confronted Andrew. Instead I've been made to look a fool by his and Blake's lies. I'm going to go out and talk to Andrew."

Jo went to open the car door but Gibbs took hold of her hand. She tried to pull away but he held firmly onto it.

"Wait a minute, just wait a minute. I only found out when I went to the golf club, which was after I spoke to you. I wasn't even intending on coming here, but when I discovered Andrew was not at the club dinner, my suspicions about him increased and I wanted to speak to him."

Jo leant against him. "I don't understand—why is Blake is lying for him?"

Gibbs knew he was on dangerous ground. "Maybe he knows Andrew is having an affair, so he deliberately lied to the major about Andrew's whereabouts."

Jo was close to tears. "It wouldn't be the first time I suspected him of having an affair."

"The fact is, Blake lied to you as well, which means he's hiding something. God forbid it should be anything about the murders, but whichever way you look at it, we've got nobody who can truthfully corroborate your husband's movements from six p.m. on Friday night until you saw him in bed at around four a.m. the next morning."

Jo nodded.

"So, for the time being, Jo, I really need you to keep quiet about what we've spoken about. I could get in serious trouble for revealing too much information."

Jo turned away to stare through the driver's window. "I can't stand the thought of being near him. I don't want him in the house. You have to help me. If he killed his mother and that other woman, then who knows what he could do to me and the kids?"

"We don't know for certain your husband killed anyone, Jo. Granted, he's a liar, but as I've just said, it could be because he was being unfaithful to you."

She began to cry and Gibbs put his hand on her arm. "I think you and the children should go and stay with your parents for a while."

"Their flat only has two bedrooms, one of which is a storage room."

"What about a hotel then?" Gibbs suggested.

"No, I don't want to distress the kids by taking them away from home and school. I'll pack Andrew's bags, then when he returns home from the hospital I'll tell him to go and live at his mother's," Jo said firmly.

"What will you do if he refuses?"

"He won't. I'll make sure of that. If necessary, I'll get my father to call some of his old Bermondsey mates. Believe me, Andrew won't argue with them."

"Well, if he ends up being charged with anything then he won't be going anywhere, other than on remand to a prison."

Jo shook her head. "I just can't make sense of it all . . . Although Sybil and I didn't get on, she mollycoddled Andrew and he provided for her every need."

"Have you told the children that their grandmother is dead and that their father is in hospital?"

Jo shook her head again. Even though she had despised her mother-in-law, she never stopped Andrew taking the children to see her. Jo was dreading telling them, and was afraid that kicking Andrew out the house would only make matters worse.

Gibbs knew he had said too much. "You have to do what you feel is best for you and the children. I'm not going in to speak with Andrew, especially if Blake is still there. I can ring you at home later and let you know what's happening."

Jo nodded. "I'll be on my own. They're keeping Andrew in hospital overnight and the children will be in bed by eight."

"I'll call you later then."

Gibbs drove back to Peckham and went to Moran's office to update him on what he'd found out at the golf club, and about Jo Hastings' visit to her husband in hospital, as well as Blake's involvement. He had no intention of mentioning any of the more personal conversation he had had with Jo, or the fact that he would be calling her later. He also decided to tell Moran that he had only spoken with Jo Hastings on the phone, as opposed to meeting with her face to face at the hospital.

As he approached Moran's office, Jane came out, looking red-faced and distraught. Gibbs was about to ask if she was OK but she pushed past him without saying anything and headed towards the stairwell.

"What's up with Tennison?" he asked, as he entered Moran's office.

"I had to give her a dressing-down. She tends to open her mouth too often without thinking of the consequences first."

Gibbs nodded in agreement. "Her heart's in the right place, though, and she's diligent. Maybe she's a bit over keen to prove herself as a new DS?"

Moran detected the smell of alcohol on Gibbs and asked if he'd been drinking on duty. Gibbs held his hands up and admitted that he'd had "a pint" of lager at the golf club, purely to be social as the club secretary had offered him a drink.

Moran listened patiently as Gibbs went over the salient bits of his afternoon's work, making it clear that Andrew Hastings was lying about his whereabouts on Friday evening and early Saturday morning. However, there was no evidence to prove this as yet.

"Do you trust Jo Hastings?" Moran asked.

Gibbs nodded. "Yes."

Moran wasn't convinced. "By her own admission, she didn't like, or get on with, Sybil Hastings, and if she thinks her husband's having an affair then maybe she's embellished what was said in the hospital room to implicate Andrew as some form of payback."

"If you're asking whether I think she's lying, then my answer is no. I got the impression things aren't good between her and her husband. Admittedly I don't know them, but it's glaringly obvious they're like chalk and cheese—he's an arrogant, self-opinionated, prick and she's not," Gibbs replied.

"That doesn't make him a murderer."

"His mother's death means that he inherits a shed-load of money. Although he already appears to live life in the fast lane, who's to say his business isn't going under and he needs more money?"

"What does Jo Hastings make of Blake?"

"Same as every woman: a perv with wandering hands. Blake lied to Jo Hastings at the hospital and to the major at the golf club."

"I'd think twice about making wild accusations against a senior officer, Gibbs. For all you know, Andrew Hastings could have been with another woman and Blake was covering for him. I know you're not married, Spence, but you know full well blokes protect each other when it comes to affairs."

Gibbs shook his head. "OK, so Blake may know who Hastings' bit on the side is. He also knows that those close to a murder victim are considered suspects until the investigation proves otherwise. If everything's as innocent as you're suggesting, then why hasn't he even told you in confidence that Hastings is out of line?"

"If Blake doesn't suspect Hastings of anything criminal, what's there to bloody well tell me, Gibbs?"

"My gut feeling tells me that Hastings could be our murderer and Blake is hiding something from us. They're both Freemasons in the same bloody lodge—"

"That doesn't mean anything!" Moran shouted, getting increasingly frustrated with Gibbs.

Gibbs wouldn't let it go. "You know from personal experience that Freemasons protect each other. Hastings might even have something on Blake and is bribing him to lie. It's also possible the unidentified victim could be Hastings' mistress—"

"For Christ's sake, Spencer, you're letting your imagination run wild! Or perhaps you had more than one pint at the golf club and can't think straight. I can understand your suspicions about Andrew Hastings, but you are way out of line suggesting DCS Blake would lie for a murderer."

Moran had never been a Freemason, nor did he want to be. However, he had been a prosecution witness in 1977 at the Old Bailey where many Met detectives stood trial for serious corruption. During the investigation it emerged that most of the accused officers were Freemasons, and it became referred to by the press as "A Firm within a Firm." Thirteen detectives were jailed, including two commanders, one chief superintendent and five inspectors. Moran also knew that some officers, who were Masons like Blake, were honest, hardworking and diligent detectives, but Blake's lies about Andrew Hastings worried him.

Moran's phone rang and he picked it up. "Yes!" he barked. After listening for a moment, he started to look concerned. "I'm sorry, darling, I can't just drop everything . . . But if you're worried, call your mother . . . I'm going to be at work for some time, but I'll get home as soon as possible . . . I promise . . ." Moran replaced the receiver, paused, then lifted it off the hook and placed it on the table.

"The wife giving you earache?" Gibbs asked.

"Yes. Apparently little Arthur, whom we've now started calling Art, has got croup. At first she thought it was wind, but apparently it's a cough. You should be thankful you're single. And don't you dare suggest I take some time off and you take over the investigation!"

Gibbs was baffled by Moran's remark. "Why would I do that?"

"Go and type up your report and liaise with Tennison so she can update you about her investigations." Moran waved his hand for Gibbs to leave.

"By the way, did Blake tell you he was going to visit Hastings at the hospital?"

Moran looked annoyed. "Blake is our senior officer. He tells us what to do, not what he's doing!"

"He's perverting the course of justice in a murder investigation."

Moran shook his head in despair. "Do you always change the law to suit you, Gibbs? Blake hasn't even been spoken to, or interviewed by us, so he's done nothing that interferes with the investigation or perverts the course of fucking justice."

"Then you need to ask Blake why he's lying about Andrew Hastings' whereabouts on the night in question."

Moran banged his hand on the desk. "Don't tell me how to run a murder investigation, Gibbs! We don't even know if both murders are connected. If you think Andrew Hastings is involved, then bring me some hard evidence, not hot air conjecture. I could argue that Jo Hastings has pulled the wool over your eyes. She clearly hated her mother-in-law and would gain from her death. Not to mention that she may well feel inclined to strangle any woman she discovered was having an affair with her husband."

"That's ridiculous!" Gibbs retorted.

Moran laughed and shook his head with disdain. "You've only just met her, you know nothing about her, and haven't even bothered to confirm her movements for that Friday night. Blake has had an unblemished career and though he might be considered by many to be a perv, not one woman has ever made an official complaint against him."

"We both know that's because he's a senior officer and they're frightened of losing their jobs."

"For Christ's sake! Why have you and Tennison got it in for Blake? Let it go, or you'll both be off this investigation. Do I make myself clear?"

Gibbs glowered, but said nothing.

"I'll take that as a yes, shall I? Go and write up your notes for the case file and concentrate on identifying the woman in the alleyway. And I don't want you casting any aspersions about Blake to the team. Just keep what we discussed between us for now."

In the CID office Gibbs found Jane sitting at her desk, checking the house-to-house folders. From the subdued look on her face he could see she was still upset and asked if she had a minute to have a chat. She followed Gibbs into his office and he shut the door behind her, sitting down at his desk.

"Don't let Moran get to you, Jane."

"What do you mean?"

"He told me he gave you a dressing-down about opening your mouth without thinking. If it's any consolation, he's just had a pop at me as well. He also noticed that I'd had a pint at the golf club—just to be social, of course."

Jane raised her eyes at Gibbs. "You know Moran doesn't like drinking on duty. And you smell like you've had more than one pint, Spence."

"Christ, don't you start on me as well. Hang on, you're wondering if I'm back on the bottle, aren't you?" Gibbs asked, looking directly into Jane's eyes.

"I'm just concerned, Spence. To be honest, you looked a bit hungover this morning at the Hastings flat."

"My drinking problem was three years ago, Jane, and you haven't worked with me since. I spent time in the police nursing home drying out. I do still drink, but just to be social. And I don't touch spirits anymore. I had a glass of wine with my girlfriend last night and she got a bit frisky, hence me looking a bit tired this morning."

Jane felt that Gibbs was being honest with her. Since she had worked with him previously, he certainly seemed more confident and at ease with himself, so she decided not to press him about the drinking.

Gibbs continued. "Moran had a go at me because I badmouthed DCS Blake, even though I felt I had every reason to."

Jane nodded. "Moran had a go at me because I said Blake might not be completely impartial, due to his friendship with Andrew Hastings—"

Gibbs interrupted. "There's a lot more to distrust about Blake than that, Jane. It wouldn't surprise me if he's telling Hastings everything about the investigation as we speak. Pull up a chair—I'll tell you about my enlightening day. But first, fill me in on what you've been up to."

"There's not much to tell, really." Jane recounted her return visit to Sybil Hastings' flat with Lawrence, but that they didn't find anything suspicious. She told Gibbs about her chat with Agnes and her visit to the Samaritans, asking if he thought they should get a court order for the call logs at the Samaritans, in case one of the people Sybil had spoken to or seen may be responsible for her death.

"I'd put that on hold for now. My guess is that Andrew Hastings is responsible for his mother's and the unknown victim's murder. In fact, I suspect the girl in the alley might be his mistress."

Jane wasn't convinced. "From her calloused hands and the way she was dressed, she doesn't seem the type Andrew Hastings would mix with."

"She could have been on the game. Hastings may have paid her for sex and she threatened to tell his wife," Gibbs said with conviction, then proceeded to tell Jane everything he had told Moran about Andrew Hastings and DCS Blake.

Jane was shocked that Blake would lie for a murder suspect, but could see why Gibbs suspected Andrew Hastings may be involved in his mother's death.

"I don't know where Hastings killed them, or why, but my gut tells me he did and I'll find the evidence to prove it. I just hope Moran has the balls to challenge Blake about what he said to the golf club secretary, and why he lied to Jo Hastings about his 'mate' Andrew being with him at the dinner."

"What if Moran doesn't have the balls?"

"Then I bloody well will. I'm not scared of that tosser Blake. If he lies to us about Hastings, then he's really up shit creek."

Jane nodded. "Paul Lawrence found Sybil Hastings' will in a filing cabinet at her flat. She's left everything to Andrew."

Gibbs shook his head. "I suspected as much. According to his wife, Andrew was his mother's blue-eyed boy."

Moran was in his office, mulling over what Gibbs had said and how best to confront Blake, when the phone rang.

"Nick . . . Mike Blake here. Just to let you know, I've spoken with the hospital and they'll be releasing Andrew Hastings tomorrow, at about midday. I'll take him for a spot of lunch and bring him to the station for about half one. We can speak to him together before one of your officers takes his statement. It can't be Gibbs or Tennison, as I don't want Andrew being unnecessarily upset. He's suffered enough as it is."

"Have you had a chance to chat to Mr. Hastings about his mother's death?"

"No. I saw him at the hospital briefly, but he was still a bit groggy from the sedatives he'd been given. I just offered my condolences and said I'd see him tomorrow, then left."

Moran knew that if Jo Hastings had told Gibbs the truth about Blake's visit to the hospital, he was lying yet again. He wanted to ask Blake if he knew what Andrew Hastings was doing on the Friday evening, but Blake ended the call. Moran sat back in his chair, annoyed at his indecision. He knew he'd have to tread delicately where Blake was concerned, as there could be a valid explanation behind his actions. He also knew any unfounded accusation against Blake could be the end of his career as a detective and would scupper any future chance of achieving further promotion. What concerned Moran most was how close Blake was to Andrew Hastings. He wondered if Hastings had some sort of control over Blake, and if he did, that suggested Blake might be a corrupt officer.

Moran felt tired and confused. He desperately needed to work out a strategy about how to deal with Andrew Hastings and ultimately confront DCS Blake about his lies. But he needed to get home to help Fiona. She didn't seem to be getting over the baby blues and he was worried about her behavior. He wondered whether he should call Fiona's mother in Norfolk and ask if she would come and stay for a bit. He didn't particularly relish the idea of his mother-in-law staying, but he really didn't know what else to do.

CHAPTER SEVEN

After a restless night, Jane left for work early to finish typing up her reports. It was 8 a.m. and she was the only one in the office. She was glad of the peace and quiet so she could concentrate. She'd just been to the canteen to get a coffee, and some toast and marmalade, when the office phone rang. She answered it via the link to her own desk phone.

"Peckham CID, can I help you?" Jane said politely.

"Yes, I was trying to get hold of Detective Inspector Gibbs. Is he there?" It was a well-spoken woman with a soft voice.

"DI Gibbs is not in yet, but he should be here shortly. Can I take a message, or a number he can ring you back on?"

"I'm Tamara, his girlfriend. He called me last night at about six p.m. to say he'd be working late. I haven't seen or heard from him since. I've tried ringing his flat, but there's no answer. I'm rather worried about him, especially as I know he's working on a murder investigation."

Tamara was clearly very anxious, but Jane didn't have a clue where Gibbs was and wasn't sure what to say. She felt slightly annoyed that she was having to make excuses to Gibbs' girlfriend about his whereabouts.

"Spencer was very busy yesterday, and was still in the office when I left last night," Jane said, wondering if he had lied to her about his drinking and was actually crashed out somewhere after a night in the pub. "Can you just hold on a second, Tamara?"

Jane dashed across the room to Gibbs' office, opened the door and looked inside. He wasn't at his desk, or on the floor asleep, as she'd hoped. She hurried back to the phone.

"Sorry, I got distracted by someone asking me a question. Spencer didn't have his car, as it was in the garage, so if it was really late when he finished work he may have stayed at the local police section house overnight."

"But why didn't he phone me? They must have phones at the section house, don't they? Oh God! What if something happened to him on his way there?"

"If anything had happened to him I think we'd know, Tamara, so try not to worry. I'll see if I can find out where he is and get him to ring you as soon as possible."

Just then a beaming Gibbs walked into the office, carrying a cup of coffee and a dripping bacon bap in his hands.

"Morning, Jane. How are you this fine day?" he asked, taking a big bite of the bap and causing the red sauce to dribble over the sides of his mouth.

Jane put her hand over the mouthpiece. "It's Tamara. She's got herself all worked up, wondering where you've been all night!"

"Shitttt" he muttered, grabbing the receiver from Jane.

Jane was pointing to the side of her mouth, hoping Gibbs would realize his was covered in sauce before he wiped it all over the phone. It was too late.

Jane heard Gibbs groveling to Tamara, saying that he'd been out on an all-night observation and had only just got back to the station. He was claiming that he hadn't been able to call her as he had been confined to the observation van in case the suspect turned up.

"I'm really, really sorry, Tamara. I promise I'll take you out for dinner tonight to make up for it . . . Love you too, sweetie." Gibbs made a few kissing sounds, then put the phone down.

Jane gave him a sideways glance, knowing full well there had been no overnight observations.

"You got a problem?" he asked.

"Not at all, guv, not at all." Jane noted that Gibbs was wearing the same clothes as yesterday.

He went to his office and kicked the door shut. No sooner had Jane sat down to continue typing her report than the phone rang again. She thought Gibbs might have heard it and answered it from his office, but he didn't. Jane sighed. She would probably have got more peace and quiet if she'd sat at home typing up her reports. She answered the phone.

"Could I speak with Spencer Gibbs, please?" a woman's voice asked.

Jane could tell it wasn't Tamara. "I'll just see if he's available. Who's calling, please?"

"Jo Hastings."

Jane was wary about disturbing Gibbs in his bad mood. "I'm afraid he's busy at the moment. Can I take a message?"

"Actually, I forgot to tell him something last night and would rather speak to him personally. I'll ring back later. Thank you." Jo Hastings put the phone down.

Jane wondered if Gibbs had spent the night with Andrew Hastings' wife. She knew it wasn't her business but she hoped he would not have been so unprofessional.

Professor Dean Martin was unable to attend the mortuary until late morning. Sybil Hastings' body lay on the mortuary table, still fully clothed in the expensive fur coat, a black turtleneck jumper, skirt, tights and leather boots. As Andrew Hastings was still in hospital, Jane identified the body to Professor Martin as Mrs. Sybil Hastings, whom she'd first seen in the boot of the Allegro.

Jane was thankful that the body had been held in cold storage, so the overriding smell of decomposition was not as strong as it had been when she had first been discovered. Seeing Sybil Hastings' face, Jane felt a tinge of sadness as she realized that she wasn't much older than her own mother.

DS Lawrence took some photographs before the pathologist and Martin removed the clothing, which Lawrence then placed in separate exhibits bags. Moran had a large notebook open and pen in hand, ready to take down details of Martin's findings and conclusions.

Martin stood over the now naked body, taking measurements of every stab wound whilst Lawrence recorded the position and size on a female post-mortem body diagram form. He had suggested that Moran should wear a protective face mask as he had a very young baby and should avoid the possibility of picking up any infections.

Martin pointed to the bruising around the chest injuries. "The high number of injuries suggests a frenzied attack, with great force behind the stabbing motion. The shape of the bruising around some of the entry wounds is consistent with the weapon having a small circular hilt of some sort. There are also marks to her right palm, consistent with raising the hand to defend herself from the blows."

"What sort of knife are we looking for?" Moran asked, muffled behind the mask.

Martin said he wasn't sure the injuries were caused by a knife, but wanted to check the back and internal injuries before commenting further. Once all the wounds were measured and photographed, the pathologist helped Martin turn the body over, revealing a number of wounds to the back of the head, neck and right shoulder blade.

"These injuries are all similar in shape and size to the frontal ones, so I'm confident the same weapon was used to inflict all of the stab wounds. The pattern and position of the rear injuries indicate the suspect chased the victim, stabbing her as she ran. Also, the rear injuries are predominantly to the right side, which suggests the attacker was right-handed."

All the injuries were painstakingly photographed and measured before the body was rolled onto its back. As Martin proceeded to cut the chest cavity open with a large scalpel, Jane recalled her first post-mortem as a probationer. The smell of the internal organs had nearly made her faint, but now she had got used to it. She found the workings of the human body fascinating, unlike Moran, who was sucking his breath in and out behind the mask covering his mouth.

Having measured the depth of injuries and removed the internal organs, Martin took a close look at the heart. "Most fatal stab wounds to the chest involve the heart or the aorta." He pointed to a cut section at the top of the heart. "There you go: the left anterior descending coronary artery, which supplies blood to the left side of the heart muscle, has been severed. Her death would have been pretty quick once that had occurred."

"At least it wasn't slow and painful," Jane remarked.

Martin looked at her over the rim of his glasses. "Sadly, it was probably the last injury to her body, and inflicted while she was in a prone position on her back."

Jane realized the sheer terror that Mrs. Hastings must have been in at the time of her death. Initially attacked from the front, she tried to defend herself, then running for her life she was repeatedly stabbed in the back, before falling to the ground and rolling over to see the fatal blow coming towards her. Jane felt a shiver run through her body as she thought about it. She wondered if Gibbs was right about Andrew Hastings being a murderer. Although she thought Hastings was arrogant and objectionable, he had no criminal history of violence and so far there was no direct evidence against him.

It was another half an hour before Martin completed his examination of the body, brain and all the internal organs, taking blood and urine samples, which he placed in small glass phials and handed to Lawrence.

At midday Martin finally removed his pathology gown and handed it to the morgue attendant. "Cause of death was obviously the fatal stab wound to the heart. As for the weapon, the entry wounds are narrow with abraded edges, as opposed to fish-tailed, which you'd get from a knife. Also, the bruising from the hilt of the weapon is circular, so you could be looking for something like a screwdriver or chisel."

"Unusual weapon to use in a stabbing," Jane remarked.

"I've seen it before, but not often," Martin replied.

Lawrence said there was no screwdriver, chisel or similar implement in the victim's car. Any suspect murder weapon they found could now be compared to the injury measurements, both on the body and her upper clothing. He also added that the killer could be a tradesman of some sort and it might be worth checking if Sybil Hastings had had any work done in her flat recently. Jane said she would check with Agnes, adding that the murder weapon may have been close to hand when an argument started and that the killer lost his/her temper, grabbed it and in a frenzied attack stabbed her to death.

Moran sighed. "The type of weapon doesn't get us much further."

"Well, looking for a screwdriver is better than looking for a needle in a haystack," Martin said, grinning at Moran.

"Is there any change in your opinion on the time of death, since you attended the scene to view the body in the car boot?" Moran asked.

"No. She died on the Friday within the same time frame as the unknown victim, give or take an hour or two. And before you ask, DCI Moran, I can't confirm if the same person is responsible for both murders. Both victims are women and were found in close proximity to each other, but with Mrs. Hastings there are no signs of any form of sexual assault or strangulation."

Moran looked at Lawrence. "I really need the lab to pull out all the stops on this, Paul. Right now, forensics might be our only way to link or disassociate the two murders."

"The lab was closed at the weekend, so the scientists have only just started working on the fibers and blood grouping on the unknown victim's coat this morning. There's a good chance the blood may have come from the suspect."

"Get Mrs. Hastings' fur coat checked as well—it's covered in blood."

"The suspect's blood may be the same blood group as both or one of the victims, plus there's—"

"I don't want to hear about problems. I need results, and evidence that gives me answers, so get working on it." Moran banged his notebook closed, tossing his mask into the bin. He thanked Professor Martin and stomped out of the mortuary.

"Unpleasant bugger, isn't he?" Martin said.

CHAPTER EIGHT

Moran was taken aback when DCS Blake walked into his office, accompanied by a subdued-looking man that Moran hadn't seen before.

Blake shook Moran's hand. "Good to see you, Nick. This is Andrew Hastings. He's just been discharged from King's and I'm taking him home, but I thought we'd pop in here first. I've explained that you need to speak to him about his mother and her last known movements, as it will assist the investigation."

Moran shook hands with Hastings. "I'm sorry for your loss, Mr. Hastings. Please take a seat. Are you feeling better? It must have been terribly traumatic for you."

"Obviously I'm still deeply shocked, but under the circumstances I'm bearing up." Andrew sat in the chair on the other side of Moran's desk, opposite him.

Blake looked at Andrew. "DCI Moran won't keep you any longer than necessary, as he understands you need to be with your wife and children at this sad time."

Moran didn't want to interview Hastings in Blake's presence without another officer there. "With your permission, I'd like to ask someone in to take notes of our conversation."

Hastings frowned. "Is that really necessary?"

Blake nodded to Hastings. "It will speed things up, Andrew. Notes need to be taken and made into a statement. The statement can be put together in your absence and you can read and sign it later."

"Please excuse me whilst I see who's free in the CID office. I'll organize some coffee as well." Moran stood up and left the room.

Jane was on the phone when Moran approached her. She looked up at him and mouthed "nearly finished."

"I'm really sorry, Agnes . . . If there is anything I can do to help, please let me know." Jane put the phone down and turned to Moran. "Agnes went to the hospital this morning to see Andrew Hastings. He informed her that she was no longer needed as a housekeeper and would have to find somewhere else to live."

"Heartless bastard! Seems he's not as shocked about his mother's death as he likes to make out."

"His behavior is very odd," Jane added.

"Blake's just brought him in from the hospital for an informal interview about his mother. I want you to take the notes whilst I talk to Hastings, with Blake in attendance."

Jane was surprised. "I thought you didn't want me or Gibbs anywhere near Hastings or Blake? Wouldn't it be better if you used Edwards?"

"No. You know from what Gibbs found out at the golf club that Hastings is lying."

"Then surely Gibbs should sit in," Jane replied.

"The interview needs a subtle approach. I can't risk using Gibbs as he's got it in for both of them and is liable to let rip with his accusations, which won't help if Blake lies to me again."

"You've already spoken to Blake?" Jane asked, taken aback.

Moran hesitated. "Yesterday, late afternoon. I asked him if he'd spoken to Hastings about his mother's murder and he said he hadn't. I'm beginning to think there may be some substance to Gibbs' belief that Blake is hiding something. I don't know why, but I just hope and pray it's nothing to do with the murders. It could all turn nasty. I need someone present to cover my back and take notes of everything that's said. Are you OK with that?"

"Yes, sir," Jane replied, glad that Moran trusted her and relied on her integrity. "Will you be asking Hastings about both murders?"

"We'll start with his mother's and see what happens. I need you to grovel a bit and apologize to Hastings about the way he found his mother's body. We need to keep him sweet."

Jane realized that the more Andrew Hastings thought he had the upper hand, the more crushing it would be when Moran tripped him with up his lies.

"Do you mind getting some coffee and biscuits while I tell them that you'll be taking the notes?"

Jane made her way to the canteen whilst Moran returned to his office.

"I know it may not be to your liking, Mr. Hastings, but the only officer available to take notes is WDS Tennison."

Hastings sighed. "Well, let's hope she's a better note-taker than she is an investigator."

Although Moran had only just met Hastings, he could understand why Gibbs thought he was an arrogant prick.

Carrying the tray of hot drinks and biscuits, Jane used her foot to knock on Moran's office door. It was opened by Blake. On seeing Jane, he took a step back to get a better look and asked if she was DS Tennison.

"Yes, sir," Jane replied.

This was the first time Jane had met Blake. He was in his late forties, around 5⊠10⊠, and was wearing a dark blue three-piece pin-striped suit and shiny black shoes. His greased-back black hair and staring eyes made him look like Bela Lugosi, the famous *Dracula* actor. She thought Blake might at least have had the manners to take the tray from her, and could almost feel him leering at her bottom as she leant over and placed the tray on Moran's desk. She turned to Andrew Hastings and handed him a coffee.

"I'd like to apologize, Mr. Hastings. I'm sorry your mother's body wasn't found earlier, and I can't begin to imagine how you must be feeling. I want you to know we will do everything we can to find who did this terrible thing to Mrs. Hastings."

"Let's hope so," Hastings said bluntly.

"We all learn from our mistakes, Tennison, and DCI Moran tells me you're one of his best officers," Blake said ingratiatingly.

Moran handed Jane a large notebook and pen, before picking up a chair and placing it to the left of his. He invited Jane to sit down, with Andrew Hastings sitting opposite him. Blake remained standing. Moran started the questioning by asking Hastings for his mother's full name and date of birth. They then spent a bit of time going over Sybil's background, from the time she met Henry and married him, to Henry's death and then her move to Viceroy Court.

"We are pretty sure your mother wasn't killed during a robbery as none of her property seems to have been taken—other than her car keys. Do you know if your mother had any enemies, or anyone she'd argued with recently?" Moran asked.

Hastings eyes were red as he shook his head. "No, there's no one I can think of. If she had, I'm certain she would have said something to me. My mother was a kind and generous woman. She didn't have a bad bone in her body. It's totally beyond me why anyone would want to hurt her. She was a Samaritan, you know."

"Yes, Agnes told DS Tennison about her Samaritan work. DS Tennison visited the Soho branch to see if there was a link."

"Was there?" Andrew asked, with a concerned look.

Jane answered. "We don't know yet, Mr. Hastings. They're still helping us with our enquiries."

"I once asked her about her work there. She told me it was private and confidential and that she'd never reveal it to anyone. Why would someone she tried to help want to kill her?" Hastings asked, welling up.

Jane felt that Hastings was being genuine and wondered if Gibbs was wrong about him, and was making his suspicions fit a preconceived notion of guilt because he disliked him. Moran then turned the subject to the last time Hastings had seen his mother. Andrew said it was on Tuesday, when they played a round of golf at the Coombe Hill club together. He had also spoken to her on the Thursday about playing that Sunday, but she had told him she was going to be busy.

"Did your mother say anything about what she was doing on the Friday or at the weekend?" Moran asked.

"No, not a thing. When Agnes phoned me on Sunday morning, I thought my mother might have gone to a hotel on her own for the weekend."

"Has she done that before?" Jane asked.

"Yes, a few times she's gone to the Grand in Brighton, but usually in the summertime, and she lets us know beforehand."

Moran told him they'd check with the Grand, just in case his mother had been there. Moran looked at his watch and told Hastings there were just a few more questions he needed to ask.

"I don't want you to take this the wrong way, Mr. Hastings, but I need to ask you what you were doing on Friday and Saturday."

Jane noticed a slight change in Hastings' demeanor. He licked his lips and sat up, but before he could reply, Blake stepped forward and put his hand on Hastings' shoulder.

"I've explained to Andrew that he might be asked some probing questions about his movements in order to eliminate him from the investigation. He understands that it's 'par for the course.'" Blake laughed at his own golf pun.

Hastings forced a smile. "I realize you have a job to do, DCI Moran, but I can assure you I didn't kill my mother. Even though she was planning to leave everything to me in her will, she had already put what money she had into a trust for her grandchildren. I do inherit the flat, but I helped her buy it with my own funds. After my father died, I took my mother in and paid for everything, even setting up a monthly income from the family business, which is paid directly into her bank account."

Moran looked at Jane. She wondered if he, like her, thought Hastings was becoming a bit defensive. Moran turned back to Hastings.

"It is obvious that you cared a great deal for your mother, but you haven't answered my question regarding your movements on the Friday and Saturday."

Hastings sighed. "On Friday I was playing golf all day at Coombe Hill with Michael, then I attended the club dinner in the evening." He looked at Blake, who nodded.

"Yes, that's right. The bar closed at midnight and Andrew went home at around half twelve," Blake stated.

"I got back home just after one a.m. and went straight to bed." Hastings sat back in his chair and once again looked at Blake.

Jane felt as if she was watching a rehearsed play, in which Hastings and Blake were the lead characters, trying to convince the audience they were honest, upright citizens. It was clear to her that the two of them were lying. Jane looked at Moran again, who appeared uneasy and hesitant.

Blake noticed Jane's expression. "Is something wrong, Sergeant Tennison?"

"No, sir, I was just trying to indicate to DCI Moran that I'm ready for him to ask the next question."

Moran looked at Blake, then back at Hastings. "I believe you won a medal on Friday for coming second in the golf competition?" Moran asked.

Hastings frowned and directed his answer at Blake. "What's that got to do with my mother's murder?"

Blake stared at Moran. "I don't know, Andrew. As it happens, I forgot to tell you that you left your medal on the table at the dinner, so I took it home for safekeeping."

Moran shook his head and sighed with disbelief at the unashamed way Blake was protecting Hastings.

Blake continued. "Andrew is obviously tired and emotional and should be with his family. It seems to me he's told us everything he can, so I think we should call it a day for now and I'll take him home." Blake grabbed his coat from the stand in the corner of the room.

"I'd be happy to conclude the interview when you and Mr. Hastings tell me the truth about where he really was on the Friday evening," Moran said calmly.

"I object to your insinuations!" Hastings shouted.

Blake put his hand on Hastings' shoulder to calm him down, glaring at Moran.

"As I said, Nick, it's best we terminate this interview."

"You getting all of this down, Tennison?" Moran asked irately, looking at Blake and Hastings.

"Yes, sir, I am. Every word." Jane sided with Moran.

Moran flexed his shoulders and took out his notebook. "DI Gibbs attended Coombe Hill golf club yesterday and made enquiries about Sybil Hastings. Major Whitehead, whom I'm sure you both know well, told DI Gibbs that Andrew Hastings didn't stay for the prize-giving meal as he'd gone home because one of his children was unwell."

"Well, he's obviously mistaken me for someone else, hasn't he, Michael?" Hastings looked at Blake for support, but Blake remained quiet. Hastings continued. "I find it disgraceful that DI Gibbs is able to go around tarnishing my good name at the golf club."

Moran wanted to make them both sweat. "Actually, it was DCS Blake who told the major you had gone home, and the

major told Gibbs that he gave Blake your runners-up medal."
Moran turned and looked at Blake, frowning. "Why are you
lying for him?"

Blake licked his lips and asked Jane to leave the room so he
could "discuss things in private" with DCI Moran. As Jane stood
up, Moran put his hand on her arm to indicate that she should
sit down again.

"Tennison stays, and if Mr. Hastings continues to lie, I will
arrest him on suspicion of murder."

"I didn't kill my mother!" Hastings shouted at Moran.

"He's telling the truth, and I know that as fact," Blake said.

"Well, you're both doing a good job of perverting the course
of justice."

Blake looked at Hastings. "This is getting out of hand,
Andrew. For God's sake, just explain where you were."

Hastings sighed and lowered his head. "I was with Katie Oliver, the wife of another club member who was at the golf dinner.
Knowing Katie would be at home on her own, I skipped the
meal and prize-giving to go and see her."

"You are having a relationship with her, I take it?" Moran
asked, and Hastings nodded. "How long were you with her for
that night?"

"From about six p.m. until just after midnight, when Michael
phoned me to say that Katie's husband had just left the club. I
got home about quarter to one and went to bed."

"I'll have to speak with Mrs. Oliver to confirm that what you
have told me is true."

Blake looked subdued. "I can confirm he was there. I called
Katie Oliver's house from the golf club. She answered, then I
spoke to Andrew to tell him it was time to leave as her husband
was on his way home. If you must speak to her, then I'd be grateful if you did it at the station and off the record, to prevent her
husband from finding out the situation."

Moran agreed. He knew that Blake was more concerned about his own reputation, especially if Mr. Oliver found out Blake was aware Hastings was screwing his wife.

Moran opened his desk drawer, took out a prepared pro forma and slid it across the table to Hastings.

"Sign that, please. And before you ask, it's an authority for me to have access to all your personal and business bank accounts."

Hastings looked at the form and slid it back towards Moran. "No. You know I didn't kill my mother, so you've no right to look into my personal or business affairs."

Moran looked smug. Jane sensed he wanted to teach Hastings and Blake a lesson and she was right.

"I can't rule out that you didn't pay someone to kill your mother while you were with your mistress. If needs be, I will go to court and get a judge's order on the grounds that you lied in a murder investigation and that you are a suspect—which won't look too good for you or DCS Blake."

"Sign the fucking form, Andrew!" Blake bellowed.

Hastings reluctantly signed the form.

"You can go now," Moran said to a visibly furious Hastings.

Jane was impressed by Moran's calm restraint. She couldn't believe how stupid Blake had been to risk his career for someone like Andrew Hastings. Perhaps Hastings did have something on Blake? Jane's thoughts were interrupted as Moran told her to take Hastings downstairs whilst he continued to speak to DCS Blake.

After everyone else had left the room, Moran looked Blake in the eyes.

"You caused me and my team to waste valuable time with Hastings. All you had to do was speak to me in private about his affair and where he was, then we could have avoided all of this confrontation. Has he got something on—?"

Blake anticipated the question. "I'm not corrupt, and he hasn't got anything on me. It was a little lie to the major that got out of hand. I was just trying to stop any scandal breaking out in the clubhouse about Andrew and Katie Oliver, that's all. It was silly of me and I apologize."

Moran had a good idea why Blake had lied. "This is the Freemasons' old pals act, isn't it? He's lied for you when you've been out of line."

Blake looked annoyed. "My private life has nothing to do with you."

"When you lie in a murder investigation, it bloody well does. But don't worry, I'll do my best to keep a lid on it . . . for now."

"And what about DS Tennison?" Blake asked.

Moran said that he would speak to her, but couldn't guarantee her silence.

Blake picked up his coat. "If there's anything more you need to assist your investigation then just ask."

Moran shook his head. "I don't need anything from you, Blake. It might be best if you take yourself off the investigation. You could always injure yourself playing golf!"

"You know I can't do that without the top brass asking questions. But I'll give you free rein to investigate the murders and keep myself in the background."

"I can live with that. I'll keep you updated on any developments."

Blake nodded and left the room.

Moran sat at his desk with his head in his hands. He was exhausted, and realized he was back at square one. He had two victims, one still unidentified, and although he felt the murders were probably linked in some way, he had no evidence to prove it. Did he have one or two killers on the loose? Or worse: two men acting together, who had a lust for attacking and killing women of any age? Whatever the case, he knew he had to find who was responsible before there was another murder.

Taking a deep breath, straightened the papers on his desk. His office phone rang and, picking it up, he heard his baby son wailing in the background.

"Yes, I'll be home soon, Fiona . . ."

CHAPTER NINE

It was quarter past nine on Tuesday morning. Jane was in the CID office with Gibbs, Edwards and the rest of the team, waiting for an update meeting with DCI Moran. The meeting was supposed to have started at nine but Moran still hadn't arrived. Jane was talking to Gibbs as they looked at a wall covered with photographs of the crime scenes, post-mortem results and Sybil Hastings' full details. The information regarding the unknown victim was still blank. Missing persons checks and further house-to-house enquiries had turned up nothing to take the investigation forward.

Moran walked in, sipping coffee from a polystyrene cup. He was unshaven, his grey suit was creased and he was wearing the same shirt as the previous day. He was normally meticulously neat and tidy with his appearance, but today he looked exhausted, and had bloodshot eyes and dark circles surrounding them.

Gibbs whispered to Jane: "Looks like he's been dragged through a hedge backwards. He hasn't even bothered to change his shirt."

"You're a fine one to talk," Jane retorted.

Gibbs looked puzzled.

"You came in yesterday morning in the same gear you wore on Sunday. Moran's under a lot of pressure with two murders on his hands and no suspects." She raised her eyebrows at him.

"Yeah, well, we're all under pressure, Jane," Gibbs replied.

"We don't all have babies that keep us up all night, though," Jane defended Moran.

"Sorry I'm late. Heavy traffic."

Gibbs whispered again: "He was probably on nappy duty."

Moran briefed everyone on the events of the previous day.

"Myself and WDS Tennison interviewed Andrew Hastings yesterday. It seems unlikely he was directly involved in either of the murders as his alibi has been corroborated." He deliberately avoided any mention of DCS Blake's initial lies.

"He could have paid someone else to kill his mother," Gibbs said.

Moran gulped some of his coffee and nodded towards Gibbs. "I am aware of that, DI Gibbs. Hastings has begrudgingly given written authority for his bank and business account details to be handed over to us. Edwards, I want you to collect them and go through them."

"I'll give Edwards a hand checking the accounts," Gibbs said, then whispered to Jane, "Even if there's no large transfer or withdrawal of money, Hastings could have had cash tucked away to pay a hitman."

Jane shrugged. "I think you're wrong about Hastings."

"We'll see," Gibbs replied.

"How are the house-to-house enquiries going, Tennison?"

"All of Copeland Road and the flats on the Rye Lane side of Bussey Alley have been done. So far we haven't found anyone who saw anything suspicious or could identify our unknown victim."

"I'd like you to widen the house-to-house then. Copeland Road is a horseshoe shape so take in all the streets that run between it."

"Yes, sir. Could I have some more uniform assistance?" Jane asked.

"I'll speak with Chief Superintendent Blake. I'm sure he'll be obliging and arrange for more officers from the surrounding stations."

Moran then went around the room asking each detective if they had any information that could help. There was a morose silence in the room as no one had anything positive to say.

DS Lawrence entered, carrying a forensic folder and looking a lot happier than anyone else in the room. He stopped in his tracks as he realized everyone was staring at him.

"I hope you've got something good for us, Paul?" Moran asked, seeing the smile on Lawrence's face.

"Yes, sir, very good. The lab's managed to link your two murders."

Everyone in the room perked up. One officer shouted out jovially, "Hail the savior who comes bearing good news," and there was a ripple of laughter. Moran was visibly relieved and smiled for the first time that morning.

"Come on, Paul, don't keep us on tenterhooks," he joked.

Lawrence took some paperwork out of a folder. "OK. Blood grouping first. The smears on the unknown victim's blue coat are not her blood group, but they do match the blood group of Mrs. Hastings."

"So, the smears on the coat must have come from contact between our two victims, or the killer transferred Hastings' blood onto the coat," Jane remarked.

"Possibly, but the killer could also be the same blood group as Mrs. Hastings or the unknown victim, which won't help if the smears on the coat came from an injury to the suspect."

Gibbs shook his head. "Then the blood grouping doesn't take us much further, or positively link the two crimes if the coat smear could be the suspect's blood."

"I thought you said you had something positive for us, Paul?" Moran asked.

"I do, I was just dealing with the blood grouping first and saving the best till last." Lawrence smiled. "Fibers from the clothing of the unknown victim were found on the rear seat of the Allegro, as well as two hairs that match in color and length."

Moran looked pleased. "So the Allegro was used to transport the victim before she was dumped in Bussey Alley."

"Most probably, yes, but she could have been a willing passenger in the car prior to the murder. Fibers from Mrs. Hastings' fur coat were also found on the unknown victim, but again they could have got there innocently or by the killer carrying both bodies and transferring fibers from one to the other in the process. On the balance of probabilities, I'd say both victims were killed by the same person, probably at or about the same time. It's also reasonable to assume the killer, or killers, are male."

"Any idea where they were killed?" Edwards asked.

Lawrence shook his head. "Only the victims know that, and I'm not a psychic. We also found some tweed fibers in the car, similar in color and texture to DI Gibbs' tweed suit."

Everyone looked at Gibbs, who wagged his finger and was quick to defend himself. "Hey, I never went near the inside of the car or the victims. And I can assure you I'm no murderer, guv!"

There was more laughter around the room.

Lawrence continued. "The tweed fibers were mostly on the driver's seat in the car, with a few on both victims. They could have come from something the killer wore or from something Mrs. Hastings had previously worn."

"I'll check with Agnes, the housekeeper, to see if Mrs. Hastings has any tweed outfits," Jane said.

"Strange the killer didn't dump Mrs. Hastings as well," Edwards said.

"Maybe he saw something in Copeland Road that made him panic after he'd dumped the first victim, and he ran off before he could dump Hastings," Jane suggested.

"He probably couldn't drive the car away because of the flat tire," Edwards added.

Lawrence had more forensic evidence to reveal. "I found a half-full can of petrol in the boot of the Allegro. There wasn't a single fingerprint on it, just what appears to be glove marks."

"If the killer wore gloves to hide any fingerprints, then they might already have a criminal record," Jane remarked.

Moran nodded. "Good point, Tennison. I'll have a word with the collator and get him to draw up a list of everyone on our patch who has form for assault on females."

Lawrence continued. "I'm surmising here: if the petrol can didn't belong to Mrs. Hastings, it's possible the killer may have intended to drive her body somewhere secluded, pour petrol over her and the car, then set light to the vehicle. But as Edwards suggested, the flat tire prevented that outcome."

"If that had happened in another police force area like Kent or Surrey, then we'd never have had any reason to connect the two murders," Moran said.

"I'll ask Agnes about the petrol can," Jane said.

"Call her now, please, Tennison, while we all take a quick break. You can use my office phone. In the meantime, the rest of you can grab a tea or coffee from the canteen. I want you all back here in ten minutes."

After the break, everyone was back in the office, waiting for Jane to return. When she walked in, all eyes were on her.

"Agnes confirmed that Mrs. Hasting had a tweed outfit, but she doesn't think she's worn it since last winter. She often went grocery shopping with Mrs. Hastings and has never seen a petrol can in the boot of the Allegro."

Lawrence responded, "I'll need to go to Mrs. Hastings' flat to seize the tweed outfit as evidence. The lab can do a comparison to the tweed fibers we recovered in the Allegro and on the victims. If they don't match to Mrs. Hastings' clothes, it's even more likely they came from something the killer wore."

"Maybe Andrew Hastings has a tweed suit?" Gibbs asked, noticing that Moran was frowning. "I'm just saying. He may have driven his mother's car at some point, and tweed suits tend to be worn by the posher gentleman."

"Not always—you wear one," Edwards said wryly to Gibbs.

"DI Gibbs has made a valid point," Lawrence remarked.

"You could get Blake to ask Hastings?" Gibbs looked at Moran.

"I'll see. We all need to step up our game and identifying our unknown victim will be a big step forward. I think it's time we set up a full press conference and reveal to the public that both murders may be linked. Edwards—arrange for an artist's impression of the unknown victim's face to be made for the press release. Somebody out there must know her."

"They might be too scared to come forward," Jane suggested.

Moran agreed. "I'll ask Blake if we can offer witness confidentiality and a reward. We need to catch this bastard before—"

The duty sergeant walked in looking very somber. "Sorry to interrupt, sir, but we just received a call from the manager of the Peckham Rye homeless hostel on East Dulwich Road. The body of a young woman with a possible head injury has been found in one of the rooms. I've got a uniform panda car with two officers en route to check it out and seal the scene, pending your attendance."

"Is she a resident?" Moran asked.

"I doubt it, sir. The hostel is for men only."

There was an unnerving silence as Gibbs drove Moran and Jane to the East Dulwich hostel. Although just over a mile from Peckham Police Station, which was surrounded by deprived housing estates and urban decay, East Dulwich was a very different area, with many large detached and terraced Victorian and Edwardian homes. It was a short distance from Peckham Rye Park and Common, which together made up 113 acres of open recreational grassland, ornamental and water gardens, a lake and woodland. Sadly, the East Dulwich Road end of the park was still littered with rotting rubbish due to the dustbin strike and was a stinking eyesore for the residents.

As they passed Bussey Alley, Jane noticed the look of anxiety on Moran's face. The silence was broken by a call on the car radio from the PC who was at the hostel scene. Moran picked up the radio and told the officer to go ahead.

"I've had a quick look at the victim, sir. She's clearly dead and the hostel manager has put a blanket over her. She's lying on the floor, face down. There's blood around her head and on the carpet next to her is a broken wine bottle, as well as a pair of ladies' knickers."

"Seal the scene off. I'll be with you shortly." Moran banged the radio mike against the dashboard. "I hope to Christ this isn't connected to the other two murders!"

Neither Gibbs nor Jane said anything, wondering if the killer had struck again. Gibbs parked in the street outside the three-story red-brick Edwardian house, which had been converted to a hostel eight years ago by the local council. Lawrence pulled up behind them in his own vehicle and took his crime scene case out of the boot. An elderly uniform PC was standing on the white washed stone steps of the building waiting for them. He opened his notebook as Moran approached.

"Good morning, sir. My colleague is standing guard outside the scene. The hostel cleaner, Gladys Jackson, a fifty-two-year-old black female, found the body in room six this morning. She's currently with the hostel manager in his office. All the residents on the premises have been told to remain in their rooms until informed they can leave by the CID." The officer paused as he flicked over a page in his notebook. "The hostel has twelve bedsit-style rooms over three floors, and provides accommodation for male-only residents—down-and-outs, alcoholics and drug abusers. The manager lives in the basement area."

"Good work. Radio the station for me and get them to send Professor Martin to the scene, please."

Lawrence smiled to himself, knowing that Moran was calling Martin to the scene to avoid incurring his wrath again.

Moran turned to Lawrence. "Paul, you can start photographing the scene and commence a cursory examination before Prof Martin arrives. Myself and Gibbs will speak with the manager."

"Would you like me to assist DS Lawrence?" Jane asked enthusiastically.

"No, I want you to speak to the cleaner, Tennison."

As they entered the building through the large wooden door, the pungent smell of stale smoke and damp permeated the air. The interior was grubby, with stained and torn white wood-chip wallpaper and a threadbare carpet. The manager's office was small and cramped, even more so now with five people in it. The room was unkempt, with two chairs and a wooden desk that was propped up with some folded cardboard under one leg to stop it wobbling. A rotund man in his fifties, wearing a coffee-stained white polo shirt and black trousers, was sitting at the desk with a cigarette in his mouth, reading the *Sun* newspaper. The distraught-looking cleaner was sitting opposite him, still wearing her light blue button-up housecoat and headscarf. Her hands shook as she sipped at a cup of tea.

Moran stepped forward. "I'm DCI Moran from Peckham CID. This is DI Gibbs and WDS Tennison. I take it you're the manager?"

The man put the paper down. "Yeah. This is Gladys, the cleaner. She found the body. I knew something was up when I heard her screaming."

"You heard the victim screaming?" Moran asked.

"No, Gladys screamed when she found the poor girl in room six."

Moran turned to Gladys. "It must have been a terrible shock, Gladys. WDS Tennison will need to ask you a few questions, if you feel up to it?"

A nervous Gladys nodded. Moran asked the manager if there was another room that WDS Tennison could use to interview the cleaner. The manager stubbed out his cigarette and said there was a communal room down the hallway. Jane smiled at Gladys, helped her up and the two of them left the room.

"Who occupies room six?" Moran asked the manager.

"I've already got his hostel residents' form out." He handed it to Moran, who moved closer to Gibbs so that he could read the details as well. The form showed room six was let six weeks ago to a Ben Smith, aged 19, date of birth August 26, 1959.

Gibbs got out his notebook and jotted down the name and date of birth. "Can you describe him to me, please?" he asked.

"Ben's a skinny lad, about five ten, with blond hair—I reckon it was dyed cause his eyebrows were dark. Oh, and he had a tooth missing at the front, about here," the manager said, pointing to the left side of his teeth, just off the center.

Gibbs noted the details. "Did you speak to him much?"

"Nope, only when I filled out his registration form. Told me he couldn't read or write. From what I heard, he kept himself to himself and didn't mix with the other residents, though I don't blame him, as some of 'em in here are right low life. Half of 'em use the sinks in their rooms to piss in, some even have a dump in 'em. Dirty bastards, they are."

"Why was Ben Smith here?" Moran asked.

"Social services referral. He was homeless and had a drugs problem."

"How many residents are in their rooms at the moment?" Moran asked.

"Most of them! The lazy bastards don't get up until after midday, when the pubs open. Or they stagger down the road to the off-licence, then get pissed in the park."

Gibbs closed his notebook and put it back in his pocket. "I'll nip out to the car and radio the station to tell everyone in the CID office to come to the hostel right away so we can interview all the residents."

"And get a criminal record check done on Ben Smith," Moran added.

Gibbs nodded and left the room.

"You reckon Smith killed her then?" the manager asked.

"We don't know yet," Moran replied, irritated by the manager's manner and attitude.

"I read in the paper about that bird who was murdered in Bussey Alley. That bastard Smith could have done her as well, you know. She were strangled, weren't she?"

"Can we stick to this incident, please. Are women allowed on the premises?" Moran asked.

"Rules is residents ain't allowed any guests outside of visiting hours, which is ten to eleven in the morning and three to four in the afternoon in the communal room, and one visitor only. But it's almost impossible to enforce. We have a hostel warden on duty day and night, but the residents bring people in through the fire exit doors, or someone distracts the warden so they can sneak people in. All the residents have a front door key and a room key, but often the front door is just left on the latch because the druggies and drunks amongst them regularly lose their keys and start banging on the door at all hours of the night."

"I'll need the details of the day and night duty wardens."

"No problem. I could ring Eric and get him to come in early—he's on the late shift all this week."

"That would be helpful. In the meantime, I'd like you to remain on the premises while I view the scene. Where is room six, please?"

"First floor, turn right and it's the end room on the left."

Jane was in the communal room with Gladys. Like the entrance area, it was shabby, but reasonably neat and tidy. There was a TV and pool table, as well as a small kitchen area with some tables and chairs at the far end. Jane sat the trembling Gladys down at one of the tables.

"I'm sorry, love, but I didn't catch your name earlier," Gladys said with a Jamaican accent.

"I'm Detective Sergeant Jane Tennison." Jane reached out and held her hand. "I know it must have been an awful shock for you this morning. The good thing is I don't need you to tell me what you saw as the uniform officer has already informed me."

Gladys squeezed Jane's hand and started to cry. "It was awful, officer. There was a lot of blood and her knickers was on the floor."

"Did you know the man who occupied room six?"

"He said his name was Ben. Young lad, he was, face like a baby and lovely blond hair, though I think it was dyed. I can't believe he'd do a thing like that," Gladys said, becoming more distressed.

"Did you ever chat to him?"

"A few times. He was always very pleasant and asked how I was and if I had any grandchildren. I told him I didn't—me and my Winston couldn't have kids, you see. He said he had a young niece and nephew, but didn't get to see them or his sister very much as he didn't get on with his brother-in-law. He seemed quite sad about not seeing them."

"Did he say where they lived?"

"No, never."

"Any signs he'd had women in his room before?"

"Not that I noticed, but I think he was a heroin user. I found a burnt spoon and rubber tube under his bed one morning while he was out. You get to know what those things is used for when you work in these sorts of places. Mind you, the people ain't as bad in here as you'd think, they just don't have anyone to love and care for 'em, and sometimes choose the wrong path in life."

Jane warmed to Gladys, who was becoming less distraught. She seemed to be an honest and upright woman with a kind heart, and clearly didn't judge people for the problems they had.

"When did you last see Ben, and how did he seem?"

"I'm not sure exactly when it was—maybe a couple of days ago. I was putting on me coat, about to leave, and he was on his way out. He asked me how I was. I said fine and he left the hostel."

"I'll need to get a full statement from you, Gladys, but I think you've been through enough today and probably want to get back home to your husband."

Gladys looked down. "Winston died a few years ago. He was robbed and banged his head badly on the pavement. They said a bleed on the brain killed him."

Jane felt embarrassed. "I'm so sorry, Gladys, I didn't realize."

"It's all right, dear, you weren't to know. Your lot caught the thugs who done it—they got ten years each, but I think they should have got life. They stole mine."

Jane thanked Gladys for her assistance, then went to see how Lawrence was getting on. As she was walking along the corridor towards the first-floor stairs, she came across Moran talking to Gibbs.

"Edwards is on the way here with more troops. There's no trace on criminal records for a Ben Smith with the date of birth the manager gave us. This seems pretty cut and dry, guv, what with the body being in Smith's room and he appears to have done a runner," Gibbs said.

"Let's hope so, Spencer. How'd it go with the cleaner, Jane?" Moran asked.

Jane briefed them on what Gladys had told her, emphasizing the finding of the heroin paraphernalia under the bed.

Moran frowned. "If Smith was a junkie who was referred to the hostel by social services, then I'd have thought he'd have a record for drugs-related offences."

"The manager could have got Smith's birth date wrong on the residents' form," Gibbs remarked.

"It's possible. Run a check with social services later. Let's have a look at the scene and see what Lawrence has to say."

They went upstairs to room six. Lawrence had wedged the door open and there was a strong smell of stale alcohol and nicotine in the room. The victim was lying face down. Blood had run through her light brown hair and down the side of her face, forming a deep red pool on the cheap grey carpet. The woman was wearing a brown embroidered knee-length shearling coat, red corduroy skirt and black patent leather calf boots.

Already gloved up, Lawrence knelt beside the body, placing the jagged upper half of a broken white wine bottle in a box to preserve it for fingerprints. Jane could see the uneasiness on Lawrence's face as he turned and looked at them.

"Did the bang on the head kill her?" Moran asked.

Lawrence shook his head. "It's more likely this did," he said, and slowly lifted back the collar of her coat to reveal a blood stained white cord. "For some strange reason it looks like the killer pulled the collar up in a pointless attempt to conceal the cord on this victim as well as the unidentified one. The cord looks to be the same type and it's tied in a slip knot as well."

Moran looked shaken. It wasn't what he wanted to hear. He banged his hand on the doorframe. "Fucking press are going to be all over this and crucify us . . ."

"On the positive side, at least we have Ben Smith's details and his description now, guv," Gibbs interjected.

"That could be a fucking alias for all we know. Is there anything to identify her?"

"No. Her coat pockets are empty and there's no sign of a handbag," Lawrence replied.

"I want you to carry out a thorough fingerprint examination of this room and get every lift checked against criminal records ASAP," Moran said anxiously.

"I was going to do that anyway, sir. I'll start with things most likely to have been touched recently by the suspect. That said, we will probably get a lot of hits against criminals as the room would have been used by a lot of residents with previous convictions."

"Just do it, Paul," Moran barked.

"Good to see there's peace and harmony in the work place." Professor Martin smiled as he approached, slipping on a pair of latex gloves. "This has been a busy few days. So what have you got for me this time?" he asked.

Moran wasn't amused by Martin's frivolity.

Lawrence attempted to lighten the tense atmosphere. "Our victim awaits you . . . As do we, with baited breath, Professor." Lawrence bowed towards Martin and waved his arm in a subservient manner.

"Await, yes, but I fear the victim does not breathe, otherwise I would not have been called here," Martin replied and looked at Moran, who was still not amused.

Jane remembered being upset by the dark humor when she first joined the police. However, it didn't take her long to realize it was police officers' way of dealing with traumatic situations to make them more manageable. She remembered Lawrence once saying to her, "If you didn't laugh, Jane, you'd cry."

Lawrence confirmed that he had photographed the room and body, then showed Martin an exhibits box filled with bits of broken glass and the jagged half of the white wine bottle.

"These were on the floor around her and there's still some fragments in her hair. There was also a pair of torn knickers on the floor, which I've packaged."

Martin knelt beside the body and looked closely at the back of her head and at the rope. He then hitched up the coat and skirt, reached into his pocket and pulled out a plastic tube containing a thermometer. Removing the thermometer, he took a rectal temperature of the victim.

Martin stood up. "The injury to her head is obviously from the wine bottle, and with her eyes and tongue protruding, I would say she was strangled with the cord. I can be more exact about the mechanics of her death once I've examined her at the mortuary."

Martin asked Lawrence to place a plastic body sheet beside the right side of the body, then they slowly turned the victim onto her back on top of the sheet. Even though Jane knew what to expect, it was shocking to see the woman's bulging eyes and protruding tongue, which were classic signs of strangulation. The victim's face was contorted and bloodstained, but Martin estimated she was in her early to mid-twenties. He picked up her left arm and, holding it just above the elbow joint and wrist, he tried to move it up and down.

"Body's rigid from rigor mortis, so she's been dead for at least twelve hours or longer. Taking into account the body temperature and skin discoloration, I'd say she was killed between six p.m. and ten p.m. yesterday evening."

Moran looked at his notebook. "The hostel manager said visiting hours were three to four in the afternoon, so she must have snuck in and come to the room."

"She might be a hooker?" Gibbs remarked.

"I'll be able to tell you more when I do a full post-mortem on her, but if I were a gambling man, I'd say that this poor soul was murdered by the same person as your first victim. She's not wearing any rings, so might be single, but she's got a distinctive mole on the right side of her lip, which might help with identifying her," Martin said.

"DS Lawrence and the lab have forensically linked Mrs. Hastings' murder to the unknown victim," Moran said.

"Then you have a multiple killer at large, DCI Moran," Martin said coldly.

Moran felt someone looking over his shoulder and turned to see that it was the hostel manager.

"She looks a bit of a mess. I told you some of the residents here were low life. Hope you catch that bastard Ben Smith. They should bring back hanging for the likes of him. Or burn him at the stake, like the good old days."

"You shouldn't be in this area; it's a crime scene," Moran said in a raised voice.

"I just came to tell yer Eric's here."

"Who's Eric?" a puzzled Moran asked.

"The warden who was on late shift. Silly bugger said he let a woman in last night to visit Smith."

Moran and Gibbs went to interview Eric in the manager's office whilst Jane stayed to assist Lawrence. Edwards had now arrived from the station with six colleagues and they were interviewing the residents in the communal room.

Eric was in his late fifties, grey-haired and softly spoken.

"It was about seven p.m. when I heard someone knocking on the front door. I opened it and there was a young woman standing there. I'd never seen her before and asked what she wanted."

"What was she wearing?" Moran asked.

"Pardon?"

Moran sighed. "You've never seen this woman before, but you let her in?"

"I've let lots of people in I've not seen before."

"Out of visiting hours?"

"Well, no, but—"

"Can you describe what she was wearing?" Moran asked.

"Oh right. Yes: a long dark coat and red dress, I think. She was a young lass, pretty with brown hair. It was cut in a bob style like me daughter's. She said she'd come to see Ben Smith. I told her visiting hours were over, but she said it was urgent she speak to him." He went silent.

Moran was becoming irritated. "Well, go on, then what happened?"

"She seemed a bit anxious and I said I'd go get him, but she said it was a private matter. She knew he was in room six . . ."

"So you just let her in?"

"Yes. I thought she might be his social worker, because in God's truth, we do have some right tarts coming in and out, but she looked quite respectable. Was she a social worker?"

"We don't know yet, Eric, but we'll check it out. Did you hear any noises coming from the direction of Smith's room, or see him at all that evening?" Gibbs asked.

"No, nothing. I never saw Ben. I was in the communal room for a while, chatting with some of the residents and playing cribbage. I didn't think any more about the woman and assumed she'd left after she'd seen Ben." Eric's eyes started to well up and he took a handkerchief out of his pocket and blew his nose. "Will I lose me job over this?"

Moran put his hand on Eric's shoulder. "You could never have anticipated what happened to her and what you've told us is very helpful. If there's anything else you think we should know, then please contact me at Peckham CID, OK?"

Eric nodded and blew his nose again.

"Sorry to interrupt you, sir." Jane entered the room. "DS Lawrence has found something of significant interest that he wants you to see."

"I'll be with you in a minute." Moran turned back to Eric. "Do you know if Ben Smith was ever visited at the hostel by other woman?"

"Not as far as I know."

"Have you ever seen him out and about with other women?"

"No. The few times I've ever spoken with him he's always been polite and well mannered."

Moran smiled. "Thanks for your help, Eric. I'm sure the manager won't mind if you want to take the rest of the day off."

"No, thanks, I'd rather work, to be honest."

When Moran and Gibbs arrived back at room six, Lawrence held up a tweed jacket.

"This was in the wardrobe. Not the kind of thing you'd expect a homeless junkie to wear."

"It's probably nicked," Gibbs remarked.

"Or bought from a charity shop, like yours was, Gibbs," Lawrence jested. "I'll need to get it examined at the lab, but under my magnifying glass it looks to be very similar to the fibers we found on the other two bodies and from the Allegro. Talking of which . . ." Lawrence motioned towards Jane, who held up a set of keys on a fob.

"I found them wedged up behind the basin in here," she said, displaying the badge on the fob. It had a blue background with a red crown and large silver italic style "VP" on it.

"Does the badge mean anything to you?" Lawrence asked.

Moran and Gibbs looked at each other and in unison said "no."

"It's the Allegro Vanden Plas Princess badge, and I'll bet these are Sybil Hastings' keys," Jane said.

"You little beauty, Tennison," Gibbs exclaimed.

"Good find, Jane," Moran added.

"Thank you, sir. There's no purse, house or car keys in the room that might belong to the victim, so the suspect might have nicked them."

"There's still a holdall and men's clothes in the wardrobe, as well as in the chest of drawers. Looks like Smith left in a hurry," Lawrence added.

Jane looked pensive. "I was just thinking . . ."

"Don't spoil the moment, Jane," Gibbs interjected wryly.

She continued: "There's a high mortality rate amongst the homeless, not just due to drugs and alcohol, but also from suicide due to depression. People contemplating suicide often call the Samaritans."

"And your point is?" Moran asked.

"Maybe Ben Smith phoned Samaritans and spoke with Sybil Hastings. She could have arranged to meet him?"

"She's really on a roll today," Gibbs said, impressed by her train of thought.

Moran agreed. "Get a court warrant to seize the call logs from the Samaritans, and check out the people Mrs. Hastings dealt with." He patted Jane's shoulder. "Good girl, Tennison."

CHAPTER TEN

Jane and Edwards had driven the CID car straight from the hostel to the magistrate's court to obtain a warrant, and were now on the way to the Samaritans branch in Soho to seize the documents relating to the callers Mrs. Hastings had dealt with.

"Moran looks like he's got the weight of the world on his shoulders at the moment," Edwards said.

"That's hardly surprising—he's got a maniac on the loose and three murders to deal with," Jane replied.

"WDS Tennison from DI Gibbs . . . you receiving, over?" Gibbs' voice boomed from the radio.

Jane picked up the receiver. "WDS Tennison receiving, over."

"Where are you?" Gibbs asked.

"En route to the Samaritans in Soho with a warrant."

"OK. An 'all stations' telex we sent out has turned up a call to Kentish Town nick about a missing teacher, Eileen Summers, aged twenty-three," Gibbs relayed.

Jane looked at Edwards. "Pull over while I get my notebook out."

"Did you get that, Tennison?" Gibbs asked impatiently.

As Edwards parked at the side of the road, Jane opened her notebook and pressed the radio transmitter button. "Yes, guv. Go ahead with the details. Over."

"Summers works at Southfield Primary school in Kentish Town. She was reported missing by the headmistress, Mrs. Rowlands. I've a gut feeling Summers is the East Dulwich murder victim. The misper form described her as having a mole beside her right lip and a bob haircut. She also wears a coat that matches the victim's," Gibbs said.

"What are the circumstances of her going missing?" Jane asked Gibbs.

"Summers was at work yesterday but didn't turn up this morning. Mrs. Rowlands repeatedly tried ringing Summers' flat but got no answer. She was concerned, so called Kentish Town."

"Shall I delay executing the warrant at the Samaritans . . . over?" Jane said.

"Yes, go to the school first and get back to me as soon as you've spoken to the headmistress."

"On way, guv . . . Tennison out," Jane said and replaced the handset on the radio holder.

"Looks like things are starting to step up," Edwards said as he put the car into gear and moved off.

The two-story Victorian-built school was imposing, with its English Renaissance-style features, fancy gables, colorful brick-work and terracotta ornamentation. As they walked across the playground, the noise of happy children enjoying their after-noon break filled the air. Groups of boys were kicking a foot-ball about and the girls were playing hopscotch or skipping to the song "Pease pudding hot, pease pudding cold." Jane smiled to herself, fondly remembering her own primary school days. Edwards couldn't resist stepping into the boys' football game and trying a bit of "keepie uppie." He only managed three and lost control of the ball, which caused the boys to mockingly chant "rubbish."

"Oi, watch this, mister!" a young boy shouted. Flicking the ball into the air with his foot, he proceeded to make Edwards' effort look lame. The other boys counted, shouting out the num-bers for Edwards' benefit, and by the time they had reached the school entrance, the young footballer was already up to twenty.

"I hate kids," Edwards said jovially, as he held the door open for Jane.

Mrs. Rowlands was in her office doing some paperwork. She was in her early fifties and looked rather dowdy, dressed in an ankle-length heavy brown skirt, white frilly shirt and grey cardigan. Jane informed her that they were police officers and had come about Eileen Summers. Mrs. Rowlands stood up and, with a warm smile, shook their hands and invited them to sit down.

"That was quick. I only reported Eileen missing at Kentish Town a few hours ago. The officer I spoke to took down Eileen's details, but said that because she was an adult, and there's no evidence she's in immediate danger, police enquiries wouldn't commence until twenty-four hours had elapsed."

"There's been a development, Mrs. Rowlands, but we're not sure yet if it involves Miss Summers. Do you have a photograph of her I can have a look at, please?" Jane asked.

"Has something happened to Eileen? Was she involved in a car accident on the way to work?" Mrs. Rowlands nervously asked, walking over to a filing cabinet in the corner of the room.

"I'll be able to tell you more when I've seen the photograph." Jane didn't want to unduly alarm her.

"Eileen's never missed a day since she's been here. She teaches the nine- to ten-year-olds, and is one of the best young teachers I've ever come across. The children absolutely adore her, as do the parents and staff." Mrs. Rowlands spoke with a tremor in her voice, anxious about what could have happened. She pulled out a folder from the cabinet with "Year Five—Class Photographs" written on it. She took out the most recent picture and handed it to Jane. "That's Eileen, in the middle." Mrs. Rowlands pointed.

Jane looked at the photo of the young and attractive teacher, her face glowing with warmth and pride as she sat amongst the smiling young children. Jane thought of the poor victim strangled to death in room six at the hostel, her bulging eyes and bloodstained face flashing into her mind as she looked at the picture. She was in little doubt that Eileen Summers was the murder victim in Ben Smith's room. Jane looked at Edwards, who hadn't seen the body, and nodded.

"She's dead, isn't she?" Mrs. Rowlands exclaimed.

Jane had been in this position many times before, but this time it felt different. She knew Eileen Summers' death would have a devastating effect on the entire school.

"We are investigating a murder that occurred in Peckham last night. Having seen the body, I'm almost certain that it is the same woman in this photograph."

Mrs. Rowlands was close to tears, but kept her composure and asked Jane what had happened. Jane gently told her that Eileen had been strangled and that they had a suspect they were currently looking for. Jane asked if she could have Eileen's parents' contact details, and Mrs. Rowlands went back to the filing cabinet.

"Here we are . . . Her parents live in Manchester. Eileen came to London to teach a couple of years ago and lives on her own in Chalk Farm. I think she may have gone up to see them over half term."

Edwards took the folder from Mrs. Rowlands and jotted down Eileen's address, as well as the parents' details, in his notebook.

"Did she have a boyfriend?" Edwards asked.

"Not that I know of. But she could have done."

"Did she ever mention the name Ben Smith to you?" Jane asked.

Mrs. Rowlands paused. "Not that I recall . . . Is he the suspect you spoke of?"

"It's a name that has come up in the investigation and he's someone we're interested in tracing." Jane was keen to change the subject and asked how Eileen had seemed on Monday.

"She was in good spirits and was happy to be back teaching the children. She really did love them so much."

"Did Eileen have a car or did she use public transport to get about?" Jane asked.

"She had a car—a green 1973 Morris Minor. She hadn't had it long."

Jane jotted the details down.

"I appreciate your help, Mrs. Rowlands. I know Eileen's death must be a terrible shock to you. Could I ask that, for now, you say nothing about this to anyone as we've yet to inform Eileen's parents or make a press release."

"Yes, I understand, officer. I'll do whatever is best under the circumstances."

"Mrs. Rowlands, it is a very difficult thing to ask of you, but would you be prepared to identify the body for us? The mortuary is in Lewisham," Jane asked tentatively.

"Yes, of course. I could be there after school, at about five o'clock, if that's suitable?"

Jane nodded and thanked her again, whilst Edwards jotted down the mortuary address and handed it to Mrs. Rowlands.

Before leaving the school Jane phoned the office and asked to speak to Moran. She was informed that he'd gone to the postmortem, but that Gibbs was available. Jane updated him on what had happened at the school and told him that she now had an address for Eileen Summers as well as for her parents in Manchester. Gibbs took down the details and said he'd contact Manchester CID to instruct them to inform the parents.

"Mrs. Rowlands has agreed to ID the body at the mortuary after school today. Edwards and I are now going to the Samaritans, if that's OK?" Jane told Gibbs.

"Go and check out Eileen Summers' flat first. Force entry if you have to."

"Another gut feeling?" Jane asked.

"No, but there could be some paperwork or something that might help us find Ben Smith."

Eileen Summers lived in Ferdinand House, near Chalk Farm tube station. It was a 1930s grey and red brick, four-story, council-owned building with no lifts.

"Christ! Is there nowhere in London that's rubbish-free?" Edwards remarked, observing the large overflowing council rubbish bins.

"Mind the rat!" Jane shouted.

"Where?" Edwards exclaimed in a squeaky voice, jumping to one side.

"It's just darted under the bin over there," Jane said, trying not to laugh.

"I thought things might be a bit better this side of London, but it's just as much of a shithole as Peckham."

"At least there's no burnt-out cars or graffiti here, and once the rubbish is cleared away this place won't look half as bad."

"What exactly are we looking for?" Edwards asked, as they climbed the stairs to Eileen's flat.

"Anything that might help us. Hopefully she'll have something that can help us trace, or link her to, Ben Smith, such as an address book with names and contact details," Jane replied.

"He'll be well gone by now," Edwards remarked unenthusiastically.

"Well, if he killed all three women, he didn't run off after the first two, did he?"

"Then maybe he's hiding out somewhere. We should be back in Peckham, hassling the drug dealers for info, not wasting time here."

Jane was becoming annoyed with Edwards' attitude. "Just stop moaning about what we should be doing and get on with the job at hand."

Edwards sullenly continued climbing the stairs. Arriving at Eileen's flat on the top floor, he peered through the letter box. An elderly male, in his mid-seventies with a hunched back and walking stick, came out of the flat next door.

"What you doing snoopin' about? I'll call the police."

"We are the police." Edwards showed his warrant card. "Who are you?"

"I'm Frank, Eileen's neighbor."

"I'm Detective Sergeant Tennison. We're making enquiries about Eileen Summers. She's been reported missing, so we're just checking to see if she may have returned to her flat."

The neighbor looked surprised. "I saw her last night. She's a lovely young lady. Gets me newspapers and does me shoppin', as I'm pretty much house-bound these days. I was a prisoner of war, you know—captured by the Japs and held in Changi prison until the end of the war. They treated us terribly and killed a lot of me mates. Me right leg was badly broken while I was being tortured for information." He gasped for breath and had a coughing fit before he could continue.

Jane felt sympathy for the old man but was keen to find out more information about their latest victim.

"When did you last see Eileen?"

"About five last night. She was going to the chippy down the road—got me a lovely bit of plaice and a portion of chips. I offered to pay but, bless her, she refused to take me money. She's a teacher, you know. Loves her job, and the kids. You sure she's not in?"

"We tried knocking but there's no answer." Jane didn't want to upset the old man by telling him that his neighbor was now dead. "Obviously we're concerned she might have had an accident indoors, so we'll have to force entry to check it out."

"There's no need to do that—I've got a spare key. Eileen leaves it with me in case of emergencies, and I also water her plants when she's away." The old man went into his flat and returned a minute later with the key.

Jane took it. Lawrence had taught her that it was always worth keeping latex gloves in her bag. She pulled some out and handed a pair to Edwards. They both put them on and then let themselves into Eileen Summers' flat. There was a strong smell of joss sticks, which Jane knew was sometimes used to cover the smell of cannabis, but she doubted Eileen was a user. The first room, to the right of the corridor, was the kitchen. It was very tidy, with a spotless electric oven and spotless work surfaces. It reminded Jane of her own small kitchen and it suddenly struck her that Eileen was very similar to her, being a single professional woman who was enjoying her career whilst maintaining her independence.

Jane noticed a knife, fork and plate in the kitchen sink, with remnants of white fish and tomato sauce on it. She opened the bin and saw the discarded fish and chip newspaper.

Edwards called out to her. "Someone's turned the place over, Sarge."

Jane hurried into what was obviously Eileen's bedroom. The dressing table and bedside cabinet drawers were all half open, or pulled out completely. The mattress had been pulled off the bed and on top of the cabinet there was an open and empty jewelry box.

"No forced entry, so whoever did this must have had a key," Jane remarked.

"Well, I think we can rule out the old boy next door," Edwards replied.

"Eileen Summers didn't have any house keys in her pocket, and no handbag or purse was recovered," Jane stated.

"Then that bastard Ben Smith must have burgled the place after he murdered her. You need cash or valuables to sell if you're a heroin addict on the run."

"It's possible, but we don't know that for certain." Jane looked around the room.

"It's bloody obvious, I'd say," Edwards exclaimed, going over to pick up the empty jewelry box.

"Don't touch it! You might smudge any prints on it," Jane said firmly. "We need Lawrence down here to start fingerprinting the place."

Edwards nodded.

"I want to speak to the neighbor again. Edwards, you go and radio the station for DS Lawrence to attend."

Frank's living room was filled with military memorabilia and photographs, of which he was clearly very proud. He picked one up of himself and his colleagues and showed it to Jane.

"Most got killed in the war or died in the prison camp."

Jane was unsure about telling Frank that Eileen was dead, but she knew he would eventually find out through the newspapers or TV. She gently encouraged him to sit down.

"I'm sorry to have to tell you this, Frank: Eileen was killed last night, and we're treating her death as murder."

Frank was beside himself and tears rolled down his face.

"Is there anyone I can call to be with you?" Jane asked.

"I ain't got no family . . . Eileen was like a daughter to me . . . She was so kind . . . What am I going to do without her?" Frank wiped his nose on the sleeve of his jumper.

Jane comforted Frank, sitting on the edge of the chair with her arm around him. She didn't know what to say and it was terrible to see a man who'd survived horrific torture and the horrors of war in such emotional pain. A feeling of sadness overwhelmed Jane as she thought about her parents and remembered the pain they suffered when her younger brother had drowned. She had cried at the time but had been too young to really understand what grief was. It was clear that Frank's only connection with the outside world had been through Eileen Summers, and now that world had ended for him.

Edwards entered and realized that Jane had informed Frank of Eileen's death. He took Jane to one side.

"Lawrence is attending Summers' post-mortem. I spoke to Gibbs and he's sending a couple of SOCOs down to start printing the flat. I'll stay with Frank for a bit whilst I wait for them to arrive. You may as well head off to the Samaritans." He handed Jane the CID car keys.

"Thanks." Jane looked at her watch. It was quarter to three. She felt physically and emotionally drained, and would have liked to go home and execute the Samaritans warrant the next day.

"Did you have a look in the living room for an address book?" Jane asked Edwards, about to hand him Eileen's flat key.

"You said not to touch anything."

"I'll have a quick look before I go." Jane held onto the key.

Eileen's living room had also been ransacked, but Jane noticed a phone on a small side table and next to it was an address book. Wearing gloves, she picked it up and flicked through it, but didn't see the names of Ben Smith or Sybil Hastings. There was also the latest edition of *Woman's Own* magazine on the table, which Jane flicked through to see if any phone numbers or names had been scribbled in it. She suddenly came across a Samaritans advert giving a phone number, and Jane could see that the top right corner of the page had been folded over, as if to bookmark it. She wondered why Eileen Summers had done this and whether there could be a connection to Sybil Hastings.

CHAPTER ELEVEN

Moran and Lawrence were once again in attendance at Ladywell mortuary. Professor Martin was concluding his post-mortem on the hostel victim as the coroner's officer entered and told Moran that DI Gibbs was on the phone.

After speaking to Gibbs, Moran returned to the mortuary, looking slightly less stressed. He told Martin and Lawrence that the body was believed to be that of Eileen Summers, a 23-year-old teacher from Chalk Farm, and explained the circumstances that had led to the headmistress reporting Summers as missing, finally updating them on Jane's subsequent visits to the school and Eileen Summers' flat.

"Tennison's having a pretty productive day," Lawrence remarked.

Martin laughed. "At this rate, she'll be the first plonk in the Met to make DCI and run a murder squad."

"Yeah, and pigs might fly," Moran retorted.

Martin handed Lawrence the blood and urine samples he had taken during his examination. "There was undigested fish and chips in the stomach. Your victim must have eaten them shortly before her death."

"No sign of fish and chips wrappers at the crime scene," Lawrence said.

"Edwards told Gibbs that Eileen Summers bought herself and her neighbor fish and chips at about five p.m. last night," Moran put in.

"My time of death estimation is pretty good then." Martin smiled.

The pathologist had removed the brain and placed it on a small work table, where Martin now proceeded to examine it.

"There's no major damage to the skull or brain. The blow to the head with the wine bottle didn't kill her, though it would have knocked her out. The hyoid bone in her throat is broken due to strangulation, which is the primary cause of death. Like your first victim, the suspect straddled her from behind as he strangled her. The cord is the same type as found on the first victim, as is the slip knot, and both ends are cut and frayed."

"Sexual assault?" Moran asked.

Martin nodded. "The torn underwear at the scene was an obvious indication, but there are also scratch marks on her inner thighs and vaginal bruising consistent with rape. I've taken swabs for semen. I also suspect, from the injuries to her back, that the rape occurred whilst she was face down and unconscious, which may explain why no one heard any screams."

The duty leader at the Soho Samaritans was polite and helpful, but had clearly been very shocked to hear about Sybil Hastings' death.

"Would you like something to drink while you go through the paperwork?" he asked Jane as he pulled out copies of all the sheets relating to Sybil Hastings' duties for the previous six months.

"A coffee would be nice," she replied.

"I'll get one of the volunteers to bring you one. I was wondering," he added, "can I tell the other volunteers about Mrs. Hastings?"

"Well, seeing as they're all trusted Samaritans . . . But I'd appreciate it if you didn't go into any detail."

He looked relieved. "Of course. Now I'll leave you to it."

Jane decided to start looking from the previous Thursday, when Sybil Hastings was last on duty, and work backwards. As she looked through the records of calls and one-to-one meetings, Jane saw nothing that leapt out at her. Two of the calls

Sybil dealt with were from women and one from a man who had become paralyzed after a serious car accident. The names Ben Smith and Eileen Summers weren't recorded anywhere, and there was nothing to suggest any of the callers were teachers or homeless drug addicts.

She closed her eyes for a moment, feeling exhausted, and knew that it would be better to look at the documents back at the station, with the assistance of Edwards and Gibbs.

There was a knock at the door and a pretty young woman in her mid-twenties, dressed in jeans and a turtleneck jumper, came in carrying a cup of coffee and some biscuits on a plate. She looked as if she'd been crying.

"Are you OK?" Jane asked.

"Yes . . . sorry . . . I just heard about Mrs. Hastings. I can't believe anyone would want to harm her. She was so gentle and kind." She put the coffee and biscuits down on the desk.

Jane picked up her coffee and took a sip. "Thank you. What's your name?"

"Alice. Alice Hodges."

"Had you known Mrs. Hastings long, Alice?"

"A few months. She was training me to be a Samaritan, so we worked the same shifts."

"Were you working together last Thursday?"

Alice nodded.

"How did she seem to you?"

"She was fine to start with. Then she took a call that seemed to bother her. It was unusual because one of the most important parts of our training is not to show any emotion or distress when dealing with a caller."

"What time did the call come in?"

"Between quarter past and half seven, I think."

Jane checked the call log for that evening. "According to the records, the last call Mrs. Hastings dealt with was at 7:10 p.m., from a woman whose husband had repeatedly assaulted her. After that there's no record of her dealing with another call before she finished at eight p.m."

Alice closed the office door and sat down opposite Jane. "Mrs. Hastings started to make some notes on a call sheet. Then she picked up a bit of paper, put it on top of the call sheet and started writing on it. I thought it strange at the time, as she told me every call should be logged and filed."

Jane realized the importance of the information and instantly forgot about her tiredness. She took out her notebook to make some notes. "Did you hear what was said during the call?"

"Only bits. I was sat next to Mrs. Hastings at the time, completing the paperwork from the last call for filing. It was a female caller, and I think she had a northern accent."

Jane remembered Mrs. Rowlands telling her that Eileen Summers was from Manchester. "I need you to take your time and think hard, Alice. Try to remember anything strange that was said during the conversation."

Alice sat quietly, her eyes closed, trying to remember the call.

"She asked the caller if the boy's mother was aware of the situation, and the last thing she said before she put the phone down was: 'When you find out where he was treated, you must tell the police.' That's really all I can remember."

"Did you hear any names during the conversation?" Jane asked.

Alice shook her head. "No names, and Mrs. Hastings didn't say anything to me about the call afterwards."

"What did Mrs. Hastings do with the notes she made?"

Alice paused. "She folded the call sheet and bit of paper up and put them in her handbag."

There had been no call sheets in Mrs. Hastings' handbag when she had searched it. Jane wondered if her killer had destroyed the notes because it linked them to Sybil Hastings.

She also realized the note could be somewhere in Mrs. Hastings' house and decided to contact Agnes about it later.

"Did you or Mrs. Hastings deal with any other calls or visitors that night?" Jane asked.

"I dealt with the next two calls, under Mrs. Hastings' supervision. I think you have copies of the call sheets?"

Jane looked through them and saw the two calls. She heard sniffing and looked up to see Alice wiping tears from her face.

"I should have told the leader about that call, shouldn't I? Do you think if I had, Mrs. Hastings might still be alive?" She looked distraught.

Jane leant forward. "Don't blame yourself, Alice. You're in no way responsible for what happened. You've done the right thing by telling me about the phone call. It could really help the investigation. As far as I'm concerned, this conversation is just between us, and you won't get into any trouble."

Alice smiled gratefully, as Jane jotted down her office phone number. "Call me if you remember anything else about the call or just anything you think might be significant."

Jane was keen to get from Soho to Ladywell mortuary before 5 p.m., to make sure everything was ready for Mrs. Rowlands to identify Eileen Summers. She turned on the CID car siren but didn't like driving at high speed. Other officers found it exhilarating, but Jane constantly worried about having a police vehicle accident or "POLAC," as it was known in the police.

She arrived at the mortuary at ten to five and was shocked to see that Eileen Summers' body had been left on a trolley in the storage area, with just a white sheet over it. She pulled back the sheet and could see that Eileen's tongue was still slightly protruding from her mouth and her face still had blood smears on it. Seeing the morgue attendant, Jane asked him to make the body presentable and take it to the small chapel for identification by the victim's head teacher.

The attendant casually leant over and pushed the victim's tongue back in her mouth. "I should get more warning about preparing a dead body to be taken to the viewing room. There ain't anything more I can do to make her look better without proper notice," he said gruffly.

"Please go and get the viewing room ready," Jane said sharply.

The disgruntled morgue attendant walked off, muttering to himself.

Jane soaked a sponge in water and used it to wipe the blood from Eileen's hair and face. She could now see how pretty Eileen Summers had been, almost angelic.

"What a waste of a young life," she said sadly, patting Eileen's hair and face dry with a towel.

She took her own hairbrush from her handbag and gently brushed Eileen's hair, then used a rubber band she found in a drawer and tied it in a ponytail. She had never touched a dead body so intimately before and began to feel quite emotional. She applied a bit of make-up to Eileen's face and placed the white shroud over her neck to cover the strangulation marks, then stood back, satisfied that the young woman now looked at peace.

Mrs. Rowlands wept as she stood beside Jane and formally identified Eileen Summers' body. It was the first time Jane had seen the dignified headmistress really break down. Mrs. Rowlands leant forward and kissed Eileen's forehead.

"If I'd had a daughter, I'd have wanted her to be like Eileen. She was a wonderful woman and teacher, so kind and thoughtful. She loved all the children and they loved her. I don't know what the school will do without her. She's irreplaceable."

Jane could feel herself welling up. The identification of a body in a murder investigation had become a routine task since she'd been in the CID and she had become desensitized to it. But somehow this was different. She reached out and took hold of Mrs. Rowlands' hand, squeezing it.

"I promise you we will do our very best to find whoever killed her."

Mrs. Rowlands wiped the tears from her cheeks and looked at Jane. "I spoke with the school secretary, who told me something about Eileen that might be relevant to your investigation."

Jane lead Mrs. Rowlands to the coroner's office so they could speak in private, then took out her notebook and nodded that she was ready.

"On Monday morning, just after ten a.m., the secretary answered a call from a well-spoken man who said he was a friend of Miss Summers and needed to speak to her about a personal matter."

"Did he give his name?" Jane asked.

"He said he was Mr. Smith, but he didn't give a first name."

Jane's breathing quickened. Was that their suspect, Ben Smith? "What happened?"

"Miss Summers was in the school yard, supervising the children during their morning break. The secretary kept an eye on the children while Eileen took the call."

"Did anyone overhear the conversation?"

"No, Eileen was alone in the secretary's office when she spoke with the man. The secretary said it wasn't long before Miss Summers came back out to the yard and she seemed fine. Do you think the call might be connected to her murder?"

Jane kept her voice neutral. "Obviously I can't say too much about the investigation, but the information you've just given me may be useful and will certainly be followed up. I'll also need to take a full statement at some point, with more details about Eileen Summers' employment at the school."

Mrs. Rowlands nodded. "That's fine, and I'm quite happy to do it now, if it would help."

It was 7:30 p.m. before Jane completed the detailed statement and left the mortuary, much to the annoyance of the morgue attendant, who had to wait around until she'd finished. Driving home, she wondered if Eileen Summers had been lured to the Peckham hostel by Ben Smith because he intended to kill her. It seemed strange that he had not tried to dispose of Eileen's body, as he had done with the other two. But Jane's excitement that the investigation was now moving forward was tempered by frustration: although the murders had been linked by forensics, there was nothing to help them find Smith quickly before he killed again.

It was just after 8 p.m. when Jane got back to her flat. She didn't have the energy to cook and opted for a takeaway sausage and chips instead. She'd got to know the owner of the local chippy after an incident one night when a drunk was being obnoxious and Jane had stepped in and told him to get out before he got arrested. As a result, the owner always gave her a larger than normal portion of chips, which she always felt was a bit of a waste as she never ate them all, but she appreciated the gesture.

After she had eaten, Jane had a long soak in a hot bath. It had been a tiring and emotional day, not only investigating the murders but comforting the grieving friends and colleagues of Eileen Summers. Jane had been impressed by Mrs. Rowlands' dignified manner at the school, but had seen the pain and hurt come pouring out at the mortuary when she identified Eileen's body. She wondered how Mrs. Rowlands would cope with informing all the parents, and especially the children who had lost a teacher they loved so dearly.

Jane was bone-tired when she went to bed, but no matter how hard she tried, she couldn't sleep. She sat up and read through the notes in her notebook, going over the details of the case.

As she thought about her conversation with Alice at the Samaritans about the call that "seemed to bother" Mrs. Hastings, she remembered Alice telling her that Mrs. Hastings had written on one of the call sheets and then on a separate bit of paper, both of which she folded up and put in her handbag. Jane jumped out of bed, went to the living room and opened her briefcase containing the Samaritans call logs. She hurriedly removed the call sheet log Alice had made under Mrs. Hastings' supervision, after the suspicious call. Jane ran into the kitchen and placed the call logs on the table, before getting a torch from the kitchen drawer.

"Please, please let there be something there," Jane said to herself. She had learnt about indented writing from an old Hackney case. Lawrence had shown her that when a document is written whilst resting on top of other papers, impressions of the writing were transferred to the underlying sheet and could sometimes be seen if illuminated with side-lighting.

Jane could have kicked herself for not thinking about it earlier, realizing that even if she didn't have the original sheet Mrs. Hastings had written on, she had the one that was underneath it. She turned off the kitchen light and shone the torch at an angle across the sheet. There were definitely some faint impressions of writing, but her torch wasn't anywhere near as good as the forensic ones at the lab, so it was impossible to read what Sybil Hastings had written. Jane carefully placed the two call logs between two pieces of cardboard to preserve them, feeling at least she could get some sleep now, knowing she had found what might be a vital clue in the investigation.

CHAPTER TWELVE

Jane woke up early. Despite the fact that she hadn't had much sleep, she felt buoyant. She phoned the lab to speak to DS Lawrence and was told he'd had a very late night and wasn't expected in until 9 a.m. Jane then phoned the station and told the duty sergeant she would be in a bit later as she had to see DS Lawrence at the Met lab. As she drove to Lambeth, she looked forward to showing him what she'd found.

After parking her car in the underground car park, she went to Lawrence's office on the first floor, where he was writing up a report.

"Morning, Jane. Always a pleasure to see you. Have you heard? There's been a big development overnight on the investigation."

"No, what's happened?" she asked eagerly.

Lawrence smiled and got up from his desk. "Take a seat while I put the kettle on and I'll fill you in."

He shook the kettle to check the water level then switched it on.

"What brings you to the lab? Something for us to look at?" he asked, sitting back down.

"Yes, but I want to hear about the big development first."

"The fingerprint lab worked all night developing and examining the prints we lifted at the hostel murder scene and Eileen Summers' flat. Bad news is they didn't find any trace of the unknown victim, or Mrs. Hastings' fingerprints. The guys were red-eyed after doing countless side-by-side comparisons against criminal records. Good news is they found a match to prints on Eileen Summers' jewelry box and bedroom drawers, which also matched a print on the wardrobe door of Ben Smith's hostel room." Paul put a spoonful of coffee in two cups. "I've got no milk—is Coffee-Mate OK?"

"Black, no sugar is fine for me. I thought Gibbs ran a check on Smith's details at the CRO and it was negative?"

"Smith is an alias." Lawrence handed Jane a mugshot and criminal record sheet, with the name "Aiden Lang" on it. "Ben Smith was not referred to the hostel by social services. Turns out the hostel manager was letting the room illegally and pocketing the cash."

As Lawrence made the coffee, Jane looked at the mugshot of Aiden Lang. He only looked about seventeen, with a fresh complexion and high cheekbones.

"His hair is light brown, not blond," Jane commented.

"That mugshot was taken a few months ago. Lang is currently wanted on warrant for non-appearance at Hampstead Magistrates Court on assault and theft charges, so he probably used the alias and dyed his hair to avoid arrest. He also has previous convictions for possession of cannabis and taking a motor vehicle." Lawrence handed Jane her coffee.

"He looks so young. Not at all like I imagined him," she remarked.

"Well, I've learnt that murderers come in all shapes and sizes, Jane. What's really sickening is the way he raped those two young women as he strangled them to death."

Jane nodded. "He's a monster, and he'll undoubtedly keep on killing until he's caught."

"I've told Moran about Lang and the fingerprints. He's arranged a press conference at Scotland Yard, in the lecture theatre at midday. He wants everyone on the team there for an eleven a.m. meeting in the briefing room beforehand, so he can be brought up to speed with everything before facing the press."

"I think Eileen Summers might have phoned the Samaritans and Sybil Hastings dealt with the call on the Thursday evening before she was killed on the Friday." Jane picked up her briefcase and took out the call log, which was still protected by the two sheets of cardboard.

She briefed Lawrence on her visit to the Samaritans in Soho, and her conversation with Alice Hodges. She then handed Lawrence the call sheet.

"The details of this call were written by Alice. Mrs. Hastings wrote something on the previous call sheet, which she didn't file, for some reason. Obviously I'm hoping the indented writing from Mrs. Hastings' notes might reveal some details of the caller, or maybe even the suspect. During the conversation there was also mention of a boy receiving treatment somewhere. I looked at the call sheet in the dark using my house torch—there's something there, but I couldn't make it out. Can you do a proper examination on it for me, Paul?"

"Well done for preserving it between the cardboard, but it'll have to go in the 'awaits' pile for now, Jane. I'm up to my eyeballs with forensic work on the case. I still need to compare Mrs. Hastings' tweed suit with the fibers on the bodies and from the Allegro. And we both need to be at the Yard for eleven."

Jane pursed her lips and gave him a "please, just for me" look.

Lawrence laughed. "You're very hard to resist, Tennison. There's a new bit of equipment called the Electrostatic Detection Apparatus—ESDA for short. It was invented recently at the London College of Printing. At present, we're the only force that's got it on trial. It's much better than using a light source, and brings up indented handwriting that's invisible to the human eye."

Jane finished her coffee and followed Lawrence into a room with "Questioned Documents & Handwriting" on the door. In the corner was a blue steel box, about the size of a briefcase, marked ESDA. On the top was a bronze plate covered with pin-size holes and there was a rectangular metal wand attached to the side. Lawrence placed the Samaritans call log, written by Alice, onto the brass plate, then stretched a piece of cling film over the document. He turned on the ESDA. It began to whirr then vibrate, and Jane watched as the air was sucked through the pinholes, pulling the document and cling film firmly down on the bronze plate.

Lawrence picked up the wand attachment and told Jane to stand back as he was about to run a few thousand volts of static electricity over the document. Jane took two big steps back as Lawrence waved the wand across it. He lifted the brass plate at a 30-degree angle and gently poured black toner from a jar over the cling film. He explained how the toner would bring up the unseen indented areas of the document onto the cling film. He replaced the wand and tapped the plate, removing the remnants of the toner. Jane was transfixed as darker traces showing the indented impressions slowly appeared on the cling film against the grey background, and the indented writing began to reveal itself. She could identify different styles of handwriting, some on top of each other, and it was hard to separate them.

Lawrence shrugged. "That's one of the problems: bloody machine is so sensitive it can pick up three or four layers of indented writing, which actually makes it difficult and time-consuming to find what you're looking for." Lawrence then made the indented images permanent by placing clear sticky-backed plastic over the toner, thus producing a fixed, transparent image. He then made a second copy and handed it to Jane for the case file back at the station.

"The documents section will need some samples of Mrs. Hastings' handwriting, as well as Alice's, to help narrow down who wrote what."

"I've got other call logs that Mrs. Hastings and Alice filled out. Will they do?"

Paul nodded. Jane opened her briefcase and handed him a folder.

"I'll get a handwriting expert to look at them and the indented writing. It could be two or three days before they get around to it as they're examining documents in an IRA case for the Bomb Squad, whose work always takes precedence over everything else."

"Thanks, Paul."

"Right, it's just after ten, so we'd better make our way over to the Yard for the press conference. We can grab a sandwich and coffee in the canteen, if you want."

"Sounds good to me," Jane said as she put the copy of the indented writing in her briefcase.

Arriving at Scotland Yard, they went straight to the briefing room, where Gibbs and the rest of the murder team were waiting. Moran didn't look happy.

"Where have you been, Tennison? I expect you to be in the office by nine a.m. at the latest."

"I spoke to the duty sergeant and explained that I had to go to the lab. I thought he'd have told you."

"Well, he didn't. I need to know what you're doing so that I can be kept up to speed with developments," Moran said tersely.

Gibbs was quick to defend Jane. "In fairness, Jane did phone me several times with updates yesterday, as you were out the office. Her findings were in the report I left on your desk."

Moran looked slightly embarrassed. He clearly hadn't had time to read Gibbs' report.

"Well, we're all very busy, but in future a phone call would be appreciated, Tennison. Is there anything you haven't told DI Gibbs that I need to know about?"

Jane quickly updated him, focusing on the indented writing and the phone call Eileen Summers had taken at school, from a man calling himself Mr. Smith.

Moran nodded. "Good work. I appreciate the labs document section are busy with the Bomb Squad stuff, but keep chasing them up for a result. Right, moving on . . . Just so you all know, the press are all over the fact that three murders have taken place in Peckham." Moran picked up a newspaper from the desk and held it up.

"As you can see, the headlines in the tabloids are 'Peckham's Murder Mile' and 'Peckham Rye Killer Strikes Again.' The press is inferring all three murders are linked and are the work of the same killer. It's also been leaked that Mrs. Hastings' body was discovered by her son."

"Well, that's obviously come from that prick Andrew Hastings," Gibbs interjected.

Moran ignored him. "The press is calling us inept and clueless. The Commissioner is livid and wants DCS Blake and me to explain the complexities of the investigation to the press and release the fact we now have Aiden Lang as a suspect, with forensic evidence to suggest he's responsible for all three murders."

Edwards and another officer entered the room.

"Sorry we're late, sir," he said sheepishly.

"Where have you two been?" Moran bellowed.

"Making enquiries at Hampstead Police Station about Aiden Lang's arrest for assault and theft—just as you instructed us to do first thing this morning, sir," Edwards replied.

Moran looked embarrassed again. "Uh, yes, sorry, Edwards. Things have been a bit hectic this morning. What've you got for us?"

Jane noted that she hadn't got an apology from Moran for his brusque manner.

Edwards flicked open his notebook. "We spoke with the uniform officer who last arrested Aiden Lang. The circumstances were . . ." Edwards paused to look at his notes. "The officer was walking past the public toilet block at Hampstead Heath at about two p.m., when he heard a commotion in the men's. He entered the block and found Lang assaulting the victim—an accountant in his early thirties. The PC broke up the fight, and the accountant said Lang had attacked him and stolen his wallet. The wallet was in Lang's possession and he was duly nicked."

"Did Lang admit the offences under interview?" Moran asked.

"Yep. His excuse for committing the offence was because he was homeless and needed money."

"What address did he give as his last residence for the charge sheet?" Moran asked.

Edwards turned a page in his notebook. "The Golden Lion pub in Soho. Said he worked there and lived in a small room above it. He didn't get on with the landlord so left and had been living rough in the West End. He also said he had a married sister who lived in south London, but he didn't get on with her husband, so he didn't visit her."

Gibbs nodded. "That doesn't mean he doesn't keep in contact with her. Find out who she is and where she lives, Edwards."

"The Samaritans branch Mrs. Hastings worked at is in Soho," Jane said.

"The Golden Lion is a gay boys' pub in Dean Street, just off Shaftesbury Avenue," Edwards added.

Gibbs opened his eyes wide in mock surprise. "Didn't take you for a shirt-lifter, Edwards!"

Edwards grinned. "Takes one to know one, guv. Funny thing is, the officer who arrested Lang said the area on Hampstead Heath where the incident happened is commonly known as

'Gobblers Gulch,' where men go cottaging and looking for a blow job in the men's toilets."

"What's 'cottaging'?" a young detective asked.

Edwards laughed. "It's a term used when referring to anonymous sex between poofters in a public toilet, or where they're cruising for someone to have sex with. Some toilets have glory holes they stick their todgers through . . ."

"Shut up, Edwards, and stop behaving like a school kid," Jane said sharply, annoyed at the way he was treating the subject as a joke.

"Anything else to add, Edwards?" Moran asked.

Edwards adopted a more serious tone. "The arresting PC suspected there was more behind the incident, but he had no evidence to prove it. Lang was charged and appeared at the local magistrates court the next day, where he pleaded guilty and was released on bail pending a probation service report by social services. He obviously did a runner as he failed to reappear at court for sentencing."

Moran thought for a moment. "Tennison and Lawrence, I want you two to go to the Golden Lion and speak to the landlord and staff. And do a thorough search of the room Lang stayed in there."

Lawrence frowned. "Can I send a local SOCO to meet Tennison there? I've got a huge backlog of stuff to deal with at the lab."

Moran shook his head. "Sorry, Paul, you've been to all the crime scenes and the post-mortems. I value your experience and I know I can trust you not to miss anything of forensic value."

Lawrence didn't look happy, but knew he couldn't argue.

Moran continued. "I agree with the arresting PC. Something doesn't add up about Lang's arrest in the toilets. Gibbs, I want you and Edwards to visit the accountant who was robbed by Lang. It's possible they might have met for sex and are old acquaintances. Find out if there's more behind the incident."

"Why do I always get the shitty jobs?" Edwards muttered under his breath.

Moran glared at him. "You got a problem, Edwards? And before you answer, I'm not in the mood for any more of your frivolous remarks."

Edwards looked chastened. "I just remembered something, sir. Although Lang's mugshot doesn't show it because his mouth's closed, the arresting officer said he had an upper front tooth missing on the left side of his mouth. Believe it or not, Lang told the officer it was knocked out when someone robbed him."

Moran looked happier. "Good, that should help with identifying him." He cleared his throat. "I want Lang traced and arrested within the next forty-eight hours. All of you need to keep up the hard work. We can't rest until he's found. There must be a connection between our three victims and Lang, and finding it will lead us to him. I don't believe any of the murders are random, so it's more likely the three women were lured to their deaths, especially as neither Summers nor Hastings were from Peckham. Likewise, I suspect our unknown victim isn't either."

Jane spoke up. "The Kentish Town primary school that Eileen Summers taught at, and her home address in Chalk Farm, are not far from Hampstead Heath, where Lang was arrested."

"Good point. Revisit Eileen Summers' school and see if Lang was ever a pupil there."

"But Eileen is only twenty-three, so she couldn't have been a teacher when he was at primary school," Jane argued.

"Don't question, Tennison, just do as I ask. It may be that Lang is an ex-pupil with a grudge against the school and he decided to take it out on one of the teachers. I know there's more questions than answers right now, and the press are about to give me a grilling, so let's find Lang before he kills again. Or we might all find ourselves back in uniform."

Jane bit her tongue as Moran left the room. The impending press conference had clearly made him edgy.

"Well, if he's a gay boy, he shouldn't be hard to break," Gibbs remarked.

"He might just squeal like a piggy . . . Weee . . . Weee." Edwards grinned, adopting a hillbilly accent in imitation of the film *Deliverance*.

Some of the officers laughed as everyone began to leave the room.

"Now that was a great film." Gibbs laughed.

"Yeah, remember that bit where Burt Reynolds shot the pervert hillbilly with a bow and arrow, then buried him?" Edwards added.

Jane noticed Lawrence shaking his head sadly at his colleagues' childish and narrow-minded behavior.

As Jane left the team meeting, she saw Moran speaking to Blake in the corridor. She would have liked to have gone into the press conference, but Moran had made it clear he wanted them out on the streets doing everything they could to find Aiden Lang.

Blake lit a cigarette, inhaled deeply and let out two streams of smoke through his nostrils. "Have Summers' parents given us the OK to release their daughter's name to the press?"

"Yes. They're coming down today to do an official ID on the body," Moran replied.

"I think it's best you take the lead at the press conference, Nick. I don't want to steal your limelight. Besides, you know a lot more about the case than I do, so you're also in a better position to fend off any dodgy questions."

Moran frowned. "I can take the flak, but if they start to criticize my detectives, then I expect you to step in and defend them. They've hardly slept and haven't stopped grafting since day one."

"Of course I'll support them. I'm also confident you'll have Lang arrested and charged by tomorrow night. It will be a big deal, and could lead to calls for your promotion to detective superintendent, which I of course will recommend." Blake stubbed his cigarette out in the ashtray on the hallway table. "I'll do the introductions, then hand over to you."

As he led the way to the conference room, Moran resisted the urge to kick Blake up the backside for his condescending manner. Moran wondered how he'd feel if he told the press the investigation had initially been hindered by Blake and Andrew Hastings' lies.

As Blake and Moran entered the conference room, the high-pitched whine of camera flashes charging up was followed by a strobe of pulsating light as the flashes popped, creating a slow-motion effect as the two officers walked over to the podium. Blake introduced himself as the senior officer overseeing the investigation and Moran as the lead investigator, then made a brief statement.

"I am pleased to tell you that DCI Moran has identified a single male suspect in all three murders. He will give further details after he has briefed you on the current state of the investigation and appealed for the public's assistance."

For a moment the room went silent. This was information the press were not expecting. It was also something Moran had intended to keep to the end. He nodded to one of his detectives at the back of the room, who was operating a slide projector between two television cameras.

Moran pointed to the projection screen behind him. Photographs of Eileen Summers and Sybil Hastings, and an artist's impression of the unidentified victim, came up on the screen. Moran gave a detailed description of the unknown victim, followed by the others: who they were, where their bodies were found, and brief details of how they had been murdered. He did not reveal that a similar rope had been used to strangle two of the victims.

Blake suddenly stepped forward, as if wanting to show his involvement.

"To date we have had no one reported missing across the country who matches the unidentified victim's description. I would appeal to anyone who thinks they might know her to get in contact with the Peckham incident room."

"Do you have any connection between the three victims?" a member of the press shouted out.

Blake didn't answer, looking at Moran.

"Not at present. However—"

"How strong is the evidence against your suspect?" Moran was interrupted as the cameras started to flash again and a barrage of questions were shouted out.

"One at a time, please . . . One at a time." Blake raised his voice and pointed to a journalist.

"More to the point, how many more women will be killed before you arrest him?"

Moran tried to remain calm. "I am not prepared to go into the exact details, but there are forensic links between all three murders, pointing to our prime suspect: this man." Moran paused as the mugshot of Aiden Lang appeared on the screen, then gave his age and physical description, including his missing tooth and the fact that his hair was believed to be currently dyed blond, and added that he had used the alias Ben Smith. As Moran was about to appeal for the public's assistance in finding him, Blake stepped forward again.

"Obviously someone out there knows Lang and we also believe he has a sister who lives in South London. I would appeal to her, or anyone who knows his whereabouts, to contact DCI Moran's incident room. If you see him, do not approach him as he is obviously very dangerous and prone to violence."

"What else are you doing to trace Lang?" a newspaperman asked.

Blake was quick to answer. "Everything we can, of course. All-ports warnings have been sent out and every force in the country has been issued with his photo—which we're also distributing nationally, in the press and on television."

"In less than a week three murders have been committed within a mile of each other. What makes you think you'll find him now, DCS Blake?" someone else piped up.

"I have every confidence that, with the help of the public, DCI Moran will arrest Lang before he commits another murder."

Some of the press laughed out loud, and one shouted out, "But you haven't a clue where Lang is!"

Moran decided he'd had enough and cut Blake off before he could answer the question.

"We only identified Lang yesterday after a fingerprint analysis revealed he was using the name Ben Smith. I have a dedicated team of officers working day and night to find Lang, and we need the press to help us, not hinder us by accusations of incompetence. It's not good for the victims' families or the morale of the investigating officers. Let me assure you my team will arrest Lang and bring him before the courts. Every one of them is determined to solve these horrific murders and give the grieving families and friends the answers they need." Moran paused as he picked up his paperwork. "I'm sure DCS Blake would be happy to answer any further questions. I need to get back to my investigation and support my officers in their work."

There was a buzz of conversation in the room as the journalists looked at one another. Moran seized the moment to exit the room as a flurry of further questions were directed at Blake, delighted to be leaving him in the proverbial "shit."

CHAPTER THIRTEEN

Lawrence sat silently looking out of the passenger window of the "Jaffa cake" as Jane parked outside the Golden Lion. He certainly didn't seem his normal enthusiastic self, chomping at the bit to examine the crime scene and find forensic evidence that could break open the investigation.

"You were very quiet in the meeting, Paul. Are you OK?"

He didn't look at her. "I'm fine, just really tired. There's a load of work piling up at the lab, and with everything Moran wants done, it's just getting bigger and bigger. The danger is that when you get tired, you make mistakes and miss things that might be important."

Jane smiled. "*You*, miss something? As if! You could sleepwalk your way around a crime scene and still find more than the rest of us put together."

Lawrence sighed. "Believe me, Jane, I've made mistakes. I've been lucky so far, and I've been able to hide or rectify them before anyone else notices."

Jane thought for a moment. "What do you reckon to this Aiden Lang? I mean, if he is gay, as Edwards was inferring, then why would he rape two of the victims?"

"Maybe he's bisexual," Lawrence replied brusquely.

"Never thought of that," Jane admitted.

Once again Lawrence didn't look at her, clearly not wanting to discuss Aiden Lang. Jane shrugged and got out of the car. Lawrence followed.

The Golden Lion had many original features dating back to the late seventeen hundreds. The exterior carved oak façade, interior rustic oak floor, and ornate red and gold ceiling all suggested the pub's former glories and a time when Soho first became known for its theatres and music halls. Now it was busy with lunchtime trade and the customers were predominantly male.

Jane and Lawrence approached the bar and she asked the barman if the landlord was available. He bent down, lifted the wooden trap door to the cellar and shouted, "The Old Bill's here, John—they want to speak to you!" The conversation in the pub went quiet as everyone looked towards the bar.

The landlord, John Davis, was a portly man in his fifties, with greasy hair and a beer belly. He was dressed in a white open-necked shirt with a sweat-stained collar, black trousers and brown suede shoes. Once they were seated in the corner, out of earshot of the staff and the regulars, Jane briefed him about the murders and showed him a photo of Aiden Lang.

"Yeah, that's Aiden. He was working here as a trainee barman up until seven or eight weeks ago. I rent the rooms out on the first floor to the bar staff. Aiden had one, but his replacement's living in it now—he's the bloke you spoke to behind the bar."

"Did Aiden have blond hair when you last saw him?" Jane asked.

"No."

"What about a missing upper tooth?"

"Yeah, on the left side."

Lawrence picked up his forensic bag and looked at Davis as he stood up. "I need to search the room for anything that might help us find Lang, or assist the investigation, so if you could tell me where it is, I'll get on with it. We're pressed for time."

"It's on the first floor, second room on the right. The barman's got the key. The top floor's all mine if you need to search it."

"No, Lang's room is the only one I need to see." Lawrence walked off to get the room key from the barman.

"So why did Lang stop working here?"

"I sacked him after I caught him with his fingers in the till. He denied it, but I told him I saw him slip the money in his pocket. He said he was going to pay it back, but I didn't believe him. I went to get the money out of his pocket and he pushed my hand away, so I thumped him. Truth is, it was me that knocked his tooth out. I didn't mean to, it was an instinctive thing. An accident, if you see what I mean."

"It's still assault, Mr. Davis. But under the circumstances, I think we can forget about it. So tell me, why did you hire Lang in the first place?"

He laughed. "His boyish good looks attracted the gay punters. I gotta tell you, officer, Aiden was a well-spoken lad, who always dressed in fashionable gear. Apart from the thieving incident, he was never any bother. I suspected he might have a drug problem, 'cause his eyes used to look a bit too big for his head sometimes." He shook his head. "I can't believe he'd murder anyone, especially a woman, considering it's a fair bet he was gay. I never saw him get aggressive when any of the male punters grabbed his arse or squeezed his bollocks. Sorry, pardon my language."

Jane shrugged. "I've heard worse. Did Lang ever mention if he had any family? A sister, perhaps?"

Davis paused. "Not that I recall. I never asked Aiden about his personal life, to be honest."

"Was he in a relationship with any of the punters, or anyone you know of?"

"Don't know. I did tell him I was against staff having relationships on the premises, but what he did outside the pub was his own business."

Jane showed him pictures of Sybil Hastings, Eileen Summers and the artist's impression of the unknown victim. "Do you recognize any of these women?"

Davis took his time looking at the pictures before shaking his head. "Sorry, I don't recognize any of them. We don't get many women in here, and if we do, they're usually lesbians. Can I show these pictures to my bar staff?"

"Sure. I'll nip upstairs and see how my colleague is getting on."

Davis pointed Jane towards the door that led to the staff accommodation.

"Find anything of interest?" Jane asked Lawrence, entering the dingy room.

"No. I've had a good look around. But the barman said he chucked anything out that Lang had left behind."

"Are you going to dust for fingerprints?"

"What for? We know he lived here, so finding his prints won't prove anything or help us find him." Lawrence picked up his bag. "Have you finished downstairs?"

"Just about."

"I'll wait in the car then."

Jane handed him the car keys, then went to retrieve the victims' pictures from the landlord, who was standing next to Aiden Lang's replacement. As Jane approached the barman, he held up the black and white artist's impression of the unidentified victim.

"Last Thursday or Friday afternoon, a woman who looked a bit like this came in and asked for Aiden. I told her he'd been sacked for stealing cash from the till. She looked upset and walked out."

"Can you tell me anything more about her?"

The barman thought for a second. "She had brown hair, shoulder-length—a sort of sandy color and parted in the middle."

"How old would you say she was?"

"I dunno, late twenties, early thirties?"

"Can you remember what she was wearing?"

"Bloody hell, I only saw her for a few minutes. Her coat was buttoned up so I didn't see what was under it."

"Was the coat blue?" Jane asked, realizing the woman's description was very like the unknown victim's.

"It could have been, but I can't remember now. It's freezing cold; everyone who comes in here is wearing a coat."

"OK, thanks for your help." Taking the artist's impression back, she walked quickly out to the car, got in and turned to Lawrence.

"The barman gave a description of a woman who came to the pub looking for Aiden Lang. It could've been our unidentified victim. She seemed upset when he told her Aiden had been fired for stealing."

"Well, that's something positive to tell Moran," Lawrence agreed, but his tone was unenthusiastic. "Can you drop me off at the lab, please?"

Paul was silent on the journey back. Jane knew he had been working long hours and could see he looked tired, but was still surprised by his uncharacteristic behavior.

Gibbs and Edwards were on their way to Highgate, one of London's most affluent suburbs, to see the accountant who had been robbed by Aiden Lang.

"What's this accountant's name again?" Gibbs asked Edwards.

"Mr. Poofter?" Edwards smirked.

Gibbs laughed. "That might be why he only gave his work address on his victim statement."

"Yeah, I'll bet he's married and doesn't want his wife to know what happened."

"Well, he'll be in for a shock when we turn up at his office unannounced. Best I ask the questions."

"I won't argue with that." Edwards snorted.

Arriving at the elegant building, they guessed that Peter Barnes was a wealthy man. Gibbs spoke with the receptionist, who rang Barnes then escorted them to a plush office. Barnes was in his late thirties and well dressed in a three-piece pin-stripe suit, white shirt, silk tie and black brogues. He was six foot tall, well groomed and athletic-looking.

"Good afternoon, officers," he said, holding a hand out to Gibbs. "What can I do for you?"

"We'd just like to ask you a few questions about Aiden Lang, Mr. Barnes, the man who robbed you a few weeks ago in the toilets at Hampstead Heath."

"That was some time ago now. But it was a terrifying experience. To be honest, I don't know what he'd have done to me if the constable hadn't intervened."

Gibbs nodded sympathetically. "You were in the wrong place at the wrong time, I guess."

"Indeed. I won't be going there again, that's for sure."

"As a matter of interest, what were you doing on Hampstead Heath that day?" Gibbs asked.

Barnes pushed a hand though his hair. "I, uh, was out, um, visiting a client and got caught short on the way back to the office. So I, uh, popped into the toilets on the Heath. If I'd known it was a thief's hangout, I certainly wouldn't have gone there," he added.

"It's not renowned for thieves, actually, but it is a notorious haunt for gay men looking for blow jobs," Edwards told Barnes, unable to resist putting some pressure on him.

"Well, that's news to me . . . and another reason I'll avoid the area," Barnes said with a nervous smile.

"Had you ever met Aiden Lang before at the Heath toilets?" Gibbs asked.

"No, I had not, and I resent your insinuation that I was there for anything other than a pee."

Gibbs held his hands up. "I wasn't insinuating anything, Mr. Barnes."

Barnes didn't look convinced. "I'm very busy, officers, and have a business to run. I don't know anything about Aiden Lang—other than that he's a criminal. If you don't mind, I'd like you to leave."

"Lang is also a triple murder suspect," Edwards said evenly.

Barnes now looked like a rabbit caught in the headlights.

"How did your wife take it when you told her you were robbed in a toilet on Hampstead Heath?" Gibbs asked.

"She was upset . . . of course."

"Best we speak with her then. What's your home address?" Edwards asked.

Barnes stiffened. "I will not be spoken to like some criminal! Please leave now."

"You leave us no choice than to arrest you for perverting the course of justice in a murder investigation, Mr. Barnes. You are not obliged to say anything—" Gibbs began.

"All right, all right." Barnes' body seemed to go slack. "I'll tell you what happened, but please don't say anything to my wife. She'd leave me and take the children."

"I'm not interested in your home life, Mr. Barnes, just your association with Aiden Lang," Gibbs said.

Barnes looked relieved. "I'd never met or seen Aiden Lang before that day. I'd had a working lunch with a client in the Jack Straw's Castle pub next to the Heath. When I left, Lang approached me in the car park and propositioned me."

"Why would he approach you in particular?" Edwards asked.

"I don't know. He might have seen me at the toilets before with another man. We went to the toilets, then . . . in a cubicle he performed oral sex on me and demanded ten pounds. We'd originally agreed a price of five pounds, so I handed him a fiver. Lang became aggressive and started screaming at me.

He grabbed me round the throat and took my wallet. The PC turned up and arrested him. I assume, like me, he didn't want the officer to know what we'd been doing."

Gibbs gave him a curt nod. "Thank you for your time, Mr. Barnes. If we need to speak to you again, we know where you are."

Barnes said nothing as they walked out of his office.

"Where to now?" Edwards asked as they got in the car.

"Jack Straw's Castle. We can have a bit of lunch and a pint, and ask a few questions about Lang in case he's still a regular."

Edwards didn't look very excited about Gibbs' suggestion, but he knew he had no choice in the matter.

Arriving at the top of Hampstead Heath, it was easy to find Jack Straw's Castle, an imposing building that stood alone like a sentinel looking down over the greenery. They spoke with the landlord over lunch and showed him pictures of Lang and the victims, but he didn't recognize any of them and neither did any of his staff. Already uncomfortable with the idea of enjoying a pub lunch whilst on duty, Edwards felt like it was a wasted visit. Gibbs, however, had one more idea up his sleeve. Leaving the pub, he told Edwards to park the car up near the toilets, so they could keep observation for a while and see if Lang, or anyone else who might be cruising for gay sex, turned up.

Edwards cheered up. "We'll be the dog's bollocks in the office if we get Lang." He grinned.

It wasn't long before they saw a youth hanging around outside the toilets. He was then approached by an older, camp-looking man, who was walking a small black and tan Yorkshire terrier. The two men then went into the toilets.

"You don't think the dog's involved in a threesome, do you?" Edwards joked.

Gibbs laughed. "Let's have a word and see if either of them know Lang or have seen him in the area."

Edwards sighed. "Can't we wait until they come out? If we go in there we might get one of them SID things, like gonear."

Gibbs laughed even harder. "It's gonorrhoea, you pillock, and STD, which is short for Sexually Transmitted Disease, and you can't catch them off a toilet seat or urinal, so shift your arse."

When they got to the toilet, the two men were just coming out.

"That was a quick one," Edwards quipped as he held his warrant card up to stop them.

"Pardon?" the older man said.

Edwards gave them a stern look. "Gross Indecency in a public toilet is a criminal offence under the Sexual Offences Act 1956."

But the man showed no sign of being intimidated. "As a barrister, I'm fully aware of that offence, officer, as is my son here, who's currently studying law at university."

Edwards shook his head. "Yeah, good try, mate—these toilets are a well-known haunt for you bum bandits."

The older man looked incensed. "We've just met up to go for lunch in Jack Straw's Castle. I hope, for your sake, you're not implying that we have just committed a sexual act in the toilets?"

Gibbs realized the man was telling the truth and quickly stepped in to defuse the situation. He apologized for any misunderstanding and told the two men they were looking for a murder suspect who frequented the Heath and showed them a picture of Lang, but neither the solicitor nor his son had seen him before. Gibbs thanked them for their assistance and hoped they had an enjoyable lunch.

The barrister nodded at Gibbs, then turned to Edwards.

"I suggest you don't jump to blinkered conclusions in future, officer. My son and I could just as easily have mistaken you and your colleague for a gay couple, but we're not as narrow-minded as you. Good day."

When the pair were out of earshot, Edwards muttered, "Fucking wankers. I reckon that lawyer is a closet poofter like our Mr. Barnes."

Gibbs shook his head. "You need to wind your neck in and change your attitude, Edwards. We could have ended up with a serious complaint there."

Edwards looked at him in surprise. "What? You make remarks about poofters as much as I do."

"That's just having a laugh amongst ourselves. I don't have a problem with gay men. To be honest, I couldn't care less if Aiden Lang is a gay rent boy; the fact he's brutally murdered three women is what makes me detest him."

"I need a pee." Edwards stomped off to the toilets with a disgruntled look.

Gibbs waited a few seconds before sneaking into the toilets and creeping up behind Edwards, who was muttering to himself about queers. Gibbs reached out and squeezed Edwards' bottom, making a startled Edwards jump forward, urinating on his trousers and shoes.

As Gibbs burst out laughing, Edwards turned and shouted angrily, "That's not funny, guv. Look at the state of my bloody trousers!"

After dropping Lawrence off at the lab, Jane rang Moran to update him about the visit to the Golden Lion and the woman who'd been looking for Aiden Lang. Moran also had some positive information.

"We've had a call from a woman in Kilburn called Brenda Matthews. She was so distressed it was hard to understand what she was saying, but anyway, the gist of it is she thinks her daughter Helen may be the unidentified victim. Everyone's busy so I'll get the local plods to visit her."

"I'm on my way to Eileen Summers' primary school in Kentish Town to see Mrs. Rowlands. Kilburn's nearby so I could follow up on Brenda Matthews first," Jane said, hoping he'd say yes.

"OK, do that. The address is flat forty, Bronte House on the South Kilburn Estate."

Jane parked in the street outside Bronte House, an eighteen-story concrete tower block in South Kilburn. The grass area outside the block was littered with rubbish bags spilling out rotting waste due to the bin strike. But Jane knew the rundown appearance of the estate was also due to the area's drug problem, which brought a lot of crime to the neighborhood.

Brenda Matthews lived on the tenth floor and Jane knew before she even pressed the lift button that it would be out of order—probably not through any mechanical fault, but deliberate damage caused by some of the many young criminals and hooligans who lived on the estate. Jane, like so many of the unfortunate residents, had no choice other than walking up the stairs.

She was breathing heavily when she reached the tenth floor, and thanked her lucky stars Mrs. Matthews didn't live on the eighteenth. She waited a few moments to get her breath back, then knocked on the flat door. It was instantly opened by a small woman in her mid to late fifties. She wore glasses, had short wavy hair with a few grey streaks, and was casually dressed in a brown shirt, brown and white checked knee-length skirt, with a white apron over it and slippers. But what Jane noticed most was the tremor in hands and the distraught look on her face.

She also immediately saw a strong resemblance to the unknown victim.

"Brenda Matthews?" Jane asked as she showed her warrant card and the woman nodded. "I'm Detective Sergeant Tennison. I've come about the call you made to the incident room regarding your daughter, Helen. Can I come in and speak to you?"

"Are you investigating them murders in Peckham?"

Jane didn't answer. She could see Mrs. Matthews was unsteady on her feet, so took her gently by the arm and helped her onto the settee. The living room in the small two-bedroom flat was neat and tidy, though sparsely furnished, with just the settee, an armchair, side dresser in one corner and a small dining table pushed up against the wall, along with three wooden chairs. In another corner of the room there was a small cardboard box overflowing with Dinky and Corgi toy cars, some Action Man dolls and accessories.

Jane got Mrs. Matthews a glass of water from the kitchen and handed it to her. Once Brenda had taken a few sips, Jane sat next to her on the settee and noticed an old wedding picture on the wall.

"Is your husband at work, Brenda?"

"I'm a widow. He died some years ago in a car accident."

"Oh, I'm sorry. I can imagine this is very distressing for you, Brenda, but can I ask why you called the incident room?"

Mrs. Matthews' lower lip trembled, and she began to cry. "I'd been out shopping for groceries and bumped into my neighbor on the landing. She'd watched the lunchtime news about the murders in Peckham and said a drawing of one of the victim's looked just like . . . my Helen." She paused to wipe her eyes. "I'd seen in Monday's paper about them two women who was murdered in Peckham, but it didn't say no names." She turned to Jane with a pleading look. "I'm scared, so scared . . . Please tell me it's not my Helen."

Jane felt desperate for her, but couldn't help wondering, if it was Helen, why she hadn't reported her daughter missing earlier. She decided, rather than prolonging the agony asking painful questions about Helen, to resolve the situation in a more direct way.

"Do you have a photo of Helen I can look at?"

Mrs. Matthews pointed to a picture on a wooden side dresser. "There's one of her with my grandson Simon at the fun fair. He'd just turned nine."

Mrs. Matthews began to rock back and forth, clutching her hands together below her chin, as if praying for Helen's safety. Jane realized the box of toys in the corner must be Simon's. She got up to look closely at the photograph. It was a poor quality black and white picture, taken from a distance, which made it hard to be certain if the victim was Helen.

"Please, God, officer, tell me it's not my Helen," Mrs. Matthews sobbed.

Jane could see Brenda was in shock and she really didn't want to take her to the mortuary to view the body in case it wasn't her daughter.

She crouched down in front of her. "It's hard to say from that photo. Do you have another picture, a close-up, perhaps?"

Mrs. Matthews pointed to the chest of drawers. "There's some photos in the top drawer. One of them is her and Simon in one of them Woolworths photo booths what takes pictures of you."

Jane opened the drawer and immediately saw an A4-size school photograph. Sat in the middle of the children was a smiling Eileen Summers. It was the same picture Mrs. Rowlands had shown Jane when she first visited the school. Jane's heart raced as she rummaged through the drawer. She found the black and white passport-sized photo booth picture of Helen and Simon, who was sitting on his mother's lap, with his arms around her neck. Jane held it next to the school photo and could see Simon sitting on the floor in front of Miss Summers.

There could be no doubt anymore: Helen Matthews was the killer's first victim, and there was now a definite connection between her and Eileen Summers. Mrs. Matthews could tell from the somber look on Jane's face that her worst fears were true.

"The dead girl's my Helen, isn't it?"

Jane nodded, unable to find any consoling words.

Mrs. Matthews began rocking back and forth on the settee, holding her arms tightly around herself. She realized that Brenda had no idea Eileen Summers had been murdered, and thought it best not to tell her yet.

Jane sat down next to her on the settee and held her hand. "I'm so sorry, but I will need you to formally identify Helen at the mortuary. I will be there with you, but we don't have to do it right away. My main concern at this moment is obviously for you and Simon. Is he at school just now?"

Helen nodded as she continued to rock back and forwards, her eyes still filled with tears.

"We will also need to notify Simon's father."

Mrs. Matthews shook her head. "Helen was a single mother and never told anyone who Simon's father was, not even Simon. Oh dear God, how am I going to tell him his mother's dead? I need to see Simon. Can we go to his school?" Brenda pleaded.

"Yes, of course. Brenda, I know you are very upset right now, but I just need to ask you a few important questions about Helen before we go and see Simon. Is that OK?"

Brenda nodded.

"I'll also need to search her bedroom."

"Helen doesn't live here; she has a place of her own."

"Whereabouts?"

"Number four Willbury House, on the Hilldrop estate. It's near Tufnell Park tube station."

Jane jotted down the address, realizing that answering questions was somehow helping Mrs. Matthews to keep from completely collapsing. "I don't mean to pry, Brenda, but does Simon live with you?"

"Sometimes. But it's just so Helen can go out and work. She's a cleaner, you see. It's hard for her to earn money when Simon's not at school. During the school holidays he spends most of the time with me. He's been with me over the half term."

Jane was a little confused about the arrangements concerning Simon, as she knew he must have returned to school on the Monday just gone.

"I take it you made the arrangements about Simon before the half term started?"

"Yes and no. We'd spoken about it beforehand but then Helen came here last Friday afternoon to see Simon."

"What time was that?"

"About three thirty, I think. Helen gave me some money for looking after Simon. She said she'd been busy and doing lots of extra hours cleaning."

"Are you looking after Simon this week as well?"

"Well, I didn't think so, but then again I wasn't sure, cos I thought Helen said she'd collect him from me on the Monday evening after school. When she didn't, I thought maybe Helen said she'd pick him up on the Tuesday from mine after school, but again she didn't. I was a bit annoyed with her, to be honest, and neither of us has a phone, so after I dropped Simon at school this morning, I went to her flat to see what she was playing at, but she wasn't there." Mrs. Matthews started to cry again at the realization her daughter was already dead when she went to the flat.

"Did you speak with any of the neighbors?" Jane asked, realizing Mrs. Matthews wouldn't have got an answer at Helen's flat.

"No. I thought she might have been at work. I put a nasty note through the letter box about her responsibilities as a mother." The memory sent her into a fit of sobs.

Jane rubbed her arm. "It's not your fault, Brenda. You weren't to know what had happened to Helen, and she never saw the note."

There was more that Jane wanted to ask Mrs. Matthews about her daughter, especially about how she seemed when she came to her flat last Friday, which must have been shortly before she was murdered. But she realized talking about Helen's last known movements would simply be too upsetting. She would speak with her in more depth later. Instead, she told Mrs. Matthews that they would go to the school, see Simon and speak with Mrs. Rowlands, the headmistress. The prospect of seeing Simon seemed to calm her down, and Jane was able to help her down the stairs and into the car, before driving the short distance to the school, the dark clouds overhead making the silent journey feel even more oppressive.

Twenty minutes later, Brenda Matthews sat in numbed silence in the headmistress' office as Jane took Mrs. Rowlands to one side and told her that Helen Matthews had also been murdered.

Mrs. Rowlands was clearly shocked, but kept her composure for Mrs. Matthews' sake. "Is there no end to this madness? You do have a hard job, Sergeant Tennison. I don't know how you cope with so much death and misery."

"I sometimes wonder myself, Mrs. Rowlands," Jane admitted. "But I have a job to do and that's what keeps me going, I suppose."

Mrs. Rowlands smiled sadly. "Your DCI Moran rang me this morning. He told me there would be a press release at lunchtime, naming Eileen as one of the victims. I was going to hold an assembly with the teachers, children and parents at the end of class today and inform them."

"Mrs. Matthews doesn't know about Eileen yet. I couldn't tell her earlier due to the state she was in. She'd like to see her grandson and then, if she's up to it, I'll take her to formally identify Helen's body. I asked her on the way here if there was anyone who could look after Simon, but she doesn't appear to have any other family in London. Do you have a contact number for the local social services so I can arrange—?"

"I am happy to look after Simon," Mrs. Rowlands interjected. "If Brenda agrees, that is, and wants to view Helen's body. He knows me, so he'll feel safe. I can take him home, and you and Brenda can collect him later. And if they both need a room for the night then I've plenty of space."

"That's very kind of you," Jane said gratefully.

"It's the least I can do under the circumstances. Are you going to tell Simon about his mother's death now or later?"

Jane thought for a moment. "Now is probably best. I'm not sure if Mrs. Matthews is up to it, but I best ask her if she wants to." Jane walked over to Mrs. Matthews. "Would you like to tell Simon about his mother? or I can, if you want?"

Mrs. Matthews looked pale as she shook her head. "I'm sorry, I just can't do it . . . Please could you tell him for me?"

"Of course." It was what she had expected Brenda to say. But Mrs. Rowlands sensed Jane was anxious and quietly asked if she was OK.

"Yes, it's just a new situation for me. I've informed adults about the loss of a loved one many times during my career, but never a child."

"I can do it if you like, officer. I have had previous experience in these types of situations."

"Thank you. But as Brenda has asked me to, I feel I should."

Mrs. Rowlands smiled. "You'll be fine. The best way is to be caring and use words that are simple and direct. I'll go and get Simon."

Jane nervously rehearsed in her mind what she was going to say as she waited for Mrs. Rowlands to return with Simon. In her desire to get it right with Simon, she had forgotten about how traumatic it would be for his grandmother, so sat in the chair next to her.

"I know you must be dreading this, Brenda, but we all need to be strong for Simon. I'm not going to tell him anything about what happened to his mum, just that she's passed away."

Mrs. Matthews nodded, and Jane told her about Mrs. Rowlands' offer of a room for the night and to look after Simon if they went to the mortuary.

Just then Simon came into the room, with Mrs. Rowlands holding his hand. The small blond-haired boy looked a picture of happiness as he shouted out: "Nana" with a big smile that revealed his braces. He bounded over to his grandmother and gave her a big hug. As Mrs. Matthews hugged him back she couldn't control her emotions and started to cry.

"Why are you crying, Nana?" Simon asked, his smile turning to a curious frown.

Mrs. Matthews pointed a trembling finger at Jane. "This is Jane, Simon. She's a police lady and wants to speak to you about Mummy."

"Is Mummy in trouble?" he asked nervously, with a noticeable lisp.

Jane crouched down to his height, smiled and put her hand out. "Mummy's not in trouble, Simon."

Simon stepped back from Jane and looked at his grandma.

"Is Mummy in trouble because of me, Nana?" he asked, his bottom lip quivering.

Mrs. Matthews forced a smile. "It's OK, Simon. Jane is a nice lady and has been very kind to Nana."

Simon looked at Jane, who held her hand out again, and this time he took hold of it.

"Nana's crying because something's happened that's made us all sad." Jane paused to take a deep breath.

"Is Mummy sad because I shouted at her?" Simon asked as a tear rolled slowly down his cheek.

Jane squeezed his hand, struggling not to cry herself. "No, Simon, you've done nothing wrong and Mummy loves you very much. We're sad because Mummy had an accident and has gone to heaven."

Simon looked confused and didn't reply. Jane wondered if he'd understood what she'd said.

After a few moments, he said, "Only dead people go to heaven. Is my mummy dead?"

"Yes, Simon, and she's with God now, who will be looking after her," Jane replied, her voice choking.

He looked quizzical. "Why did Mummy die?"

Mrs. Rowlands crouched down beside Jane. "Jane doesn't know yet, Simon, but although Mummy's gone to heaven, she will always be here in your heart." She gently touched his chest with her hand before continuing. "And Nana will look after you now, just like Mummy did."

Simon turned and looked at Mrs. Matthews, who stepped forward and hugged her grandson, whilst struggling to control her emotions.

"Nana has to go with Jane for a while," she said, squeezing Simon tightly.

A panicked look came into Simon's eyes. "Where are you going, Nana?"

"Mrs. Rowlands is going to look after you and I'll see you later. OK, sweetheart?"

Simon clung to his grandmother. "I want to come with you, Nana," he cried.

"We can do the viewing tomorrow," Jane said.

"I'd rather do it now, thank you," Mrs. Matthews insisted, trying to gently detach herself from the weeping Simon, who wouldn't let go.

Mrs. Rowlands knelt beside him. "You can come and see my house, Simon, and have whatever you want for your supper. Do you like ice cream?"

Simon turned, looked at Mrs. Rowlands and nodded. "Do you have chocolate flavor?"

Jane made a quick phone call to the mortuary before leaving the school, and told the coroner's officer she was bringing Brenda Matthews over to identify the unknown victim, who was possibly her daughter.

Once in the car, she decided to broach the subject of Eileen Summers' murder.

"I know it's been a harrowing day for you so far, but I've some other sad news I have to tell you."

Mrs. Matthews looked dejected as she stared out the car window. "What can be worse than my daughter's death?" she muttered.

"There have been three murders so far, Brenda—not two, like you thought. The most recent happened on Monday evening, but the body wasn't discovered until Tuesday morning in a hostel in East Dulwich."

Brenda slowly turned and looked at Jane. "Who was she?"

Jane was saddened that she assumed it was another woman. "Simon's teacher, Eileen Summers."

Brenda's breathing became shallow. "Oh God, no ... Not her as well. Simon adored Miss Summers."

"Mrs. Rowlands had reported her missing. She didn't want to worry the children so said she was ill. Obviously, Helen and Eileen are connected through the school."

"Who's the other victim?"

"A woman called Sybil Hastings. Does the name mean anything to you?"

Brenda shook her head.

"Did Helen and Eileen socialize together?" Jane asked.

"I don't know . . . they might have. Helen rarely went out, and if she did I'd usually look after Simon for her." Fresh tears came as she spoke about her daughter.

There was so much more Jane wanted to ask. What was the connection among the three women? What dark secret had led to their deaths? But for now all that would have to wait.

CHAPTER FOURTEEN

Pulling up in the small car park at Ladywell mortuary, Jane reflected on how it had become like a second work place over the last few days. Guiding Mrs. Matthews through the double doors, Jane took her to the waiting room and informed the coroner's officer she was here to identify the body. He told Jane that DCI Moran was currently in the chapel of rest with Eileen Summers' parents, who had travelled down from Manchester. Jane hadn't expected him to be at the mortuary, and realized she'd forgotten to phone him with the news that Helen Matthews was their unidentified victim. Jane asked the coroner's officer if he would inform Moran that she was with Brenda Matthews in the waiting room, and having seen a photograph of Helen Matthews, Jane was one hundred per cent certain she was their hitherto unknown victim. He said he would and left.

Jane returned to the waiting room and sat with a pale-looking Mrs. Matthews. She explained the viewing procedure and the fact that Mr. and Mrs. Summers were presently viewing their daughter's body.

The waiting room door opened and DCI Moran walked in with Eileen Summers' parents. Mrs. Summers was wiping her eyes with a handkerchief already sodden with tears, whilst her husband held her by the arm, the effort of keeping his emotions in check obvious from his haggard expression.

Jane stood up. "Brenda, this is DCI Moran, who is leading the investigation."

Moran took her limp hand in his. "I'm deeply sorry for your loss, Mrs. Matthews. Myself and my officers are doing everything we can to find the man we believe is responsible for these horrendous crimes. If you'll excuse me, I just need to have a quick word with WDS Tennison." He tilted his head to one side for Jane to follow him.

Moran closed the door and walked a little way down the corridor before turning around and facing Jane.

"I'm sorry I didn't ring you, sir, but Mrs. Matthews didn't have a phone, and I had to take her to the school to see her grandson, Simon. I'm certain our unknown victim is Helen Matthews. Her nine-year-old son Simon is in Eileen Summers' class at Southfield Primary." She felt the emotion of it all welling up again. "Telling him his mother was dead was one of the hardest things I've ever done."

Moran put his hand on Jane's shoulder. "You're doing a good job, Jane. Cases like this get to us all, one way or another. Being compassionate and listening to people shows you care, and in turn makes you a better detective. Just don't allow your emotions to affect your work or cloud your judgment." He opened his notebook and began flicking through the pages.

"I spoke with Mr. and Mrs. Summers before the identification. Eileen spent half term with them and told her mother she had concerns about a boy in her class being abused."

"My God, was it Simon Matthews?"

"Eileen never divulged any details about the boy or his family to her parents. Apparently, she did speak with the boy's mother and told her the child had become withdrawn at school, and his classwork was not as good as usual. The mother dismissed Eileen's thoughts as rubbish and stormed off."

"So, it could have been Helen Matthews who Eileen Summers spoke to."

"Under the circumstances it seems likely, but we can't know for sure." Moran tapped his notebook with his pencil. "It's strange—Summers didn't say anything to Mrs. Rowlands, the headmistress?"

"If she had, I'm sure Mrs. Rowlands would have told me. Maybe Eileen was worried she might lose her job if she was wrong," Jane suggested.

"Either way, the abuse issue needs to be resolved. Get a statement from Brenda Matthews with as much detail as possible about Helen, her acquaintances and relationship with Simon."

Jane gasped. "Are you suggesting his mother was abusing him?"

Moran shrugged. "I didn't say that, but it can't be ruled out. We also need to find out if Helen Matthews knew Aiden Lang."

Jane could see that was a valid point, but wondered if there was more behind it. "Are you thinking Lang may have abused Simon?"

"He could have had access to Simon if he knew Helen Matthews. Gibbs interviewed the accountant, who admitted paying Lang for oral sex in the toilets at Hampstead Heath."

Jane rolled her eyes. "And therefore, being a homosexual, he must also abuse children?"

"No, not necessarily, but he could have a liking for young boys as well," Moran said defensively.

Jane thought back to Moran's advice about not letting your feelings cloud your judgment. But it seemed he had convinced himself that Lang was responsible for all the murders and sexually abusing Simon Matthews.

"On that basis, it doesn't make sense that Lang, as a homosexual, would rape two of his female victims," Jane argued.

That seemed to be the last straw for Moran. "What's your bloody problem, Tennison? In my time in Vice I came across men who swung both ways—particularly rent boys doing it for the money."

"I wasn't challenging you, sir," Jane insisted. "Just giving an alternative viewpoint. Like you said yourself, Eileen Summers' abuse fears could be wrong. When I first saw Simon he seemed quite happy, until I told him about his mother."

Moran glared at her. "How many abused children have you dealt with in your short career?"

"Well, none yet, but—"

"People who abuse children always scare them into silence. I want you to interview Simon, but not on your own. Get social services involved. They deal with this sort of thing regularly and can assist with the interview. They can also arrange counseling for the poor lad after all the trauma he's been through."

"Yes, sir, I'll get a statement off Brenda after she's identified her daughter's body," Jane said brusquely, turning to walk away.

"I haven't finished yet," Moran snapped. "Do you have an address for Helen Matthews?"

"Yes, sir." She opened her notebook to the relevant page and handed it to Moran, who wrote the address down in his book.

"I'll get Lawrence to check the address out for any forensic evidence that might help us." He tossed Jane's notebook back to her.

The morgue attendant approached and told Jane the body was ready for viewing. He apologized about what had happened before and said he'd done a better job this time. Jane thanked him and said she'd be a couple of minutes.

Jane and Moran returned to the mortuary waiting room. Brenda Matthews and Mrs. Summers were sitting holding hands and consoling each other, unified in grief. Then Moran ushered the Summerses out with him, leaving Brenda Matthews staring disconsolately at the wall.

Jane took a deep breath. "I know this will be hard for you, Brenda, and you can spend as much time as you want with Helen. I will be with you, but if you want to be alone with her, that's fine." From the distant look on Brenda Matthews' face, Jane realized she hadn't heard a word. She stepped into her line of sight. "Are you OK, Brenda? We can go and see Helen now, if you're ready."

Mrs. Matthews answered in a flat voice: "Mrs. Summers said her daughter had been raped and strangled. Did he do the same to Helen?"

Jane had planned to divulge this information after the viewing and now regretted it. "The pathologist couldn't be certain about any sexual assault, but it's possible she was."

Brenda Matthews started to retch, but as she hadn't eaten since breakfast, there was nothing in her stomach to come up. It was another five minutes before she was composed enough to go with Jane to the chapel of rest.

Helen Matthews' body had been well prepared by the morgue attendant. He'd closed her eyes, washed her hair and face, and arranged the shroud neatly so it concealed the strangulation marks on her neck. Although her skin was pale, Helen Matthews looked as if she was in a peaceful sleep. Jane gave the attendant a nod of approval.

"Is this your daughter, Helen?" Jane asked, trying to keep her voice steady.

Mrs. Matthews nodded. Jane had expected her to break down, but she remained composed as she leant forward and kissed her daughter on the forehead. She then removed her wedding ring and lifted the shroud from Helen's side, revealing her right hand.

"I wanted her to have this when I died." She placed the ring on her daughter's right ring finger and kissed her one last time.

After the identification, Jane took Mrs. Matthews to the bereaved interview room at the mortuary. It was sparsely furnished with just a desk, four chairs and white painted brick walls. The heat blasting from the large cast iron radiator made it stuffy. Jane opened an A4-size notebook, placed it on the table and took her pen from her jacket pocket.

Brenda Matthews watched her forlornly. "Will the statement take long? I should be with Simon."

"I'm just going to take some notes for now, then write your statement up later. I can bring it to you to read over and sign tomorrow."

"Thank you." Her voice was almost a whisper.

"If you want, I can speak with the victim support organization, who can help you and Simon through this terrible ordeal," Jane offered.

"I can't afford anything like that, but thank you for offering."

Jane smiled. "It won't cost you anything, Brenda. They're a new national organization, and have trained volunteers. They offer practical and emotional support to victims and witnesses of serious crime."

"If you think it would help me and Simon,. then yes, I'd like to speak with them."

Jane nodded. "I think it would be good to share your feelings with someone who's not connected to the investigation."

Sooner or later, Jane was going to have to tell Brenda Matthews that Simon might have been sexually abused. Her first instinct was to wait until Mrs. Matthews had recovered from the shock of seeing her daughter's body, but she knew there was no "good" time to deliver this disturbing news.

"What I'm about to tell you is quite distressing. We have reason to believe Eileen Summers was concerned about one of her male pupils being abused. Obviously Helen and Eileen Summers are connected through Simon, so it's possible—"

Grief turned to anger as Brenda Matthews interrupted her. "How dare you suggest my daughter abused her son! Helen was a good mother and worked hard to provide for Simon. She'd never even smacked him and hardly ever raised her voice. Now if you don't mind, I want to see Simon." Brenda stood up and pushed past Jane. "I'll make my own way to Mrs. Rowlands."

A flustered Jane got up and followed her. "Brenda, please listen to me, I don't believe for one minute it was Helen. I know it's a difficult subject to discuss, and the last thing I want to do is upset you. My concern is if Simon was abused, it could be connected in some way to Helen's murder."

Mrs. Matthews turned around sharply. "If Simon was being abused, Helen would have told me."

"If Helen did know, or just suspected, she may not have wanted to upset you. Please . . . there's just a few more things I need to ask. Then we'll finish, and you can be with Simon."

Reluctantly, Brenda returned to her seat and Jane sat down opposite her.

"I wish to God I didn't have to ask you such upsetting questions, Brenda. Unfortunately, we don't know which boy Eileen Summers thought was being abused. It may not even be Simon, but we need to be sure either way."

Brenda sighed. "I appreciate you're only doing your job, but if Simon was being abused, I know he would have said something to Helen or me."

Jane remembered what Moran had told her. "Sometimes children are threatened by their abusers and too frightened to say anything. Did Helen have a boyfriend or any friends who had regular contact with Simon?"

"She dated a man about two years ago, but that's all over. As far as I know, she hasn't been seeing anyone since. She hasn't any close friends—she's always too busy working."

"I'd still like to interview Simon with a social services officer who specializes in child welfare."

Mrs. Matthews looked worried. "They'll take Simon away from me if he was abused!"

Jane shook her head. "That won't happen." She pulled the photograph of Aiden Lang from her pocket. "Have you ever seen this man before? His hair may have been dyed blond since the photograph was taken."

Mrs. Matthews looked closely at the photo. "No. Who is he?"

"His name is Aiden Lang. He also uses the name Ben Smith. Eileen Summers' body was found in his hostel room."

Mrs. Matthews put her hand to her mouth. "Did he kill Helen as well?"

"We don't know for sure. We are doing everything we can to trace Aiden Lang and have released his picture to the press."

"I hope he rots in hell." Mrs. Matthews pushed Lang's photograph back across the desk.

"How did Helen seem when you saw her on the afternoon of Friday sixteenth of February?" Jane asked.

"A bit moody, as I recall. I thought it was because she was tired after taking on the extra cleaning work over the half-term break."

Jane flicked back a couple of pages in her notebook. "You said before that Helen visited about three thirty p.m. Can you remember when she left?"

Mrs. Matthews thought for a moment. "It wasn't long after . . . between four and four thirty, I think."

"Did Helen say where she was going when she left your flat on the Friday?"

Mrs. Matthews shook her head. "No. I just assumed she was going to do another cleaning job."

"Do you know where Helen did her cleaning work on Fridays?"

"No. It was various places for cash-in-hand. I know she did some work for a dentist in Harley Street."

"Do you know the name or address of the dentist?"

"No, but Helen said he was a nice man. He fitted Simon's braces for him."

"That must have been expensive." Jane wondered how Helen had been able afford dental treatment in a posh Harley Street clinic.

"He did the work for nothing because she was his cleaner. Simon had crooked front teeth and Helen had mentioned it to the dentist. Mind you, Simon wasn't too happy, seeing as the braces gave him a lisp and some of the boys in his class started teasing him and calling him Jaws, after that big bloke with the scary teeth in the Bond films."

"Children can be very mean to one another at that age without even realizing it. Did Helen tell Miss Summers about the bullying?"

"No. She just had a word with the two boys—put the fear of God in them. Believe me, they soon stopped calling Simon names." Mrs. Matthews smiled at the memory, then suddenly started to cry. "I just can't believe I'll never see my Helen again. And the thought Simon may have been abused is unbearable."

Jane quickly made a note to make enquiries about Helen Matthews' cleaning work in Harley Street, then put her hand gently on Mrs. Matthews' shoulder.

"I'll arrange the interview at social services and be in touch tomorrow, Brenda. I've got a few things to do back at the station now, I'm afraid. Will you be OK if I get a uniform patrol car to take you to see Mrs. Rowlands?"

Mrs. Matthews nodded as she blew her nose on a tissue and wiped the tears from her cheeks.

Jane was exhausted, physically and emotionally, but made sure she updated Moran before she left the office. Driving home to an empty fridge, she stopped at a kebab shop and chose a chicken shish with salad. At least it was healthier than a doner kebab, she thought wryly to herself as she got back in the car.

Once home, she wolfed down her kebab, had a relaxing bubble bath and went straight to bed. But sleep eluded her as the events of the day replayed themselves in her mind. So many lives had been changed for ever. The thought of little Simon losing his mother was almost unbearable, but Jane knew that even Andrew Hastings, as obnoxious as he was, must be suffering at the loss of his own mother. Jane suddenly found herself welling up as she thought of the three dead women, their families and how happy times could turn to misery and grief in the blink of an eye. She thought again of her own parents, and how it must have been for them when her brother drowned aged three. She was only four herself then, and didn't really understand what had happened at the time, but right now she imagined herself in the mortuary viewing her brother's body with her parents. In the darkness, her tears began to flow.

The bedside phone rang. Jane didn't want to speak to anyone, but knowing it might be something to do with the investigation, she reluctantly picked it up. It was Paul Lawrence.

"Hi, Jane, sorry to bother you at home. I just wanted to apologize for my surly behavior today. I hope I didn't upset you."

Jane took a moment to compose herself, but her voice sounded hoarse. "You didn't. We're all under pressure, Paul, and I know you've got a lot more on your plate than most of us."

"You OK?"

Jane wanted to pour out her feelings, but was scared Paul might think she wasn't coping. "Yes, I'm fine. I've had a busy day and I'm tired, that's all."

Paul wasn't convinced. "Are you sure? If there's anything bothering or upsetting you, you know you can tell me in confidence. It's better to let it out than bottle it up."

There was such obvious concern in his voice, Jane began to well up again. "I know it's stupid, Paul, and it's not like me, but I feel like I'm on an emotional rollercoaster and can't get off." She began to tell him about her day. She was speaking so quickly, he could hardly keep up with her, let alone get a word in himself. In the end, he just let her pour out her feelings and listened.

". . . and ever since I got home I can't stop thinking how sad it all is. To be honest, I don't even know why I'm crying."

"You're crying because you care, Jane," he said finally. "Shedding a tear, even as a police officer, is nothing to be ashamed of. Believe me, I've had many a blubber under the sheets when I've got home from some horrific crime scene. Especially where children are the victims. You're strong, Jane, a good detective, and although you may not think it, well respected."

"Thanks, Paul." Jane sniffed and took a deep breath. "Did you do a search at Helen Matthews' house?"

"Not personally. I was busy at the lab. Moran sent Edwards and two SOCOs to the address. Just like Eileen Summers' flat, the place had been ransacked but there was no forced entry. Aiden Lang's fingerprints were found on the dressing table drawers and the wardrobe."

"He must have stolen Helen's house keys when he murdered her and went looking for money and valuables," Jane mused.

"Certainly looks like it. Moran's now worried the three women's murders may be linked to sexual abuse on Simon."

"Then that means Simon could be in danger!" Jane exclaimed.

"It's OK," Paul reassured her. "Moran already thought of that. Simon and his grandmother are staying at Mrs. Rowlands' and there's an armed PC at the front and rear."

There was a brief silence before Paul continued. "I was just wondering—and I know it depends on how the investigation is going—but would you like to come round to my place for dinner on Saturday night?"

"That would be lovely, thank you, Paul."

"Do you like beef Wellington?"

"I do. And I'll bring a nice bottle of red to go with it. Are you still at the same address?"

"No, I moved from the mews house."

Jane grabbed a pen and notepad off her bedside table and wrote down the new address.

"Pop into the lab tomorrow if you want to talk more," Paul said finally.

"I'm going to Harley Street. Helen Matthews was a cleaner for a private dentist there, so I want to speak with him."

"OK, take care then."

She put the phone down and realized how much better she felt after speaking to Paul. She smiled to herself as she snuggled up in bed. Paul was a very attractive man, and maybe it would be nice if something did develop between them.

CHAPTER FIFTEEN

Jane woke refreshed, which she put down to a mixture of sheer exhaustion and Paul Lawrence's kind words making her feel more relaxed. After breakfast, she looked through the Yellow Pages and found twelve dental practices in Harley Street, then phoned the office and told Gibbs she was going to make enquiries about Helen Matthews.

It was a cold but sunny morning, and Jane decided to walk from her flat to Harley Street, an area renowned around the world for its high quality private medical and dental clinics and hospitals. Jane walked at a brisk pace and arrived at Harley Street in fifteen minutes. Standing at the north end of the street, she admired the rows of large Georgian townhouses, most of which were now used as clinics, with their beautiful detailing: cast iron balconies, arched doorways and vast first-floor windows. Jane couldn't help but notice how devoid the street was of rubbish, compared to other parts of London. She saw a man dressed in overalls come out of a building, carrying two bags of rubbish which he threw into the back of a large open-back lorry. She realized that it was a private company who the wealthy residents must have hired to clear their refuse.

The receptionists at the first two clinics told her snootily over the intercom that they'd never heard of Helen Matthews. She was just looking at her list for the next address when she saw DCS Blake coming out of one of the buildings further up the street. She wondered at first if he was on police business, but then noticed he was holding his hand to the side of his mouth, as if he was in pain. He didn't appear to see her as he got into the passenger seat of an unmarked police Ford Granada, which immediately drove off. Jane wondered how he could afford to be treated in Harley Street, even on a DCS' pay, and decided to take a look.

She walked up the white marble steps to the large wooden double doors and saw that there were four dentists listed on the plaque. She was about to press the intercom when the door was opened by a woman in a long camel hair coat making her exit, allowing Jane to slip inside. The interior oak-paneled reception hall was even bigger than Jane had imagined, with two large chandeliers, a grey and white marbled floor, and matching wide staircase with oak banisters to the upper floors.

"Do you have an appointment, madam?"

Jane looked to her left and saw a smartly dressed lady in her early thirties sitting behind a Georgian mahogany desk, partially hidden beneath the stairs. Jane got out her warrant card, introduced herself, and asked if Helen Matthews worked at the surgery as a cleaner.

"She does, or rather she did. Helen hasn't turned up for work this week."

"Did you hire Miss. Matthews?"

"No, one of the dentists did."

"Which one?"

"I think it was Mr. Simmonds," the receptionist said vaguely.

"Do you know if he fitted Helen Matthews' son with braces?"

The receptionist frowned. "I doubt that very much. This is a private clinic, not an NHS practice," she added dismissively.

Jane took no notice of her superior tone. "Can you check the patient cards for me, please? His name is Simon."

The receptionist huffed as she pushed her chair back, opened one of the filing cabinets behind her and flicked through the "M" files. "There's no Simon Matthews on record."

Jane realized it was possible Helen Matthews worked as a cleaner at more than one dentist's in Harley Street, but a gut feeling told her she was in the right place.

"I'd like to speak with Mr. Simmonds, please, so I'd be grateful if you could tell him I'm here."

"I'm afraid he's busy with patients all day. If you'd like to leave me your contact details, I'll speak with him later and get back to you."

Jane decided it was time to bring the receptionist down a peg or two.

"I'm here on official police business. Mr. Simmonds can decide whether he wants to speak to me, *not you*. So please kindly inform him I'm here before I do it myself."

The receptionist went pale, then quickly scuttled off to speak with Mr. Simmonds.

She returned a minute or two later, all her haughtiness gone. "Mr. Simmonds said he'll speak with you as soon as he's finished with his current patient. The waiting room is to the left of the stairs. Please help yourself to a hot drink and biscuits," She added with an ingratiating smile.

Jane's curiosity got the better of her. "As I was walking here, I could have sworn I saw a friend of mine leaving. Michael Blake? Poor chap looked to be in quite a bit of pain, which is probably why he didn't see me. Is he all right?" Jane asked in a concerned voice.

The receptionist leant forward and whispered, "I'm not supposed to divulge any information about our clients or their treatment, but seeing as he's a friend of yours . . . He had an emergency appointment with Mr. Simmonds for terrible toothache." She laughed, covering her mouth with her hand. "I know it must have been bad as normally he's quite flirtatious, but today he was in and out without even telling me how gorgeous I looked."

Jane forced a smile. "He's quite a character is our Michael. Must be expensive, though, being treated here." She suspected Blake was taking advantage of his rank getting treatment at a reduced fee, which was against the rules but not uncommon.

"Any fees for treatment are strictly between the dentist and the patient, of course. Though rates for individual clients can differ," the receptionist added with a conspiratorial smile.

Jane nodded. "Mum's the word."

The waiting room was three times the size of Jane's lounge, with red velvet curtains, matching Edwardian sofas, armchairs and antique sideboards. Jane poured herself a coffee from a sterling silver pot into a Wedgwood teacup with matching saucer. There were three choices of milk and cream in little silver pourers, and delicate silver tongs for the sugar. She didn't feel hungry, but the chocolate biscuits looked very tempting. An immaculately dressed couple sat on a sofa by the window, looking as if they were preparing for a night out at the theatre rather than waiting to be seen by the dentist. The woman had a sable coat over her knees and sparkled with gold and diamond jewelry.

Jane put her cup down on the table, beside the neat piles of *Tatler*, *Vogue* and *Country Life* magazines. Deciding those were more suited to the elegant couple on the sofa, she picked up a copy of the *British Dental Journal* and started flicking through it. The articles seemed mostly technical and rather boring, but one featuring a picture of a handsome, blue-eyed, blond-haired man in a dental coat caught her eye. The subject of the piece was a dentist called David Simmonds, who had been awarded a Certificate of Merit for Outstanding Services to the Dental Profession. Jane thought Simmonds looked familiar, but she couldn't recall having ever met him. She looked over at the woman with the sable coat.

"Excuse me, this is my first time here. Do you know if this is the same Mr. Simmonds who works here?" Jane asked, holding up the picture in the magazine.

The woman smiled graciously. "Yes, my dear, it is. He's a wonderful dentist and exceedingly charitable, too. He does work for the poor people, you know."

Jane ignored her snobbish remark and started to read the article. Simmonds, she read, was raised in a South London council flat. In the early fifties he passed a scholarship exam for a boys grammar school in Tulse Hill, and when in 1956 the General Dental Council created bursaries for poorer families, Simmonds applied and was accepted to study dentistry at the renowned King's College Dental School in South London. After qualifying, he applied for a commission in the army as a dentist, was accepted for the Royal Army Dental Corps and posted to a military base in Germany as a lieutenant.

Jane was absorbed by the story of Simmonds' upward climb, and impressed by what he'd achieved. The receptionist walked into the waiting room and bobbed her head towards Jane.

"Mr. Simmonds can see you now, Miss Tennison."

The lady with the sable coat promptly stood up and insisted that she was Mr. Simmonds' next patient, and didn't seem at all mollified by the receptionist's assurance that Miss Tennison would not be long, glaring at Jane as if she'd just tried to steal one of her diamonds.

As they walked up the marble stairs to the first floor, the receptionist apologized for not addressing Jane as Sergeant Tennison, but explained that she didn't want anyone to know the police were on the premises making enquiries, as it might reflect badly on the dental practice.

Jane forced herself to smile. "Oh, I quite understand."

The receptionist knocked on Mr. Simmonds' surgery door, and it was opened by a young and very attractive dental assistant. Jane could see a tall blond-haired man in a white medical smock with his back to her, putting some ivory-handled dental implements into an autoclave sterilizer.

"This is Sergeant Tennison, Mr. Simmonds." The receptionist left the room, closely followed by the dental nurse.

Simmonds turned with a smile and put his hand out. "Please, call me David."

Jane shook his hand, noticing he was wearing an expensive gold Rolex watch, and thought he looked younger and even more handsome in the flesh.

"My receptionist mentioned you were looking for Helen. We've been wondering why she suddenly stopped turning up for her cleaning job. Left us in a bit of a pickle, actually. She's not in any trouble, is she?"

"I'm sorry to have to tell you, Mr. Simmonds, but Helen's body was found in an alleyway in Peckham last Friday. I'm afraid she was murdered."

Simmonds was clearly shocked. "Oh my God, that's terrible! What happened to her?"

"She was strangled and sexually assaulted."

Simmonds looked shaken as he sat down on his dental high stool and shook his head in disbelief. "I heard something on the radio about the murders in Peckham. There was no mention of Helen's name."

"We only found out who the victim was yesterday when her mother identified her body."

"It must be awful losing a daughter like that. What about Simon, Helen's son? How is he?"

"He's with his grandmother. I don't think he fully understands what has happened yet."

"That poor boy. Please tell Helen's mother how sorry I am for her loss, and if there's anything I can do for her or Simon to contact me."

"Of course. I'm sure Mrs. Matthews will appreciate your kind words and offer of assistance. I believe you fitted Simon with braces?"

"Yes, about four weeks ago. Helen told me some of the kids at school teased Simon about his 'goofy teeth.' She asked if I could give her any advice on what to do . . . about his teeth, that is, not the bullying. Helen brought Simon to the clinic and, after examining him, I told her braces would solve the problem."

Jane found herself warming to Simmonds. "I believe you did the work for free?"

"Yes. I knew Helen couldn't afford it, and probably struggled to make ends meet as a single parent, so I wanted to help her out."

Jane was curious. "I spoke with your receptionist about Simon. She checked the dental files and there was no record of him having treatment here."

Simmonds smiled and nodded. "That's right. To be honest, I did the work on Simon out of hours and didn't keep a record. I was worried the other dentists in the practice might be upset if they found out I was doing dental work for free."

"How long had Helen Matthews worked here?"

Simmonds paused. "About ten months. I was socializing with a colleague who was moving to York. I mentioned I was looking for a cleaner and he recommended Helen. I got her in on a trial basis, but she was very thorough, so I hired her. In fact, she was the best cleaner we've ever had."

"Can you recall when you last saw her?"

Again, Simmonds thought. "To be honest, no, other than one evening a week or so ago when she brought Simon in for a braces check-up. Helen's hours here were generally ten a.m. to two p.m. and I would be dealing with patients, so I saw her only rarely. The treatment rooms are cleaned by the dental auxiliaries, as the equipment is very expensive and there are anesthetic drugs stored there. Helen cleaned all the other areas and my flat on the top floor. She also did some ironing for me, so I'd leave her wages in an envelope on the living room table."

"Would you happen to know where else Helen worked as a cleaner?"

"I'm sorry, I don't."

"Could you give me the name of the colleague who recommended her?"

"Peter Brown. I've got his York number in my flat. I can call him and ask if he knew where else Helen worked."

"That would be helpful, thank you," Jane said, and Simmonds started to walk towards the door.

"It's OK, you don't have to do it right now," she assured him. "I'll give you my work number and you can ring me at the office if he's able to help. Have you ever heard the names Aiden Lang or Ben Smith? Perhaps Helen Matthews mentioned them to you?"

Simmonds thought about it for a second. "No. Are they friends of hers?"

Jane handed him a picture of Aiden Lang. "Smith is an alias used by this man. His real name's Aiden Lang."

Simmonds looked closely at the picture. "No, he doesn't look familiar. Is he a suspect?"

"We believe he may be responsible for the murder of Helen and two other women."

Simmonds shook his head sadly. "He looks so young. Would you like me to show the other dentists this photograph?"

"There's no need for now," Jane said, and he handed her back the photo. "But thank you for your time and your assistance."

"Would you be kind enough to let me know the details of Helen's funeral, please? I would like to attend and pay my respects."

"It may be quite a few weeks yet before the coroner releases her body for burial. But as soon as I know, I'll be in touch."

On her way out, Jane popped into the waiting room and picked up the dental journal she had been reading.

"Would it be all right if I took this?" she asked the receptionist.

"I'm sure that would be fine. We have a couple of copies, I think."

As Jane rolled up the journal and slipped it into her coat pocket, the receptionist leant forward and spoke in a whisper. "If you're still looking for Helen Matthews and she turns up here, should I phone nine-nine-nine?"

"I'm sorry to tell you that Helen Matthews has been murdered. I've been trying to find out where else she worked."

The receptionist gasped, put her hand to her mouth and rocked backwards on her chair.

"Do you know where else Helen worked as a cleaner?" Jane asked.

"No. I didn't really know her and we rarely spoke."

Jane pulled out the picture of Aiden Lang. "Have you ever seen this man before?"

The receptionist took her time studying the photograph. "He looks familiar . . . Has he got a tooth missing?"

Jane felt a little surge of adrenalin. "You know him?"

"Not personally, no, and he's not a patient here. But working as a dental receptionist has made me notice people's teeth more. I can't be sure, but a week or so ago I left the clinic and it wasn't until I got to Oxford Circus tube station that I realized I'd left my purse in the reception desk drawer. I had to walk all the way back to the clinic and I saw a young man, like the one in the picture, standing by a car outside the clinic. He looked at me and I said, 'Good evening.' He smiled and nodded. I noticed he had a tooth missing here." She pointed to the right side of her mouth. "When I came back out a few seconds later he was still there by the car, talking to the driver who had his window open."

"Can you remember what color his hair was and what he was wearing?"

"Let me see . . . He had a dark jacket on with the hood up over his head, so I couldn't see what color his hair was, and I'm not sure about his trousers, but they might have been flares. He seemed quite smart."

"What time was this?"

"Well, I left work at just after six p.m. It's ten or so minutes to Oxford Circus. I realized I'd forgotten my purse and turned back. That's another ten minutes, so it must have been about six thirty."

Jane nodded, eager to get more details. "What about the car? Can you remember the make or color?"

"Definitely dark, and it was big. It might have been a Mercedes like Mr. Simmonds has."

"What did the driver look like?"

"Well, it wasn't Mr. Simmonds. He was white and looked older than the young man in the coat. I didn't really get a good look at him."

"Can you remember what day it was?"

"No, but it was either the beginning of last week or the end of the week before."

"Would you recognize either of the men again?" Jane asked, desperately hoping for a positive answer.

"Maybe the younger one with the missing tooth."

"Thank you." Jane wasn't sure how this new information could help the investigation, but she was keen to get back to the station and share it with Moran.

CHAPTER SIXTEEN

Jane walked to her flat to collect her car, which was parked in a side street. As she drove back to Peckham, she wondered if Helen Matthews had taken Simon to see Simmonds for his braces check-up on the same evening the man who looked like Aiden Lang was outside the clinic. If that person was Lang, then it was possible he was waiting for Helen and Simon. She also wondered about the man in the car, but realized he could simply have been a waiting mini cab driver, or someone who had stopped to ask directions.

Entering the Peckham CID office, Jane couldn't help but notice they were running out of space on the far end wall, which was now covered with crime scene and pathology photographs of the three victims, as well as other notes about the investigation. The civilian clerk told Jane that DCI Moran had said he wanted a full office meeting when she returned, adding that he was not in a good mood. They were no nearer to finding Aiden Lang, even though they'd had a slew of calls about possible sightings of him after the press release. The press was also hounding Moran, demanding constant updates on the state of the investigation, as were the top brass at the Yard.

Jane took a deep breath and made her way to the meeting room. She'd just taken her place with the rest of the team when a weary-looking Moran entered with DI Gibbs, who in contrast seemed to have a spring in his step and looked quite animated. Jane wondered if it was Tamara who made him so perky, or, as she'd previously suspected, Andrew Hastings' wife, Jo. If it was the latter, she had a terrible feeling he was playing with fire.

Moran laboriously went over all the developments since the last team meeting: the connections among the three women, the suspected sexual abuse of Simon Matthews, and the fact that Aiden Lang's fingerprints had been found in both Helen Matthews' and Eileen Summers' flats, which had been ransacked.

Moran took a gulp of coffee before continuing. "Obviously we can't tell when Lang left his fingerprints in the women's flats. In my opinion, it's more likely he entered Eileen Summers' flat after she was murdered. With respect to Helen Matthews, it could have been before she was murdered. It's also possible she knew Lang, allowed him in her flat and he abused Simon, then when Helen found out he murdered her." He turned to Jane. "Have you spoken with social services about interviewing Simon Matthews?"

"Not yet, sir. I was visiting a dentist Helen Matthews worked for this morning. I was going to ring social services after the meeting."

"It needs to be done and quickly, so get it sorted. Simon Matthews may know a lot more about Lang than we bloody well do right now. Did the dentist have any useful information?"

Jane briefed the team about her visit to the Harley Street clinic, but without mentioning that she'd seen DCS Blake.

"Did you show Simmonds Lang's mugshot?"

"He didn't recognize him." Jane paused to find her notes of what the receptionist had told her about the man who looked like Lang.

"Has anyone got anything positive to tell me about Lang's whereabouts?" Moran asked, with an edge of sarcasm in his voice.

"Yes, sir," Jane said. "I just need to find the page." As she flicked through her notebook, Moran continued.

"I want you to organize house-to-house enquiries in the blocks of flats where Helen Matthews and Eileen Summers lived, Tennison." He looked at Edwards. "I want you to make enquiries about Lang in every gay bar in the West End."

Edwards didn't look happy. "Gays don't like the Old Bill, so it's hard to get anything out of them."

"Unless you pay for it, sweetie," a detective chipped in, mimicking oral sex with an up and down hand movement whilst pushing his cheek out with his tongue.

There was more laughter in the room. Jane was on the point of telling them to grow up when Moran exploded.

"The lot of you cut the jokes and start taking this fucking investigation seriously! Someone out there must know where Lang is—he can't just disappear off the face of the earth. I've checked with the passport office and he hasn't got one, which means he must still be in the country."

Jane raised her hand.

"What?" Moran snapped.

"I didn't get to finish telling you about my enquiries at the dental clinic."

Jane heard someone mutter, "Here we go. Miss Marple is off again."

Jane ignored the remark. "I showed the receptionist Lang's photo. She told me she'd seen a man who looked like Lang standing outside the clinic. This was about a week or so ago, around six thirty p.m. and he was standing next to a car with another slightly older white man in the driver's seat, who she didn't get a good look at. The man who looked like Lang wore a jacket with the hood up, so she couldn't see the color of his hair."

"It could be any Tom, Dick or Harry then," Moran said sourly.

Jane felt Moran was unfairly taking his frustrations out on her. "Maybe. But the receptionist also said the man in the coat had a tooth missing. From what Simmonds told me, it's possible Helen Matthews attended the clinic that evening with Simon."

Jane felt vindicated as this new information brought silence to the room as everybody focused their attention on her.

"Which tooth was missing?" Moran asked.

It dawned on Jane the receptionist pointed to the right side of her mouth and Lang's missing tooth was supposedly on the left. She began to wish she'd spoken in private with Moran, but realized she had to be honest about what happened at the clinic.

"I've just realized the receptionist indicated the missing tooth was on the upper right side of his jaw," she admitted in a disconsolate tone.

There were a few sighs around the room and some officers shook their heads, which only made her feel worse, but then she remembered something she had come across many times when taking statements from a witness.

"But it's not uncommon for witnesses to mix up left and right when face-on to a suspect, and I believe that could be a possibility here. I don't think we should rule out Lang as the person the receptionist saw."

Gibbs nodded in agreement. "I was once at a PM with Prof Martin when he referred to the left hand as the right until DS Lawrence corrected him."

"I read in the news once about a man who had the wrong limb amputated because a doctor made the left/right error," Edwards chipped in.

Moran seemed pleased. "Any other revelations you'd like to share with us?"

"It could be the man in the car was an accomplice who was involved in the murders," Jane said.

There were murmurs of disagreement around the room.

Moran shook his head. "Every piece of forensic evidence we have points to one killer. Professor Martin said all Hastings' stab wounds were from the same weapon, plus Summers and Matthews were strangled with the same type of cord."

Jane persisted. "I'm just suggesting two killers is a possibility we should consider. From what we know of Lang, he's quite slight. Moving two bodies in one evening would have been hard work on his own."

"Stop muddying the water, Tennison," Gibbs said a little harshly. "Summers' body was in his bloody hostel room."

"You also seem to be forgetting Lang's fingerprints are all over Summers' and Matthews' flats, and jewelry was stolen," Moran added.

She looked at Gibbs. "You said Lang was gay. If that's right, then maybe an accomplice raped Helen Matthews and Eileen Summers."

"Maybe Lang swings both ways." Gibbs shrugged.

Moran vented his frustration on Jane. "Maybe I should do a new press release and say: 'Sorry, I screwed up, as one of my less experienced detectives thinks I'm wrong and there are two maniacs on the loose.' Let me assure you, Tennison, I've already considered that Lang may have had an accomplice, but you tell me one bit of hard evidence that supports that theory."

Gibbs, fearing Jane was digging a hole for herself, changed the subject. "The workload is mounting up, sir. Is there any chance of extra staff on the team?"

"I'll speak with DCS Blake," Moran replied. "But for the moment, you will all have to work the weekend. Sort it out amongst yourselves and split into two teams. One lot can work Saturday and the other Sunday."

Some officers looked pleased, knowing that as it was on short notice they would get double pay and days off in lieu. Others weren't so happy, particularly those with families or those who had made plans for the weekend.

"Which day are you working, guv?" Gibbs asked, assuming he'd be doing the other day in charge.

"Both, and so will you," Moran told him firmly. "I want contact numbers for everyone in case I need to call you all in. And if I do, you'd better not be pissed. Right, any questions?"

No one said anything. Moran walked over to Jane.

"After you've arranged the Simon Matthews interview with social services, come to my office." He strode out of the office.

Jane exchanged a look with Gibbs, then picked up the phone. She contacted Peckham Social Services to arrange the interview for 1 p.m. the next day. Jane then rang Brenda Matthews. They had a brief conversation and Jane told Brenda she'd pick her and Simon up on Friday from Mrs. Rowlands' at midday.

Jane trudged along the corridor to Moran's office, suspecting he was going to give her a bollocking for undermining his authority in public. The dark look on his face told her she was right.

"I don't like people challenging my views in front of junior officers. It's not what I expect from anyone, let alone you as supervising DS, who should lead by example."

Jane sighed. "I wasn't challenging you, sir. I was merely offering an alternative viewpoint, which I felt should be considered. But I accept I may well be wrong."

Moran seemed satisfied. "Good. I appreciate that every theory must be considered—but on the evidence, not wild flights of fantasy. You are very perceptive and have the makings of a good detective, but you still have a lot to learn, so think before you speak. What you said in that meeting could diminish the respect your colleagues have for you. When that happens, you can end up becoming ostracized by the rest of the team. If something's troubling you, or you want to voice your opinion, you can always speak to me or Gibbs on a one-to-one basis. OK?"

Jane nodded.

"Everything arranged for the Simon Matthews interview?"

"Yes, sir. It's tomorrow, one p.m., at Peckham Social Services."

"Good. Now go and get your reports for the case file up to date."

Leaving Moran's office, Jane frowned as she saw Gibbs walking towards her.

"What's up?" he asked.

She shrugged. "You tell me. I was ridiculed from all sides, especially by you and Moran. I thought we were friends."

"We are, Jane," Gibbs insisted. "I wasn't having a go at you; I was just trying to make you see reason. This investigation is getting to everyone—the long hours, lack of sleep, all of that. We all want to find Lang. If he kills again, all hell will break loose in the press—not to mention Scotland Yard."

Jane sighed. "I sometimes feel like I can't say anything without someone jumping down my throat. If I was one of the lads, you'd all be patting me on the back and saying, 'Good job, son.'"

Gibbs smiled. "But you're not one of the lads. You're WDS Jane Tennison and should be proud of what you've achieved in your career so far. You've got more savvy about you than detectives with a lot more experience. All the same, sometimes it's better to think before you speak. Weigh up the evidence against what you suspect might have happened. Gut feelings aren't a bad thing, just don't put them forward until you have firm facts and evidence to support them."

"Have you been speaking to Moran about me?" she asked.

Gibbs raised his hands defensively. "No, I haven't."

"Well, he said virtually the same thing to me."

Gibbs gave her a sly look. "Then one of us must be right, Jane. Listen, don't take it personally; consider it as constructive criticism and keep your focus on the investigation." Gibbs reached into his jacket pocket, pulled out two tickets and held them up. "My band's playing at the Churchill Arms in Chelsea Friday night. I'd really like you to come and meet my girlfriend. You can bring someone, if you want."

Jane instantly thought about asking Paul Lawrence. As she reached to take the tickets, Gibbs leant forward and kissed her quickly on the lips.

"I've always wanted to do that . . . but it doesn't mean I want to shag you." Gibbs walked off with a contented smile.

Jane rolled her eyes. "And I wouldn't let you."

Gibbs turned and gave her a thumbs up. "Good. I'm already spoken for."

Moran appeared out of his office. "The duty sergeant just called me. He said there's a woman at the front counter claiming to be Aiden Lang's sister. Pop down and check her out, will you? See if she's got any ID. She could be press trying to pull a fast one."

"And if she's legit?" Jane asked.

"Bring her to my office and the two of us will interview her."

CHAPTER SEVENTEEN

When Jane saw the woman sitting on a bench in the foyer below a wanted poster of Aiden Lang, she realized she wouldn't have to ask for ID. The resemblance was striking. She was a few years older, probably in her early thirties, very petite, with dark shoulder-length hair that was parted in the middle. She was casually dressed in a long white and brown afghan coat, blue turtleneck jumper and a red and white cotton ankle-length hippie skirt with drawstring waist. She was looking at the floor whilst nervously twisting the multi colored beads that hung around her neck.

"I'm Detective Sergeant Jane Tennison, Miss Lang."

There was sadness in her eyes as she looked up. "My surname's Peters. Lang is my maiden name. I'm Aiden's sister." She spoke softly but clearly.

"Thank you for coming to the station. I believe you want to talk to a detective about Aiden?"

The woman nodded and slowly stood up.

"My DCI would like to speak with you. I'll take you to his office." said Jane. "What's your first name?" she asked, as they walked up the stairs to the first floor.

"Hilary."

"Do you live in Peckham, Hilary?"

"No. I live in Woolwich with my husband. He's a market trader in Beresford Square."

"I know that area. I worked at the forensic lab in the Royal Arsenal buildings, across from Beresford Square," Jane added, trying to make Hilary feel more at ease.

Jane introduced Hilary to Moran, who shook her hand and invited her to take a seat. Jane could see from his expression he'd also been struck by the likeness to Aiden Lang.

Moran smiled. "Thank you for coming in. Would you like a tea or coffee?"

"No, thank you."

"Are you happy for WDS Tennison to take notes of our conversation?"

Hilary nodded. Jane sat down and opened an A4 notebook. She thought Moran would get straight to the point, but first he asked her for some personal details.

"Just for the record, would you mind giving me your full name, date of birth, address and family circumstances, please."

"Hilary Peters. Twentieth of February 1949. I live at sixty-four Wellington Street, Woolwich, with my husband John and our two children. John's a market trader and I'm a yoga teacher," she added timidly.

"How old are your children?" Moran asked as he wrote the details down.

"Charlotte's five and Duncan is seven."

"They're at school, I take it?"

Hilary nodded. "Yes, at St. Columbus Primary."

Jane also recorded the details, assuming Moran wanted to check Hilary's details with Woolwich Police and criminal records—standard procedure in a criminal investigation, even with witnesses.

Moran put his pen down. "I take it you're aware your brother's wanted on suspicion of three murders?"

Hilary was clearly trying to control her emotions, and didn't answer immediately.

Moran tapped the table with his pencil. "I have to say, you've certainly taken your time getting in touch with us. Could you tell me why?"

She coughed into her hand. "Well, I never really watch television and didn't pay much attention to the murders, until I saw Aiden's picture and realized he was . . . a suspect. To tell the truth, I wasn't even sure about coming here, because I know my brother is not capable of murder."

Moran shrugged. "We have a lot of evidence that shows he is, including his fingerprints in two of the victims' flats. Do you know where your brother is at present?"

Hilary was visibly shocked. "No, I haven't seen him for at least two months. But I've spoken to him on the phone."

"And when was the last time you spoke with him?" Moran asked.

"A week or so ago. He phones every so often to see how me and the children are."

Moran sat up. "Did he say where he was calling from?"

"From a payphone in Peckham, I think, only because he said that's where he was living, but he didn't tell me an address or anything."

Moran told Hilary her brother had been living at a homeless hostel in Peckham and the hostel was near where the first two victims were found.

Hilary looked stunned. "Why are you so sure Aiden killed them?"

"The most recent victim was found in your brother's hostel room and he's not been seen since."

Hilary gasped and put her hand to her mouth. "No. No, you're wrong. Not Aiden. He's never hurt anyone."

"He's also wanted for failing to appear at court on assault and robbery charges, which he admitted when originally arrested."

Hilary shook her head in disbelief, though Moran had omitted the full details of the incident.

There was a knock on the door and DI Gibbs entered, apologized for interrupting and handed Moran a file. Moran handed him a different file and asked him to get it typed up ASAP. Jane thought it odd that Gibbs would interrupt such an important interview unless the file he had handed Moran contained vital information. Jane looked questioningly at Moran, but he ignored her and continued his questioning.

"What did you and your brother talk about during this phone call?"

Hilary seemed to get her emotions back under control and spoke calmly. "It was brief. I did most of the talking and asked him how he was doing. He seemed fine and said he'd ring next week."

"Has your brother visited you recently at home?"

"Like I told you, not for a long time. Aiden and my husband don't get on. Aiden doesn't visit on a regular basis, but when he does it's always when my husband's at work."

"Why don't they get on?"

Hilary paused, avoiding eye contact with Moran, and started fiddling with her beads again.

"I could of course ask your husband what the problem is, but I'd prefer to hear it from you, Mrs. Peters," Moran said bluntly.

Hilary took a deep breath and looked at Moran. "My brother Aiden is gay. Because of his sexuality, my husband won't talk to him or allow him in our house. My parents disapprove of him, too, but I don't. I don't judge Aiden. I accept him for who he is—a kind, gentle and loving person."

Moran paused to let Jane catch up with her notes.

"Where do your parents live?"

"They moved to Betts Hill in Sussex five years ago."

"Is it possible your brother could be there?"

She shook her head. "You don't understand. They completely disowned him. They don't speak to me, just because I keep in contact with Aiden."

"Does your brother have a boyfriend?"

"I don't know. I don't ask him about his private life. Why do you keep saying 'my brother' all the time? Does it upset you to call him Aiden?" Hilary asked, her agitation growing.

Jane could sense from the steely look on his face that Moran thought Hilary was hiding something to protect her brother.

He leant forward. "We suspect your brother has been sexually abusing the nine-year-old son of one of our murder victims. Do you know Helen Matthews?"

Jane knew they had no evidence that Lang had abused Simon Matthews, so Moran was using this assertion as a scare tactic.

Hilary didn't seem scared, but she was certainly offended. "Aiden is not a monster! He would never abuse or hurt a child, and whoever told you he did is lying!" she said in a raised but steady voice.

"You didn't answer my question, Mrs. Peters."

"I don't know anybody called Matthews," Hilary insisted firmly, "or the other victims that were in the paper. If I knew where Aiden was, I swear to you I'd tell him to give himself up and clear his name."

"Why are you being so defensive? What are you hiding?"

"Why are you treating me like a suspect?" Hilary retorted sharply. "I came here to offer you my help in finding Aiden."

Jane thought the pressure to get results had made Moran too aggressive, and they were now in danger of losing the one person who could possibly get Aiden to give himself up. It was as if Moran was convinced that Hilary had come to the station fishing for information and was actually harboring her brother. Jane contemplated taking over the interview to try to placate her, but before she could, Moran was on the attack again.

"I have officers on the way to your home address as we speak, Mrs. Peters. Is your brother there?" he asked bluntly.

Hilary frowned. "I'm telling you the truth. I haven't seen Aiden and he hasn't been to my house in months."

Jane knew Moran was lying about the search to intimidate Hilary, since they hadn't known her address before the interview.

"DI Gibbs is currently organizing a thorough search of your premises," Moran continued. "The officers attending will also speak with your neighbors about your family. If we find your brother, or any trace of him, you will be arrested for perverting the course of justice."

Jane was shocked at Moran's underhandedness as she realized he must have discussed his intentions with Gibbs before the interview. It was now obvious Moran had slipped Hilary's details into the folder he'd handed Gibbs when he came into the room earlier.

Hilary shook her head in disgust. "Why do you need to involve my neighbors? Now they'll think my husband and me are guilty of harboring a murderer!"

Moran shrugged his shoulders, as if to say he had no choice.

Jane watched as Hilary sat upright, took some deep breaths to calm herself, then glared at Moran with contempt. "I pity you, Mr. Moran. You are a homophobic bigot, who perceives that gay men must be sick in the head and therefore more likely to be child abusers and murderers. You need to open your narrow little mind and understand that being gay doesn't make you a bad person. You seem incapable of considering the possibility someone else murdered those poor women. I know Aiden didn't do it. You can tell me till you're blue in the face that he's guilty—but I'll never believe you."

Moran shrugged again, but Jane could see it was just bravado. Hilary had struck a nerve.

"Sermon over?" he asked.

"I was prepared to help you and persuade Aiden to give himself up, but now I want nothing more to do with you. Aiden is a far better person than you will ever be. If I do hear from him, you'll never know about it, but rest assured I will tell him to keep running as he'll never receive any form of justice from the likes of you." Hilary stood up, leant forward and looked Moran in the eye. "Unless you're going to arrest me for something I haven't done, I'd like to go."

Moran looked at Jane and nodded towards the door. "Show her out."

Hilary was silent as they walked downstairs to the foyer. Standing together at the front steps, Jane decided she had to say something so Hilary didn't think she condoned Moran's behavior.

"I'm sorry for the way DCI Moran treated you. I had no idea he'd sent officers to your house."

Hilary's face relaxed slightly. "I could see that from the way you looked at him. But you shouldn't be the one apologizing, officer. I know Aiden better than anyone. He's confided in me all his life, and believe me, he is incapable of murder. I hope, for all our sakes, you find the person who did do it."

For a moment Jane thought back to the discovery of the first victim. "This may sound strange, Hilary, but was Aiden ever in the boy scouts, cadet corps or anything like that?"

Hilary frowned. "No. Why do you ask?"

"It's just something to do with the investigation. Has he ever done any type of job where he'd have learnt to tie different kinds of knots or ropes?"

"No, that would be impossible for him."

"I don't understand."

"My brother was born with a partially clasped left thumb."

Jane was puzzled. "What does that mean?"

"Aiden's thumb is slightly deformed. It faces in towards the palm of his hand, so he can't straighten it. Every pair of shoes he ever had were slip-on as he can't tie a shoelace because of his thumb."

"Do you know if Aiden was working?"

Hilary sighed. "He was, at a pub in Soho. I was told he got sacked for stealing from the till. I expect it was to feed his drug habit."

Jane recalled the cleaner mentioning the needle and spoon in Aiden's hostel room. "Was he a heroin user?"

"Heroin? I don't think he was on that stuff. Cannabis was his weakness, though he did tell me he occasionally popped a tablet of speed."

Jane remembered her conversation with the barman at the Golden Lion, who said a woman came in looking for Aiden. Jane looked at Hilary and realized her hair color and style was similar to Helen Matthews.

"Did you ever go to the Golden Lion looking for Aiden?"

"Yes, but that was before those women were killed. If you don't mind, officer, I really need to go. My husband will be angry about the police searching our house."

Jane told Hilary she'd like to speak with her in more detail about Aiden and asked if they could meet in private. Hilary looked apprehensive, then told Jane she would think about it and maybe call her. Jane gave her the CID office phone number.

"I really am sorry about what just happened. If you want to talk, then please call me."

Jane returned to Moran's office, feeling her anger at him building.

Moran looked up. "She say anything else to you?"

"No, for some reason she wasn't in the mood for conversation," Jane replied testily. "But she did tell me she went to the Golden Lion looking for her brother. So it was probably her the barman saw and not Helen Matthews."

Jane picked up her notebook, but decided not to mention Lang's clasped thumb in case Moran just said Hilary was lying to cover for her brother.

Moran sighed. "The officers searching her house in Wool-wich just called in. So far there's nothing to suggest Aiden Lang has been there. The neighbors were shown Lang's photograph. No one recognized him."

"Looks like she was telling the truth then," Jane remarked.

Moran sensed a hint of sarcasm in her voice. "If you've got a problem with the way I interviewed her then spit it out."

Jane knew better than to get into an argument. "I'll go and type these notes up," she replied.

"You're going nowhere until you answer me," he growled.

"I don't think it would be appropriate for me to give my opin-ions, sir," Jane replied evenly. "You are leading the investigation, so you make the decisions."

Moran laughed. "I could see from the sour look on your face you didn't approve of the way I interviewed her. I don't have time to listen to how wonderful Hilary Peters thinks her brother is, or pussyfoot around being nice when she refuses to accept he's a murderer. I'm not going to be accused of failing to do my job, Tennison. Searching her house and speaking with the neighbors is a necessary part of the investigation."

"As I said, sir, you make the decisions. I'm sorry if I upset you with my sour look. It won't happen again." She was managing to keep her emotions in check, but desperately wanted to get out the room before she lost control and said something she'd regret.

"Don't try and soft-soap me, Tennison. If you think I was wrong, then at least have the balls to tell me."

Jane looked him in the eye. She recalled him telling her ear-lier he was happy for her to express her opinions as long as it wasn't in front of other officers.

"This is strictly between us. On a one-to-one basis?"

Moran looked around the room. "Well, I can't see anyone else in here, can you?"

Jane took a deep breath and spoke calmly, but without holding back. "Hilary Peters is an innocent victim of her brother's crimes, but it seems to me you treated her as if she was a criminal just because Aiden Lang is a homosexual. Hilary didn't make her brother gay, and wanting to protect him doesn't make her a bad person. Surely, as police officers, we should treat suspects' families with a bit of decency and understanding."

Moran shrugged. "Hilary Peters will get over it. What's done is done and I stand by my decision."

Jane shook her head in disbelief. "Hilary's husband hates Lang because he's gay, a poofter, faggot or any one of the derogatory terms I've heard bandied round the office. Do you really think he'll brush off his house being searched and neighbors questioned with a 'what's done is done'?"

As far as Moran was concerned, their one-to-one was over. "You can call it a day now and book off duty," he said brusquely as he picked up a folder on his desk and started reading.

Jane banged the door closed behind her and went straight to the ladies' locker room to compose herself. Standing at the sink, she looked in the mirror and was taken aback by how worn out she looked. But she didn't regret speaking her mind to Moran, and after splashing some water on her face, she felt restored.

The CID office was empty, with everyone out searching Hilary Peters' house or following up suspected sightings of Aiden Lang after the press appeal. Jane looked at the roster and saw she was off Saturday and working Sunday, which meant she could still go for dinner with Paul Lawrence. But realizing she needed something to cheer her up now, so she didn't just sit at home thinking about the investigation, Jane decided to pay a surprise visit to her parents in Maida Vale. She gathered up her things, flicked off the lights and closed the door behind her, leaving the photos of the three murdered women and Aiden Lang in darkness.

Jane still had her own key to her parents' flat, but wanting to make her visit a nice surprise rather than a shock, she knocked on the door.

The Tennisons' large flat in Maida Vale was pleasantly decorated. It had three good-sized bedrooms, an open-plan lounge with dining room, and a kitchen with a breakfast bar along one wall.

Jane's father opened the door, beaming from ear to ear. He was dressed casually in a white shirt, grey trousers and slippers. He stepped forward and gave Jane a big hug and kiss on the cheek.

"Lovely to see you, Jane. Come on in."

Jane walked into the hallway and instantly smelt the sweet aroma of home-baking. "That smell always makes my mouth water."

"Your mother's in the kitchen making some bread and scones. Mother, come and see who's here," he called.

Mrs. Tennison came out of the kitchen, wiping her flour-dusted hands on a long pink and red pinafore. It was one that Jane and her sister Pam had bought her for Christmas five years earlier.

"Jane!" They kissed and hugged. As Mrs. Tennison stepped back, Jane smiled and brushed flour off her coat.

"Sorry I've not been in touch recently—I've been really busy at work, but my DCI let me finish early today."

"I've seen the news on TV and read the papers about those terrible murders. I hope you're not on the investigation."

"I am, Mum, I am."

Her mother took a moment to consider her response. "Then maybe I spoke out of turn the other night, and I'm sorry. But you know if you ever need us we're here."

Jane was not expecting her mother to be so sympathetic, especially after their last telephone conversation had ended so abruptly.

"It's not been pleasant, Mum. But it's far worse for the families who lost a loved one."

"I'll put the kettle on and butter some scones." Mrs. Tennison hurried into the kitchen.

Jane looked at her father. "Some things never change," she said, realizing her mother didn't really want to discuss her work.

"Your mother told me she was upset and put the phone down on you the other evening. I had a word with her about being more understanding when it comes to your work as a detective. She is trying, but you know how she worries about you, especially after you got caught up in that IRA bomb."

"I was off duty when the explosion happened, Dad. It was just wrong place, wrong time."

"And then there was that IRA sleeper woman who tried to kill you."

"Natalie Wilde fooled me and a lot of other people, but I learnt a valuable lesson." Jane followed her father into the lounge and sat down on the sofa.

"How is the investigation going? Are you any nearer catching the suspect?" her father asked quietly, after checking Mrs. Tennison was still in the kitchen.

Although Jane had promised herself she wouldn't think about work for the rest of the day, she didn't mind discussing it with her father. He had always been supportive of her career choice, and had a genuine interest in her investigations, offering sensible advice or words of comfort when she felt down. Jane also knew she could trust her father to keep what she told him to himself. She filled him in briefly about the three murders—the hardest thing to talk about being that a nine-year-old boy had lost his mother.

Her father shook his head sadly. "That poor boy."

"Simon may have been sexually abused. I have to take him to be interviewed by a social services welfare officer and he'll be examined by a pediatrician," Jane said.

Jane's father could hear the pain in her voice. "That side of police work must be heart-wrenching."

"Yes, it is. But if Simon was abused, it will give us further evidence against the suspect and reveal some of his motive for the murders."

"Well, I hope to God you catch him, Jane. Cases like that make you wonder if it was right to abolish hanging."

Jane was surprised. "We don't always get it right in the police, Dad. In the past, innocent people have been convicted by a jury and hung for murders they didn't commit. To be honest, I'm not convinced our suspect acted alone. He may have had an accomplice."

"Really? Have you told your boss what you think?" Mr. Tennison asked.

"I made the mistake of airing my opinion in an office meeting and got a severe dressing-down from DCI Moran and DI Gibbs about my gut feelings and jumping to wild conclusions."

Her father nodded sympathetically. "I watched a TV documentary recently about human intuition. It said that gut feelings and instinct play a big part in a detective's search for the truth—especially knowing when someone is lying. You shouldn't dismiss a gut feeling just because others disagree with you."

Jane smiled. Her dad really was a wise old soul. "I know, and thanks for the advice, Dad. Anyway, I wanted to have a job-free evening, so if it's OK with you, can we talk about something else?"

"I'll get the slide projector and screen out. You haven't seen the slides of our last cruise, have you?"

Jane was on the point of saying she had, but didn't want to disappoint her father. "I'd love to see them, thanks."

"Tea's up." Mrs. Tennison walked in with a tray of tea and plate of fresh buttered scones and jam.

Watching the cruise slides, Jane bit into a scone and realized how much she missed her mother's home cooking. "These are the best, Mum."

"Thank you, dear. I've put some in a cake tin for you to take home. I've got a homemade steak and kidney pie, with mash and peas, for supper later."

"You're spoiling me now, Mum." Jane smiled.

Jane's father kept up a running commentary as he went through the slides, and she had to fight to stop herself from drifting off. Then the doorbell rang.

"See who it is, please, dear," her mother asked, looking at Jane.

She opened the door to a smiling Pam and her husband Tony, who was holding baby Nathan. Pam was carrying a wicker baby basket and had a patchwork baby bag slung over her shoulder.

"Mum rang to say you were visiting, so we thought we'd surprise you," Pam explained.

Tony held Nathan's tiny hand and made him wave to Jane. "Say hello to your aunty Jane, Nat."

"Nat?" Jane wasn't sure if she'd heard Tony correctly.

"It's short for Nathan. It was my idea and Mum liked it," Pam said.

Jane just smiled, even though she thought Nat sounded like a bug. Jane followed her sister and Tony into the living room.

Mrs. Tennison came out from the kitchen, delighted to see her grandson, as was Mr. Tennison.

"I've got some good news for you all," Pam announced.

"You're pregnant again?" Mrs. Tennison ventured.

"No, Mother. The date for Nat's christening is set." Pam turned to Jane. "I want you to be his godmother."

Tony handed Nathan to Jane. "We both want you to be his godmother."

"Me? Really? I don't know what to say," Jane stammered.

"That's a lovely idea." Her mother beamed.

"Of course I'd be honored." Jane felt chuffed as she cradled six-month-old Nathan in her arms.

Mrs. Tennison put her arm around Jane's shoulder. "Being a godmother is a big responsibility, dear."

"You'll be like an extra parent to Nat," Pam added.

Mrs. Tennison nodded in agreement. "You'll have an important role to play at the christening. Make sure to book a day off from work as soon as you can."

"And try not to be late," Pam added with a smile.

Jane looked into her nephew's beautiful blue eyes. "I wouldn't miss it for the world."

Nathan gurgled, burped and started to cry.

"Nat's hungry." Pam took him from Jane, then sat down to breastfeed him.

Mr. Tennison looked away.

Mrs. Tennison shook her head. "Don't be so prudish. Breastfeeding is perfectly natural."

Mr. Tennison got up from his armchair. "There's something I need to do in the kitchen."

Pam finished feeding Nathan, then handed him to Jane. "He needs burping now."

"I haven't a clue how to do that, Pam."

"Hold him against your chest, so his chin is resting on your shoulder, then support him with one hand and gently rub his back with the other. Like this."

Suddenly Nathan burped, then passed wind. It made Jane laugh, but she didn't find it so funny when he burped the second time and was sick.

"Sorry, I forgot to put a cloth on your shoulder. It's not much anyway," Pam said casually as she rubbed Jane's shoulder with the cloth.

"Does it stain?" It was one of her good work jackets.

"Don't worry, I'll clean it with a bit of disinfectant," Mrs. Tennison offered.

Jane handed Nathan to Pam. "I think he needs changing."

"This would be a good time to learn, Jane," Pam said with a smile.

"I need to clean my jacket." Jane beat a hasty retreat to the kitchen, followed by her mother.

By the time she'd returned, Pam had changed Nathan's nappy and he was asleep in the wicker basket.

During supper, Mrs. Tennison asked Jane if she wanted to stay the night, but Jane said she couldn't as she had an early start at work in the morning.

"Have you got the weekend off?"

"Just the Saturday."

"You could come and stay the night then," Mrs. Tennison said.

"We're not here, dear, we're visiting friends in Eastbourne," Mr. Tennison reminded his wife.

"We can make an excuse. Tell them I've got a cold."

"There's no need to change your plans," Jane insisted. "I've already got a dinner on Saturday evening."

Mrs. Tennison looked surprised. "Is it a work colleague?"

Pam giggled. "Well, that could be a recipe for disaster with your track record."

Jane frowned. "Very funny, Pam."

"What his name?" her father asked.

"Paul Lawrence. He's a detective sergeant like me."

"Isn't he the nice forensics man you've spoken about before?"

Jane sighed. "Yes, he is, Mother. I've learnt a lot from him since I joined The Met."

"How old is he?" Pam asked.

"What is this, the Spanish Inquisition? Paul and I are just good friends, and our relationship is purely platonic. Can we change the subject, please?" Jane didn't want to reveal that Paul was at least eight years older than her.

After supper, Pam brought Nathan down after bathing and changing him. In his soft white Babygro, he looked like a sleeping cherub. Jane lent over the wicker basket. She would've liked to pick him up and cradle him in her arms, but she was worried she would wake him. She couldn't resist kissing his cheek. He smelt of talcum powder and milk. The thought of any harm ever coming to him was so awful, she wondered if she could be a mother.

CHAPTER EIGHTEEN

It was 4 a.m. when Jane woke abruptly, with a cold sweat all over her body. She'd dreamt it was morning and she was on her way to work when she got a flat tire. When she opened the boot to get the tire jack, she discovered Sybil Hastings' bloody body, eyes wide open and staring at her.

Jane went to the kitchen and poured herself a large glass of water. She sat at the kitchen table whilst she drank it and saw the dental journal she'd brought back from Harley Street. She flicked through it until she found the picture of Simmonds. Suddenly it struck her why he looked familiar. She felt a shudder run through her body as she recalled the photograph Agnes had shown her of Mrs. Hastings and her son playing golf. She was certain now that Simmonds was one of the men in the photograph. She stood up, her heart beating wildly, and the glass of water fell from her hand and shattered on the kitchen floor.

"Oh my God," she said aloud. "Simmonds is connected to two of the victims and treated Simon."

Jane cleaned up the broken glass, knowing she would not be able to get back to sleep after this revelation. So she sat in the kitchen drinking strong black coffee and reading the rest of the article about Simmonds. He'd been born and raised on a Peckham council estate, where he witnessed the daily suffering of others, and became determined to help those in the community less fortunate than himself. To that end, he set up a small NHS surgery in his mother's house in Peckham after she passed away, where he also treated the homeless and those on benefits without charge, for which he had been awarded the Certificate of Merit for Outstanding Services to the Dental Profession.

Jane checked the date of the journal: January 1979. She wondered why Simmonds hadn't mentioned his Peckham practice. She had found him pleasant and helpful, and he was obviously well respected within his profession. She sighed, realizing there was no reason for Simmonds to tell her. Maybe it was just a coincidence. She took a sip of coffee, wondering if her gut instinct was leading her astray. Then it suddenly crossed her mind that Helen Matthews could also have worked at the Peckham practice and therefore might have come across Lang somewhere in the neighborhood. She made a note in her notebook to speak with Simmonds again, wondering about the possible sighting of Lang outside the Harley Street practice.

Jane went over all her notes on the case, jotting down her new thoughts. Was it possible that Simmonds had lied about knowing Lang because the two of them were involved in the murders of the three women? She contemplated sharing her suspicions with Moran, but after the run-in she'd just had with him, she decided to wait until she had more evidence to support them.

Jane checked Yellow Pages for dental practices in Peckham. There were only a handful, and not all of those listed the dentists' names, but Simmonds name wasn't there. Of course, it was possible Simmonds didn't advertise his Peckham practice. She glanced at the kitchen clock. It was nearly 8 a.m. But she didn't feel tired. Her thoughts about the case had energized her and she was eager to follow them up. She decided that the first thing to do was go to Mrs. Hastings' flat in Regent's Park to confirm that the man in the golfing photo was Simmonds.

Before she left, Jane phoned the office. Edwards answered.

"Edwards, it's Jane. Can you book me on duty and let Moran or Gibbs know I'm going to make some further enquiries at the Samaritans office in Soho, then I've got to take Simon Matthews to social services for his interview."

"Yeah, will do."

"Any positive leads on Aiden Lang yet?"

"Not a thing. The sightings we followed up came to nothing." He seemed fed up with the lack of progress. "You going to watch Gibbs' band tonight?"

It was the last thing she was thinking about. "I had a restless night. I'll probably give it a miss."

"You should go. It would do you good to let your hair down and mix with the team more often."

It was true that she rarely socialized with her work colleagues. "OK, I'll see how I feel later."

Arriving at Viceroy Court, the same porter let her in.

"Good morning, officer. Can I see your warrant card, please? And you'll need to sign the visitors' book."

Jane looked bemused. "You know who I am."

"Yes, but as you know, rules are rules."

Shaking her head, Jane showed her card and signed the book.

"Do you want this?" the porter asked, plonking a plastic bag down on the table.

"What is it?"

"Mrs. Hastings' car radio cassette player. I fixed it for her. I can put it back in the car if you want."

Jane picked the bag up and handed it back to the porter. "The car's still at the police lab. Can you keep it for now?"

"Suppose so. Cost me a couple of quid to fix it. Do you think it will be all right if I used it in my car?"

"I don't know. You'd best speak with Mr. Hastings about it."

The porter nodded as he opened the lift door. "I hope you catch the bloke who murdered Mrs. Hastings and those other women. Hanging would be too good for him."

When Jane knocked on the door of the flat, she was surprised when it was opened by a bleary-eyed and unshaven Andrew Hastings, still wearing his dressing gown.

"What do you want?" he asked, regarding Jane with obvious disdain.

Jane tried not to let his attitude affect her. "I just need to ask Agnes a couple of questions about your mother."

"She's moved out to her sister's." He started to close the door.

She remembered Agnes telling her she was no longer needed as a housekeeper and would have to find somewhere else to live. But she was determined to get a look at the photograph if she could. "Then you might be able to help me, Mr. Hastings. I'll only take a minute or two of your time."

He opened the door. "I suppose you'd better come in then. Are you any nearer finding that queer bastard who murdered my mother?"

Jane knew the fact that Lang was gay hadn't been released to the press. She suspected DCS Blake was keeping Hastings updated on the investigation and had told him about Lang's sexual orientation.

"Not yet, Mr. Hastings. But I can assure you we're doing everything we can to find him."

Jane followed him into the living room. It was in a state of disarray. Dirty plates, cups, knives and forks were on the coffee table, along with a half-eaten curry in a tinfoil container. There was also an empty whisky bottle and crushed beer cans on the floor. The ashtray was full of cigar stubs and, not surprisingly, the room smelt strongly of stale cigar smoke. Hastings didn't seem bothered about it and didn't apologize for the mess. Jane wondered why he was now living at the flat.

"Was it you or Moran who told my wife I was having an affair?" he asked abruptly.

Jane was taken aback.

"I didn't, and neither did DCI Moran. It's not our job to get involved in your private life," she replied.

"Well, someone from your Keystone Cops department must have said something to her. She's kicked me out the house and I've had to move in here."

Jane realized it must have been Gibbs since he was the only person on the team who had contact with Jo Hastings. She suspected he was still in contact, but in more than a professional capacity.

Jane quickly changed the subject. "As part of the investigation we're speaking to people who played golf with your mother. They could help with regards to her movements on the day she died."

She moved over to the photograph Agnes had shown her. She was certain now it was David Simmonds standing beside Andrew and his mother.

Jane pointed to the picture. "Agnes showed me this picture when I was last here. Obviously we'd like to speak with them and—"

Hastings interrupted. "The other woman's Lady Helen Woosnam, but she's died since the photograph was taken, which must have been at least three years ago. The other chap is David Simmonds. I haven't seen him at the club or any functions for ages. He's not much of a golfer," he said dismissively. "I reckon he only joined so he could drum up business for his Harley Street dental practice."

Jane was excited that Hastings had confirmed Simmonds' identity but didn't want to make her interest in him obvious.

"Oh, was your mother a patient of his?" she asked, as casually as she could.

Hastings nodded. "Yes, along with quite a few other members of the golf club."

"Thanks for your time, Mr. Hastings. I'm sorry I didn't have any positive news for you on the investigation. But I'm sure DCS Blake will keep you updated of any developments."

She felt elated as she got in the car. She now had Simmonds directly connected to Sybil Hastings, as well as Helen and Simon Matthews. Jane remembered Simmonds telling her he'd heard the news about the murders on the radio. She knew Helen Matthews hadn't been identified at that point, but Sybil Hastings' name had been released to the press. It seemed strange, if Simmonds had listened to the news, that he didn't mention Sybil Hastings was a patient. If Simmonds was hiding something, she'd have to tread carefully from now on.

Realizing she still had a bit of time before she had to pick up Brenda and Simon Matthews, Jane decided to go back to Harley Street, ask Simmonds a few open-ended questions and gauge his reaction. She knew it was risky, but Simmonds didn't know she'd read the dental journal, or that she'd discovered Sybil Hastings was a patient of his.

Jane parked her car a few minutes' walk away from Harley Street. She felt strangely nervous and wanted time to compose herself. She knew she had to be careful with her line of questioning, as the last thing she wanted was for Simmonds to think she now considered him a suspect.

Jane walked up the marble steps, took a deep breath and pressed the intercom.

"Who is it, please?"

Jane recognized the receptionist's voice. "It's Detective Sergeant Tennison."

A buzzer sounded and the electric latch on the door was released.

"Good morning, Sergeant Tennison. How can I help you?" the receptionist asked with a wide smile that showed off her gleaming white teeth.

"I'd like to speak with Mr. Simmonds, please."

"I'm afraid he's not here today. He works in his Peckham practice on Mondays and Fridays, treating his non-paying patients." She beamed.

"Oh, I thought he owned the Peckham clinic but someone else ran it for him."

"No. He does all the work there himself."

"Can you give me the address?"

"Certainly." She proceeded to write the address on a piece of paper.

"Do the other dentists mind him working in the Peckham clinic?" Jane asked.

The receptionist looked up at Jane. "This is Mr. Simmonds' clinic and they work for him, so he can do as he pleases, but between you and me, it does annoy some of them."

Jane recalled Simmonds had told her he hadn't kept a record of Simon Matthews' treatment in case the other dentists in the practice were upset he was doing dental work for free. This was clearly a lie if he owned the business.

"You can't please everyone," Jane said.

"Unless you're Mr. Simmonds," the receptionist replied, and handed Jane the address.

61 Brayards Road. Jane knew from the house-to-house enquiries that Brayards Road was close to Copeland Road, where Sybil Hastings' body had been found. Jane thought about asking the receptionist when Mrs. Hastings had last attended the clinic, but worried she might tell Simmonds.

As if she was reading her thoughts, the receptionist leant forward and whispered, "I heard on the news Sybil Hastings was a victim. She was a patient here, you know."

Jane hesitated. She didn't want the receptionist to think that Simmonds hadn't shared that information with her. "Yes, Mr. Simmonds told me. He was most upset, especially with

Helen being a victim as well. I expect he didn't talk about it so as not to worry you."

"He's so considerate," the receptionist agreed.

"Yes, he is," Jane said, slipping the address in her pocket. She looked at her watch and realized she'd have to get a move on to pick Brenda and Simon Matthews up. "Thanks for your help."

Jane ran back to her car, then headed to Mrs. Rowlands' house.

Jane sat with Brenda and a frail-looking Simon, who was clutching his grandmother's hand, in the social services waiting room. It was painted a dull grey, with wooden chairs lined along the wall and a small coffee table with a few tattered magazines on top. Jane was disappointed to find it was as dreary and unwelcoming as police station interview rooms.

A tall woman in her mid-forties with short brown hair walked in, accompanied by a woman in her early thirties, casually dressed in a red turtleneck jumper and grey skirt. The older woman introduced herself as Mary Williams, the senior child care worker.

Jane stood up, shook hands and introduced Brenda and Simon.

Mrs. Williams knelt in front of Simon. "Hello, Simon. My friend Claire wants to show you our special children's room. It's got lots of toys in it. Would you like to see it?"

Her colleague smiled and put her hand out towards Simon.

Simon looked anxiously at his grandmother. Jane felt for the boy, who didn't really know what was happening.

Brenda hugged Simon, then took his hand and placed it in Claire's. "It's OK, sweetheart. The nice ladies just want to speak to you about how you're feeling since Mummy died. There's nothing to worry about."

Reassured by his grandmother, Simon left the room with Claire as Mrs. Williams waited behind to speak with Jane and Brenda.

"The interview with Simon will probably be about an hour or so, then there'll be a physical examination by the pediatrician. You're welcome to wait here or there's a café just up the road."

At the café, Jane ordered two coffees and teacakes. Brenda sat quietly as she picked at her teacake and pushed the pieces around the plate.

"Don't worry, Brenda. Mrs. Williams and her colleagues are well trained and very experienced. They'll make sure Simon feels at ease, and so will the doctor who examines him."

"I think you're right about Simon being abused," Brenda said, with deep sadness in her eyes.

"I'd prefer to be wrong," Jane replied.

"I spoke with him last night. Not in detail—it makes me sick to my stomach to even think about it. It's not right Simon should have to suffer so much pain. He's done nothing wrong, he's harmed no one . . ." Brenda's voice trembled as she held back the tears.

"I know it hurts more than anyone can imagine, Brenda, but you need to tell me what Simon said last night."

"I asked him if anyone had touched him down there . . . you know. He didn't answer, but he was upset. He started to cry. I told him it was OK to tell me if someone had touched him." Brenda paused and took a deep breath. "Simon said his mummy had asked him the same question. He said he didn't want me to get cross like she did and . . . leave him." Brenda was struggling to get the words out.

Jane noticed a few people in the café staring at them, and she decided it was best to continue their conversation away from prying eyes and ears. She took Brenda to her car, which was parked nearby, and asked what else Simon had told her.

"I didn't want to push him too much as he was obviously distressed talking about Helen. He told me when he saw his mummy last Friday, she said he'd have to go back to the dentist to have his braces checked. He told her he didn't want to go because he didn't like the dentist touching him, and his mummy looked angry and left." Brenda began to sob.

Jane patted her arm. "You're doing really well, Brenda. Did Simon say anything else about the dentist touching him?"

Brenda shook her head and wiped the tears from her eyes. "I couldn't bring myself to ask. He looked so upset. I just hugged him, told him he'd done nothing wrong and his mummy wasn't angry with him. I told him he must tell the social workers the truth."

"Did Helen tell you or Simon where she was going?" Jane wondered if it was to see Simmonds.

"No. I was in the kitchen cooking supper when all this was happening. When I came out Helen had gone. I asked Simon where she was. He said she'd gone to a cleaning job. Helen can be a bit impulsive at times, so I didn't think anything of it. Do you think the dentist might be involved?"

Jane didn't want to reveal her suspicions, but this was a big step forward.

"I don't know. Mrs. Williams' interview with Simon will be critical to the investigation. That and the pediatrician's expert opinion will be strong evidence if he did. For now, I'd ask you not to say anything about the dentist to Mrs. Rowlands or anyone else. Come on, shall we go back?"

Brenda nodded, wiped her eyes again with a tissue and blew her nose.

As they sat together in the social services waiting room, Jane was on the point of phoning Moran and telling him her suspicions about Simmonds. She was sure when he heard Simon had been sexually abused, Moran would straight away send a team to arrest him and get a warrant to search the Harley Street and Peckham clinics. She was about to go and make the call when Simon came into the waiting room with Mrs. Williams. He was sucking a lollipop and smiled to see his grandmother again.

"I told the truth like you said, Grandma." He took another lick of the lolly as Brenda gave him a big hug.

Whilst Brenda and Simon chatted, Jane took Mrs. Williams to one side and recounted what Brenda had just told her.

Mrs. Williams nodded. "Simon told us about his last conversation with his mother and his fear of the dentist. However, in my professional opinion and that of the doctor who examined him, he has not been sexually or physically abused in any way."

Jane was shocked. "Are you sure?"

Mrs. Williams looked offended. "I understand it's not what you wanted to hear, Sergeant Tennison, but let me assure you I am experienced enough to know when a child has been sexually abused."

"I didn't mean to be rude, but it's hard to understand why Simon would lie to his mother about it."

"I don't believe Simon did lie to his mother," Mrs. Williams said.

Jane was confused. "But he told her the dentist had abused him."

She shook her head. "No, he only said he didn't like the dentist touching him. Even as adults we don't like having needles and probes stuck in our mouths, so imagine how a child must feel. The bullying at school, being called Jaws because of his braces, also added to his dislike of the dentist. In his mind it was the dentist's fault the other boys picked on him."

Jane felt disheartened. "How could his mother have been so wrong?"

"She never asked him what he meant by being touched, so misconstrued what he'd said. Children don't always understand the importance of context in what they say. They can also have difficulty in expressing themselves clearly. Sometimes the listener hears what they want to hear, especially if they have a preconceived notion that something bad may already have happened."

Jane knew what Mrs. Williams was telling her made sense, but still found it hard to accept she was wrong. "Simon's teacher, Miss Summers, had a boy in her class who'd become withdrawn, and she suspected he was being abused—"

Mrs. Williams interrupted. "If she said as much to Simon's mother, it could explain any preconceived notion she had about him being abused. I fear his teacher may have misread things. It was the bullying about his braces that was affecting his behavior."

Jane thanked her lucky stars she hadn't shared her suspicions with Moran and ended up making a fool of herself.

"What about our suspect, Aiden Lang? Is there a possibility he could have abused Simon?" Jane asked.

"We showed Simon a picture of Lang from a newspaper cutting. He didn't recognize him. People who abuse young children have a specific sexual interest in them. It's nothing to do with being homosexual, or indeed a lesbian," Mrs. Williams added.

"What if Simon's abuser threatened to harm him or his mother? He might have been too frightened to tell you what happened."

"That can happen, of course, but I don't believe it did in Simon's case. He said he didn't tell his grandmother because his mother told him not to, plus he didn't want his grandmother to be upset. The only sexual act he spoke about was with a young girl his age about a year ago. They touched each other playing doctors and nurses, which is all part of growing up. I'll type up a full report and hand-deliver it to the station, along with the pediatrician's, for your case file."

Jane was worried Brenda would be upset that she had put Simon through a traumatic experience for no reason, but there was nothing but relief on Brenda Matthews' face when Jane took her to one side and explained that Mrs. Williams and the pediatrician were of the opinion Simon had not been abused.

"I only wish Helen could have been with us to hear it for herself," Brenda said tearfully.

"I'll drive you and Simon back to Mrs. Rowlands."

"It's all right. I'll take him to the café for some ice cream as a treat first. He likes trains and tubes, so we'll make our own way back."

They walked out of the social services building together.

Jane turned to Brenda. "I'll be in touch as soon as we have any developments. See you later, Simon."

"Bye, bye, Jane." Simon smiled as he trotted off towards the café holding his grandmother's hand.

Jane watched them go with mixed emotions: happy that Simon hadn't been abused, but angry with herself that she'd got it all so wrong about David Simmonds. She nipped back into social services and tried calling Moran to update him, but he was at the Yard with Blake and wasn't expected back in the office.

Walking to her car, Jane reflected on Mrs. Williams' words about "misconstruing" information and Moran's advice about not letting her emotions cloud her judgment. Sitting in the driver's seat, she slammed the palm of her hand against the steering wheel. "You bloody idiot, Jane!"

CHAPTER NINETEEN

Jane arrived at the Churchill Arms to watch Gibbs' band just before 8 p.m. She'd dressed casually in jeans, a red dagger collar shirt, which she'd tied at the waist, and black boots. The pub was packed and virtually the whole team were there, although the band hadn't started. Gibbs came over, dressed in a white frilled shirt, tight leather trousers and blue suede shoes, and sporting a large peace sign medallion. She was pretty sure it was the same outfit she'd seen him in at the Helen Matthews murder scene.

He kissed her on the cheek. "Hey, great to see you. How you doing?"

"Bit of a disastrous day, if I'm honest. Luckily Moran was at the Yard when I got back to the office, so I didn't have to incur his wrath again by telling him the result of—"

Gibbs put his hand over her mouth to shut her up. "Rule one: no job talk tonight; rule two: let your hair down and have a good time; and rule three is: you let me buy you a drink."

Jane said she'd have a small glass of white wine, but Gibbs came back from the bar with a large one. An attractive girl in her early twenties, with shoulder-length dyed blond hair, came over and stood beside Gibbs. She was wearing a low-cut, figure-hugging short white satin dress and knee-high red leather high-heeled boots.

"Tamara meet Jane; Jane meet Tamara." Gibbs caught Tamara's eye and touched the side of his nose.

As they shook hands, Jane noticed there was a trace of white powder at the base of Tamara's right nostril, which she hurriedly wiped off.

"Sorry, Gibbsey. Nice to meet you, Jane. Gibbsey's told me a lot about you." Tamara's cut-glass accent was pure Sloane Ranger.

"Really? What's *Gibbsey* been saying?"

Gibbs wagged his finger at Tamara to say nothing but she didn't seem to notice.

"That you're a bit sensitive, but tenacious, with plenty of balls."

Jane laughed and turned to Gibbs with just a touch of sarcasm. "Thank you, Gibbsey, that's very kind of you to notice. Gibbsey talks about you all the time, Tamara." Jane paused to make Gibbs wonder what she was going to say next. From the anxious look on his face, it had worked.

"And having met you at last, I can see why. You look stunning, just like Debbie Harry."

"Well, thank you, Jane, that's very kind." Tamara beamed.

Gibbs looked relieved. "We need to get ready and tune up, Tamara."

"I just need the loo again. Nice to meet you, Jane. We'll catch up later." She headed off to the toilets.

"She gets nervous before a gig," Gibbs explained.

"I just hope she doesn't get you in trouble."

"What do you mean by that?"

"Well, that wasn't sherbet dip on the end of her nose, was it?" Jane said in a hushed voice.

"It's just a tiny bit to steady her nerves. And before you ask, I'm not doing any drugs."

"If Tamara gets nicked for possession, you could be in serious shit, even out of a job."

"It's OK, she's a good girl, and I know what I'm doing when it comes to relationships." Gibbs made his way through the crowd and onto the stage.

Jane wondered if he'd been having a dig about her past relationships as she watched the band going through a quick sound
check and a final tune-up, before launching into Bachman-
Turner Overdrive's "You Ain't Seen Nothin' Yet." Jane got herself
a second glass of wine and started to relax, letting the music
drive her anxieties about the case from her mind. She was glad
that she'd decided to come along and was impressed with the
band, who sounded better than she'd imagined. Gibbs had a
surprisingly good voice, and as the lead guitarist he didn't hit
a bum note. Tamara was lead singer in the next number, which
was Blondie's "Sunday Girl," and Jane reckoned when it came to
Debbie Harry, she had the voice as well as the looks. She found
herself singing along with Tamara as she belted out the lyrics.

The woman standing next to Jane didn't agree. "Spencer's
great on guitar, isn't he? Pity about the singer, though. She looks
more like Diana Dors than Debbie Harry—and sounds more
like her, too."

Jane didn't recognize her, but her voice was familiar. She was
very attractive, mid-thirties, with long blond hair and dressed in
a red boob tube, black flared trousers and stilettos. The woman
waved at Gibbs to catch his attention, and Jane could see Gibbs
looking surprised as he gave her a discreet nod of acknowledge-
ment. Jane had an idea who she was but wanted to be sure.

"Hi, I'm Jane. I work with Spencer at Peckham."

"I'm Jo. We're just friends. Have they been going long?"

"Yeah, they've done a few numbers."

"Nice to meet you," Jo said, moving closer to the front of the
stage.

Jane already suspected Gibbs and Jo Hastings were more
than "just friends," and couldn't believe Gibbs would be so stupid as to invite her to the gig with Tamara performing alongside him. She wondered if Jo just wanted to surprise Gibbs or

if she wanted to find out if he had a girlfriend. Either way, Jane couldn't wait to see what happened next.

When the band took their break, Tamara went off to the loo again and Gibbs took the opportunity to speak with Jo.

He looked anxious. "Hi, Jo. I wasn't expecting you. I didn't think rock music was your kind of thing."

She stepped closer, rubbing her body against his. "I thought I'd come and see how well you performed . . . outside the bedroom," she said with a brazen smile.

Jane saw Tamara approaching from behind and looked forward to seeing how Gibbs dealt with the situation.

"Hi again, Jane. Are you enjoying the show?" Tamara asked, looking the picture of innocence.

"Yes, thanks, Tamara. Your voice is terrific," Jane said enthusiastically.

Jo Hastings frowned. "She's all right, but you should do more solos, Spencer. Can you sing 'Kiss You All Over' for me?" she added with a suggestive smile.

"I'm sorry, love, I don't know that song," Gibbs said, as if he didn't know her.

Jo leant forward and kissed him on the lips. "I'll play it for you later, then," she said in a seductive voice.

"Who the fuck's the geriatric?" Tamara hissed, glaring at Gibbs.

Gibbs shrugged, as if he had no idea. "Come on, we need to get back on stage." He grabbed her by the hand, but she pulled away.

"Are you screwing this trollop?" Tamara asked loudly.

The people nearby turned and stared, wondering what the commotion was about. Gibbs looked as if he wished the ground beneath his feet would open and swallow him. He knew Jo was a streetwise London girl with a sharp tongue who wouldn't put up with being insulted like that. But to his and Jane's surprise, Jo remained calm and collected.

"My, my, the schoolgirl doesn't realize you prefer older women. Well, you run along back to the classroom, darling, while I educate Spencer in the finer things of life."

Jane stepped back, waiting for it all to kick off. But Tamara wasn't the fighting sort; she seemed more of a daddy's girl who got what she wanted by looking upset and turning on the tears.

Suddenly Tamara slapped Gibbs hard across the face. "It's over, Gibbsey. I never want to see you again," she shouted, pushing her way out of the pub.

Jo glared at Gibbs and slapped his other cheek. "I hope that hurts as well. If you'd been up front about having a girlfriend, it wouldn't have been a problem. It's lying about it that pisses me off." She followed Tamara out of the pub.

Jane wasn't sure if Gibbs' cheeks were redder from the slaps or the sheer embarrassment. She looked at him sadly and shook her head.

"For someone who reckons he knows how to handle women, I'd say you just killed two birds with one stone."

Gibbs forced a smile. "Well, as Doris Day said, '*Que sera, sera*' Now, if you'll excuse me, Jane, my fans await."

He jumped up on the stage and announced that, due to an unforeseen incident, Tamara had to leave in a hurry, but the band would play on.

Soon he was back in his element, singing and playing guitar solos, which brought a rapturous roar of approval from the audience. Jane found herself singing along with the crowd and even having a dance with her colleagues.

When Edwards got a bit drunk and started coming onto her, Jane had to tell him firmly to "back off," hoping he wouldn't remember in the morning.

"This next song is for a good friend of mine," Gibbs announced, winking at Jane.

Jane hoped to God he wasn't going to break into a romantic song, but quickly realized she should have known better when Gibbs began singing Rod Stewart's "Da Ya Think I'm Sexy."

Jane laughed along with the crowd, feeling more relaxed than she had in ages.

CHAPTER TWENTY

Jane had a long lie-in on the Saturday morning and didn't get up until ten o'clock. After a filling breakfast of Weetabix, followed by a chunky bacon and egg sandwich, with percolated coffee, she felt re-energized, but decided she wouldn't think about the investigation or look at her notebook for the whole day. She set about cleaning the flat and doing her washing and ironing. The household chores always gave her a feeling of independence, as her mother had done everything for her when she'd lived at home.

The flat tidy and gleaming, she spent the afternoon lazing on the settee, watching the weepy *Lease of Life*, starring Robert Donat and Kay Walsh, about the vicar of a small Yorkshire parish who is dying from cancer. It was early evening when the film finished. Happily wiping the tears from her eyes, Jane switched off the TV and went to her bedroom. Opening her wardrobe, she looked for something suitable to wear for dinner with Paul Lawrence. She knew it was informal and looked for something smart but casual. She eventually decided on a white shirt, light brown sleeveless pullover, matching gabardine knee-length skirt, skin-color tights and brown leather shoes with a braid trim. She had a shower, then dried her hair and put on some hair spray. Before leaving, she picked up the dental journal for Paul to have a look at.

En route to Paul's, Jane stopped at an off-licence. She asked the cashier for a nice red wine to go with beef Wellington and he recommended a Cabernet Sauvignon. It was the most she'd ever paid for a bottle of wine, so she hoped Paul appreciated it.

The journey to Paul's 1930s semi-detached two-bedroom house in Fulham didn't take long. She rang the doorbell and

Paul, wearing an apron, welcomed her with a hug and kiss on the cheek. She handed him the wine.

"You look gorgeous, Jane, and thanks for this." He looked at the wine. "Cabernet Sauvignon . . . Perfect choice."

Jane just smiled, not wanting to look stupid by admitting she'd never tasted it before.

"Come on through while I finish making supper. I changed my mind about the beef Wellington, actually. Do you like Spanish paella?"

"Yes, I love it," Jane fibbed, having no idea what it was.

"I first tried it in Benidorm on holiday. The fish one's all right, but I'm cooking a chicken one tonight. The magic ingredient is saffron, apparently."

"Sounds lovely," Jane said. As she walked through the living room, she remarked how modern it looked with its stone fireplace, orange leather sofa, matching armchairs and ottoman, a light brown shag pile carpet and wood paneled walls.

"I rented the last place I had in Sussex Mews from an aunt. The University of London's Bedford College were expanding their campus and made her an offer she couldn't refuse. I had to mortgage myself up to the hilt for this place, but I like it here."

In the kitchen, Paul opened Jane's bottle of wine, poured her a glass and one for himself. Whilst he cooked, Jane recounted what happened to Spencer Gibbs at the pub gig.

"I wish I'd been there," Paul laughed. "But Gibbs better hope Andrew Hastings doesn't find out. Or he may get more than a slap from him—" He was interrupted by the doorbell.

He was stirring the paella at a crucial moment, so Jane went to open the door. A man in his mid-thirties, wearing a black winter coat, was standing in the porch, holding a bunch of flowers.

"Jane Tennison?" he asked, and she nodded. "These are for you." He handed her the flowers.

Jane couldn't believe Paul had gone to the effort of surprising her with a flower delivery.

He came into the hallway. "Everything OK?"

"Thank you for the flowers, Paul. They're beautiful. Do you have any loose change?"

Paul and the man at the door burst out laughing.

Jane gave Paul a bemused look. "What's so funny?"

The man stepped into the hallway and closed the front door.

"This is Stuart, my friend. I invited him to dinner so you could meet him," Paul explained.

"I feel like a right fool." Jane blushed.

The three of them chatted in the kitchen as Paul put the finishing touches to the paella. Stuart explained that he was a jewelry designer for Dunhill and Paul showed her the elegant cufflinks he was wearing, which were a Christmas present from Stuart. Jane instantly warmed to him, feeling he shared many of Paul's endearing qualities.

"Excuse me while I nip to the loo," Stuart said.

"What are you thinking?" Paul asked Jane.

"Nothing," Jane replied, wondering to herself.

"What do you think of Stuart?"

"He seems lovely. An absolute gentleman, like you."

"He's more than that—he's my partner. We're in a relationship."

Jane nodded. "I thought so, but wasn't totally sure. I didn't want to put you in an awkward position by asking anything that might seem offensive."

Paul gave her a relieved smile. "I wanted to tell you after we'd visited the Golden Lion. I was angry about the homophobic remarks Edwards and the others were coming out with at the office meeting. I know they think it's just a joke, but I don't, and it's impossible for me to say anything without raising suspicion."

"People like Edwards are idiots and best ignored."

"You're a good friend and take people as you find them, Jane. That's why I decided to tell you about Stuart. I wish there were more police officers as understanding as you."

Jane knew that not all police officers were homophobic, but knew it would be many years yet before the force as a whole was truly accepting of gay men and women.

She went over to Paul and gave him a big hug. "Whatever happens I will always be on your side, Paul."

As if on cue, Stuart returned to the kitchen. "If I didn't know you better, Paul Lawrence, I'd be jealous."

Jane let go of Paul and gave Stuart a hug. "I'm pleased for both of you. You're clearly meant for each other."

During dinner, Paul asked Jane how her side of the investigation was going. She told him about her visit to social services, the result of their interview with Simon Matthews and her suspicions about David Simmonds.

"It's clear Simmonds didn't sexually assault Simon, but there's things about him that just don't add up. He's not very forthcoming, for some reason. He never told me he knew Sybil Hastings, or that she was a patient of his, or about his dental practice in Peckham. I think Helen Matthews was his cleaner there as well."

"Have you told Moran all this?" Paul asked.

"No—or the result of the social services interview. He's already given me a dressing-down about jumping to conclusions without supportive evidence. There's still some questions I'd like to ask Simmonds, but Moran would probably tell me to back off."

"If I were you I'd sit down and go over everything you've got with a fine-tooth comb, and then see what you can find out about his past."

"I've brought a dental journal with an article about him. I was going to leave it for you to read."

"I'll have a look now—while you and Stuart do the washing up." He smiled.

"Very crafty!" Jane grinned.

Jane did the washing whilst Stuart dried.

"Paul and I have such a good relationship, but his erratic working hours mean we don't get to see each other as much as we'd like." Stuart sighed.

Jane nodded sympathetically. "Paul's highly respected for his forensic work. He's always in demand to attend murder crime scenes, often in preference to his fellow lab liaison sergeants."

"I appreciate he has a difficult job and unsociable working hours—I'm just grateful he puts our relationship first whenever he can."

Paul came into the kitchen brandishing the magazine. "Very informative. However, it does leave me wondering if Simmonds is hiding something from you."

"The few lines about him being in the army are interesting. It was a long time ago now, though," Jane added.

"I worked with the Army SIB on a murder at the Royal Artillery base in Woolwich a year ago."

"What's SIB?" Stuart asked.

"Specialist Investigation Branch," Paul explained. "I still have a few contacts at SIB, Jane. I could make some discreet enquiries about Simmonds' army career if you wanted?"

"Oh, that would be fantastic, thank you. I've brought my notebook with me. I was wondering if—"

Paul's red Trimphone rang before Jane could ask him if he would look over her notes of the investigation to see if he felt there was anything she'd missed or should follow up.

"That better not be work," Paul said with a frown as he got up to answer it.

After a moment, she heard Paul telling the caller politely but firmly that he was not the on-call lab liaison sergeant. But instead of putting the phone down, he continued to listen, his expression changing from annoyance to concentration.

"Bloody hell! Are there any other parts nearby? Give me the location." Paul grabbed a pen and paper and started writing. "I'll be with you shortly. Make sure the area is totally sealed off. Tennison's here with me. I'll let her know and we'll meet you there."

He put the phone down and turned to Jane. "That was Edwards. Someone walking his dog in Peckham Rye Park found a human forearm by the piles of rubbish."

"Oh my God. Please don't let it be connected to our cases."

Lawrence was already shrugging on his overcoat. "It could be a coincidence, but Peckham is becoming a favorite place to dump dead bodies."

CHAPTER TWENTY-ONE

Jane had never driven at such high speed as she followed behind Lawrence, who had a police siren and blue lights on his car. There was a three-quarter moon and no clouds, so visibility when they arrived at Peckham Rye Park was not bad, but it was bitterly cold. The area was crawling with police officers, who were tying blue crime scene tape from tree to tree to stop public access.

"It's like an eerie mist," said Jane, looking out across the park.

"As the food decays, the bin bags produce bacteria and molds, which in turn produce heat, which creates steam, and this is the mist effect," explained Lawrence, picking his way across the grass.

Edwards was blowing on his hands to keep them warm when he spotted them. He nodded and started to lead them over to the center of activity. A putrid smell emanated from the steaming pile of rubbish at least six feet high that ran along the edge of the park.

As they walked across the park, Edwards sidled up to Jane. "Sorry if I interrupted your evening in with Lawrence, Sarge. I must say you're looking well dolled up. Anything I should know about going on between you two? Wink wink, nudge nudge, say no more," he concluded, imitating a popular Monty Python sketch.

Jane thought she'd have some fun and hopefully shut Edwards up at the same time. "Well, you did . . ." She paused deliberately as Edwards' mouth gaped open. Jane leant closer. "Unfortunately you spoilt the moment with your phone call," she said with a straight face.

Lost for words, Edwards scuttled ahead. Lawrence, having heard every word, caught her eye, and they grinned mischievously at each other. Ahead of them they could see Moran and Gibbs standing next to the night duty uniform inspector, who was shining a large torch onto a pale shape on the grass.

Moran turned when he saw them. "Thanks for getting here so quickly." He looked stressed.

Lawrence said nothing as he put on some latex gloves. It was as if his brain had switched into another mode, now that he was in his domain: a major crime scene. Lawrence knelt, picked up the ten-inch forearm and held it under the inspector's torch to get a closer look.

"From the serration on the wrist, the hand's obviously been cut off using a saw. Same with the elbow end," Lawrence remarked, pointing to the saw marks.

"Is it male or female?" Moran asked.

Lawrence shrugged his shoulders. "I can't say."

"Should I get Professor Martin here?"

"I don't think it's worth it for one body part, and in any case, it's fairly certain the murder and dismemberment took place elsewhere," Lawrence replied.

"Are those bite marks in the middle?" Jane asked.

Lawrence nodded. "Not human, though. Could be a dog, but more likely to be a fox."

"The man who found the forearm said there was a fox nearby," Edwards put in.

"Foxes are scavengers. They'll rip rubbish bags open to get to food. The piles of rubbish dumped in the park are like a banquet to them." Lawrence pointed to a couple of rubbish bags that had been ripped open.

"There could be other body parts in amongst all these rubbish bags," Jane said.

"Some bits may even have been taken by foxes. They like to bury food to consume later, so this whole park will need searching," Lawrence added.

"Shit! Right, I want the whole area searched," Moran told the uniform inspector standing beside him.

"It's over a hundred acres," the inspector replied hesitantly.

Moran glared at him. "I don't care how fucking big it is, it has to be done sooner rather than later. Firstly, get every available officer from the surrounding divisions and the SPG down to the scene to start going through the rubbish bags. Tell the traffic police to attend with every available arc light they have—and I want every detective on the team called in to assist in the search."

"Yes, sir," the inspector said sheepishly and scuttled off to organize the search teams.

Moran looked anxiously at Gibbs. "The press will be all over this by morning. I want as much done as possible at the scene before they turn up in their droves fishing for information. Searching the bin bags for any other human remains is the priority."

"No doubt the headlines will say the Murder Mile Killer has struck again," Gibbs added.

"We don't know for sure if this is linked to the other murders. The forearm could be a man's," Moran said, but he didn't sound very convincing.

"This murder could have happened before Lang went on the run," Gibbs suggested. He turned to Lawrence. "How long ago do you think the body was cut up?"

"Hard to tell. It doesn't look that decomposed, but if it was in a bag on the exterior of the pile, the cold might have preserved it. Professor Martin will be able to give you a better time frame."

Moran held a hand up to get their attention. "Look, we keep this in-house for as long as possible and say we're looking for a murder weapon after an anonymous tip. And tell the man who found the forearm it wasn't human, just a bit of pig."

Jane and Lawrence exchanged glances. Moran was clearly desperate to avoid further damaging press coverage, but no one argued with him.

"Seeing as we're going to get covered in shit, is there any chance someone could bring down some overalls and gloves?" Edwards asked.

Moran shook his head. "Not at this time of night."

"I've got a box of latex gloves in the car," Lawrence offered.

"If you find any other body parts, tell Lawrence. He can look at them and make sure they're discreetly placed in clean black bin bags for removal to the mortuary."

Lawrence followed up on Moran's order. "Preserve the original bin bag and contents for fingerprinting. There could be an old envelope with an address on it, or other paper stuff we can fingerprint that will lead us to whoever is responsible."

Moran patted Lawrence on the back. "I'm glad you're one of us, Paul, 'cause someone with your knowledge could get away with murder."

"What the fuck!" Edwards shouted.

Everyone swiveled in his direction, then turned to look where he was staring.

"There, over there! That fox has something big in its bloody mouth." Edwards pointed, then started running. "Drop it, you mangy animal," he shouted, but the fox only looked up and casually sauntered off. As Edwards chased it, his shoe slipped off. "Stop! Do you hear me? Stop, I'm a police officer!" He picked up his shoe and threw it, hitting the fox and causing it to drop whatever was in its mouth. The fox looked at Edwards, picked up his shoe in its mouth and quickly disappeared into a wooded area of the park.

Everyone was trying not to laugh as Edwards limped back through the damp grass.

"Did you see that? The bastard nicked my shoe!" he moaned.

"That fox simply has no respect for the law." Lawrence grinned.

Gibbs started laughing. "The fox will probably take it down the charity shop in the morning. What was in its mouth, anyway?"

"Looks like a hand, or what's left of it." Edwards handed it to Lawrence in the handkerchief he'd used to pick it up.

"The other hand must be around here somewhere," Gibbs said.

"Not if the victim's Captain Hook," Edwards joked.

"Shut up, Edwards. I've had enough of your stupid jokes," Moran snapped.

"We might be able to identify the victim from fingerprints on the hand," Jane suggested.

Paul shone his torch on it. It was a left hand, but the fingers and thumb had been chewed down to the knuckle, making fingerprinting impossible.

Lawrence put the hand in a plastic property bag. "There could be more than one dismembered body hidden in this rubbish."

Moran looked downcast. "Then start searching. I need to inform DCS Blake. I'll be back at the station if you need me."

Jane looked at the huge pile of rubbish as Moran trudged off wearily. This certainly wasn't how she'd expected her evening to turn out.

Within an hour there were nearly fifty uniform officers and detectives methodically searching the piles of rubbish, using high-powered torches and arc lights. There were muttered complaints about the stench and the cold, but Gibbs told them to shut up and get on with it, as the harder they worked, the quicker they'd get through the pile and the sooner they'd get home for a bath or a shower. Jane felt herself retching at the foul smell of rotting food and other household rubbish like soiled nappies, but agreed with Gibbs.

It wasn't long before their work started to pay off. By 2 a.m. they had found two upper arms, a thigh and a size 10 left foot in three separate bags. Edwards, who was searching next to her, called out to DS Lawrence that he'd found something in a bin bag. As Lawrence approached, Edwards pulled a lower leg out of a bin bag and held it up.

"It's quite hairy and as the foot was size 10 it must be a man that's been murdered and cut up," Edwards declared.

"Probably," Lawrence replied. "But not all women shave their legs, and I can't say if any of the parts are from the same body yet. I'm afraid it's possible that more than one person has been killed, dismembered and then dumped on the pile."

Jane grabbed another bin bag, shone her torch inside and started to rummage around with her gloved hand. She pulled a stinking chicken carcass and some soggy newspapers out and shone the torch in again. What she saw next shocked her to the core. Dropping the bag, she stepped backwards so quickly she fell onto her backside. Edwards rushed over and helped her up.

"You OK?"

Jane's heart was hammering in her chest, her breath came in short gasps, and she couldn't speak. Edwards looked in the bag, then instantly turned away and vomited onto the grass. Paul hurried over and opened the bag, at first not understanding what he was seeing, then carefully reached in with both hands and pulled it out.

The three of them found themselves looking at a human head.

Her hand shaking, Jane shone her torch onto it, the light making it look even more like something out of a horror film. The skin had been removed, revealing muscle tissue, blood vessels and sinew. The eyes bulged from the peeled sockets, as if frozen in terror at the moment of death.

Gibbs joined them and let out a low whistle. "Jesus. Whoever did that is one sick, evil bastard."

When he heard about the gruesome discovery, Moran quickly returned to the scene with DCS Blake. They too were shocked when Lawrence showed them the skinned head and for a few seconds both were too dumbfounded to speak.

Then Blake turned to Moran. "I doubt this murder is connected to the three females. It's a very different MO and the victim is most likely male. This has the hallmarks of a gangland killing and dismemberment to dispose of the body."

Lawrence was sealing the bag. "We haven't found any genitalia yet, sir."

Blake ignored Lawrence. "You've got enough on your plate already, Nick. I'll get another team to run with this."

"When do you think you'll complete the search of the bin bags, Paul?" Moran asked.

Lawrence looked at his watch. It was just after 5 a.m. "Hopefully by about eleven a.m."

"Thanks, Paul. I'll contact Professor Martin and arrange a post-mortem for midday."

Moran walked over to Jane, who was covered in muck from searching the bin bags. "I heard you found the head."

"Yes, sir. It was a bit of a shock." Jane blew her now untidy fringe from her eyes.

"But you're OK now?" Moran asked.

"Yes, sir."

Moran noticed how disheveled Jane looked and could smell the rotting rubbish on her clothes. "Don't take this personally, but . . ."

"But what?"

Moran smiled. "You stink and look a mess. I suggest you go home to get washed and changed before the post-mortem—and don't be late." Moran walked off.

Jane sighed. "Not another bloody post-mortem," she said to herself.

Moran, Gibbs and Jane were in the mortuary examination room waiting for Professor Martin. DS Lawrence had already laid out the recovered body parts on the post-mortem table in anatomical order and photographed them. Lawrence had also done Scotch tape lifts on each part to retrieve any fibers from the skin. The search had so far recovered the skinned head, a lower half of a torso cut just below the breast line and above the genitals, left and right upper arms, one right forearm and chewed up left hand, left thigh, left lower leg and foot, all of which were in varying states of decomposition. Lawrence had taken a rough measurement from the top of the head to the heel of the left foot. He estimated their victim was five foot ten to six feet tall. He also surmised that the missing upper torso, genitalia and other body parts had either been dumped elsewhere or taken by foxes.

"What happened at social services with Simon Matthews?" Moran asked Jane.

"I did try and ring you, sir, but you were at the Yard. Mrs. Williams, the senior child care worker, interviewed Simon, and a doctor examined him. They were both of the opinion he had not been sexually assaulted."

"So why did Miss Summers suspect that he had been?"

"It would seem Simon was subdued because he was being bullied and Summers misread the signs," Jane answered, careful not to mention Simmonds.

"Well, I'm relieved the lad wasn't abused. At least we can put that to bed now and concentrate on finding Aiden Lang. Brenda Matthews can return to her flat, if she wants, but I'll still keep an armed guard with her until Lang's under lock and key."

To everyone's surprise, DCS Blake suddenly walked in.

"What's he doing here?" Gibbs whispered to Moran.

Moran answered in a low tone, "I don't know . . . He never told me he was coming. Hopefully he'll just be a silent observer."

Professor Martin walked in and slammed his clipboard down on an empty mortuary slab. "I hope you lot appreciate I'm missing my Sunday lunch in the pub for this—" He froze, shocked to see what was laid out on the PM table. "Jesus wept. I've been a pathologist for twenty-five years and never seen a flayed head like that! I hope the poor bugger was dead or at least drugged when it was done to him."

The four detectives looked at each other in horror. Even in their worst imaginings, it hadn't occurred to them that the flaying could have been done whilst the victim was still alive.

"You said *him*, Professor. Is the victim definitely male?" Blake asked.

Martin picked up a scalpel. "Long time since I've seen you in a mortuary, Blake. Haven't they got you driving a desk at the Yard now you're a DCS?"

Blake looked offended. "I'm overseeing this murder and the three women's."

Martin looked at Lawrence. Whilst Blake's attention was still drawn to the assembled body parts, he raised his eyebrows and mouthed the word "wanker." Lawrence nodded in agreement.

The professor stood over the lower torso and proceeded to cut it open with the scalpel. He felt around inside the torso. "Well, this bit is male. And I'd say all the parts you've recovered so far are from the same body." Martin removed the intestine, bladder and other organs, then placed them in a round plastic kitchen bowl.

"The bladder is intact with some urine still present." He picked up a syringe, punctured the bladder, then withdrew the urine, before ejecting it into a small plastic bottle. Using a different syringe, he withdrew some blood from an artery in the left thigh. He handed the blood and urine samples to Lawrence for drugs and poisons testing by the toxicology lab.

Martin then proceeded to examine each body part. "The last dismemberment case I worked on was in the late sixties. It was a gang killing in East London—"

"I told DCI Moran this might be gang related." Blake nodded, looking pleased with himself.

Martin looked displeased. "How astute of you, Blake. I was going to say the victim had been lured to a flat where he was stabbed to death, then dismembered. They put the bits in bags and threw into the canal at Bow. Silly buggers didn't realize that a torso underwater will still bloat from gases created by decomposition." Martin laughed, as if it was a fond memory. "So of course it floated to the surface."

"Was it the Krays?" Jane asked.

"Everyone suspected them, but it was never proved," Martin said.

"If it wasn't for the man walking his dog, we might never have found the body parts," Jane mused. "People have been avoiding the park because of the rotting rubbish and the rats. Whoever dumped the body probably assumed the rubbish bags would be carted off to a landfill site when the bin strike ended and nobody would be any the wiser."

Blake threw her a dismissive look. "Well, that's pretty obvious, Tennison."

Martin shook his head at Blake's rudeness, then turned his attention to examining the cut edges of the dismembered parts with a magnifying glass. "The marks left by the teeth of the saw blade on the bone suggest a hacksaw rather than a thicker and larger handsaw."

Lawrence got his camera out. "I'll take some close-up scaled photographs of the cut marks on the bone. If we recover any saws, I can do some test cuts on pig bone to see if they produce the same striation marks."

Martin looked closely at the left hand through the magnifying glass. "The fingers and thumb were cut off at the knuckle joint, before the fox had a nibble. Again, most probably with a hacksaw."

Blake looked shocked. "Whoever did this doesn't want the victim identified. The flayed head makes him unrecognizable and removing the fingers suggests the victim might have a criminal record and could be identified."

Martin moved onto the head, which had been hacked off where the neck met the shoulders. He slowly peeled back the layers of neck muscle with a scalpel, revealing the underlying bone and cartilage.

"No signs of bruising on the neck or muscle tissue, and the hyoid bone isn't fractured or broken." Martin shone a torch in the eyes. "No petechial hemorrhages in the eyes, either. I think we can safely rule out strangulation as the cause of death, but I'll just check the tongue to be sure." He slowly opened the mouth. "Jesus, they've even cut out his tongue!" he exclaimed.

Everyone stepped forward to get a closer look.

"Cutting out the tongue is a common gangland punishment for police informants," Blake pointed out.

"I think we have become rather saturated with Hollywood gangster movies, don't you?" Professor Martin commented.

He spent the next two hours going over every inch of the recovered body parts. Eventually he took off his latex gloves and mortuary gown, and turned to the detectives.

"The victim could have been stabbed or shot in the heart, since we don't have that organ. It's also possible the artery on the missing left thigh was severed and he bled to death. To be honest, I can't give you definitive cause of death."

"Can you give an estimate of his age or time of death?" Moran asked.

Martin sighed. "Hard to tell his exact age with no face. It could be anywhere from twenty to thirty. There are also many variables to consider regarding time of death. The decomposition on some parts is more advanced than others. The parts could have been kept in a fridge or freezer before being dumped. A best-guess scenario would be seven, maybe six days ago—but don't quote me on it."

Moran looked glum. "There'll probably be hundreds of mispers across the country who fit his size and age range. We don't even have a definitive hair color."

"We know he's got blue eyes," Gibbs said, trying to sound positive.

Moran frowned. "Well, that should crack it, Spence. Maybe I should circulate an appeal for information poster of the flayed head with: *Do you know this man?* scrawled across it!"

"Might be worth getting a forensic odontologist to check the teeth against dental records of male mispers," Gibbs countered.

"That could cost a bloody fortune. Check Missing Persons first for any likely matches, and then I'll decide about the odontologist."

"Do you think, in your professional opinion, this murder is linked to the murder of the three women?" Blake asked Martin.

"That's not for me to decide, DCS Blake. My job is to give the cause of death from a pathologist's viewpoint. I'll have my report done by mid-week. Now, unless there's anything else, I'm off home."

Blake looked at Moran. "In my opinion, this murder has all the hallmarks of a gangland killing."

Moran nodded. "Well, the first thing I'm going to do is put out a press release making clear it has no connection to the three female victims."

CHAPTER TWENTY-TWO

Jane arrived at work at eight o'clock on a freezing Monday morning and went straight to the collator's office on the ground floor. Every police station had a collator, and at Peckham it was PC Burt Oliver, a rotund officer with a bald head. He had worked there for nearly twenty-five years, and there wasn't much he didn't know about the criminal underworld. He received and collated information about criminals in the division and dispersed intelligence to the beat officers about criminal trends and people suspected of particular crimes. His accumulated knowledge was invaluable, and he was highly respected by everyone in the station. He also happened to be a genuinely nice man who had time for everyone, male or female.

"What can I do for you, Sergeant Tennison?" He smiled as Jane entered his office.

"It's about the dismembered body in Peckham Rye Park."

"Yeah, I heard about the flayed head. Must have been a real sickener for the officer who found it."

Jane nodded, but decided not to tell Burt it had been her. She was eager to get to the point of her visit. "Whoever skinned the head also cut out the tongue. DCS Blake is convinced it's a gangland murder. He thinks the tongue was removed because the victim was a grass."

Burt laughed. "That's more the mafia's style, not your South London mobsters."

"Even so, I was wondering if you knew of any local gangs who're at war with each other?"

"I haven't heard anything on the grapevine recently. Mind you, Eddie Harrison might be trying to reclaim his manor."

"Eddie Harrison? I've not heard of him."

"That's probably because you've always worked north of the big divide," Burt laughed.

Jane knew he was right. The Met was a sprawling force, covering over six hundred square miles of London, and it was hard to keep tabs on everything that was going on. She'd only ever worked at Hackney and Bow Street, in the West End, and felt she hardly knew what went on south of the river since she'd just arrived in Peckham.

Burt continued. "Eddie and his brother Charlie are serious South London gangsters. They pretty much ruled South London in the sixties when they were known as the 'torture gang.' Charlie got sentenced to fifteen years. He's still inside, but Eddie was released only recently after an eight-year stretch. While they were inside, some other villains took over their patch, and did very nicely out of it."

"What did the Harrisons do?" Jane asked.

"They pulled rivals' teeth out with pliers, cut off toes and fingers with bolt cutters, nailed people to the floor. Basically they got pleasure from other people's pain."

"No, I meant how did they make their money?"

"Oh, fraud and extortion mostly."

"Do you think the dismemberment could be the work of Eddie Harrison or one of his henchmen?"

"It's possible. But like I said, I've not heard anything. Between you and me, there's a guy who used to work for them as an enforcer called The Clown. There's a sort of mutual respect between the two of us. I can have a word with him, see if he's heard anything."

"That's a strange nickname for a villain," Jane remarked.

Burt chuckled. "He liked making people smile with a razor. He'd cut their mouth open from ear to ear, so it looked like a clown's smile." Burt drew a finger across his face to illustrate what he meant.

Jane winced. "If he's capable of that, then maybe he skinned the head and cut out the tongue."

"I doubt it. He's been in a wheelchair since a rival gang threw him off a roof five years ago. He still drinks in the villains' pubs and keeps his ear to the ground, though. More to the point, in my experience, people like the Harrisons wouldn't skin the head or remove the tongue of a grass. They'd want their rivals to know exactly who it was."

"Why?" Jane asked.

"Because it sends out a message not to mess with them."

"Thanks, Burt. As ever, you've been a fount of wisdom."

Jane went up to the CID office, thinking about what Burt had told her. The clerk handed her a large brown envelope with her name on it from Peckham Social Services. She also told Jane that Moran wanted a team meeting at 10 a.m.

Opening the envelope, Jane found it contained two reports. One was from Mary Williams, detailing her interview with Simon Matthews, and the other was from the pediatrician. Jane started to scan Mary Williams' report but quickly realized it didn't contain anything she hadn't already discussed with her. Jane sighed as she put the report back in the envelope and wrote on the front: *Social Services Reports—Simon Matthews—No Further Action.*

Jane was about to give the CID clerk the envelope, so it could be filed with the case papers, when she recalled something Lawrence had said at dinner on Saturday night. He had called her tenacious, and advised her to go over everything connected to Simmonds with a fine-tooth comb. Despite Moran's insistence that they focus on Lang, something about Simmonds was nagging at her. Jane also knew she lacked experience in child abuse cases, so looking at the types of questions Simon was asked would also be beneficial.

She removed the report from the envelope and read it again. What stood out this time was the part where Simon said his mum was angry because he told her he didn't like the dentist touching him. Jane remembered Mrs. Williams telling her a listener hears what they want to hear if they are already convinced something bad has happened. It struck Jane that even if Helen Matthews had dismissed Eileen Summers' fears about Simon being abused, it might still have created doubt in her mind. In turn, it was possible that the doubt became a conviction when Simon told his mother he didn't like the dentist touching him. Jane flicked through her notebook. Brenda Matthews had said Helen could be impulsive and had confronted the bullies who tormented him. Jane wondered: was it possible that a volatile Helen went to Peckham that Friday to confront Simmonds?

Jane flicked through her notebook to the time she first met Agnes. She'd asked her if she knew where Mrs. Hastings was going when she left the flat on the Friday afternoon. Agnes said Mrs. Hastings was going to see a friend from the golf club. Jane now knew that Simmonds wasn't just Sybil Hastings' dentist, but she also played golf with him—so he could surely be considered a friend. It was reasonable to assume that Sybil Hastings would have known Simmonds worked in Peckham on a Friday. Even more significant was the fact both Mrs. Hastings and Helen Matthews were murdered on the same Friday, around the same time, and their bodies were found in Peckham a short distance from each other.

Then a possibility struck her. Jane picked up her desk phone and rang the Kentish Town Police Station communications room.

"It's WDS Tennison from Peckham. I'm on the Helen Matthews murder investigation. I wonder, could you do me a favor and radio the uniform PCs who're guarding Brenda Matthews and her grandson Simon? Mrs. Matthews hasn't got a phone and I need to know where Simon had his braces fitted and where the check-ups were done."

"No problem, Sarge. Hang on and I'll radio the officers."

Jane waited anxiously for the next two minutes before the comms officer came back on the phone.

"Mrs. Matthews thought it was at Harley Street. Simon didn't know exactly where it was. He said his mum took him there on the underground, then a train. The dentist's was in a house, with a room like his grandmother's, where they had to wait to see the dentist. Is there anything else you need to know?"

"No, that's fine for now. Thanks for your help."

Jane got a tube map out of her desk drawer and laid it on her desk. Looking at the map, she realized that if Helen took Simon to Harley Street from her home address, the most direct route was by tube or bus. Jane knew Peckham had no tube stations, so if Helen went to Simmonds' Peckham practice in Brayards Road, she'd have taken Simon on the tube, then the train to Peckham Rye railway station—just like he'd said. Jane was now certain Simmonds had lied because he didn't want anyone snooping around his Peckham clinic.

Jane was determined to prove to Moran that Simmonds had repeatedly lied to her. She knew, as it was a Monday, that the Peckham practice would be open. Jane put her coat on and left the office.

The ten-minute walk from the police station gave Jane time to think. She decided she'd speak with the dental receptionist first, casually asking if Simon Matthews was a patient there, and if Helen was the cleaner. She didn't want to make Simmonds suspicious, so would explain to him that Brenda Matthews had told her Simon was treated there and gauge his reaction.

As Jane walked along Brayards Road, she realized how close it was to Bussey Alley and Copeland Road, where Helen Matthews and Sybil Hastings' bodies had been discovered. Arriving at the 1930s terraced house, Jane felt her heart racing. She could hear the high-pitched whirr of a dentist's drill from inside and, feeling a little more relaxed knowing Simmonds was working on a patient, rang the bell. She stepped back, her warrant card in her hand, and waited. The sound of the drill stopped and a few seconds later the door opened.

"Good morning, I'm—" Jane was surprised to see Simmonds, dressed in his white dentist's coat.

"Sergeant Tennison, what can I do for you?"

Jane had to think quickly. "I'm sorry, Mr. Simmonds, I didn't mean to interrupt while you were with a patient. I just wanted to ask you a couple of questions."

He looked at his watch. "I'm going to be at least another fifteen to twenty minutes with my patient, so—"

"It's OK. I don't mind waiting." Jane stepped past Simmonds into the hallway.

Simmonds pointed to a door on the right. "I use the lounge as a waiting room. Please help yourself to tea and coffee—it's in the kitchen at the end of the hallway."

"No receptionist today?" Jane enquired.

"I don't bother with one since I'm only here two days a week."

The lounge turned out to be a world away from the opulent Harley Street surgery waiting room. Though clean and tidy, the furniture was very old-fashioned, with dark wood side cabinets, a brown sofa, two armchairs, a coffee table, and a worn red and brown Axminster carpet. The floor-to-ceiling white curtains were pulled back and Jane could see neat rear garden with a large shed on the left. The flock wallpaper had long since faded and the fireplace was covered over with a thin sheet of plywood. On the mantelpiece above it was a picture frame containing mounted fishing flies of various colors, with odd names such as Damsel Nymph and Goat's Toe printed under each one.

Jane noticed some well-thumbed *Reader's Digest* magazines on the coffee table, along with a copy of the dental journal with the article about Simmonds. She bent down to pick the journal up and caught a faint smell of bleach. She stepped back from the table and, looking underneath, could see a patch of carpet that was discolored. She also spotted four table leg impressions in the carpet a few feet away and realized the table must have recently been moved. She knelt and touched the carpet. It was dry, but definitely smelt of bleach.

She looked at her watch. Only five minutes had passed since Simmonds had let her in. She had time for a quick look around before he was finished with his patient. Jane crept slowly up the hallway stairs, gently turned the handle on the door to the first bedroom on the left and eased it open. The sickly sweet smell of mothballs permeated the small room, which was full of cardboard boxes. There was also a clothes rack filled with old-fashioned women's blouses, dresses and coats. Jane remembered reading that Simmonds' mother had died about six years ago.

Jane gently closed the door and turned towards the room opposite. A floorboard creaked, and she froze on the spot. Carefully sidestepping the creaking floorboard, she slowly opened the door. The room was clean and tidy, with the same dated furniture and decor as downstairs. Jane stepped into the room and looked around. Faded photographs hung on the walls, and hanging on the back of the door were a woman's nightdress and dressing gown. The dressing table had a powder puff and spray perfume bottle on it, and a vase with fresh flowers. Jane realized this must have been his mother's bedroom, and it had been preserved like some sort of shrine to her memory. Jane looked in a couple of the dressing table drawers, but they were empty.

Jane noticed a photograph of a casually dressed Simmonds on the bedside table, and picked it up to have a closer look. Simmonds was holding a large fish by the gills in one hand and a fishing rod in the other. Stuck on the picture was a brown and gold Dymo printer label with *Salmon Fishing—River Spey—1978*. Jane thought it a bit creepy Simmonds should put a year-old picture next to the bed of his dead mother. Jane had her back to the door when she suddenly heard Simmonds' voice.

"What are you doing?" His voice was calm but there was an edge of anger to it.

Startled, Jane dropped the photograph and heard glass breaking as it hit the floor.

Simmonds stepped into the room with a furious look on his face, a large metal dental syringe held menacingly in his right hand.

He saw Jane's anxious look. "It's novocaine . . . to numb the pain." He held the syringe up and pressed the plunger, causing a clear liquid to spurt. A few drops landed on Jane's coat.

Simmonds bent down and picked up the broken picture frame. "I was just about to give my patient an injection when I heard footsteps upstairs."

Jane thought quickly. "I was looking for the toilet, then I saw the photograph. My father's a keen fisherman and I couldn't help noticing the size of the salmon you caught in the picture."

"You must have missed the notice in the living room," Simmonds said with a forced smile as he placed the picture frame on the bed. "It says the toilet's at the far end of the kitchen."

"I'm sorry about the picture. I'll clean up the glass. Do you have a dustpan and brush?" Jane asked, even though she was anxious now to get out of the house and away from Simmonds.

"It's fine. I'll do it later," he insisted. "I need to get back to my patient, so if you don't mind waiting downstairs, I shouldn't be much longer." Simmonds ushered Jane out of the bedroom.

"Would it be all right if I came back later? I've got another appointment," Jane told him as she walked down the stairs.

"I finish about five p.m., so if you'd like to come back then I'll be free."

Jane nodded as she opened the front door. "I'll try and do that, work permitting, of course."

"Have a good day, Sergeant Tennison." Simmonds smiled and shut the door.

Jane concentrated on walking at a normal pace, in case Simmonds was watching her from a window. As soon as she rounded the corner, she stopped and took some deep breaths to calm her nerves. It felt as if her visit had been a big mistake.

She'd uncovered nothing and now Simmonds would be wary of her. She looked at her watch and saw it was ten o'clock.

"Shit!" she exclaimed and started to run back to the station. To cap it all, now she was going to be late for Moran.

CHAPTER TWENTY-THREE

Moran was already addressing the team when Jane hurried into the CID office. He frowned at her and opened his mouth, as if he was about to reprimand her, but she had her excuse ready.

"Sorry I'm late, sir. I was checking something out with the collator and didn't realize the time." She saw Lawrence and went over to stand next to him without waiting for a response from Moran.

Edwards nudged the officer next to him and nodded his head towards Jane and Lawrence. No doubt he'd told everyone she and Lawrence were an item.

Lawrence leant towards Jane and whispered, "Where've you been?"

"Simmonds' Peckham practice. He caught me snooping around," Jane whispered back.

Lawrence looked shocked. "What happened?"

"I'll tell you all about it later."

Moran looked pointedly in their direction. "Is there something the pair of you would like to share with the team?"

There were some sniggers around the room.

"Sorry, sir, I was just asking DS Lawrence if I'd missed anything important," Jane replied.

Moran frowned. "Luckily for you, you haven't. But in future, I expect you to be on time when I call a team meeting."

"Yes, sir. It won't happen again."

"Good. Now, unless you have something positive to add, I'd like to return to the subject of finding Aiden Lang."

Jane felt like she had a lot to add to the investigation, but now was definitely not the time to air her suspicions about Simmonds.

She wanted to ask Paul's advice before broaching the subject with Moran.

Moran continued. "Have the gay pubs in Soho been checked out, Edwards?"

"Yes, sir. Myself and other members of the team have visited numerous pubs. Some of the gay punters recognized Lang's mugshot, but no one has seen him around Soho since the murders started."

"What about local drug dealers—was Lang getting his fix from any of them?" Moran asked.

A detective raised his hand. "We've spoken to local informants and all known drug dealers we could trace, but again, nothing positive so far. It's possible Lang may go further afield than Peckham to get his drugs."

"Then widen the bloody search for drug dealers," Moran said, looking frustrated. "Since the last press appeal, we've received a shedload of possible sightings of Lang. Any of them look promising?"

There was silence in the room as everyone looked around to see if anyone was going to speak up.

"Come on, surely one of you must having something positive." Still there was silence.

Moran's gloom seemed to deepen. "Even if you think it might be irrelevant, for God's sake tell me."

The CID clerk raised her hand. "I re-circulated the all-ports warnings and sent another round of telexes about Lang out to all UK police stations."

"Have we heard back from any of them?" Moran asked.

"Not yet, sir."

Moran slapped the table. "Damn it, Lang can't have disappeared off the face of the earth!"

Edwards raised his hand. "Is it worth speaking to his sister again?"

Moran shook his head. "Hilary Peters doesn't like police. There's no way she'll talk to us."

Only because of the way you treated her, Jane thought to herself.

"What's happening about the dismembered body? Are we investigating that as well?" Gibbs asked.

Moran nodded. "I discussed it with DCS Blake after the post-mortem. Due to all the press coverage, the Commissioner has taken a personal interest in our investigations. Blake wants to speak with him first before reallocating the Peckham Rye case to another team. But until I hear back from him we're stuck with that case as well."

Gibbs snorted. "Blake's frightened to make a decision. It's bloody obvious the dismembered body isn't connected to the three women's murders."

Moran sighed. "I agree. But it's out of my hands until the Commissioner makes his decision. For now, I want to split the team in two. One half can concentrate on finding Aiden Lang and the other, led by DI Gibbs, can investigate the Peckham Rye case."

Gibbs frowned and shook his head, as did a number of other members of the team.

"Can we at least have more officers to assist us?" Gibbs asked.

Moran shrugged. "I've also asked Blake that very question and—"

Gibbs didn't let him finish. "Yeah, yeah, and he'll ask the Commissioner, blah, blah, blah."

Moran slammed his notebook down on the table. "For fuck's sake, the lot of you grow up and stop acting like children. I don't like what's happening as much as the rest of you. But until we find Aiden Lang, the top brass, press and public won't stop hounding us. Remember, I'm the one who's neck's on the line with the Commissioner—not yours! But let me assure you of one thing:

if I find out a sighting of Lang wasn't properly investigated and he slipped through the net, then I will personally make sure the officer concerned is out of the CID and back in uniform."

The room fell silent. No one needed to be told about the pressure Moran was under and how stressed he was. And they also knew Moran meant what he said if they screwed up.

Moran composed himself before continuing. "The sooner we can find out who the dismembered man is, the sooner we can make some progress. Once we know who he is, we will be able to identify his criminal associates."

Jane stuck up her hand.

"What, Tennison?"

"I had a word with Burt, the collator. He isn't aware of any current gangland disputes, but—"

Moran cut her off angrily. "What is it with you, Tennison? Why do you have to put a damper on everything I say? The collator is a uniform officer who's never been a detective. He has no experience of a murder investigation!"

"He does have twenty-five years of experience of working in Peckham," Lawrence said in Jane's defense.

Encouraged, Jane continued. "Burt told me Eddie Harrison recently got out of prison. He suggested he might be trying to 'reclaim his manor.'"

"I was a DC at Rotherhithe when they first came on the scene. The things they did to people who crossed them were unbelievable," Lawrence chipped in.

Jane nodded. "Burt said they cut off fingers and toes, pulled teeth out with pliers."

Moran took a deep breath, then let it out slowly. "Thank you, Tennison. You and Lawrence have made your point. DI Gibbs can follow up on what Eddie Harrison has been up to since he got out of prison."

"Burt has an informant he can speak to," Jane said.

"Am I not making myself clear, Tennison?" Moran gave her stern look, then turned to Lawrence. "Anything from forensics that might help us?"

"Not in locating Lang. On the positive side, the lab found fibers matching the tweed jacket in Lang's room on all three female victims."

Jane had a sudden flashback to the moment Simmonds surprised her in the bedroom at Brayards Road. She had been so anxious, she hadn't taken in the significance of the fishing photo before she dropped it. Simmonds had been wearing a tweed cap, matching tweed jacket, waistcoat and trousers.

"What was the outcome of the social services interview with Simon Matthews?" a detective asked.

Moran looked at Jane. "Tennison?"

Jane didn't hear him. She was picturing Simmonds standing over her in his mother's bedroom holding the syringe. A cold shudder ran through her body.

"I think she's on another planet, sir," the detective quipped.

Moran nodded at Lawrence. "Wake Tennison up, Paul."

Lawrence was about to give her a nudge with his elbow when Jane came back to the moment, knowing she had to share what she had just found out.

"I saw a photograph of Simmonds this morning, sir. He was wearing a three-piece tweed suit. I'm almost certain the jacket was the same one found in Aiden Lang's hostel room."

"Christ, she's off again," Edwards whispered to Gibbs.

"What on earth are you on about now, Tennison?" Moran asked.

Jane looked agitated. "We might be wrong about Lang being a lone killer. For some reason, Simmonds has repeatedly lied to me. I can also prove he and Sybil Hastings were friends!"

For a moment there was a stunned silence in the room. Then Moran gave full vent to his anger.

"I want to know exactly what you've been doing behind my back!"

Jane tried to stay calm. "Can I speak with you in your office, please, sir?"

"*No!* You'll explain yourself here and now!" Moran barked.

Before she could answer, DCS Blake strode into the room. "Moran, I need to speak to you in private."

"I haven't finished my meeting," Moran snapped, incensed by Blake's interruption. "Carry on, Tennison."

"It's not a request, Moran, it's an order," Blake retorted. He glared at Jane and pointed his finger at her. "You as well, Tennison."

Feeling herself coloring, Jane followed Blake to Moran's office. As soon as the door was closed, Blake turned on her.

"What were you doing snooping around David Simmonds' dental clinic?"

Jane realized Simmonds must have phoned Blake as soon as she'd left. And it made her more convinced he was hiding something.

Moran looked bemused. "You were at Harley Street this morning, Tennison?"

"No," Blake told him. "She was at Simmonds' Peckham clinic and he caught her upstairs rummaging around in his dead mother's bedroom. He wanted to make a formal complaint. Fortunately, I persuaded him to let me deal with it."

Moran's expression darkened. "What on earth were you playing at, Tennison?"

Jane knew she had no choice now. She had to tell them everything.

"I was looking for evidence."

"Evidence of what?" Blake shouted.

"I believe David Simmonds is connected to the murders of the three women and—"

Blake's eyes widened with anger. "David Simmonds is a personal friend. He's highly respected in his profession and absolutely above reproach."

Jane stood her ground. "He may be highly respected, sir, but he's a liar. I know he's been hiding something—"

Blake jabbed his finger at Jane. "You've lost your mind, Tennison!"

Jane looked at Moran in desperation. "Believe me, sir, I'm not wrong this time. I didn't want to say anything to you until I found some evidence to back up my suspicions—and now I have. Please hear me out."

Blake was at boiling point. "I've had enough, Tennison. As from right now, you're off the investigation. You should be thanking me for persuading Simmonds not to make an official complaint about you."

Jane decided to go for broke. "I suggest your thoughts about Mr. Simmonds are clouded by bias, sir."

Moran shook his head, silently pleading with Jane to shut up.

"I could have you kicked out the force for an illegal search, not to mention insubordination. Now get out of my sight!" Blake ordered.

Jane didn't move. "Simmonds is your dentist as well as a friend, isn't he?"

"You really are pushing your luck, Tennison. Simmonds is a member at my golf club, but not my dentist."

"I saw you coming out of his Harley Street surgery last Thursday morning."

"You're mistaken, Tennison. I'm afraid I couldn't afford Harley Street dental prices."

Blake's blatant lie only served to fire Jane up further. "The receptionist told me you had a toothache. She also said Simmonds doesn't charge friends his normal rates. I got the distinct impression you were a regular there. In fact, she said you're often quite flirtatious towards her," Jane added calmly.

Blake glared at her, finally lost for words.

Moran now saw which way the wind was blowing and changed tack. "Accepting a gratuity is against police regulations and a disciplinary offence."

Blake started to squirm. "The receptionist is wrong. It was a one-off. I was in a lot of pain and Simmonds kindly said he'd treat me, that's all."

Moran could smell blood. "So you won't be on Simmonds' records as a regular patient—or have illegally claimed back any private dental treatment fees?"

"This is not about me, Moran; it's about Tennison. She's a loose cannon. Her search of Simmonds' Peckham practice is not acceptable behavior. She's off the investigation and that's an end to it." Blake turned towards the door.

Moran stopped him in his tracks. "You lied for Andrew Hastings. But I still had the decency to hear you out, so I suggest you do the same for Tennison."

More than a little surprised at his firmness, Jane gave Moran a grateful nod.

Blake stopped and looked at his watch. "This better be worth my time, Tennison."

There was a knock at the door and Lawrence entered, carrying a folder that he handed to Moran. "The forensics update report," he explained.

"Thank you, DS Lawrence, but we're busy," Blake said tersely.

Moran closed the door. "Lawrence stays. He's dealt with all the crime scenes, so he needs to hear what Jane has to say."

"If you say so," said Blake begrudgingly.

Moran looked at her. "Go on, Jane."

She took a deep breath and began. "David Simmonds treated Simon Matthews at his Peckham clinic, not Harley Street as he'd suggested. In fact, he never even mentioned he had another practice in Peckham."

Blake looked unimpressed. "How is that in any way suspicious?"

"I believe Simmonds didn't want us snooping around his Peckham practice. It was only by chance I found out."

"It's common knowledge he works there on a Monday and Friday. He's even received an award for his charitable work."

"It may be to his patients and golfing friends, but I wasn't aware of it," Moran interjected. "Carry on, Jane."

"I believe Helen Matthews thought her son was being sexually abused by Simmonds—"

"Are you seriously suggesting Simmonds is a pedophile?" Blake spluttered.

"No. I'm suggesting Helen Matthews *thought* he was when Simon told her he didn't like the dentist touching him. I think Helen was angry, which explains why she left her mother's flat in a hurry without saying where she was going. This was late afternoon on the Friday she was murdered. It makes sense she went to confront Simmonds. Think about it: why else would she be in Peckham that day?"

"Do you have any physical or eyewitness evidence she went there?" Moran asked.

"No. But her body was found a stone's throw from the Peckham clinic—as was Sybil Hastings in the boot of her own car."

"You think Simmonds murdered Mrs. Hastings as well?" Moran asked in surprise.

"This just gets better and better," Blake muttered sarcastically.

"I don't know for certain. But I know for a fact Simmonds knew Sybil Hastings."

"How?" Moran asked.

Blake answered for her. "She and Simmonds are members of my golf club, so it's not surprising he knew her."

"Simmonds told me he'd listened to the news on the radio about the murders in Peckham," Jane continued. "Sybil Hastings was named as a victim, and yet Simmonds never told me she was a patient of his. I only found out they played golf together because of a photograph at Mrs. Hastings' flat. If Simmonds had nothing to hide, then why not tell me he knew Mrs. Hastings?"

"News of the murders was also on the radio before any of the victims were officially named. Do you know exactly when Simmonds listened to the news report?" Blake asked.

Jane realized he'd made a valid point. "No, sir."

"What time did Helen Matthews leave her mother's flat, Jane?" Lawrence asked.

Jane got her notebook and flicked through it. "Brenda Matthews said it was between four and four thirty p.m."

"And Sybil Hastings? What time did she go out on the Friday?"

Jane flicked back through her notebook again. "Agnes, the housekeeper, said it was late afternoon. She couldn't remember if Mrs. Hastings said she was going to see a friend from the golf club," Jane added meaningfully.

"What are you thinking, Paul?" Moran asked.

"Professor Martin said Matthews and Hastings died within the same time frame, which was anywhere between two and eight p.m. From what Jane just said, we can now narrow it down to anywhere between four and eight p.m."

Jane picked up on Paul's observation. "When I was at Simmonds' Peckham practice, I noticed bleach had been used to clean something off the carpet in the living room. Sybil Hastings was stabbed to death."

Blake shook his head. "The stains could be from anything and goodness knows how old."

Jane shook her head. "The stains had to be recent. Plus Simmonds was dressed in a tweed outfit in the photograph I saw in his mother's bedroom. DS Lawrence found the same type of jacket in Lang's hostel room, even though I was told that it wasn't Lang's style."

Moran looked at Lawrence. "What did the lab say about the fibers on the tweed jacket you recovered?"

"After microscopic examination of both longitudinal and cross-sectional samples of the fibers, the lab concluded the ones from Lang's jacket are exactly the same as the one's found on the victims."

Jane shook her head. "But we don't know for certain it's Lang's jacket."

Blake looked exasperated. "Are you seriously suggesting Simmonds planted the tweed jacket in Lang's room?"

"I don't know for certain, but I do know there are things that just don't add up or make sense at the moment. The only thing that's clear is that Simmonds has been lying to me."

Blake was rubbing his cheek uneasily.

"Something troubling you, sir?" Moran asked innocently.

Blake hesitated before speaking. "On the Thursday morning I visited him in Harley Street, Simmonds asked me if I was working on any interesting cases. I was in pain with my tooth and didn't say much. I only told him I was in overall charge of the murders in Peckham. I didn't know Sybil Hastings was a patient of his, but I didn't bring up her name—I just wanted him to sort my toothache out."

Moran looked him in the eyes. "Did he ask you anything else?"

Blake sighed. "Just how the investigation was going. I told him we were looking for a suspect, and the forensic evidence, by way of fibers and fingerprints, was overwhelming proof he was the murderer."

"Did you mention the name Aiden Lang or Ben Smith to him?" Jane asked.

"I can't remember for certain. But I probably did refer to Lang since we'd released his name at the press conference," Blake answered.

Jane was taken aback. "I asked Simmonds if he knew Aiden Lang just minutes after you'd been with him. He told me the name wasn't familiar."

Moran sat back in his chair. "Well, I have to admit, from what Jane's told us, it seems Simmonds *is* hiding something. The thing is, all the forensic evidence points towards Aiden Lang killing Hastings and Matthews—not to mention the fact that Summers' body was found in his hostel room."

"All you have against Simmonds is supposition, whereas the evidence against Lang is solid. I doubt a magistrate would grant a search warrant for Simmonds' Peckham and Harley Street premises," Blake said.

Moran agreed. "We don't even have anything to connect Simmonds and Lang."

"Lang had a tooth knocked out. Maybe he was a patient of Simmonds at the Peckham clinic," Jane suggested.

Moran shrugged. "But even if Lang was a patient, then it's only circumstantial evidence. We need to directly connect the two of them to the murders."

Blake stood up. "If they are working together, your priority must be to arrest Lang. He'll be the weaker of the two, and easier to crack in an interview, especially with all the forensic evidence against him. He won't want to take the blame on his own and may turn Queen's evidence against Simmonds. Right, I'm going back to the Yard to update the Commissioner."

Jane was surprised he had accepted that Simmonds was a legitimate target of the investigation.

"What about the dismembered body? Is another team taking it over?" Moran asked.

"Yes. I'll arrange for a handover tomorrow morning." Blake left the room.

Moran looked at Jane and Lawrence. "Neither of you say a fucking word. I for one am very relieved he's handing the case over. I don't know about you two, but I could do with a coffee and sandwich after that. Either of you want anything?"

Jane and Lawrence both said a coffee would be great.

"Stretch your legs and we'll reconvene in fifteen minutes. Jane, can you tell Gibbs to join me in the canteen. I'll bring him up to speed, then we can all discuss a plan of action regarding Simmonds."

"Yes, sir."

Lawrence asked Moran if he could use his desk phone to ring Fingerprint Bureau at the Yard to find something out.

"Help yourself." Moran left them alone.

Lawrence was just picking up the phone when Jane put a hand on his arm.

"Paul, do you think someone with a partially clasped thumb could tie a slip knot and strangle someone?"

Paul put the phone down. "What else haven't you told us?"

Jane explained what Hilary Peters had told her about her brother's disability, adding that she hadn't yet said anything to Moran.

"It depends how bad the disability with his thumb is, I guess. Also, if someone else had tied the slip knot, then Lang would still be able to pull the rope and tighten it round the victim's neck. The landlord at the Golden Lion never said anything about Lang's thumb, so he was clearly able to serve drinks."

"Did you recover any shoes from Lang's hostel room?"

"I think so. All the items seized will be recorded in the exhibits book by the SOCO."

"Can I borrow your magnifying glass?" Jane asked.

"My case is in the CID office. Help yourself."

Jane went to the CID office. There were a few members of the team at their desks, writing up reports or making phone enquiries. Gibbs was talking to the CID clerk. Jane told him Moran was in the canteen and wanted to speak with him. She was getting Lawrence's magnifying glass from his case when Edwards approached her.

"We all thought that tosser Blake was wrong to call you out in front of the team like that. Is everything OK?"

"Yes, thanks. Blake got the wrong end of the stick about something, but he's calmed down now."

Jane went over to the crime scene wall and looked at the hostel room photographs to see if she could see any footwear on the floor or in the wardrobe. There was just a pair of brown suede shoes by the end of the bed, and using the magnifying glass she could see they were slip-on.

Something small on the floor also caught her eye, but it was hard to make out. Using the magnifying glass Jane looked closer. She could see it was blue and red, but that was all. Jane got the exhibits book with the list of items seized from Lang's hostel room from the case file and started reading. There was no mention of a small blue and red object recovered from the wardrobe. Jane realized Lawrence had left the hostel to attend Eileen Summers' post-mortem and the SOCOs must have missed it. Lawrence would no doubt be furious with them.

"You got a moment, Edwards?" Jane asked.

"Sure." Edwards got up from his desk.

Jane handed him the magnifying glass and put her finger next to the blue and red object.

"Can you make out what that is?"

Edwards moved the magnifying glass up and down to focus it. "Pity there wasn't a close-up. It could be a tiny bit of cloth, but there's also a metal glint, which I suppose might be from the flash of the camera . . . Hold on, from the color and shape, I think it could be a fishing fly."

Jane frowned. "I'm not in the mood for any silly games, Edwards."

"I'm being serious. I'm a member of the Met Police Angling Society, I'll have you know. I've been fishing since I was a kid. Mostly coarse fishing, but I know a bit about fishing flies."

Jane explained to Edwards about the picture she saw of Simmonds salmon fishing and the framed set of fishing flies in his Peckham clinic.

Edwards paused. He looked deep in thought, then went over to another section of the photographs and looked closely at the pictures of the ligatures. "That's interesting. So Simmonds is a keen fisherman then?"

Jane shrugged. "Maybe. The picture I saw was taken on the river Spey in 1978. Why do you ask?"

"The Spey is famous for fly-fishing. It costs a fortune to fish there, so he must be keen. The thing is, fishermen use different types of knots for tying hooks, lures and flies. It's just dawned on me that a slip knot, like the one used on two of the victims, is also used by fishermen," Edwards concluded with a smug grin.

"This is one of those rare times when I could kiss you, Edwards," she exclaimed.

"Well, if you feel the need right now . . ." Edwards closed his eyes and puckered up.

Jane gave him a quick peck on the cheek. "Could you go see if the object is still in Lang's wardrobe at the hostel?"

"Sure. Is Simmonds a suspect now?"

"I'll tell you later," Jane said, removing the wardrobe and rope photographs from the wall.

When she got back to Moran's office, he was already there with Gibbs, who was putting down a tray of coffees and biscuits.

Lawrence was on the phone. "Thanks. I'm in DCI Moran's office at Peckham. Ring me when you've finished checking." He put the phone down.

Jane put the ligature photographs down on Moran's desk.

"I know this may sound crazy," she began, "but Edwards knows quite a bit about fishing and how fishermen tie a line to a fishing fly. He told me they use slip knots, just like the ones on the ligatures."

"From what we know of him, Lang doesn't seem like a fisherman to me," Lawrence said.

"I know I should have said something earlier, but Hilary Peters told me her brother has a partially clasped left thumb." Jane waited for Moran to reprimand her, but he remained silent.

"And your point is?" Gibbs asked.

"He can't tie a shoelace, let alone a slip knot or fishing fly, but Simmonds must know about different types of knots."

"That's impossible to prove without an admission or eyewitness," Gibbs said.

Jane reminded them about the photograph she'd seen in his mother's bedroom.

"There was a label on it with: 'Salmon Fishing, River Spey, 1978.' Edwards also said you'd have to be a keen fisherman to go there as it's so expensive. In the waiting room I saw a frame containing different types of fishing flies."

"Edwards' observations, and the photo of Simmonds, are thought-provoking. But it doesn't prove Simmonds tied the ligatures," Gibbs countered.

Jane frowned. "You're beginning to sound like Blake." She put the wardrobe photograph on the table and handed Lawrence his magnifying glass.

"Edwards thinks that might be a fishing fly." She pointed to the small blue and red object.

Lawrence looked at it with the magnifying glass. "It's hard to say what it is. Rather than take Edward's word for it, check the list of items seized from Lang's room."

"I did. It's not listed. I've sent Edwards to the hostel to see if it's still there."

"Bloody SOCOs better hope it is," Lawrence muttered darkly.

"It's a good spot by you and Edwards, Jane, but even if it turns out to be a fishing fly, it's hardly a connection between Simmonds and Lang," Gibbs said.

Moran picked up the magnifying glass and looked at the photo. "I'm not questioning your suspicions about Simmonds, Jane, but Gibbs is right."

"Is Simmonds married or in a relationship?" Gibbs asked.

Jane was caught out by the question. "I don't know."

"There was no mention of him being married or having a girlfriend in the dental journal article," Lawrence added.

Jane cast her mind back to her first meeting with Simmonds. "He told me he lived in a flat above the Harley Street clinic, and that Helen Matthews cleaned and ironed for him, which kind of implies he's single."

Moran's desk phone rang. He picked it up. "DCI Moran." After a few seconds he looked at Lawrence.

"It's Fingerprint Bureau for you."

Lawrence took the phone. "Are you certain?" He looked surprised. "OK. Thanks for that." He put the phone down.

They could all sense something was troubling him.

"What's up, Paul?" Moran asked.

"It's odd. The fingerprints we recovered from Helen Matthews' and Eileen Summers' flats are all from the first or second finger of Lang's right hand."

"What's odd about that?" Gibbs asked.

Perplexed, Lawrence shook his head. "There's none from his other right fingers or left hand."

Gibbs was confused. "Excuse me if I sound a bit dim, Paul, but I don't see what the problem is. No two people have the same fingerprints, and Lang's were in two of the victim's flats. That's indisputable evidence he was there."

Lawrence took a deep breath. "I think we should get a forensic odontologist to check the teeth in the severed head."

"It would be a waste of time and money," Gibbs argued. "I ran a check on mispers. There's no one reported missing with blue eyes who fell within the height or age range of the victim."

"We need an odontologist to determine whether or not recent dental work was carried out to replace any missing teeth," Lawrence argued.

"Why?" Gibbs asked.

"Because it's possible the dismembered body in the mortuary is Aiden Lang."

"Jesus Christ!" Moran looked incredulous. He opened his notebook and looked at his post-mortem notes. "I'm sorry, Paul, but that's impossible. Professor Martin said the victim whose body parts were found in Rye Park could have been dead for seven days. The earliest Lang could have broken into Summers' flat was the Monday night she was murdered—which was six days ago. So if that's the case, unless he's risen from the dead, the dismembered body can't be him."

"Don't take this the wrong way," Lawrence answered, "but if I killed you then cut your fingers off, I could use them to leave your fingerprints wherever I wanted."

Moran closed his eyes as he worked out the implications of what Lawrence had just said. If the dismembered body was Aiden Lang, then whoever had killed him had also murdered the three women. And they were back to square one.

CHAPTER TWENTY-FOUR

When Moran, Lawrence and Jane arrived at Ladywell Mortuary, Peter Carey, the forensic odontologist from Guy's Hospital, was already there waiting for them. Entering the mortuary examination area, they could see the flayed head had already been placed on a table by the pathologist.

"Bloody hell, it's even worse than you described, Sergeant Lawrence," Carey remarked.

Although Lawrence, Jane and Moran had already seen the head, it still made them wince. Carey gowned up before attaching dental forceps to the four corners of the mouth to hold it open. The upper and lower teeth, as well as the gums, were now all fully exposed, making the wide-open mouth look like an evil, smiling clown.

"We think the victim may be—" Moran started to say.

Carey was quick to hold his hand up and stop him. "Sorry, DCI Moran. It's best I don't know anything about who you think it may be, or the victim's background. I don't want anything to influence my examination."

Using a pair of dental probes, Carey started to examine the teeth and make notes.

"It's strange looking into a mouth with no tongue. The teeth are in good condition, though, and I would estimate an age range for the victim of between eighteen and twenty-two years. The upper left lateral incisor has recently been replaced with a temporary plate."

"Could we have things in layman's terms, please?" Moran asked.

"Your victim's wearing a plastic plate, which has a false tooth attached to it. I'd say it's just a temporary replacement used while the gums and supporting bone are healing." Carey put his fingers into the mouth. He unclipped the temporary plate and handed it to Lawrence. "There should still be a plaster mold in existence for this plate. It would have been made by whoever did the dental work. If you find the plaster mold, I'll be able to tell you if it was made for this poor chap."

"Who makes the plates?" Lawrence asked.

"A dental lab, usually, though some dentists do it themselves."

"I noticed you made notes on a diagram. Would the dentist have done the same?" Moran asked.

"Most certainly, yes. And they should have taken X-rays of the teeth prior to any examination."

"Would the dentist have used novocaine?" Jane asked.

"Yes, when the abutment tooth was prepared for the temporary plate. And when the new plate was fitted."

"Could a novocaine injection kill someone?" Jane asked.

"It's possible, if the patient had an unknown allergy to the drug. They could suffer a severe hypersensitive reaction, which could result in death. And if injected into a blood vessel in a large quantity, novocaine can cause heart seizure and death in anyone."

Jane made a mental note to contact Hilary Peters to see if she knew where and when her brother Aiden was last treated by a dentist. And if he was allergic to novocaine.

"What makes you ask about novocaine, officer?" Carey asked.

"We think a dentist may be involved in the murder and dismemberment of our unknown victim," Moran replied.

Carey didn't look surprised. "It takes all kinds to make a world. I can assure you I won't say anything outside of this room," he said, removing his surgical gloves. "If your victim had a tongue, I'd expect to find the needle wound and traces of novocaine around it."

"Could a toxicology test find novocaine in other parts of the victim's body or the blood?" Lawrence asked.

"I doubt it if his death was from an instantaneous heart seizure. The decomposition of the dismembered parts will also affect the blood and destroy any traces of novocaine."

"So we'll have no way of telling if he was given a fatal dose of novocaine?" Moran said, the disappointment clear in his voice.

"There's something new that might be worth a try," Carey suggested. "The toxicology department at Guy's Hospital have been doing some ground-breaking work testing vitreous humor for drugs."

Moran perked up. "What's vitreous humor?"

"Fluid contained within the globe of the eye, between the retina and the lens. It's suitable for post-mortem chemical analysis. Vitreous is relatively isolated from blood and other body fluids that are affected by decomposition," Carey said, picking up a needle and syringe from the equipment trolley.

Jane and Moran cringed as Carey pushed a needle into one of the eyeballs and slowly withdrew the vitreous into the syringe. He then ejected it into a small glass container.

Carey held up the eye fluid. "I'll take this direct to Guy's toxicology department for urgent analysis." He pointed to the head. "Your victim had previous dental treatment—a couple of fillings, at least. It might have been done by someone other than your suspect dentist. If so, a written record and X-rays of his treatment should still exist. If you find them, I can do a comparison and tell you if it's the same person."

Moran waited until Carey had left the post-mortem room to speak with his colleagues.

"Good work, Paul. After what Carey said, it looks like you were right about the dismembered body being Aiden Lang."

"We still have to prove it," Lawrence replied. "But if that is Lang, and Professor Martin is right about the time of death being seven days ago, then he certainly can't have murdered Eileen Summers."

Jane picked up on Lawrence's observation. "If Lang was involved, or knew about the first two murders, he would have posed a serious threat to Simmonds." The inference was that Simmonds had murdered Lang.

Moran kicked the leg of the mortuary table in frustration, causing the severed head to wobble. "Getting Lang to confess would have been our best chance of nailing Simmonds. Now it's gone."

Jane knew she had to take some of the blame. "Because of my stupidity at his Peckham practice, Simmonds must know we suspect him. He'll probably have destroyed every shred of evidence linking him to the three women and Lang's murders."

Moran wasn't in the mood to reprimand her. "What's done is done, Jane."

"Simmonds is clearly a highly intelligent man. He's always been one step ahead of us all," Lawrence said reassuringly.

"Are you going to arrest Simmonds?" Jane asked Moran.

"Not yet. Even intelligent men make mistakes. And there's more than one way to skin a cat," he answered with a wry smile.

Driving into the station yard, Moran and Jane saw Edwards striding towards them. As they got out of the CID car, Edwards held up a plastic property bag.

"I found it, guv. I've used one of these myself a few times fishing for trout. You're not going to believe what it's called," he added with a grin.

Moran peered at the bag. "I've no idea, Edwards. Why don't you tell us?"

"A Bloody Butcher!"

Moran smiled. "Good work, Edwards. Now tell me, when did you last visit the dentist?"

Edwards looked confused. "I don't know. About two years ago."

Moran smiled. "Then you're just the man for the job."

"What job?"

"The one that might rattle Simmonds' cage enough to make him slip up and lead us to some evidence."

Twenty minutes later a peeved-looking Edwards walked into the CID office, followed by Moran and Lawrence. Everyone stopped what they were doing to gawp at him. His hair was a tangled mess and his face was smeared with dirt. He was dressed in worn black trousers, which just about covered his ankles, a jumper with holes in it, a coat with what looked like vomit stains down the front, and scuffed shoes, one of which had no laces. A few of the detectives started to laugh.

"Edwards didn't need to change his clothes, guv. He already looked like a down-and-out," one of them quipped, setting off another round of laughter around the room.

Moran glared at them. "Stop it, the lot of you, and listen up. After consulting with a forensic odontologist, I believe the dismembered body is that of Aiden Lang. As DI Gibbs briefed you earlier, our prime suspect is now the dentist David Simmonds. However, the evidence that Simmonds killed him, and the three female victims, is weak and circumstantial. If we want to nail him, we need hard evidence. To that end, Edwards here has volunteered to go undercover."

There was a ripple of applause, and Edwards visibly relaxed.

"Where did he get the clothes?" Jane asked Lawrence quietly.

Lawrence chuckled. "As luck would have it, there was a down-and-out drunk in the cells. He was happy to get a few quid and a tracksuit in exchange for his clothes."

Moran continued. "It's likely Simmonds suspects WDS Tennison is on to him. However, DCS Blake has spoken with him on the phone. Simmonds has been told Tennison is off the case and being investigated by A10 for breach of police regulations and an illegal search of the Peckham dental premises. Hopefully Simmonds now thinks Tennison's career is over and he's in the clear."

"Do you think Simmonds will fall for it, guv?" a detective asked.

Moran nodded. "As it's come from Blake, yes. They're . . . members of the same golf club, so hopefully Simmonds will believe what he's told."

There were a few raised eyebrows around the room, but no one asked exactly what the relationship was between Blake and Simmonds.

Moran put his hand on Edwards' shoulder. "Edwards is going to the Peckham surgery under the pretext of a bad toothache. I'm hoping to rattle Simmonds' cage a little. Hopefully it'll provoke him into doing something that will lead us to the evidence we need to arrest him on suspicion of murder."

"What if he rumbles I'm Old Bill?" Edwards asked anxiously.

"If you play your part right, he won't. But even if he does, Simmonds won't risk arrest by harming a police officer. We're putting a wire on you as well, to record everything he says."

Gibbs held up a covert microphone. "Slip your jumper off so I can put this on you."

Edwards started to panic. "No! No, wait a minute, I'm not sure I can do this."

Gibbs just grinned. "Come on, Edwards. You can do this. And who knows, there might be a promotion in it for you if you can get Simmonds to spill the beans."

Moran stepped in. "Just cut all this bullshit and get on with wiring him up, Spence."

Edwards reluctantly pulled up his grubby jumper. "It's just that dentists scare the shit out of me, guv."

"By your own admission you haven't been to one in ages, so you're bound to need some work done. That's what we need. All you have to do is fake a bit of toothache, then ask Simmonds if he'll take a look," Moran assured him.

Gibbs tightened the strap of the listening device across Edwards' chest. "Simmonds made a name for himself treating the homeless. He'll welcome you with open arms."

Edwards frowned. "I won't be able to say much if I've got my mouth wide open and he's sticking things in it."

Moran patted him on the shoulder. "You'll be fine. If Simmonds says you need fillings, just say you'll think about it and leave."

"We've got officers in observation vans and unmarked cars. We'll all be listening in and ready to tail Simmonds," Gibbs added.

"You know what you got to say?" Moran asked.

"Yes, guv, you been over it with me five times already," Edwards sighed. "Engage Simmonds in conversation about Aiden Lang and the Peckham murders and the search of the hostel."

"And the code if you're in trouble?" Moran asked.

"Use a sentence with the word red in it," Edwards replied.

Gibbs held his hand up. "Can I have a bit of silence, please?" He nodded to the surveillance officer in the far corner of the room. "You ready for a test?"

The officer held his hand up and put on a headset, which he plugged into a radio on the table.

"OK, Edwards, give us a sample of your best South London accent," Gibbs said.

"My name is Michael Caine," Edwards said in flat voice.

The surveillance officer gave the thumbs up to acknowledge he'd received the transmission.

"Right, then, we're good to go." Gibbs patted Edwards on the shoulder.

"I need the loo first," Edwards said sheepishly.

"Pee in your pants—it'll go with the disguise," a detective shouted.

There was a chorus of laughter, followed by more applause for Edwards.

Jane didn't join in. Instead, her face wore a look of concern. From her experience at the Peckham surgery, Edwards was not going to have an easy time.

Half an hour later, Edwards nervously approached Simmonds' Peckham surgery. Although he'd done a sound test before leaving the station, he now had no way of knowing for sure if his colleagues were still receiving him. It was too risky to wear any form of earpiece to receive calls. He looked at his watch, then, knowing everything was being recorded for evidential purposes, lowered his head and spoke quietly into the covert listening device attached to his chest.

"It's four thirty p.m. . . . Monday twenty-sixth of February 1979 . . . I'm outside sixty-one Brayards Road, SE15." Edwards took a deep breath, rang the doorbell and held his hand to his right cheek, as if he was in pain. He waited, then rang the doorbell again. "Christ, I don't think he's in."

A few seconds later, Simmonds opened the door wearing a white dental coat.

"Me name's George Jenkins. I'm from the hostel up the road. I heard you could sort me toof ache out for noffin." Edwards did his best to sound as if he was in pain.

Simmonds invited him inside. "I'll have a look and see what I can do to help. You'll have to wait until I finish with my current patient, though."

"I'll wait all night if you can fix it." Edwards moaned.

Simmonds showed him into the lounge. "Can you read and write, George?"

Edwards nodded. "Just about."

Simmonds handed him a personal details form and pen. "I'll need you to fill this out, please. Help yourself to coffee or tea from the kitchen. I'll be with you as soon as I can."

Simmonds returned to his surgery room and Edwards started to fill out the form. He suddenly heard the unmistakable high-pitched whirr of the dental drill, and just managed to stop himself swearing out loud. He made himself a coffee and went to sit in the lounge, enduring a nervous twenty minutes before Simmonds ushered his previous patient out of the door and invited Edwards into the surgery.

Edwards cautiously sat down in the dental chair.

"Do you live here in Peckham?" Simmonds asked.

"Not exactly. I've been homeless for almost a year. But I've got a meeting about benefits, so I can get off of the streets."

"So you've been living rough, then?"

"Nah, I've been in a down-and-outs hostel but I've been warned about staying there because of all them murders round here."

"Yes, it's very sad." Simmonds used the foot pump to raise the dental chair.

"The Old Bill was all over the hostel after they found that woman's body in some bloke's room."

Simmonds made the chair recline. "I'm sure. Well, let's hope they catch whoever did it. I feel so sorry for the families who've lost a loved one."

"They said on the news they don't know who the cut-up body in the park is . . . I reckon it was the same person done it who killed them women."

Simmonds didn't seem interested in that line of conversation. "Can you tell me which tooth it is that's causing you pain?" he asked, picking up a small dental mirror and probe.

"It's one of them back ones." Edwards pointed with a grubby finger.

Simmonds put the probe into Edwards' mouth. "I'm going to tap your teeth, George. I want you to tell me if you feel any pain."

Edwards grimaced as he felt the probe touch his back tooth. "Yeah, that hurt."

"Looks like you've got some decay there."

"Do I need a filling?"

"Yes, I'm afraid so. I'll give you an injection to numb the tooth, hollow it out, remove the decay and put a filling in. I can assure you it will be quick and painless."

Edwards was trying to stop himself shaking. He was terrified of having the procedure, but even more worried that he hadn't got Simmonds to let slip anything incriminating. He knew everyone in the surveillance vehicles would be listening in and counting on him to get more out of Simmonds.

"If it'll stop me toof ache then I guess you'd better do it."

Edwards watched nervously as Simmonds filled the dental syringe with novocaine. He knew he had to try and unsettle Simmonds before the injection numbed his mouth.

"Who at the hostel recommended me?" Simmonds asked.

"Eric, the warden. He said you treated the bloke whose room the dead woman was found in. He said he used the name Ben Smith, but he was actually called Aiden somefing."

Simmonds didn't react as he squirted a little of the novocaine from the syringe. "I have so many patients, I can't remember all their names."

"Some lady detective was back at the hostel this morning, lookin' in his room and asking questions."

Simmonds stopped as he was about to put the needle in Edwards' mouth. "Did she find anything?"

"I reckon so. She was carrying a little blue and red thing in a plastic bag."

Without warning, Simmonds pushed the needle into Edwards' gum.

Edwards gripped the arms of the dental chair as he felt a sharp pain. He couldn't believe he'd allowed Moran to talk him into doing this.

Simmonds waited for a minute or so, then used the probe again, tapping it against Edwards' tooth. "Can you feel that?"

Edwards tried to say he couldn't feel anything, but his words were slurred. Simmonds picked up a dental drill and turned it on. Edwards' knuckles turned white as he gripped the chair, the horrible sound filling him with fear. As Simmonds drilled into his tooth, he was relieved not to feel any pain, but the sound of the drill still caused his heart to pump so fast he thought was going to have a heart attack.

Simmonds didn't say anything else as he finished off the filling, and the whole procedure was over in twenty minutes. He helped a still-shaky Edwards down the stairs and showed him to the door.

"You'll feel some discomfort when the injection wears off, I'm afraid. Take some painkillers if you need to." Simmonds opened the front door.

"'anks for yer 'elp, mate," Edwards replied.

Simmonds put a hand on his arm. "The lady detective you mentioned—was her name Tennison?" His voice was cold.

Edwards tried not to look surprised. "Yeah, I fink it was. You know her, then?" he added casually.

"We've met socially. She's a very interesting lady. You could say we share a common interest." Simmonds gave him a chilly smile and closed the door.

Edwards returned to the station feeling miserable as the novocaine began to wear off. He made his way to Moran's office but was finding it hard to focus his thoughts because of the pain.

Moran seemed pleased with him. "Well done, Edwards. I heard you actually had a filling done."

"Yes, sir. I'd like to say it was worth it, but my jaw hurts like mad. Did they manage to record everything?" His speech was no longer slurred, but he still didn't quite sound himself.

"Yes. Gibbs radioed in with the basics. I haven't had a chance to listen to the actual tape recording yet. The surveillance team is waiting to tail Simmonds when he leaves. Gibbs said they were feeling your pain as they listened. Apparently one officer nearly threw up when he heard the sound of the drill."

"He wasn't the only one, sir."

"Do you think Simmonds sussed you were Old Bill?"

"I don't think so. He didn't really react to anything. Apart from when I said a lady detective had been back to the hostel. That got a reaction, like he knew it was Tennison I was talking about." Edwards sighed. "I can't help feeling like I haven't achieved anything that helps us, sir."

"Don't be silly, Edwards. You should be proud of what you did. Go on, get yourself off home and get some rest."

"If this tooth stops hurting I might," Edwards grumbled.

Halfway to the door, he realized he'd hadn't told Moran what Simmonds had said at the door.

"I forgot to mention, sir: as I was leaving, Simmonds mentioned Tennison by name. He said they'd met socially. Then his parting words about her were weird."

Moran looked concerned. "What did he say?"

"That Tennison was a very interesting lady . . . and they shared a common interest."

Moran's face turned red with anger. "The conceited bastard is talking about the murders!"

CHAPTER TWENTY-FIVE

Arriving at work on the Tuesday morning, Jane went straight to Moran's office. She knew the surveillance team had tailed Simmonds from his Peckham clinic back to his residence at Harley Street. Simmonds had left the premises at 7:30 p.m., but only to dine alone at a local restaurant, and Gibbs' team were stood down at 10 p.m. whilst other officers took over the surveillance for the night.

"Morning, sir. Lawrence told me the coroner wanted further enquiries to be made to trace Lang's dental records."

"Yes, Lawrence and Professor Martin re-examined the severed hand and confirmed the clasped thumb. Lawrence also shared the odontologist's findings with the coroner. But the coroner's not willing to issue a death certificate in Aiden Lang's name without conclusive evidence. So we need his dental records. It's a long shot, but I've got some of the team making discreet enquiries at other dental practices in Peckham and other areas we know Lang frequented or lived."

"I could contact Hilary Peters. She might know if he had any fillings and which dentist did them."

"Not at the moment. Until the coroner allows for a death certificate to be issued in Lang's name, we can't tell anyone we suspect the body may be his."

"Doesn't she have the right to know we think it might be Aiden?"

"I understand your sentiments, Jane, but think what would happen if she went to the press. We'd have to say we don't know if it's him and the coroner would be livid. Get the team to help you compile a list of dentists in the areas we know Lang frequented."

The surveillance operation continued at Simmonds' Harley Street clinic all day and night on the Tuesday. As before, he left the building at 7:30 p.m. and dined alone at the same local restaurant. The detectives watching Simmonds began to wonder if he knew, or suspected, he was under observation. A frustrated Moran called for a full office meeting at ten o'clock on the Wednesday morning.

The team had a dejected air as they gathered in the CID office. Moran entered the room and called for attention.

"Thank you for all your hard work and long hours on surveillance over the last two days, even though it didn't get the result I'd hoped for. On the positive side, if it wasn't for Tennison's dogged determination, we'd still be looking for Lang and David Simmonds might never have become a suspect. DCS Blake spoke with the Commissioner, and they agreed we have grounds to arrest and interview Simmonds on suspicion of murder. A magistrate has also issued search warrants for Simmonds' Peckham and Harley Street surgeries."

The atmosphere in the room instantly lifted. Moran got the warrants out of a folder.

"I'd ask Edwards to lead the search at the Peckham clinic, but I'm worried he might have a flashback to his nightmare experience," Moran joked.

Everyone, including Edwards, laughed.

Jane was surprised when Moran handed her the warrant for the Peckham address.

"You and Lawrence execute the warrant for Brayards Road. Rip the place to bits, if necessary. Same with the Harley Street practice, Gibbs."

"I'll get another lab sergeant and SOCOs to assist us," Gibbs replied as Moran handed him the warrant.

Moran read out the names on each team. Jane wondered if Simmonds was expecting to be arrested. If so, she was certain he would have a well-rehearsed cover story and alibi. He would also, no doubt, be able to afford the best barristers in London.

Moran shoved his hands into his trouser pockets. "Right, now everyone, be aware that Simmonds is highly intelligent but also arrogant. I guarantee, if he's our killer, he will have made mistakes and it's our job as a team of detectives to find them."

Jane and Lawrence went to the Peckham surgery with two SOCOs and a uniform PC, who was to stop any unauthorized people entering the premises, as well as record the police officers who came and went. They had been informed that Simmonds was at his Harley Street practice and were eager to get in and do a thorough search. Lawrence rang the doorbell, just in case they were mistaken, but on the third ring he stepped back and one of the SOCO officers used a sledgehammer to break open the front door, which yielded easily, having only one small Yale lock.

Lawrence stepped into the hall and told the SOCOs to wait whilst he assessed what needed to be done. Jane and Lawrence put on some latex gloves and went into the living room. She showed him the discolored area on the red and brown Axminster carpet.

Lawrence placed his forensic case to one side, knelt and sniffed the carpet.

"I can smell the faint remnants of bleach. You were right. Looks like it's been used to clean a stain of some sort. When someone tries to clean up blood, the scrubbing motion pushes it down through the carpet," he explained.

Jane was on her hands and knees when he took an envelope from his pocket. "I meant to give you this earlier, but with all that was going on around Simmonds' arrest, I forgot. My contact in the SIB found out Simmonds agreed to leave the army quietly to avoid a court martial and being sent to a military prison."

Jane frowned. "I don't understand."

"He was caught in bed with an eighteen-year-old army cook. Simmonds wasn't dishonorably discharged, but let's say it had a very nasty smell to it and the army quickly swept the incident under the carpet. My contact couldn't even find a case file, so it's all hearsay evidence, I'm afraid."

"If it's true, then I would say David Simmonds was probably aware Aiden Lang was a rent boy," Jane remarked.

Lawrence opened his case, removed his camera and took some photographs of the living room, as Jane put the envelope in her bag. He placed a ruler between the stained areas and then photographed them. He took out a Stanley knife and cut the bleached area out. As he turned it over they could both see the faint remnants of what might have been blood.

"Is it blood?" Jane asked.

"I need to do a Kastle-Meyer test first," Lawrence said.

He got a small box from his bag marked *KM kit*. He opened the box, revealing three small bottles of liquid. Lawrence rubbed a small, round piece of white blotting paper against the stain on the underside of the carpet. He added a drop of ethanol to the paper from one of the bottles, followed by a drop of phenolphthalein reagent and finally a drop of hydrogen peroxide. Jane watched, fascinated, as the middle of the bit of white paper turned pink.

"Does that mean it's blood?" she asked excitedly.

Lawrence nodded. "It's only what we call a presumptive test, though. Animal blood would cause the same reaction. I'll have to do the Ouchterlony test at the lab to determine the species of origin, but the bleach could affect the grouping results. If we can group it we can check it against the victims' blood groups." Lawrence placed the pieces of cut carpet in individual exhibit bags.

Jane shrugged. "If Lang was cut up in here there would have been lots of blood."

"Depends. I had a dismemberment case where the body was cut up in a bedroom on layers of thick plastic sheeting and we didn't find any blood at all. The thing is, once you're dead the heart isn't pumping so you don't get blood spurting out everywhere when the body is cut up. The best place to dismember someone, of course, is in the bath."

Jane started to leave the room, but Lawrence grabbed her arm to stop her.

"Not so fast, Jane, there are two small stains on the carpet in the hallway I want to examine first."

Jane was surprised. "Are there? I didn't see them."

Lawrence smiled. "It's not easy on a red and brown carpet. But when you've seen as much blood as I have over the years, it's easier to spot small stains."

They went into the hallway. Lawrence stopped between the living room and surgery, put the rulers on the floor and took some photographs. Jane still couldn't see anything obvious on the worn carpet. Lawrence tested the two spots with his KM kit and both reacted for blood. He cut them out and put them in separate bags.

Jane was anxious to know Lawrence's thoughts. "What do you think? Could Mrs. Hastings and Helen Matthews have been murdered here?"

Lawrence opened the door to the surgery. "This is all hypothetical, but we know Mrs. Hastings had stabbing injuries, whereas Helen Matthews was strangled. Also, the pathologist's time of death indicates they were both murdered on the Friday evening."

Jane nodded in agreement. "It still leaves the question of who was killed first and why."

Lawrence continued. "If the blood in the hallway and the living room is from Mrs. Hastings, it suggests something happened in the surgery, or the hallway, first." Lawrence moved from the surgery to the hallway and living room as he spoke. "Then she ran into the living room, where she was stabbed, bleeding onto the carpet."

Jane thought about it. "If Mrs. Hastings and Helen Matthews came here of their own free will, it mean Simmonds, and/or Lang, hadn't premeditated the murders, doesn't it?"

Lawrence nodded. "It could be that something got rapidly out of hand."

"Like an argument. Helen believed her son Simon had been abused by Simmonds. If she came here and challenged him, he would have denied it. The thing is, I can't get my head around why Mrs. Hastings might have come here. Do you think they came here together and he killed them both at the same time?"

"It would be hard for Simmonds to have killed them both at the same time. Also, one was strangled and the other stabbed."

Jane was fired up. "But if Lang was involved, he could have stabbed Mrs. Hastings to death while Simmonds strangled Helen Matthews. Then Simmonds killed Lang, realizing he couldn't be trusted to keep his mouth shut."

Lawrence shrugged. "Only Simmonds knows the truth. Without a motive, this is all supposition."

He went back into the surgery room and looked around. "If the first two murders were not planned then the murder weapons had to be close to hand." Lawrence looked closely at Simmonds' dental tools neatly laid out on a table next to the dental chair. He picked up a dental chisel. "The tip of this and some of the other tools are like a flat-head screwdriver. I'll take them all and test them on plasticine for comparison against Mrs. Hastings' stab wounds."

"If one of the dental tools was used to kill Mrs. Hastings in the heat of the moment, then how come Simmonds used a pre-knotted cord to strangle Helen Matthews? Plus, the same knotted cord was used to kill Eileen Summers. We know she went to the hostel looking for Ben Smith, so her murder must have been planned."

Lawrence shook his head. "Sometimes the answer is staring you in the face. If you look too deep you can miss it."

He went back into the lounge and let his eyes wander around the room. Jane followed, not understanding what he was looking for. Suddenly Lawrence clapped his hands together.

"Got it! Like I said, Jane, the answer was right in front of us." He went back into the surgery.

Jane followed him. "You've lost me, Paul. What's right in front of us?"

"Actually, it's more a case of something that's missing." He removed one of the white cord ties from the surgery curtain and tossed it to Jane.

Jane examined it, instantly realizing what he was thinking. "The color's the same, but there's no slip knot and this has a tassel at either end. The cord found round our victims' necks didn't."

"The ends of the cord used on the victims were frayed. Simmonds is smart; I suspect he cut the tassels off and tied the slip knots after the strangulation to make it less obvious what the cord was originally used for."

"But we can't prove the ligature cords were from here," Jane said.

"There is some evidence to suggest they were," Lawrence said, beckoning Jane to follow him.

Back in the living room, he told her to have a good look around.

"Can you tell me what's missing in here?"

Jane scanned the room carefully, looking for a link to the ligature cords.

"No tie-backs on the curtains?"

"Exactly. There's discoloration on the curtain and hooks on the walls. There were clearly tie-backs on them at one time."

Lawrence looked at the living room curtain with a magnifying glass. "There's still some fibers on the curtains."

Lawrence proceeded to lift the fibers using Scotch tape, which he then placed onto a piece of acetate. "If these fibers match the ones on the cords used to strangle the victims, that will be powerful evidence against Simmonds."

Jane made notes of everything Lawrence said in her notebook. She knew it would form a crucial part of the interview with Simmonds. Lawrence went outside, called the SOCOs in and briefed them on what he had found so far. He told them he wanted every surface in the surgery, lounge and kitchen fingerprinted, and a thorough search for any further blood stains.

Jane and Lawrence went upstairs to the bedroom, where she showed him the broken photograph of Simmonds in a tweed suit. Lawrence agreed the bedroom was like an eerie shrine to Simmonds' mother. He looked in the wardrobes for a tweed suit but didn't find one.

Next, they looked in the bathroom, which was spotless. There was no visible sign of blood anywhere, but they could both make out a faint smell of bleach. Jane helped Lawrence remove the panel along the bathtub and the waste pipes, but again there was no sign of any blood.

"Either Lang wasn't cut up here or Simmonds has done a thorough job cleaning up," Lawrence remarked.

She followed Lawrence downstairs to the kitchen, where he checked under the sink for cleaning fluids and blood stained rags. There was a bottle of bleach, which was nearly empty, and a cleaning cloth that looked new. Jane opened a drawer and found a roll of black plastic bin bags.

"These are the same color as the bin bags the body parts were found in, but is it worth taking them as evidence if they're mass produced?"

"There's a lot of forensic evidence you can get from a simple bin bag, which I'll bet Simmonds wouldn't know."

Jane looked doubtful. "Is there?"

"When the bin bags are made, unique scratches and roller marks are left on them by the production machinery. The 'striation marks,' as we call them, can be compared side by side to see if they are from the same batch."

"So, if the striation marks on these bags are the same as on the ones the body parts were in, then they came from this roll of bags?"

Lawrence nodded. "Also, where a bin bag is torn from a roll, each tear is unique, making a physical fit between torn edges powerful and often conclusive evidence."

Impressed, Jane held up the bin bags. "If this torn end fits to one of the body parts bags, it will be enough to charge Simmonds, then?"

Lawrence smiled. "It could be the proverbial last nail in his coffin."

A SOCO entered the room. "Excuse me, DS Lawrence, but I think there's something you need to see out the back."

Lawrence and Jane followed the SOCO through the kitchen, out the back door and down the concrete steps to the garden. The SOCO pointed to some small steps that led down to a rear basement area.

"There's an old coal bunker down there, which we've searched, and there's nothing in it. Next to it is a locked door, which I think probably leads to a cellar, but we haven't looked in there yet. Do you want me to force the door with the sledgehammer?"

Lawrence nodded. He and Jane watched as the SOCO smashed the door open, revealing a damp-smelling cellar. The SOCO shone his torch around the room, lighting up various wooden crates and odd broken bits of furniture stacked against the bare brick walls. The torchlight reflected off a glass cabinet, inside which was an array of white plaster casts and red rubber molds of peoples' teeth. On a shelf beside it, stacks of airtight jars containing white plaster powder were neatly lined together.

"We'll take all those molds for the forensic odontologist to look at, just in case any of them match the dental plate in our skinned head," Lawrence said.

"What's that gurgling sound?" Jane asked anxiously.

The SOCO found a light switch and two fluorescent tube lights lit up the cellar. At the back was a large chest freezer. They could all hear the gurgling sound coming from it now. Jane followed Lawrence over to the freezer and stood beside him. His hands still in the latex gloves, he gently eased the lid open. Opening it to its full extent, they could see two compartments, one for fast freezing, which was empty, and the other larger area for storage, which was half full. Lawrence borrowed the SOCO's torch and shone it inside, revealing frozen salmon and trout heavily wrapped in cling film or in clear plastic freezer bags. There were also some plastic containers and bags with handwritten stickers describing the contents. There was shepherd's pie, lasagna, and bread and butter pudding. Some of them were marked "Mum's." Lawrence picked up a frosted-over container and showed it to Jane.

Jane shook her head in disbelief. "Some of this stuff must have been in here since his mother died. I thought her bedroom was creepy, but this is really weird."

Lawrence looked through the contents of the freezer. "No body parts, unfortunately. Odd that the quick freeze section is empty, though." He leant forward and sniffed. "Slight smell of bleach as well."

"You think Simmonds might have cut the body up and stored the parts in here?"

"Can't be ruled out." He closed the lid and ran his gloved finger over the top of the freezer. "Hardly any dust on this, compared to the shelves. I reckon it's been cleaned recently."

Lawrence knelt on the floor and turned his head sideways, so he could see the underside of the freezer handle. He had a sly smile on his face as he looked at Jane.

"What people can't see, they miss."

"Miss what?" Jane asked.

"It looks like there's some blood smeared on the underside of the handle." He turned to the SOCO. "Can you get a blood test kit, please?"

When the SOCO returned, Lawrence took a small paper swab and gently rubbed it against the inside of the handle. He handed it to the SOCO, who put some chemical drops on it and the paper instantly turned pink. Jane now knew the reaction meant it was blood, but further tests would have to be done at the lab to determine if it was human.

"Let's remove the handle, box it up and get a uniform car to take it straight to the lab for further testing and fingerprinting," he concluded.

The receptionist at the Harley Street clinic was in shock as Gibbs showed her the warrant and told her they'd come to arrest David Simmonds on suspicion of murder. Through floods of tears, she told them Simmonds was in his surgery room treating a patient. Gibbs had already told his team there could be a lot of wealthy and influential people in the building, so he wanted everything done by the book.

Gibbs knocked once on the surgery door before entering. Simmonds was standing over a patient lying back in the reclined dental chair. A young female dental assistant stood to one side.

"What on earth do you think you're doing?" Simmonds demanded.

"I am Detective Inspector Gibbs. This is Detective Constable Edwards," Gibbs answered, holding up his warrant card.

"You're a detective?" Simmonds asked, recognizing Edwards.

"Ten out of ten," Edwards replied, as he pulled a set of handcuffs out of his pocket. "David Simmonds, I am arresting you on suspicion of the murders of Helen Matthews, Sybil Hastings, Eileen Summers and Aiden Lang. You are not obliged to say anything unless you wish to do so, but what you say may be put into writing and given in evidence."

The dental assistant dropped a tray of instruments she was about to put into the autoclave. Gibbs asked her to wait downstairs and she hurried out of the room.

"What about my patient? I haven't finished his treatment." Simmonds indicated the man in the dental chair, who sat up and removed his dental bib.

"I'm sorry, but one of the other dentists will have to deal with you, sir," Gibbs said.

The ruddy-faced, white-haired patient seemed more angry than shocked. "Just as well I was having a check-up and clean rather than root canal work. My name is Arnold Davidge, and I happen to be a barrister as well as a close friend of Mr. Simmonds." He gave Edwards a withering look. "Is there really any need for handcuffs? I hardly think David is a risk to you."

Edwards caught Davidge's haughty tone. "I don't think the families of the women he murdered would share your view," he retorted.

Gibbs was quick to stop things getting overheated. "We're just doing our job, sir." He looked at Simmonds. "We have a warrant to search the premises." He held up the warrant and Davidge asked to see it.

"It's all right, Arnold. I've done nothing wrong." Simmonds seemed completely relaxed, lifting his cuffed hands and pointing to Edwards. "That officer came to my Peckham clinic posing as a homeless man needing treatment for a toothache. I also caught a female detective called Tennison searching the surgery without a warrant."

"This is outrageous and unacceptable behavior, officers," Davidge said.

"Get Simmonds out of here now," Gibbs hissed to Edwards.

Davidge got a business card out of his pocket and handed it to Gibbs. "I'll be representing David. What police station is he being taken to?"

"Peckham," Gibbs informed him.

"I'll be there to advise you during the interview, David. For now, don't say anything. Not a word, you hear me?"

Simmonds nodded as Edwards led him out of the room. Passing his colleagues and other patients who had gathered in the reception area, Simmonds kept his head bowed. The expression on his face was unreadable.

CHAPTER TWENTY-SIX

Jane and Gibbs were in Moran's office, discussing the events surrounding Simmonds' arrest.

"So if Davidge says anything about you being unlawfully at the Peckham surgery, just stick to the looking for the toilet story," Gibbs told Jane. "We got Simmonds' Mercedes taken to the lab for examination. Edwards took Simmonds' dabs when we got back to the station and is taking them up the yard. They can be checked against any unidentified prints from the hostel, in Hastings' car, and on the bin bags the body parts were found in."

Jane told them about the fridge freezer and possible blood and fingerprints on the handle.

Moran was skeptical. "I suspect Simmonds is too smart to have left his fingerprints anywhere, but it's worth a try. Did you find anything else of interest at Brayards Road?"

Jane went over everything she and Lawrence had found at the Peckham surgery and mentioned the importance of the bin liners.

"We also searched the garden shed. There were no screwdrivers or hacksaws, just gardening equipment. Behind the shed, in a recessed area, we found the remnants of a recent garden fire, which Lawrence examined. He scooped the ashes up and placed them in a bag for a thorough examination back at the lab."

Moran seemed pleased. "Good work. If the bin bags at Brayards Road are from the same batch as the ones the body parts were in, Simmonds has got big problems—not to mention he might have stashed the dismembered body in his bloody deep freeze."

Jane got out her notebook. "I made notes about the possible murder scenarios DS Lawrence suggested. I wondered if you'd like to go over them with me in preparation for the interview, sir?"

"Thank you, Jane, but you need to understand that with people like Simmonds, it's best do a cursory interview first. That way we can dictate the pace of things, soften him up and sound him out before we squeeze him by the balls in a proper interrogation."

Jane didn't argue. Moran knew what he was doing, and she would be able to observe Simmonds whilst he was being questioned.

Moran's desk phone rang. He spoke briefly then put the phone down. "That was the duty sergeant letting us know Mr. Davidge, the barrister, has arrived and wants a consultation with Simmonds. He didn't waste any bloody time. Jane, go and book Simmonds out of his cell and take him to the secure interview room so he can speak to him in private."

Jane made her way to the cell where Simmonds was being held, and waited for the uniform sergeant to open the door. Simmonds was still wearing the immaculate white dental coat he'd had on when he was arrested. He sat on the bed, sipping water from a polystyrene cup. She recalled the flattering photograph of him in the dental journal, and then the first time she'd met him at his practice in Harley Street. She had thought then that he was an attractive man, but now, sitting in a cell, his features somehow looked different. His striking blue eyes seemed vacant, and his thin-lipped mouth appeared frozen in a permanent sneer. As he stood up to face her, he seemed taller and more imposing than she remembered.

"Good morning, Detective Sergeant Tennison," he said with an off-putting smile. "Could you inform DI Gibbs that I have patients who rely on me and need important treatment?

Mrs. Lewis, who's eighty-two, needs her new dentures, then there's Mr. Riley, who has a painful abscess that needs looking at."

"I'm not here to talk about your patient list."

He smiled again. "I just wondered when I'm going to be released, that's all."

Jane couldn't believe his arrogance. "This is a murder investigation. DCI Moran will decide if and when you'll be released."

"You and your colleagues are wrong about me, Sergeant Tennison. I haven't done anything wrong."

"Mr. Davidge is here to represent you. You can have a consultation with him in private, then DCI Moran will interview you. If you'd like to follow me, please."

"Can you thank Mr. Davidge for his valuable time, but I won't be needing him."

Jane wondered what he was playing at. "But you're entitled to legal representation."

"I didn't ask for Mr. Davidge to come here. He took it upon himself to represent me. I am perfectly capable of speaking for myself and answering any questions you put to me."

"It might be better if you told Mr. Davidge yourself," Jane suggested.

He smiled. "No, I'm happy for you to tell him."

For someone who's just been arrested for murder, Jane thought his attitude was incredibly cocky. She left Simmonds locked in his cell and went to speak with Davidge in the interview room. She asked the uniform sergeant to accompany her and corroborate what Simmonds had told her.

"He's weird, right enough," the burly sergeant remarked.

Jane agreed. "I know. It's hard to tell if he's being serious or playing games."

"I've never known a murder suspect refuse to be represented or advised by a solicitor."

Davidge was making some notes when Jane and the sergeant entered the interview room.

"Mr. Davidge, I'm WDS Tennison. I've just spoken with your client, David Simmonds. He asked me to tell you he doesn't want legal representation."

Davidge looked surprised. "I'd like to hear him tell me that in person."

"The sergeant here was also present. He can confirm what Mr. Simmonds said."

But Davidge didn't give the sergeant a chance to speak.

"I think you're lying! If you think for one minute I'll walk away and allow you to fabricate evidence and concoct a false confession from my client, you are mistaken."

Jane stood her ground. "Believe me, Simmonds wouldn't be here if we didn't have evidence he was involved in the murders."

"I demand to see David now!" Davidge shouted, moving closer to Jane.

The sergeant stepped in between them. "Right, that's enough. You can leave the station of your own accord, sir, or I will forcibly remove you. It's your choice."

"You haven't heard the last of this, Sergeant Tennison. I can assure you, I will be making an official complaint." Davidge snatched up his briefcase and stormed out of the room.

Davidge's outburst was unsettling, but Jane wasn't worried as she had the duty sergeant to back her up. She went to Moran's office to update him.

"What? He seriously doesn't want legal representation?"

"No, sir. He also said he'd answer our questions," Jane added.

"Maybe he's had an epiphany moment." Moran looked pleased.

But Jane was uneasy. "Simmonds is up to something. Do you think we should get the police doctor to certify he's fit for interview? Just to be on the safe side."

"No. He might start play-acting and fool the doctor. The last thing we want is to be forced to have a social worker sitting in on the interview because the doc says he's not the full ticket. Let's stick to the plan, do the cursory interview and see what Simmonds has got to say."

Jane signed Simmonds out on his custody record for interview, then, assisted by the custody PC, took him to the secure interview room. She sat down opposite him and placed her case file folder, A4 interview book, pen, three sharpened pencils and an eraser neatly on the table in front of her. She watched as Simmonds examined his fingers. He had very large hands, and the nails were exceedingly well manicured.

He looked up sharply. "That fingerprint ink you used is very hard to clean off. As a Harley Street dentist, I must be aware of my personal hygiene. If I were a patient, I wouldn't be able bear the thought of a dentist with halitosis or dirty hands examining me."

At that moment, Moran entered holding a case file folder. Jane wondered if he had changed his mind and decided to do a more in-depth interview, referring to statements and photographs. Moran asked the PC to wait outside, then introduced himself to Simmonds, who stood up and put his hand out. Moran ignored it and told him to sit down. After this brusque beginning, Jane was surprised when Moran asked Simmonds if he'd like a tea, coffee or water.

"I'm fine, thank you," Simmonds replied.

"Can you do me a favor, Jane? I've gone and left my notebook on my desk. Do you mind nipping up and getting it?"

Simmonds raised his hand and smiled at Jane. "Actually, could I have a black coffee?"

As Jane left the room, she heard Simmonds ask Moran when he would be released. She began to wonder if Simmonds really didn't understand the gravity of his situation and was slightly unhinged.

Moran waited for the door to close. "Let's get one thing straight here and now, Simmonds: if you've any sense, you'll tell me why you murdered those three women, and what part Aiden Lang played in it."

Simmonds showed no emotion as he shook his head. "I only knew Helen Matthews through work and Sybil Hastings as a patient and friend, who I sometimes played golf with, along with her son. I have no idea who the other woman was. With regard to Aiden Lang, did you say? I have never met or had anything to do with anyone of that name."

Moran stood up, then leant over and prodded Simmonds hard in the chest. "I've got the best crime scene examiner in The Met going over your Peckham surgery as we speak, as well as a team at Harley Street."

Simmonds didn't flinch as he looked Moran in the eye. "You can beat me till I'm black and blue if it makes you feel good, but I'm not going to confess to crimes I didn't commit."

Moran sat back down with a scowl. "People like you make me sick, Simmonds. You think your money and position make you untouchable. You think you're above the law. The fact is, you're the lowest of the low—a perverted, sick monster, with no remorse for your crimes or the misery you've brought to others. You don't like the thought that a mere copper can see through your lies, do you?"

Simmonds shrugged. "You seem to have already concluded I'm guilty, DCI Moran, without presenting any evidence to support your accusations. I thought any admissions of guilt must be obtained freely and voluntarily—not under duress. Or do you prefer beating false confessions out of suspects?"

Moran stood up quickly, knocking his chair over in the process. He leant over the table with his hand raised, ready to slap Simmonds, who didn't flinch. Moran was shaking with anger as he squeezed his hand into a fist to stop himself from striking him. Moran heard the door opening, picked his chair up and was sitting back down when Jane entered.

As she handed Moran the notebook, she could see he looked angry. Although Simmonds still seemed calm and relaxed, something had clearly happened whilst she was out of the room.

"I need a break." Moran got up and opened the door. He gestured for the uniformed officer to step inside. "I'll be back in a minute."

Jane handed Simmonds his coffee. "Thank you." He smiled. There was an eerie silence as he sipped at it, his little finger elegantly raised, as if he was drinking from a bone china cup, rather than a polystyrene one.

"It seems as if I might be here for some time, Jane. Do you think I could contact my receptionist at Harley Street and tell her to cancel my appointments?"

Part of her felt she should tell him to address her as Detective Sergeant, but she decided to let it go.

"You'd have to ask DCI Moran. Seeing as you mentioned it, I didn't find an appointment book or any patient records at your Peckham surgery."

"That's because they're in box files at my flat in Harley Street. I take the appointment book and patient records to and from Peckham on a Monday and Friday. I used to keep them there, but after a break-in a year ago, I decided not to. I did report it, but no one was arrested."

"Where exactly are the box files in your flat?"

Simmonds took another sip of coffee. "In the study room on a bookshelf next to the work desk."

Jane jotted the details down and passed the paper to the PC, telling him to give it to DI Gibbs to make sure the box files were seized.

Moran returned to the interview room and the PC left. Jane could see he'd doused his face with water, as some drops had splashed onto his shirt. She told him what Simmonds had said about the Peckham patient files and the message she'd had passed on to Gibbs.

Jane thought Moran would open with some routine questions about how long Simmonds had owned the Peckham surgery, how often he worked there etc., but instead he cut straight to the chase.

"What were you doing on the day and evening of Friday the sixteenth of February?"

Jane remembered this was the date the bodies of the first victims were found.

"I worked at the Peckham surgery as usual, until about five thirty or six p.m., then went home to my flat on the top floor of my Harley Street practice. I don't think I went to my local Italian restaurant that evening. If I didn't, I would have cooked myself something, then listened to the radio or read a book."

"What exactly did you listen to on the radio?" Moran asked.

Simmonds shrugged. "I can't honestly recall now. It's hard to remember exactly what one was doing, what, two weeks ago?"

Jane knew Moran was hoping Simmonds would account for every minute detail of what he was doing on the sixteenth as it would indicate he'd prepared a cover story.

"When did you learn about the murders?"

Simmonds paused for thought. "I'd heard something on the radio but didn't take much notice at the time."

"Did you see the news coverage on TV?" Moran continued.

"No. I don't have a TV. The first I knew about Helen Matthews' death was when Jane came to see me at Harley Street."

"You mean Detective Sergeant Tennison," Moran said firmly.

Simmonds shrugged. "She didn't object when I called her Jane while you were out of the room."

Moran ignored him. "When did you hear about Sybil Hastings' murder?"

"Chief Superintendent Blake told me about it."

Moran remembered Blake saying he hadn't mentioned Mrs. Hastings' murder to Simmonds. He looked at Jane, who raised her eyebrows. She thought Simmonds was being foolhardy if he was lying, but she also knew Blake had a propensity to lie to get himself out of trouble.

"So when exactly did Chief Superintendent Blake tell you about Mrs. Hastings' death?" Moran asked.

Simmonds nodded towards Jane. "Last week. On the same morning Sergeant Tennison came to see me. He had a toothache."

Moran shook his head. "DCS Blake told me he never said anything about Hastings to you!"

"Then he's mistaken, or lying for some reason," Simmonds replied.

"If you already knew Sybil Hastings was dead, why didn't you tell Sergeant Tennison?" Moran asked.

"Because I thought my conversation with Chief Superintendent Blake was confidential and he didn't want me to tell anyone. He also told me you were looking for a suspect and the forensic evidence was overwhelming. I didn't tell Sergeant Tennison that either."

"Did he tell you the name of the suspect?" Jane asked.

"No."

"And the dental nurse who works with you will be able to confirm your version of the discussion with DCS Blake?"

"I doubt it. She was downstairs apologizing to the patient who had to wait because Chief Superintendent Blake didn't have an appointment."

Jane knew there were elements of truth in what Simmonds said, but was sure he was twisting things to support his cover story.

"You don't seem very concerned about DCS Blake and confidentiality now," she remarked.

"He's not being accused of multiple murders, is he?" Simmonds replied.

Moran looked at Jane and nodded for her to continue.

"You told me you treated Simon at Harley Street, which was another lie."

"I'm sorry, you've changed the subject. Who are we talking about now?"

"Simon Matthews. His mother Helen, your cleaner, was murdered. You told me you treated her son at your Harley Street surgery, which was a lie. Simon said it was Peckham."

Simmonds looked confused. "I don't think I ever said I treated him at Harley Street. I recall you asking if I treated him, and I told you I did."

Jane got her CID notebook out of her pocket and flicked through the pages to the notes of her first meeting with Simmonds. She had made brief notes but hadn't recorded word for word what was said, as it wasn't an official suspect interview.

"You said you didn't keep a record, as the other dentists would be upset if they found out you were doing dental work for free, which is strange as you own the practice. Surely you can do as you please? Your answer also implied you treated Simon at Harley Street—"

"That's absurd," Simmonds interrupted. "Everyone knows I have a Peckham practice. You've misconstrued what I said. You'll find a Peckham patient record for Simon in the box folders at my flat. I made Simon's braces myself at Harley Street. I didn't make a record of it, or put it through the books, for a good reason. I like to think of the other dentists as colleagues—"

"Are you saying Sergeant Tennison is a liar?" Moran snapped.

Simmonds looked offended. "I'm not accusing her of any such thing. I have no doubt she's an honest and forthright police officer. If I may ask, Detective Tennison, when did you actually make those notes?"

Jane recalled her first opportunity was after the office meeting on the Thursday. "Late afternoon, early evening, on the same day."

"Surely you must find it hard to remember exact words used in a one-to-one conversation many hours later?"

Jane shook her head. "Not at all. As a police officer I've had a lot of experience making accurate notes after a conversation, even the following day."

"What was the first thing I said to you today, then?" Simmonds asked.

Moran slapped the table, almost making Jane jump. "You're the one who has to answer the questions, Simmonds. You murdered Helen Matthews because she found out you'd sexually abused her son, didn't you?"

Jane was surprised by Moran's sudden change of tack, since they both knew Simmonds hadn't abused Simon. Was he just trying to rile him?

Simmonds scowled at Moran. "I resent your disgusting, sick allegation, DCI Moran. I am not depraved, nor have I ever treated a child without an adult being present. You can ask any of the parents of children I've treated and they'll confirm it as fact."

"Have you ever been married?" Moran asked.

"No."

"Got a girlfriend?"

"Why are you so interested in my private life?"

"Are you a homosexual?"

"You think because I don't have a wife or girlfriend I must be homosexual, and thereby also abuse children. The more I listen to you, the more I realize what a sad, pathetic little man you are, Mr. Moran."

"Were you in a relationship with a rent boy called Aiden Lang?"

"As I told you, I don't know, and have never met, anyone called Aiden Lang. The first time I ever heard the name was when Sergeant Tennison showed me his photograph. Someone else did mention it to me when—"

"When what?" Moran banged his hand on the desk.

"When you said to me, 'If you've any sense at all, you'll tell me why you murdered those three women, and what part Aiden Lang played in it.' Then, if you remember, you kicked your chair over and raised your hand to me. God knows what you'd have done if she hadn't walked into the room." Simmonds looked at Jane. "He didn't forget the notebook. He wanted you out of the room so he could beat me into confessing to crimes I did not commit!"

Jane suspected as much. She glanced at Moran, who was glaring at Simmonds. Jane felt let down by Moran's impulsive actions, which he would know could jeopardize the investigation.

"You're a liar. I never touched you. We both know you killed those women and Aiden Lang," Moran said bluntly.

Simmonds sighed. "I understand you have a job to do, DCI Moran. But why are you trying to make anything I've done or said fit your ill-conceived notion that I am the murderer? It seems to me you've failed to consider that this Aiden Lang may have committed the crimes and framed me for the murders."

Before Moran could reply there was a knock on the door.

"What?" Moran shouted.

Gibbs put his head around the door and asked if he could have a word with them both. They left the room to join Gibbs while the uniform PC entered to keep watch on Simmonds.

Moran punched the corridor wall. "He's fucking unbelievable, sitting there, cool as a cucumber. He must think we're all idiots."

Jane said nothing as she followed them down the corridor, away from the interview room.

Gibbs turned to Moran. "I just got a phone call from one of the lads searching Harley Street. They found the box files for the Peckham patients, and Simon Matthews' record was in there."

"Simmonds has already told us that!" Moran said and started to walk off.

"Has he told you there's also a file for a Benjamin Smith, and not only does his description fit, he has the same date of birth as Aiden Lang?"

Moran froze as he took this in. "No, he hasn't!"

"When I went to Harley Street, I asked Simmons if he knew Aiden Lang and showed him the photograph. I also said he might be called Ben Smith," Jane added, realizing the implications.

Gibbs stepped forward. "According to the file, Ben Smith first went to the Peckham clinic nearly two months ago. He had a missing upper left incisor, the same as the severed head. Simmonds' report noted that the socket was badly infected, with a possible abscess, and he prescribed a course of antibiotics and painkillers, before he could fit a temporary plate."

"Fuck me. So Simmonds has known Lang for about six weeks," Moran said.

"It gets better, guv." Gibbs flicked through his notes. "Simmonds fitted him with a temporary plate at his Peckham clinic on Monday the twelfth of February."

"Shit, that's one . . . two . . . That's four days before Matthews and Hastings were murdered. What else was in the file?" Moran asked, adrenalin pumping.

"In his appointments book, Simmonds has a return date for him on the following Monday, the nineteenth of February."

Moran paced up and down, rubbing at his hair. "OK, OK . . . I need to get this straight. At the post-mortem, Professor Martin estimated the dismembered victim had been dead around seven days. That's right, isn't it?"

Gibbs nodded.

"Which means that Lang's murder happened before Simmonds killed Eileen Summers." Moran rubbed his hands together. "We've fucking got him, Spence!" He turned to Jane. "When we go back in, I want you to mention that you showed Simmonds the photograph of Aiden Lang. Have you got the photo of him with you?"

"It's in a folder on the desk, sir."

"I'll let you know when to get it out."

They re-entered the interview room and sat down. As the PC left, Jane opened the A4 notebook to continue making notes.

"Do you know a young man called Ben Smith?" Moran asked.

"Not that I recall."

"That's strange, because he's a patient of yours at Peckham," Moran said.

"I've had hundreds of patients over the years. Many of them have the surname Smith, or at least claim to."

"We've had someone check the Peckham files at your Harley Street flat. There's one for a Benjamin Smith, who attended your Peckham clinic several times over the last six weeks. In fact, you fitted him with a temporary plate on Monday the twelfth of February." Moran paused to monitor the effect of this information, but Simmonds didn't react.

Moran continued. "When you first met WDS Tennison, she told you Lang used the alias Ben Smith, who we now know has the same date of birth as Aiden Lang."

Simmonds put his hands to his face. "Oh my God, I've just realized . . . it's the young man from the homeless shelter you're talking about. You're right, I fitted him with the temporary plate. I think he was supposed to come back last Monday for the actual porcelain tooth to be fitted, but he never turned up."

"So you did know Ben Smith," Moran concluded.

"He gave his name as Benjamin, not Ben."

Moran looked at Jane. "Show him the photo, please."

Jane opened the case folder and slid the picture of Aiden Lang across the table.

"I showed you this picture of Aiden Lang at your Harley Street surgery when we first spoke. Is this the man you knew as Benjamin Smith?"

Simmonds picked up the picture and studied it. "Now I remember: his hair was dyed blond, not dark like in this photo." He looked at Jane with an apologetic expression. "I didn't make the connection when we first met."

Moran couldn't keep the sarcasm out of his voice. "Well, I guess we all make mistakes. So what can you tell us about Aiden Lang?"

"I only knew him as a patient. He seemed like a nice young man, always very polite. That's really all I can say about him."

Moran nodded. "I take it you've heard about the body parts found in Peckham Rye Park?"

"Yes, it was on the radio."

"Some monster chopped the victim up and left the body parts with the rubbish."

Simmonds shook his head. "How someone could do that to another human being is beyond belief."

"The victim was Aiden Lang, the same young man you just identified as Benjamin Smith."

Simmonds looked shocked. "You can't seriously think I had anything to do with his death?"

Moran leant forward. "You wouldn't be sitting here under arrest if I didn't. We also suspect Lang's body parts were kept in a freezer before they were dumped on the piles of rubbish. You have a freezer in the cellar at your Peckham surgery, don't you?"

Simmonds shook his head in disbelief. "Why would I be so stupid as to keep Benjamin Smith's—or Aiden Lang's—dental records if I was involved in his murder?"

"Because getting rid of them would be even more suspicious."

Simmonds didn't seem to have an answer to that, and Moran sensed he was getting to him.

"The forensic officers found some bleach stains on the living room carpet at Brayards Road. I think you used the bleach to clean up bloodstains."

Simmonds found his voice again. "This is ridiculous! One of the alcoholics from the homeless shelter was sick on the carpet recently. I used bleach to clean it up."

Moran sat back in his chair. "Well, you didn't do a very good job. When the stained section was cut away, blood was found on the underside of the carpet. In your rush to clean up the blood, you actually helped to push it down through the carpet, so I'd like to thank you for that."

"Are you always so condescending to someone who's telling the truth, Moran? If there was blood on the carpet, it could have got there at any time. My mother lived alone in that house for many years. She was on warfarin to stop her blood clotting. One of the side effects was sudden heavy nose bleeds."

"You have a well-prepared answer for everything, don't you, Simmonds? If I was a juror listening to you in a murder trial, I'd probably think everything you said was perfectly plausible. But as a detective, I know better. You're lying." He paused. "I'm confident the black bin bags we found in the kitchen at your Peckham surgery will prove it." Moran let Simmonds think about that for a moment.

"Everybody has black bin bags," Simmonds said dismissively.

Moran slowly and carefully explained about the unique striation marks on the bin bags, which were being examined at the lab to determine if they were from the same roll as the ones in Simmonds' kitchen.

"Bin bags are mass produced. Thousands will have been made at the same factory and sold around the country," Simmonds declared confidently.

"You're quite right, of course, but when a bin bag is torn from a roll, each tear is unique. A match between two torn edges is conclusive evidence." Moran folded his arms and stared at Simmonds.

Simmonds sat upright and motionless. He didn't seem to have an answer and Jane sensed he was trying to work out whether what Moran had just said was true.

Moran spoke quietly. "Cat got your tongue for once, Simmonds? Or are you not quite as informed about forensics as you like to think you are?"

There was a knock on the door. "Getting a bit like Piccadilly Circus in here, isn't it?" Moran said, smiling at Simmonds.

Gibbs entered the room and handed a sheet of paper to Moran. "Just had a fax through from Paul Lawrence. I think you'll like what's on it," he added, before exiting the room.

Moran ran his eyes over the fax. He smiled as he showed it to Jane, then carefully folded it in half and ran his index finger over the fold. He held the folded page up in front Simmonds.

"This is a forensic report. Prints left by blood stained fingers were recovered from the underside of the freezer handle in your cellar." Moran paused for a response, but Simmonds didn't reply, so he continued in an increasingly confident tone.

"The fingerprints match your second and third right fingers. The blood group is the same as Aiden Lang's. And the blood on your waiting room carpet at the Peckham surgery is the same group as Sybil Hastings'. I know we can't say 'beyond a doubt' that the blood is theirs, but we can say it's not yours, as you're a different blood group. From where I'm sitting, that looks like pretty damning evidence against you. Wouldn't you agree?"

Moran leant forward, inviting a reply, but Simmonds still said nothing.

Moran sat back. "And there was me thinking you were a bit of a forensics expert. But you're just a perverted son of a bitch who's incapable of telling the truth. If you have a shred of decency or remorse, then have the guts to admit what you did."

Simmonds roused himself. "I will not be spoken to like this, Detective Moran! If you continue in this manner, I will heed my barrister's advice and respond 'no comment' to any further questions."

"So you're not prepared to answer any further questions?"

Simmonds leant forward. "No comment!" he said through gritted teeth.

Moran stood up. "I'd like you to read the questions and answers recorded by Sergeant Tennison in the interview book. If you agree they are a correct account of what was said, then sign and date each page." Moran opened the door and asked the custody PC to come in.

"Remain with Sergeant Tennison while she goes over the record of interview, then take the prisoner back to his cell."

As he shut the door, Simmonds and Tennison could hear Moran whistling "Happy Days Are Here Again."

CHAPTER TWENTY-SEVEN

Jane sat next to Simmonds whilst he carefully read through the notes of the interview. It was painstakingly slow, and Simmonds hardly said a word, apart from the odd question where he had difficulty reading what Jane had written. Eventually he had signed and dated each page. Jane stood up, closed the interview book and went back to the opposite side of the desk.

She glanced at the custody officer, about to ask him to take Simmonds to the cells.

"Tell me, how do you feel when a guilty man isn't convicted by a jury?" Simmonds asked softly.

"I've never had a case like that."

Simmonds smiled. "There's always a first."

"What do you mean by that?" Jane asked.

"You're the detective—you tell me."

"I'm not interested in your silly games, Mr. Simmonds. You pretend to be a good, upstanding citizen who cares about other people, but we both know it's all an act. You pretended to be shocked when I told you Helen Matthews had been murdered, but you already knew because you'd killed her. You even asked how Simon was and offered your help. I think your behavior is beneath contempt."

He didn't seem fazed by her damning indictment. "I meant it about Simon. I lost my own father at a young age. I know the pain and heartache the boy must be going through."

Jane was incensed. "I don't think you do. The officer here will take you back to your cell." She picked up the interview book, ready to leave.

"Please hear me out." Simmonds kept his face lowered as he took a deep breath.

Jane was surprised to see that he actually seemed distressed. The troubled look on his face was certainly unlike anything she had observed whilst Moran had been interviewing him. She sat down slowly.

"My father was killed in the war whilst fighting the Japanese," Simmonds resumed. "And my brother died in a motorcycle accident aged seventeen. My mother never spoke about their deaths. Without her strength and love I wouldn't have got over my brother's death or been a successful dentist. She was so proud of everything I achieved. She took great delight in telling anyone she met that I owned my own dental practice in Harley Street."

"I read that you bought her the house in Peckham."

Simmonds smiled. "It was the happiest I'd ever seen her when she moved in there. But I'll never forget the sound she made when they came to tell her my brother had been killed. It was a horrific accident. He was virtually decapitated. My poor mother had to go to the mortuary to identify him. He was the light of her life and it broke her heart. I don't honestly think she ever got over losing my brother, and it made her overprotective of me."

"Did you keep the house because of your mother?" Jane asked, thinking about how the bedroom was like a shrine to her.

"In some ways, yes. As my success grew I was able to develop a lucrative private practice, and eventually buy the property in Harley Street. But my beloved mother always encouraged me to help people less fortunate than myself and I knew setting up my dental practice in Peckham would have pleased her, so that's what I did. I took great care of my mother, and spent many hours cooking her favorite dishes for her and putting them in the deep freeze, so she didn't have to go shopping." He looked at Jane. "As you discovered, of course."

"Did you ever live there with her?"

He looked puzzled. "No, I had an extremely busy private practice to run, so it made sense to live in the Harley Street flat. But I saw her at every opportunity."

Jane realized he must have started the Peckham clinic after his mother had died. She felt like saying his mother would be turning in her grave if she knew what a monster he had become, but managed to bite her lip. She didn't want to alienate him when he seemed to be opening up to her.

"How did your mother die?" she asked.

"She was a munitions worker during the war, handling cordite and sulfur all day, which fatally damaged her lungs."

Jane decided to turn the screw a little. "In some ways you have been more fortunate than the families of the murder victims, though. You know how your mother died. She also lived long enough to witness your success."

"Edmund Burke once said, 'The only thing necessary for the triumph of evil is for good men to do nothing,'" Simmonds intoned.

Jane didn't understand what point he was trying to make. "Very profound, Mr. Simmonds. But it does beg the question: are you a good or evil man?"

He closed his eyes. "I am both . . . Please, dear God, I need to talk to you, Jane."

She took a deep breath. "Did you commit the murders?" she asked quietly.

It was a moment before Simmonds opened his eyes. He looked at the PC, then slowly turned to Jane. "I need to speak to you alone. I want to make a confession."

Jane could feel her heart beating fast. She turned to the PC. "Please wait outside." She remained sitting for a few moments after he was gone, then leant forward. "Did you commit the murders?"

He nodded. "I want to tell you what happened, and why."

Jane was stunned. She wondered if Simmonds was still playing mind games, but the tortured expression on his face seemed to tell her otherwise.

"I'll need DCI Moran to be present."

He shook his head. "No. I don't want Moran or any other officer in the room. Otherwise I'll tell you nothing."

Jane knew that police regulations advised another officer should be present when a murder suspect was interviewed, but it was not actually a legal requirement under the Judges' Rules of evidence. She opened the interview book and clicked her ball-point pen.

Simmonds leant over and put his hand on the book. "No notes."

"Legally I'm required to take notes, otherwise your confession may be ruled inadmissible in court," Jane told him.

"Don't worry. I'll tell you everything, then make a handwritten confession myself."

"How do I know you'll do that?"

"Because when you hear what I have to say, you'll know I'm telling you the truth."

Jane felt she was in a catch-22 situation. Reluctantly, she closed the interview book and put her pen down.

"The first thing I need you to know is that I'm not a child molester," he began. "I swear I never abused Simon Matthews."

Jane nodded. "But did Helen Matthews, his mother, think you had?"

Simmonds took a deep breath. "Yes, that's why she came to see me at my Peckham surgery."

"Do you recall what date that was?"

"Friday the sixteenth of February."

"What time?"

"Late afternoon or early evening. I'd finished with my last patient and was tidying up when the doorbell rang. Helen stormed in, shouting and accusing me of sexually abusing Simon. I told her it was lies, but she didn't believe me."

"Did she say why she thought you'd abused Simon?"

"She said he'd told her he didn't like me touching him. I couldn't for the life of me understand why he would say that."

Jane nodded. As much as she disliked the thought, she knew she'd have to be sympathetic to keep Simmonds talking.

"I think that Simon was bullied at school about his braces. It's possible Helen misconstrued what he told her, and she decided to confront you."

"She never mentioned anything to me about him being bullied."

"Did she mention anyone else expressing concerns about Simon being abused?"

"Yes. Helen only suspected there was a problem because Simon's teacher told her she thought he was being abused."

Jane raised her biro. "Would that teacher be Eileen Summers?"

"I'm sorry, I need to explain everything in the order it happened. As I was saying, I reminded Helen that she'd always been present when I treated Simon, so her accusations couldn't be true."

"If that was the case then why didn't she believe you?" Jane asked.

"I pleaded with her to realize it was absurd and she eventually calmed down. We then went into the waiting room to continue the discussion." Simmonds paused and took a deep breath before continuing.

"Helen was sitting on the sofa. I asked her if she'd told anyone else about Simon, or had been to the police. She thought my questions implied that I was guilty, so she stood up and said that was exactly where she was going. She started to walk towards the door . . . I don't know what came over me."

He looked at the floor then put his head in his hands. "Oh my God, Oh my God . . . I didn't know what I was doing at the time, but now I relive the moment over and over. I snatched a curtain tie and followed the poor woman into the hallway. She had her back to me and was about to open the front door. Something came over me . . . I wrapped the curtain tie round her neck and pulled hard . . ."

"David, the cord round Helen's neck was tied in a slip knot. Can you explain how you had time to tie it if you were acting on impulse and didn't know what you were doing?"

"I did that after she was dead, then cut the tassels off, so it wasn't obvious it was a curtain tie."

Jane kept her voice quiet and encouraging. "I see. So what happened next?"

"She was struggling and kicking. I pulled her to the ground and somehow she ended up face down on the hallway carpet. I knelt on her back and tightened the cord . . . Eventually she stopped moving."

Jane recalled Professor Martin saying that the killer had knelt on Helen's back in order to stop her getting up or struggling. It seemed Simmonds was telling the truth.

"I didn't mean to kill her. I was frightened that a sexual abuse allegation would destroy my career. I had this terrible sense of panic and didn't know what I was doing." He sighed. "I was standing over her. I couldn't believe what I'd done . . . It was all like a bad dream. Then the doorbell rang. It kept ringing and ringing. Then I heard knocking on the window and her voice asking over and over if I was there."

"Did you know who the woman was?" Jane realized she would be a valuable witness.

His reply came as a shock.

"It was Sybil Hastings. She knew I drove a Mercedes, which was parked outside, and all the lights were on in the surgery and hallway. I was worried that if I didn't answer the door she might think something had happened to me and call the police."

Jane leant forward. "Wait a minute—wasn't Helen Matthews' body still in the hallway?"

Simmonds was getting impatient. "Yes, yes. I had to quickly drag her body into the surgery, out of sight."

Jane encouraged him to continue. "OK, you're in a terrible state of panic. So then you let Sybil Hastings in?"

"Yes. She kissed me on the cheek, then asked if I was dealing with a patient. I said no—"

"Sorry, did you say she kissed you?" Jane interrupted. She thought it strange that Mrs. Hastings would greet him in that way if she suspected him of child abuse.

"I wasn't just her dentist. We were friends . . . She always greeted me with a kiss."

"Then what happened?"

"Sybil looked upset. She said that she'd received a distressing phone call whilst she had been on duty at the Samaritans on Thursday evening. I told her I was running late for a dinner engagement and asked if we could discuss it at another time. 'No,' she said, 'this can't wait.'"

Jane was sure the distressing phone call was from Eileen Summers. She realized she needed to chase up the documents section at the lab to see if they had examined the indented writing Lawrence had recovered from the Samaritans call sheet. She thought about Simmonds having a conversation with Mrs. Hastings whilst the dead body of Helen Matthews was in his surgery, only a few feet away.

"What was the distressing the phone call about?" she asked.

"Sybil said she'd had a call from a concerned teacher, who thought a young pupil of hers was being sexually abused. And she could hardly believe it, but she said the abuse was being carried out by a dentist in Peckham."

"I'm trying to keep up with you, David. Are you saying you killed Sybil Hastings because she suspected you'd abused Simon Matthews?"

Simmonds looked offended and shook his head. "No, no, no. Sybil didn't think *I'd* abused him. She never thought for one minute the teacher was talking about *me*. I'm her grandchildren's dentist. They adore me."

Jane was confused. "So why had Mrs. Hastings come to see you?"

"I'm trying to make this as clear as possible, Jane. You have to listen to what I'm saying. Sybil Hastings had come to me because she wanted to ask me if there was any dentist in Peckham I thought might be capable of such a monstrous act. I told her I would make some discreet enquires and get back to her, and then if necessary we could go to the police together. She thanked me and got up to leave." He ran his hands through his hair.

"So Sybil Hastings was murdered after she left your Peckham practice? Who by?"

Simmonds slowly looked up. His eyes were cold. "I never said she left."

Jane wondered if he was starting to play mind games again. "If you're saying you killed her, then why? Sybil Hastings didn't suspect you of anything."

"She suddenly heard a noise coming from my surgery. I realized in an instant that Helen Matthews must still be alive. Before I could stop her, Sybil opened the surgery door and saw Helen lying on the floor. She was struggling to breathe and trying to remove the cord from around her neck."

Simmonds took a sip of his water.

Jane couldn't begin to imagine the sheer terror the two women must have felt at that moment in time. She wondered if Simmonds was deliberately pausing to see if the horror of what he was describing was upsetting her. She was determined not to show it.

"You must have been panic-stricken."

"You have no idea. I was hysterical. I . . . picked up a dental chisel and stabbed Sybil. She was screeching and waving her arms as she backed away into the waiting room. Then she stumbled and fell to the floor. I will never forget what I did next . . . She lay there looking up at me and I couldn't help myself, I just kept stabbing her." He raised his right arm and made several quick stabbing gestures.

Jane could hardly believe Simmonds was admitting to brutally murdering two women, with no emotion in his voice. It was as if he considered himself to be the victim, and his actions had been forced on him by the predicament he had found himself in. Before Jane could say anything, he continued.

"I went back into the surgery. Helen was on her stomach, dragging herself towards the door. I was forced to pull the cord tighter around her neck until I was sure she was dead. I don't think you can believe what a nightmare situation I found myself in, suddenly having two dead bodies to dispose of. I had to compose myself and think what to do next. I found Sybil Hastings' car keys in her pocket. I looked out of the window and could see that she'd parked it outside the surgery. I waited until after midnight when there was no one about, then I carried Helen Matthews' body to Sybil's car and put her in the passenger seat. I went back and got Sybil's body and put it in the boot. It was a tight squeeze because she had a thick fur coat on, but I was now working on automatic pilot. I had decided that I would dump Helen Matthews' body in Bussey Alley, then drive out to the Kent countryside to hide Sybil's body in woodland and set her car alight with a can of petrol I'd already got from my own car. After I'd dumped Helen's body, I discovered the Allegro had a flat tire and I panicked. A man was walking past the car, so I decided to just leave it where it was. I went back to the surgery, cleaned up Sybil's blood, then drove home to Harley Street."

Simmonds had spittle forming in the corners of his mouth. He wiped it with his forefinger and suddenly seemed disinclined to continue.

"Did you rape or sexually assault Helen Matthews before you killed her?"

He glared at Jane. "No, I did not. I'm not a rapist. I had to protect myself. I needed to make it look as if someone else had raped her. She was already dead when I scratched the inside of her thighs and ripped her clothing. And I obviously did a good job of it, because all the headlines reported that a rape victim had been found in Bussey Alley."

After everything he'd just described, the pride in his voice was unmistakable. Jane's desire to physically assault him was almost overwhelming. She decided she needed a break to compose herself.

"Please excuse me, Mr. Simmonds, I need to take a break."

"I hope you're not using it as an excuse to tell DCI Moran or your colleagues about our conversation. I've got more to tell you and if you come back with anyone else I will deny everything."

"I'm not going to tell Moran. If I did, he'd stop the interview," Jane said, knowing that she still needed Simmonds to tell her about how he killed Eileen Simmonds and Aiden Lang.

She walked to the door and asked the custody PC to enter the room until she returned. She quickly went into the ladies'. Having to listen to Simmonds' litany of horrific assaults had really shaken her. She washed her hands and splashed cold water over her face. She took several deep breaths, then checked her appearance in the mirror.

"You can do this." She gripped the edge of the basin. "Get back in there, Tennison." She stared in the mirror at her ashen face. She wasn't sure she had the strength to hear what Simmonds was going to tell her.

CHAPTER TWENTY-EIGHT

Jane met Gibbs in the stairwell down from the canteen.

"I've been looking for you," she said.

"Moran is getting himself really pumped up for the interrogation. We've now got even more incriminating evidence from forensics, so we can charge that bastard for all four murders. Did he sign the interview yet?"

Jane nodded. "I need to talk to you, Gibbs. Simmonds is still in the interview room . . . and he's making a full confession."

Gibbs whistled. "Does Moran know about this?"

Jane clenched her fists. "No, not yet. Simmonds is getting some kind of sick pleasure in telling me in graphic detail about exactly how he murdered Helen Matthews and Sybil Hastings. He hasn't even got to Eileen Summers or Aiden Lang yet. I had to get out of the room for some air."

"Who's doing the interview with you?"

"Please, Spence, just listen to me. After Simmonds signed the record of interview, he suddenly decided to confess to me. I told him I needed another officer present and wanted to get Moran, but he was insistent he would only tell me what happened alone. He threatened that if I left the room or told Moran, he wouldn't say another word."

"What the fuck are you playing at, Jane? You know it's against police regs to do solo interviews in major crime investigations."

"I know, but it's not a legal requirement per se. The man's a sick psychopath. He's cold and calculating, but he wants me to believe he killed out of panic and didn't know what he was doing."

"Sounds like he's trying to run a diminished responsibility defense, so the murders get dropped to manslaughter. You've got everything he's said recorded word for word in the interview book, right?"

Jane shook her head. "Simmonds wouldn't let me take notes. He said he'll make a full handwritten confession after he's told me everything."

"Jesus Christ! If he doesn't, you're screwed, Jane. It will be his word against yours."

"I know that, Spence, but what would you have done? Just walk away with nothing?" Jane was frustrated.

"You'd better go and tell Moran what's been happening right now."

"I told Simmonds I needed a break. If I'm away too long he might think I've spoken with Moran and then he'll say nothing. He's telling me things only the killer could know. I'm confident a court will believe me even if he doesn't make a written confession," Jane said with conviction.

Gibbs held his hands up. "You better hope to Christ he does make a full confession. When you go back in there with Simmonds, keep calm and let him think he's running the show. I've every confidence in you, Jane. Simmonds might never have been arrested if it wasn't for you."

"Thanks, Spence. Can you do me a favor? I still haven't heard back from the lab about the indented writing on the Samaritans call sheet. Could you ring DS Lawrence and ask if he'll chase it up for me?"

"Will do. Are you sure you can handle this?"

"I don't have any other option."

"Don't let Simmonds get to you. He's not worth it."

Gibbs watched Jane walk away and immediately went in search of Moran.

Jane paused by the door of the interview room and took a deep breath to steady her nerves. She opened the door, told the custody PC to wait outside and sat down opposite Simmonds.

She checked her pen, pencils and the interview book were still on the desk.

"Are you willing to continue with your confession, Mr. Simmonds?"

"Of course. Why shouldn't I be?"

Jane got straight to the point. "Did you murder Simon Matthews' teacher, Eileen Summers?"

Simmonds looked at Jane as if she'd asked a ridiculous question. "I wouldn't have hurt anyone if that woman hadn't stuck her nose in. After disposing of Helen's and Sybil's bodies, I was totally exhausted, but I knew I somehow had to get Eileen Summers to agree to meet me, and believe me, it took a great deal of planning. Would you like to know how I lured her to the hostel?"

"You know I would," Jane replied calmly.

"It was simple, really. As a dentist I always try and relax my patients and engage them in conversation before carrying out any treatment. From previous conversations with Simon, I already knew he went to Southfield Primary School in Kentish Town, and his teacher was called Miss Summers. I have a very retentive memory, you know."

"You rang the school, didn't you?" Jane recalled Mrs. Rowlands saying that a Mr. Smith had phoned the school and asked to speak to Miss Summers.

"Yes, I called on the Monday morning and spoke to Eileen Summers. I told her I was a friend of Helen Matthews and that I had information about Simon being abused. I said I'd rather speak to her in person and gave her the hostel address. We arranged to meet in Ben's room at seven o'clock that evening."

Jane held up her hand. "You told me and DCI Moran earlier that you only knew Smith as Benjamin."

"I was lying. He told me his name was Benjamin Smith, but everyone called him Ben."

Jane was curious, and more than a little confused. "Was Ben—or rather, Aiden Lang—still alive when you made that call to Eileen Summers?"

Simmonds seemed irritated by the question. "Yes, he was still alive."

"Was he involved in the murders?" Jane asked.

"Would you stop interrupting and let me finish telling you about Eileen Summers?" he snapped.

Jane put her hands up in a calming gesture. "I'm sorry, carry on."

"I had Ben's keys for the hostel. I made my way past the porter at about ten minutes to seven, then waited in Ben's room. At exactly seven o'clock there was a knock on the door and I opened it. The young woman said she was Eileen Summers and that the hostel porter had kindly allowed her to come to the room. I introduced myself as Ben Smith and invited her in. She hesitated at first, maybe because I didn't look like a resident of the hostel. But when I told her I thought I knew who had been abusing Simon, she walked straight in. She didn't like it when I asked if Simon had said anything about a dentist abusing him, though. When she turned to leave the room, I had that terrible feeling of panic sweeping over me again. You have no notion of what it feels like—the sheer terror. I hardly remember picking up the wine bottle and hitting her with it." Simmonds blinked rapidly and took a deep breath. "Well, you obviously know I strangled her as well."

Jane recalled the ligature mark around Eileen Summers' neck. "Did you use the other curtain tie from your waiting room?"

Simmonds snorted. "I'd say that was pretty obvious, wouldn't you? But this time I made the slip knot and cut the tassels off beforehand, so it wouldn't be obvious it was a curtain tie."

Jane knew Simmonds was lying about the panic attack. He had pre-prepared the curtain tie and taken it to the hostel with the intention of strangling Eileen Summers. It was premeditated murder.

She rolled a pencil back and forth on the desk in front of her, trying to keep her voice steady. "Did you also make it look as if Eileen had been sexually assaulted?"

"Yes, God help me, I did. I used an empty Coca-Cola bottle I found in the room. I took the bottle and her handbag with me when I left via the fire escape, and threw them in a dustbin."

Jane felt sick. She didn't want to know if he had defiled Eileen Summers with the Coca-Cola bottle before or after she had died.

"You've gone very quiet, Jane."

Jane made an effort to compose herself. "I was just wondering where Aiden Lang was while you were at the hostel? He obviously gave you his keys."

"Well, he had to be in one of two places . . ." Simmonds paused.

Jane wondered if he was playing games again. "Where?"

He smiled. "Well, as he was already dead, it had to be either heaven . . . or hell. Take your pick."

Jane tried not to look shocked by his callousness. "So when did you last see him?"

"He came to the Peckham surgery on the same Monday I called Eileen Summers. He was my last patient of the day. I was going to fit a new plate with a porcelain tooth, to replace the temporary plastic one he had been wearing. But I never got to fit it. I killed him instead."

"Was this before you went to the hostel?"

"Well, obviously. As I've already told you, I'd agreed to meet Eileen Summers at seven p.m., and I don't think Lang would have given me his room key willingly—do you?"

"Did Aiden Lang know you'd killed Matthews and Hastings?"

"No."

"Then why did you kill Lang? He'd done nothing to upset or distress you like the three other victims."

Simmonds ground his teeth. "That's where you're wrong, Jane. Aiden Lang was scum. He was blackmailing me—that was why he had to die."

Jane was dubious. "What was he blackmailing you about?"

"It doesn't matter now he's dead. The thing is, I needed a scapegoat, and Ben—or Aiden Lang—was it. I couldn't look a gift horse in the mouth, could I, Jane?" Simmonds said, smiling at his play on words.

Jane hesitated before asking her next question. "I'm just trying to piece everything together, David. We know that Aiden Lang was a homosexual prostitute, a rent boy. Were you in a relationship with him?"

Simmonds looked shocked. "No, I was not! I didn't even know he was a homosexual."

Jane wanted to press him further about his sexuality and his relationship with Aiden Lang, but if he got angry he would stop talking. She decided to change the subject, but before she could ask another question, he continued.

"I never intended to kill Helen Matthews or Sybil Hastings, you know. But after I did, it made me realize how easy it was to take someone's life. It makes you feel very powerful, as if you can do anything you want. Do you understand what I mean?"

Jane kept her face blank, even though her heart was racing. "I suppose it's even more empowering when you actually *plan* to kill someone?"

He nodded enthusiastically. "Absolutely. The planning must be meticulous. As I'm sure you appreciate, Jane, the devil is in the detail."

"What were you wearing when you killed Helen Matthews and Sybil Hastings?"

"My white dental coat, of course."

"I meant specifically when you moved the bodies."

"A tweed jacket."

"Like the one you were wearing in the fishing photograph I saw in your mother's bedroom?"

"Very astute, Jane. Yes, the same one, actually. I planted my jacket and Sybil Hastings' car keys in Aiden Lang's hostel room to frame him for the murders. That was quite clever, don't you think? Rather reminiscent of a Sherlock Holmes mystery."

"So you are quite knowledgeable about forensics and fibers then?"

"I'm an avid Conan Doyle fan. I read about Holmes examining some fibers he'd found on a dead man's coat. He deduced they were shed from the murderer's jacket."

"How did you kill Aiden?" Jane wanted to know if the pathologist's theory about the novocaine was right.

"Oh, you're going back to him, are you? How do you think I killed him?" Simmonds asked with a sneer.

"When he was sitting in your dental chair you injected his tongue with novocaine. A forensic odontologist we consulted said that a lethal dose of novocaine could cause an instant heart attack."

Simmonds gave Jane a slow handclap. "Correct! What a clever girl. No doubt you have also deduced that I skinned his head and removed his fingers because I didn't want anyone to be able to identify him."

Despite her revulsion, Jane humored him. "Your plan was very ingenious. You fooled all of us at the beginning. We thought Lang was a murderer on the run. In fact, you'd probably have got away with it if we hadn't found the body parts."

Simmonds cocked his head to one side. "How did that happen?"

"Foxes scavenging for food ripped open one of the plastic bin bags."

"I must admit that's something I hadn't considered. I thought with the end of the bin strike, all the rubbish in the park would be taken to a landfill site and he'd never be found. How did you manage to identify him?"

"We could only surmise, but with reasonable certainty, that it was Aiden Lang. Officially the coroner hasn't yet formally identified his body, but I'm sure he will be able to now you've confirmed it."

He smiled. "It's the least I could do, under the circumstances."

"Where, and how, did you dismember the body?"

"I thought about taking him out to the cellar, but I couldn't risk one of the neighbors backing onto the house seeing me. So I cut him up in the bathroom, put the body parts in the black bin bags and kept them in the cellar freezer until I was able to dump them in Rye Park."

"What did you use to cut him up?"

"A hacksaw." He laughed.

"What's so funny?"

"These questions and answers are getting to sound a little like a game of Cluedo."

"This is not a game to me, David." Jane found she couldn't maintain her façade of neutrality any longer. "To be honest, I find your attitude completely sickening."

He looked chagrined. "I'm sorry. It wasn't my intention to upset you. Please carry on with your questions, Jane."

"There had been a recent fire in the garden. Was that how you destroyed some of the evidence?"

"Only the rags I used to clean up the blood, and Sybil Hastings' pocket date book, which had my name and address in it."

"What did you do with Lang's fingers? We didn't find any of them in the park."

"I put them in a bag with a large stone and threw them into the Thames from Lambeth Bridge."

"Was that after you used two of Lang's severed fingers to plant his fingerprints at Helen Matthews' and Eileen Summers' flats?"

Simmonds started rocking in his chair. "The idea came to me whilst I was cutting up the body. Because Simon Matthews was a patient, I knew where Helen lived and still had the keys to her flat. Summers' keys were in her handbag, along with a letter addressed to her. I put two of Aiden's fingers from his right hand into a jar, then went to Helen and Sybil's flats and made it look like the rooms had been ransacked by him. Really terribly clever, don't you think?"

Jane couldn't help herself from bringing Simmonds down a peg or two. "It wasn't all that clever, David. It didn't take long for our fingerprint experts to realize every print was from the first or second finger of Aiden Lang's left hand, which started us wondering."

Simmonds' rocking became more energetic. "It still fooled you, though, didn't it? Everything pointed to Aiden Lang. You'd have been none the wiser if you hadn't found his body."

"But it didn't fool us, David. Or you wouldn't have been arrested."

Simmonds stopped rocking and leant forward. "Without my confession, neither you, Moran, nor any of your so-called detectives would have enough evidence to prove I murdered anyone. Without my confession you'd have nothing!"

"Don't flatter yourself," Jane replied evenly. "You've tried to be too clever for your own good. For all the awards you've received, you're actually one of life's failures. The only positive outcome of your confession is that I can at least tell the families what happened to their loved ones and give them some form of closure. Aiden Lang posed no threat to you. He was an innocent victim, an opportunity for you to distance yourself from the murders. You used him—"

"Aiden Lang was a disgusting guttersnipe."

"He was a small-time thief. A rent boy with a drug habit, that's all."

"I told you already: he was blackmailing me. Why do I have to keep repeating myself?"

"I don't believe you." She stood up and went over to the filing cabinet in the corner of the room and took out some confession statement forms. "Are you still willing to make a written confession?"

"Aiden Lang approached me outside my Harley Street clinic when I was leaving one night."

Jane put the confession forms on the table and sat down. "When was this?"

"I don't know exactly, but it was weeks before he first attended my Peckham clinic."

"Tell me what happened."

"I was leaving the Harley Street clinic to go to my favorite Italian restaurant. He walked up to me and said something, but I didn't hear him properly. I asked what he wanted, and he said, 'It's not what I want, it's about what you want.' He then offered me . . . his services. He seemed drunk or high on drugs. I was outraged."

"If you're worried about telling me exactly what words he used, don't be. I won't be offended."

"I didn't want to repeat his foul words. But he actually said he'd suck my cock for twenty pounds or I could fuck him for forty. I told him he was disgusting and to go away or I would call the police. He laughed in my face and said if I didn't give him some money he'd start shouting in the street that I'd approached him for sex." Simmonds was becoming increasingly agitated.

"Did you give him any money?"

He nodded. "Twenty pounds. He clicked his fingers and said he wanted more. I gave him another ten and turned to walk away. He grabbed my arm and said he wanted a weekly payment. You understand why I had to pay him, don't you?"

"Not really, no. And if he was blackmailing you, why did you give him dental treatment?"

"When I first met him there was nothing wrong with his teeth, but then it became part of the blackmail deal. I met him in the West End a week later to give him more money. He said someone had knocked out his tooth and he wanted me to fix it. I agreed to do it, but at the Peckham clinic, for obvious reasons."

"Did you ever have any form of sex with Aiden Lang?"

"No! I already told you I am not a homosexual!"

From his frantic manner, Jane sensed that he was lying. It was obvious that Aiden Lang was more than just a patient to him.

Simmonds pushed his chair back and crossed his arms. "I have finished my confession. I have nothing more to say to you, Sergeant Tennison."

Jane picked up a pencil and tapped the point on the table. "I don't think you're telling me the truth." She was nervous, knowing that she herself was about to embellish the truth, in an attempt to gain further information.

"David, we have made some enquiries into your military service. We have spoken to an army SIB officer, who told us that you were found in bed with an eighteen-year-old cook in your officer's accommodation. You didn't leave the army voluntarily; you jumped before you were pushed. I think you were lucky the whole incident was covered up. Otherwise you'd have been court-martialed and sent to prison."

Simmonds was physically shaking. "It's all lies! The whole incident was a total misunderstanding."

"What, you just woke up and happened to find a young man in your bed? Listen, David, I don't care about your sexuality."

Simmonds glared at her. "It was a drunken, one-off incident. I paid the price and was hounded out of the army. My mother raised me to be a devout Christian. I do not have a girlfriend and I am celibate."

"Personally, I very much doubt the army incident was a one-off. Your denial regarding any relationship with Aiden Lang is also a lie. Did your doting, overprotective mother know why you really had to leave the army? Did she want to protect your reputation in the outside world by encouraging you to be celibate?"

"Don't you dare make insinuations about my mother!"

Jane kept going. "I think she would be turning in her grave if she knew what you had become. Perhaps you've always been envious of her love for your brother, and in some sick, perverted way, to get back at her, you dismembered Aiden Lang's body and skinned his head."

Simmonds was losing control. His hands clenched as she pressed on.

"I think you and Aiden Lang were in a sexual relationship. He wasn't blackmailing you, and you frequently and willingly paid him for sex."

Jane pushed her chair back, stood up and slid the confession forms across the desk towards Simmonds.

He leant forward. "I have a question for you, Jane: do you think I've killed anyone else?"

Jane wondered if Simmonds could have developed a lust for murder, and there might be more victims they didn't yet know about. The thought chilled her.

"Have you?"

"No, but I was this close." He held his right thumb and forefinger an inch apart. "Guess who it was?"

"Your little mind games don't bother me, David."

"But they should, Jane, they should."

"If you've killed more people, then tell me and I will listen. If you haven't, then don't waste my time—"

Simmonds suddenly stood up and pointed his finger at her. "It was you, Jane. *You* were going to be my next victim!" he shouted.

Jane reacted with fury. "Sit down NOW!" she shouted back and shoved the table hard, making him fall back onto his chair. "You don't scare me, Simmonds. You disgust me!"

The interview room door flew open and the custody PC rushed in. "You all right, Sarge?"

"Yes, everything's fine. You can wait outside." She was wide-eyed and breathing hard.

"You sure, Sarge?"

"Yes, I'm sure!" She didn't feel fine—far from it. But she needed the PC to leave them alone before she continued.

Looking uneasy, he left the room and closed the door behind him.

Jane turned back to Simmonds. "Whatever you say now doesn't matter. The career you were so proud of is over and you will spend the rest of your life in prison. You might get away with pleading diminished responsibility and be sent to a secure psychiatric hospital like Broadmoor, but let me tell you, life in there is worse than a normal prison. It's like hell on earth. I've had to listen to your sickening justifications for your crimes and watch you gloat over your success as a dentist, while pretending to care about the less fortunate. I seemed to upset you when I made reference to your mother. She had to suffer the terrible trauma of having to identify the decapitated body of her most precious son, and what did you do? You filled the deep freeze with little home-cooked meals, pretending to care about her, and yet in that same deep freeze you put the butchered body of Aiden Lang. Not content with that horror, you skinned his head, cut out his tongue and chopped off his fingers—all to hide your sexual preferences—"

"STOP IT!" Simmonds collapsed back in his chair, his mouth wide open. He started to cry, sounding like a lost child.

Jane realized her words about his mother had broken him. He still worshipped her and couldn't bear the thought of how she would view his crimes, even though she was dead.

"Are you going to make a written confession?" Jane was worried she had pushed things too far, letting her emotions get the better of her.

But Simmonds was like a deflated balloon, all the defiance gone. "Yes. I will write it. And it will all be done properly, Jane. I need you to ask Mr. Davidge to witness that I have made the statement of my own free will, and countersign it."

"I'll get the custody PC to sit with you while you make your statement."

Jane opened the door and asked the PC to come in.

Simmonds rubbed his hands over his face. "I'm feeling very tired now. Could I go back to my cell for a while?"

"Yes, of course. I'll ask Mr. Davidge to come to the station, then you can sit with him and make your statement."

"Thank you, Jane."

Jane nodded to the custody officer, who walked Simmonds out of the interview room and back to his cell. Jane felt her legs give way as she sank back into her seat and put her head in her hands, utterly exhausted.

CHAPTER TWENTY-NINE

Jane called Davidge as soon as she got back to the CID office. He seemed surprised when she told him Simmonds now wanted legal representation.

"He wants to make a written confession and have you present as a witness."

"He's confessed?"

"Yes, to the murders of three women and a young man called Aiden Lang."

Davidge paused. "We'll see about that. I'm coming to the station right now and I'd like you to advise him to do nothing until I get there."

Jane put the phone down and went to see Moran in his office. He was talking to Gibbs, who looked a little sheepish when he saw her.

"I decided it was best to tell the governor what was happening."

Moran frowned at her. "You should have told me he wanted to confess, Jane. It should have been my decision whether or not you continued to interview Simmonds."

"I'm sorry, sir. Simmonds was adamant he would only confess to me, with nobody else in the room, and he wouldn't allow me to make any notes."

"What's done is done, I suppose. As much as I'd have liked to have been there, I would probably have done the same if I'd been in your shoes."

"Do you want me to go over what he said in detail or are you happy with a condensed version for now?" Jane asked.

Moran told her a quick summary was fine and Jane recounted Simmonds' key admissions, whilst Moran jotted down notes. Then she told him about her phone call with Davidge.

"Good job, Jane. Simmonds might be lying about some things or change his story in the handwritten confession. I want you to write down his version of events in a statement, while they're still fresh in your memory. You can use my office."

"The conversation was off the record as far as Simmonds was concerned. Davidge will no doubt argue my statement is inadmissible."

"Jane, I don't give a toss about Davidge. Simmonds confessed to four murders. He was still under caution and said things only the murderer could know. A judge at trial will decide what is or isn't admissible as evidence. I'll countersign your statement as the same truthful version of events that you recounted to me."

"Thank you, sir." Jane looked at Gibbs. "Did you ask Lawrence about the indented writing?"

"Yeah. He said the lab were still working on it."

Moran stood up. "Right, Spence, you can buy me lunch. If you need me, Jane, give me a shout."

"Thank you, sir."

Jane sat quietly in Moran's office, concentrating hard on remembering everything Simmonds had said. Thankfully a lot of her suspicions had proved to be right, which helped in compiling the statement. She wondered how Simmonds had managed to appear a pillar of society for so long, when underneath his kind and gentle persona raged an unstable mind. Jane reflected on how his carefully constructed façade had crumbled to pieces when Helen Matthews said she was going to tell the police he was a child abuser and he'd snapped—causing a brutal chain reaction. Jane also wondered if Simmonds' relationship with Lang, sexual or not, had precipitated a psychological crisis that acted as some sort of catalyst for the murders. She doubted Simmonds would ever tell the truth about his sexuality or the nature of his relationship with Lang. But it didn't matter now. The important thing was that Simmonds had confessed to murdering him.

It was nearly two hours later when Moran entered the room with Gibbs.

Jane looked up. "I've nearly finished, sir."

Moran looked pleased, opening his notebook. "I just spoke with Lawrence on the phone about the bin bags."

"And?"

"Thankfully he gave me the details in layman's terms, which were . . ." Moran read from his notes. "'The striation marks on the body part bags are the same as the ones under the sink at the Peckham surgery. There's also a perfect mechanical fit on the torn edge of the bag the head was in and the next bag on the roll under the sink.' That's enough to nail him for Lang's murder even if he retracts his confession." Moran turned a page in his notebook. "Fibers from the curtain ties used to strangle Helen Matthews and Eileen Summers matched fibers recovered from the waiting room curtains. The same fibers were also found in the pocket of Simmonds' winter coat, which I'm guessing he wore when he went to kill Eileen Summers."

Jane's eyes lit up. "He's not as forensically savvy as he likes to think. What about the testing of the eye fluid for novocaine?"

"We're waiting for a result on that," Moran said.

"Everything you just said about the forensic results on the ligatures fits with what Simmonds told me in his confession."

Moran's desk phone rang. He spoke briefly with the caller. "You can take Davidge through to the interview room and tell him one of us will be with him shortly. But don't let him see Simmonds yet." Moran put the phone down.

"I'll make a copy of my statement so far for Davidge to read, then get Simmonds out of his cell so he can write his confession with Davidge present."

"Whoa, slow down, Jane. I want to read your statement before Davidge or Simmonds. You don't need to tell Davidge anything for now. Just give him and Simmons the confession forms and let them get on with it. You can finish your statement later."

"I've already finished it, sir." But she knew it wasn't a complete record of what had been said between them. She had made no reference in her statement to the fact that Simmonds had threatened her, or that the custody PC had entered the room after hearing him shouting at her. And she had omitted her comments about Simmonds' mother, and his dishonorable conduct in the army.

Jane took the cell keys from the duty sergeant and asked the custody PC to accompany her when she escorted Simmonds to the interview room. She opened the wicket on Simmonds' cell door and peered in, but couldn't see him.

Jane turned to the PC. "Has he been taken for a walk in the yard, or for a wash?"

"Not that I know of."

Jane turned back to the door and raised her voice. "Mr. Simmonds, please show yourself. Mr. Davidge is here to see you."

"I checked on him half an hour ago and he was there," the PC assured her.

"Well, he can't have bloody well escaped. Open the door," Jane told him.

As the cell door opened, she could see Simmonds lying face down by the door, with a pool of blood around his head.

"Get an ambulance!" Jane shouted.

The PC knelt and put two fingers on Simmonds' neck. "There's no pulse. He's dead."

"Are you sure?" Jane felt for a pulse herself, but there was nothing.

CHAPTER THIRTY

The PC left Jane with Simmonds' body whilst he went to inform the duty sergeant of the death. Jane couldn't believe it. She crouched down and looked at the back of Simmonds' head, but there was no noticeable injury. Could he have fallen over and split his forehead open on the floor? She slowly lifted his head. His face was covered in blood, but there was no visible injury.

"What the hell have you done to him?" Davidge shouted.

"Nothing. We opened the cell door and found him like this."

Davidge scowled at her. "I don't believe you!"

The duty sergeant approached the cell. "Back off, Davidge. Simmonds was checked half an hour ago and he was fine."

"I want Simmonds examined by an independent doctor," Davidge insisted.

"I'm calling a forensic pathologist to examine the body in situ, and a lab liaison sergeant to examine the scene," the sergeant replied firmly.

"I want to be present when that happens," Davidge told him.

The duty sergeant ushered him away from the cell. "Please go and wait in the station foyer."

As Davidge walked off, the sergeant took Jane to one side.

"I'm playing this by the book, Sergeant Tennison, and not just because Davidge is here, but to protect you, Moran and everyone else involved in the investigation."

Jane knocked nervously on Moran's door before opening it. He was on the phone with a smile on his face and waved for her to sit down.

"That's unbelievable . . . Cutting his first tooth . . . But isn't he too young? . . . Are you sure he said it? . . . I can't wait to come home . . . Yes, I hopefully won't be too late."

Replacing the receiver, Moran clapped his hands. "Did you hear that? Cutting his first tooth, which explains why he's been so ratty. And he said 'Dada'! Could just be wind, of course, but—" From the expression on Jane's face, he knew something was wrong. "What is it?"

Before she could say anything, they were interrupted by a knock at the door. The duty sergeant entered and looked at Moran.

"SOCOs finished taking photographs and Professor Martin should be here in about five minutes. I spoke with A10 and they're happy for DS Lawrence to deal with the scene."

Moran looked confused. "What? Don't tell me we've had another bloody murder. And what's A10 got to do with it?"

The sergeant looked at Jane.

Moran banged his fist on the desk. "Will someone tell me what's going on?"

Jane took a deep breath. "I found Simmonds dead in his cell."

Moran, Gibbs, Jane and the duty sergeant watched as Professor Martin and DS Lawrence carefully examined Simmonds' head. Davidge was taking notes.

"How do you think he died?" Moran asked.

"In the interests of my client, Mr. Simmonds, I'd like to see the detective sergeant's notes of his alleged confession."

Moran turned on him. "For Christ's sake, shut up, Davidge. Your client's hardly in a position to deny it now, is he!"

Martin took some medical pliers out of his bag and inserted the end in Simmonds' left ear, which was covered in congealed blood. He slowly pulled out a six-inch pencil with blood and brain matter stuck to it. Gibbs and Moran looked at each other in shock. Jane recognized it as one of her pencils, and realized with horror that when he asked to be returned to his cell, Simmonds must have slipped it into his pocket with the intention of using it to kill himself.

Martin placed the pencil in an exhibits bag. "I'd say he put the pencil a little way in his ear, then lay sideways on the floor so it was touching the ground. Once in this position he placed his right hand on his head and rammed it towards the ground, causing the pencil to penetrate the brain. He would have died slowly through blood loss and brain hemorrhaging. 'Slowly'—in this case being a matter of minutes rather than seconds."

Davidge looked stunned. "Why wasn't my client searched before being put in the cell?"

"I can assure you he was searched, and all his pockets emptied. He must have hidden the pencil somewhere in the cell," the duty sergeant replied.

"I guess this is a case where the pen, or rather pencil, is mightier than the sword," Gibbs quipped, to nervous laughter.

Davidge was white as a sheet.

"Spence, Jane—my office," Moran ordered.

"I'd like to see Sergeant Tennison's statement," Davidge insisted.

Moran sighed. "No need to be so impatient, Mr. Davidge. I've not even read it yet."

"I'm entitled to a copy on my client's behalf."

"Simmonds is hardly a client anymore, and as you can see, he isn't going anywhere. I'll get a copy of the statement to your office tomorrow morning."

Davidge walked off without another word.

Gibbs watched him go. "He'll soon lose interest. A dead man isn't going to stand trial, let alone pay him, so there's nothing in it for him."

As Moran, Gibbs and Martin walked down the corridor, Jane stayed behind to have a quick word with Lawrence.

"The pencil was mine, Paul. Simmonds must have taken it when we were in the interview room."

"Well, if I were you, I'd say nothing. He's committed suicide and that's that. If he didn't have the pencil he'd have found another way."

"But I might have pushed him to suicide."

"Don't be silly," Lawrence chided.

"I'm not. I brought up the army thing and the young cook he slept with. I also asked if he was in a sexual relationship with Aiden Lang. It seemed to affect him. Then when I said his mother would be disgusted with him, he broke down." Jane couldn't bring herself to tell Lawrence exactly what she had said to Simmonds about his jealousy towards his brother and his mother hiding the fact he was a homosexual.

"I hope you haven't put any of that in your statement, Jane. The army stuff is hearsay. There's no record of it, so A10 could say you lied to a suspect in an effort to extract a confession."

"I haven't put it in. And thanks for chasing up the indented writing."

"No problem. Pity there was . . . nothing of interest," Lawrence said hesitantly.

Jane tilted her head to one side. "Why do I get the feeling you're not telling me something, Paul?"

"It doesn't matter now. Simmonds is dead."

"It does matter to me, Paul. Did the indented writing reveal something?"

Lawrence checked to make sure no one could overhear them. "The document section still hadn't had a chance to examine it so I took a look myself. It was hard to make out, because Sybil Hastings had written a few notes across the page, not down as you'd normally expect."

"What was on it?" Jane asked apprehensively.

Paul took a piece of paper out of his pocket and handed it to Jane.

"Eileen Summers teacher . . . Dentist Peckham . . . ?"

"Lang and the women were already dead before you got the Samaritans forms, Jane." Paul put his hand on Jane's shoulder. "I only spotted some of the indented writing was across the page through experience. As the forensics officer in the case, I should have taken the time to examine it before submitting it to the document section."

"Will you have to mention the indented writing in your forensic report?"

"I don't want either of us getting hauled over the coals about something that's of no evidential value now. I'm going to say I couldn't find any identifiable handwriting or indentations that could be attributed to Sybil Hastings. Let sleeping dogs lie, learn from mistakes and move on."

The duty sergeant walked down the cell passageway towards them.

"I've had a word with the custody PC. Apparently Simmonds asked if he could have some plain paper and a pen so he could start writing his confession. The PC gave him a few sheets of A4 paper and a pen. I asked him if it could have been a pencil and he said it might have been. Anyway, that clears the matter up and should satisfy A10 since prisoners are allowed writing material."

"Thanks, Sarge." Lawrence turned to Jane. "We didn't find any confession, did we?" He lifted up the plastic mattress in Simmonds' cell, revealing a folded sheet of paper. He handed it to Jane. "Take it to Moran and let him decide what to do with it."

Jane went to Moran's office and gave him the sheet of paper. Gibbs stood beside Moran, reading over his shoulder.

I, David Simmonds, am totally innocent of the murders I am accused of. Detectives Tennison and Moran have ignored all evidence that points to the real killer being a man called Aiden Lang, whom I knew as Benjamin "Ben" Smith. I gave him a Harris tweed jacket and he repaid my kindness by stealing items of property from my premises (dental chisel, curtain tie backs) and used them in the commission of his crimes. Because of Tennison and Moran's desire to arrest a suspect AT ALL COSTS, my reputation and career have been destroyed. They have made me an outcast in a world where I was respected for my achievements and honoured for my charitable work. I find myself in a position where I have no choice other than to end my life. The police have driven me to suicide through their biased and ruthless quest to frame me.

Signed: David Simmonds

Moran looked furious. "There'll be a coroner's inquest into Simmonds' death. If these notes are part of it, the press will have a field day saying we got the wrong man for the 'Murder Mile' killings. I'm not having Simmonds laugh at us from his grave."

He tore the page in half and then quarters, before throwing the pieces into a confidential waste bag.

"Anyone have a problem with this?" Moran asked.

"Not at all," Gibbs replied.

They both looked at Jane.

"No, sir. As you said, it's all lies."

"What are you going to tell DCS Blake?" Gibbs asked.

"That Simmonds made a full confession to WDS Tennison, then committed suicide because he couldn't live with what he'd done."

"Thank you, sir," Jane said.

"Be wary of Blake, Jane. He doesn't like what you know about his involvement with Simmonds and Andrew Hastings. He won't say anything to your face, but behind the scenes he will try and persuade other people that you're not up to the job. So watch your back."

"Thank you. I appreciate the warning."

"We may still get a slap on the wrist and some words of advice from A10," Moran said.

Jane shrugged. "I've been in the firing line with A10 before. But I was naive back then. I can justify my actions from start to finish where the investigation against Simmonds is concerned—even the fact I mistook his mother's bedroom for the toilet, I reckon."

Moran laughed. "I was wrong about you, Tennison. You're much wiser than your years in the job would suggest. You're turning into an excellent detective and earning the respect of your colleagues. Next time you have a hunch or gut feeling, speak up. I for one will listen. Go and finish your statement then bring it to me to read. Make a copy as well so I can show A10 that your interview skills led to Simmonds' confession."

"Yes, sir." Jane left the room, glowing from Moran's words of praise.

Gibbs waited until Jane had closed the door. "You know A10 won't just sweep Simmonds' death under the carpet, guv? They love to screw the department whenever they can. They'll go through the investigation with a fine-tooth comb looking for any fuck ups."

Moran shrugged. "I'm not worried about being interviewed by the rubber heels, Spence. As far as I'm concerned, the 'fuck up' just left the room."

Jane volunteered to deal with the unenviable task of informing the London-based victims' families about Simmonds' arrest, confession and subsequent suicide, while Gibbs travelled to Manchester to inform the Summers family, as he'd already met them when they were in London.

Jane visited Andrew Hastings first. He was still living at his mother's flat, since his wife had apparently asked for a divorce. He was his usual arrogant self and moaned once again about the fact that he'd been arrested. Jane suspected that underneath it all, he'd been hit hard by his mother's death, but he was so self-obsessed, he found it hard to show his emotions. Jane told him the coroner had released his mother's body for burial. Hastings was quick to tell Jane that he didn't want any police at the funeral and asked her to leave.

Hilary Peters cried profusely when Jane told her that her brother, Aiden, was dead. It was of some comfort for her to know that Aiden had been framed by Simmonds and had had no involvement in the women's murders. Even Hilary's husband commented that, regardless of Aiden's sexuality, he didn't deserve to die in the way he did. Both he and Hilary were grateful for all that Jane had done as it proved his innocence, but Hilary was still scathing about Moran's bigotry and the way he had spoken about her brother.

Jane's hardest visit was with Brenda and Simon Matthews. She found it upsetting to see the bright young boy happy to see her. It showed he still had no understanding of what had happened to his mother. Brenda would have liked to see Simmonds spend the rest of his life suffering in prison and felt cheated by his suicide. Jane was about to leave when Simon came up to her holding a drawing book.

"Grandma said to show this to you, Jane, because you are so nice to me and to her." Simon opened the book and handed it to Jane.

The drawing, in pencil and crayon, had "Mummy" written at the top. Helen had a smiley face, red cheeks and brown hair, with a gold halo above her head. She was wearing a long yellow dress with angel wings. A voice balloon coming from her mouth said, "Thank you, Jane."

"You can keep it, if you like."

"That would be lovely. Thank you, Simon. Is it OK if I tear the drawing out as I don't want to take your whole book?"

Simon nodded. Jane gently removed the drawing from the book.

"I'll keep this on my bedroom wall." Jane felt herself well up as she gave Simon a hug and kiss on the cheek.

As Jane left, she looked at her watch and realized she would have to get a move on to get to the church in time for Nathan's 11 a.m. christening.

Simon was in his bedroom and opened the drawing book to the back page. He had already started a picture with the words "Bad Dentist" written at the top of the page. Picking up a red crayon, he started to draw the devil's horns on the head of the dentist. He had been too frightened to ever tell anyone about what had happened.

Jane parked and ran up the gravel driveway to the church. Her mother was pacing up and down at the doors. She was wearing a wide-brimmed hat, tailored navy suit and crisp frilled white blouse.

"You're late," her mother said sternly.

"Sorry, I got caught up with work."

"Really, Jane, there are times when family should come first."

Biting back a sarcastic retort, Jane took Simon's drawing out of her coat pocket. "I was visiting the little boy whose mother was murdered. He gave me this." Jane handed the drawing to her mother. "Things like this reassure me that what I do as a police officer is worthwhile."

Mrs. Tennison looked at the picture briefly and handed it back. "It's a lovely drawing."

Jane realized her mother hadn't looked at it properly.

"Everyone's waiting inside for you. Pinch your cheeks, dear. You look all washed out. You should have let Pam do your hair."

Jane followed her mother into the church. She ran her fingers through her hair and, even though she loathed doing it, pinched her cheeks.

Pam, Tony and his brother, who was to be the godfather, were standing at the christening font with the vicar. There was a small gathering of close family and friends sitting in the front two pews.

"You cut that fine," Pam whispered.

"Sorry, heavy traffic."

Pam gave her a knowing smile. "You shouldn't tell fibs in church."

"Can I hold Nathan?" Jane asked.

"Of course. You're his godmother!" Pam handed him over.

Jane could feel the warmth of his body through the white christening gown as she cradled him. His little face glowed with innocent happiness as he let out a gurgled laugh and smiled at her.

It was an emotional moment for Jane as the vicar baptized Nathan with holy water and made the sign of the cross on his forehead. She saw her parents' adoring glances fixed on their grandchild, whilst Pam's eyes brimmed with tears of pride as she held Tony's hand.

Jane held Nathan closer to her chest, silently vowing that she would always protect him.

ACKNOWLEDGMENTS

To my fantastic team at La Plante Global: Nigel Stoneman, Tory Macdonald and Veronica Goldstein. You keep the wheels turning and the engine running—thank you so much.

Huge thanks to all my publishers: Everyone at Bonnier Zaffre in London and New York—you are wonderful to work with and make the publishing process a joy for me. My international publishers, Allen and Unwin in Australia and Jonathan Ball in South Africa—I look forward to seeing you soon. And to the international publishers who translate my books into French, Japanese, Italian, Polish, Danish, Swedish . . . Je vous remercie, ありがとうございました, Grazie, Dziękuję Ci, Tak skal du have, Tack . . .

Thank you to all the retailers who sell my books and promote them. You are always so creative and enthusiastic, and I still get a great thrill when I see my books on the shelves.

To all the media who have reviewed, interviewed, blogged and supported me and my books for many years—thank you so much, especially to Sarah Oliver, Malcolm Prince and Graham Norton.

Last, but by no means least—to you, my wonderful readers. Thank you for reading my books and for all the wonderful messages you send me via my website, Facebook and Twitter. I really do love hearing from you, and your kind words and positive feedback are what make me continue writing. I am forever grateful.

Lynda La Plante

Readers' Club

If you enjoyed *Murder Mile*, why not join the
LYNDA LA PLANTE READERS' CLUB by visiting
www.bit.ly/LyndaLaPlanteClub?

A MESSAGE FROM LYNDA LA PLANTE...

Dear Reader,

Thank you very much for picking up *Murder Mile*, the fourth novel in the Jane Tennison thriller series. I've been so pleased by the response I've had from the many readers who have been curious about the beginnings of Jane's police career. It's been great fun for me to explore how she became the woman we know in middle and later life from the *Prime Suspect* series and I hope you have enjoyed reading this book as much as I enjoyed writing it.

I still remember the miserable "Winter of Discontent" in which *Murder Mile* is set. Looking back, it seemed like a particularly bleak time for Britain, but at the time, we just got on with our lives and made the best of it. I was interested, however, in what effect the three-day week and the many strikes we faced might have on a murder investigation—and on the police officers running it. I was also interested in what life then might have been like for the young Jane. Young women with ambition faced many barriers as they climbed the career ladder and Jane has to learn from the very beginning to stand her ground. In *Murder Mile* she also comes up against the sort of prejudice—from class snobbery to homophobia—that thankfully we rarely see today. All these experiences play in to Jane's character and will go on to form the exceptional detective she later becomes.

If you enjoyed *Murder Mile*, then please do read the first three novels in the Jane Tennison series, *Tennison*, *Hidden Killers* and *Good Friday*, which are now available in paperback and ebook. And you might like to know that the fifth book in the series, *The Dirty Dozen*, will be published in hardcover next year. The A10 investigation at the end of *Murder Mile* will result in Jane being taken off the murder squad and thrust into the "The Sweeney." If Jane's early career has often seemed a baptism of fire, it is a picnic compared with her time on the notorious Flying Squad. Here she will really learn how to toughen up—and give as good as she gets . . .

And in the meantime, there is a lot else going on! I'm very excited about the new publication and forthcoming film of my first novel *Widows*—a book and TV series very close to my heart. I'm also working on a whole new series with a central character who has really taken hold of my imagination. I'm looking forward to revealing more in due course—and if you would like more information on what I'm working on, or about the Jane Tennison thriller series, you can visit www.bit.ly/LyndaLaPlanteClub where you can join the My Readers' Club. It only takes a few moments to sign up, there are no catches or costs and new members will automatically receive an exclusive message from me. Bonnier Zaffre will keep your data private and confidential, and it will never be passed on to a third party. We won't spam you with loads of emails, just get in touch now and again with news about my books, and you can unsubscribe any time you want. And if you would like to get involved in a wider conversation about my books, please do review *Murder Mile* on Amazon, on GoodReads, on any other e-store, on your own blog and social media accounts, or talk about it with friends, family or reader groups! Sharing your thoughts helps other readers, and I always enjoy hearing about what people experience from my writing.

With many thanks again for reading *Murder Mile*, and I hope you'll return for *The Dirty Dozen*, the fifth in the Jane Tennison series.

With my very best wishes,
Lynda

TENNISON

The first book in the sensational Jane Tennison series

The Kray twins may be behind bars but the streets of London
are still rife with drugs, robbery and murder.

1973, in the East End of London, a young WPC Jane Tennison
joins the toughest ranks of the Hackney police force as a
probationary officer.

When her first case comes in, a woman savagely beaten and
strangled to death, Jane is thrown in at the deep end. But the
victim's autopsy is just the beginning of Tennison's
harsh initiation into the criminal world . . .

Praise for the Jane Tennison series:

"Classic Lynda, a fabulous read"
MARTINA COLE

"La Plante excels in her ability to pick out details that give her
portrayal of life in a police station a rare ring of authenticity"
SUNDAY TELEGRAPH

"A terrific, gutsy back story for the heroine of
TV's *Prime Suspect*"
WOMAN & HOME

HIDDEN KILLERS

**The second brilliant crime thriller in the
Jane Tennison series**

When WPC Jane Tennison is promoted to the role of detective
constable in London's Bow Street CID, she is immediately
conflicted. While her more experienced colleagues move
on swiftly from one criminal case to another, Jane is
often left doubting their methods and findings.

As she becomes inextricably involved in a multiple rape case,
Jane must put her life at risk in her search for answers.

Will she toe the line, or endanger her position by seeking
the truth?

Praise for the Jane Tennison series:

"An absorbingly twisty plot"
GUARDIAN

"Enthralling"
HEAT

"Vintage La Plante"
INDEPENDENT

GOOD FRIDAY

The third book in the brilliant Jane Tennison series

**March, 1976. The height of The Troubles. An IRA bombing campaign strikes terror across Britain.
Nowhere and no one is safe.**

When Detective Constable Jane Tennison survives a deadly explosion at Covent Garden tube station, she finds herself in the middle of a media storm. Minutes before the blast, she caught sight of the bomber. Too traumatized to identify him, she is nevertheless a key witness and put under 24-hour police protection.

As work continues round the clock to unmask the terrorists, the Metropolitan Police are determined nothing will disrupt their annual Good Friday dinner dance. Amid tight security, hundreds of detectives and their wives and girlfriends will be at St. Ermin's Hotel in central London.
Jane, too, is persuaded to attend.

But in the week leading up to Good Friday, Jane experiences a sudden flashback. She realizes that not only can she identify the bomber, but that the IRA Active Service Unit is very close to her indeed. She is in real and present danger. In a nail-biting race against time, Jane must convince her senior officers that her instincts are right before London is engulfed in another bloodbath.

The groundbreaking thriller from
the Queen of Crime Drama

WIDOWS

Facing life alone, they turned to crime together.

Dolly Rawlins, Linda Perelli and Shirley Miller are
left devastated when their husbands are killed in a
security van heist that goes disastrously wrong.

When Dolly discovers her husband's bank deposit box
containing a gun, money and detailed plans for the hijack,
she has three options. She could hand over the ledgers to a
detective. She could hand them over to the thugs who want
to take over Harry's turf. Or, she and the other widows
could finish the job their husbands started.

As they rehearse the raid, the women discover that
Harry's plan required four people and recruit hooker
Bella O'Reilly. But only three bodies were discovered
in the carnage of the original hijack—so who was
the fourth man, and where is he now?

Available in paperback and ebook now

Soon to be a major motion picture